PRAISE FOR *ANOTHER DAWN*
#1 *NEW YORK TIMES* BESTSELLING
AUTHOR SANDRA BROWN

"So steamy it'll probably leave a rectangle on the coffee table—if you can leave it down long enough."
—*New York Daily News*

"Author Sandra Brown proves herself top-notch."
—**Associated Press**

"Sandra Brown has continued to grow with every novel."
—*Dallas Morning News*

"Brown's storytelling gift is surprisingly rare, even among crowd pleasers."
—*Toronto Sun*

"Brown's forte is devising plots spiced with sexuality that keep her readers guessing."
—*Library Journal*

"Plotting and pacing are Brown's considerable strengths."
—*San Jose Mercury News*

"She knows how to keep the tension high and the plot twisting and turning."
—*Fresno Bee*

"Sandra Brown is known for her memorable storytelling."
—*Tulsa World*

Books by Sandra Brown

SANDRA BROWN

ANOTHER DAWN

WARNER BOOKS

NEW YORK   BOSTON

WARNER BOOKS EDITION

Copyright © 1985 by Sandra Brown
All rights reserved. No part of this book may be reproduced in any form or by any electronic or mechanical means, including information storage and retrieval systems, without permission in writing from the publisher, except by a reviewer who may quote brief passages in a review.

Cover design by Jackie Merri Meyer
Cover photography by Photonica

Warner Books, Inc.
1271 Avenue of the Americas
New York, NY 10020

Visit our Web site at
www.twbookmark.com

A Time Warner Company

Printed in the United States of America

First Warner Books Printing: July 1991
Reissued: March 1993, April 2001

10 9

Dear Reader,

Several years ago, my career underwent a transition with my novel, *Slow Heat in Heaven*. Before then I had written genre romances under several pseudonyms. Because so many of my new readers have expressed an interest in my earlier work, Warner Books is making these books available.

I feel that *Another Dawn*, the sequel to *Sunset Embrace*, tells a compelling love story while staying within the framework of romance fiction and reflecting the elements that characterize it, such as a high level of sensuality and a happy ending.

Thank you for your many requests to have these books reprinted, and please enjoy ...

Sandra Brown

PROLOGUE

The man lunged to his feet, clumsily drew his pistol, cocked it, and aimed.

His stocky thighs caught the edge of the table, jarring it and rocking the glasses full of liquor that stood on it. One sloshed over. A cigar rolled from an ashtray and burned a small hole in the green felt top.

Jake Langston sighed tiredly. He had come in for a game or two of stimulating poker, a glass or two of stinging whiskey, perhaps a satisfying tumble or two in one of the beds upstairs—all to fill the hours until his train pulled out.

Now here he was involved in an argument over a hand of poker with a sodbuster named Kermit something or other, who he hoped had more talent handling a plow than he had a gun.

"You calling me a cheater?" the farmer demanded. Unaccustomed to drinking any more than an occasional Saturday night beer, he was none too sober and, though his feet were well planted, he swayed like a sailor on a turbulent sea. His beefy face was perspiring and flushed. The pistol pointed directly at Jake's chest was wavering in an unsteady hand.

"I only said I'd like to see all those aces you've got in your sleeve at one time rather than having them pop up every other hand." With infuriating nonchalance Jake reached for the tumbler of whiskey near his right hand, his gun hand, and took a leisurely sip.

1

The farmer's glance nervously bounced around the barroom, suddenly aware of the spectacle he was making of himself. No one else in the cavernous room was moving. The music had ceased at the first sign of trouble. The others at the poker table had carefully ebbed away like the ripples from a stone thrown into a still lake.

The man was trying his best to appear threatening. "You're a liar. I wasn't cheating. Draw on me."

"All right."

It all happened so quickly that, later, only those standing closest could testify as to what had actually taken place. In one lithe move Jake came out of his chair, drew his gun, swept his other hand wide to deflect the farmer's arm and sent the pistol ineffectually clattering to the floor.

Kermit's Adam's apple elongated to accommodate a knot of stark terror. He looked into eyes as cold and brittle as icicles that cling to the eaves after a frigid, wet January norther. They were much more frightening than the gaping barrel of the pistol pointed at the end of his nose. He faced a body that was leaner than his by forty pounds, but menacing with its taut control.

"Pick up half the winnings you've stockpiled there. I figure you won that much fairly."

The farmer's hands fumbled with the coins and bills as he stuffed them into his pants pockets. He exuded the frenzy of a fox prepared to gnaw off his foot to escape a trap.

"Now pick up your gun real easy-like and get out of here."

Kermit obeyed. Only a miracle prevented the pistol from firing in his trembling hands as he let down the hammer and reholstered it.

"And I advise you not to come back until you learn to cheat without getting caught."

The farmer was humiliated, but vastly relieved that his heart was still beating, that he wasn't bleeding profusely from a gunshot wound, and that he wasn't going home penniless to his harping wife. He left, vowing to himself that he would never return.

The piano player resumed his jumping, jangling tune. Other patrons of the gambling hall drifted back to their tables, shaking their heads in amusement. Smokes abandoned in ashtrays were relit. The bartender immediately began to refill glasses.

"Pardon the interruption," Jake said congenially to the other players as he scooped his own pile of winnings off the table. "Divide the rest," he said of the money the farmer had wisely left on the table.

"Thanks, Jake."

"See ya."

"You could've killed him for pullin' a gun on you like that."

"Damn sure could have. We'd've backed you."

"Damn sodbusters."

Jake shrugged, turned away, and left them talking. Taking a slim cheroot out of his shirt pocket, he bit off the end and spat it on the floor. Striking a match with his thumbnail, he lit the cigar as he weaved his way through the tables toward the oak bar that extended the width of the room. According to rumor it had been shipped piece by piece from St. Louis to Fort Worth and painstakingly assembled. It was ornately carved, bedecked with mirrors, and lined with bottles and glasses that were kept highly polished. The proprietress wouldn't tolerate dust.

Brass spittoons were strategically placed along the brass rail of the bar. Spitting on the floor was not allowed in Priscilla Watkin's Garden of Eden. Hand-lettered signs posted along the bar at six-foot intervals said so.

Jake smiled. That floor, waxed to a high gloss, was now desecrated by the tip of his cigar. He also took a perverse pleasure in making sure the spurs on his boots scarred the surface the madam of the establishment took such pride in.

A grin tugged at the corners of his thin, wide lips. Priscilla. Just as his mind conjured up her name, he spotted her poised on the bottom step of the curving staircase, looking as resplendent as the Queen of Sheba. Clad in bright purple satin with black lace trim, she would catch any man's eye. Always had. When Jake had first met her almost twenty years ago, she had worn well-laundered calico. But she had turned heads even in that.

Her ash-blond hair was piled on the top of her head and decorated with a single purple ostrich plume that curled down around her cheek and flirted with a dangling jet earring. She held her head at a regal tilt.

Indeed, this whorehouse was her domain. She ruled it like a despot. If customers or employees didn't like the way she managed things, they were summarily dismissed and escorted off the premises. But everybody in Texas knew that the Garden of Eden in Fort Worth was in this year of 1890 the best whorehouse in the state.

Priscilla extended a slipper-shod foot and stepped off the bottom stair. Proudly, leaving behind her a wake of musky scent imported from Paris, she made her way to the bar just as Jake was lifting a glass of whiskey to his mouth.

"You just cost me a customer, Mr. Langston."

Jake didn't even turn his head, but nodded toward the bartender to pour him another shot. "I think you can afford to lose one or two, Pris."

It irritated the hell out of her for him to call her that. He took as much pleasure doing it as he did in scuffing the floor of her saloon. Only an old friend like Jake could get by with either one.

Were they friends? Or enemies? She was never quite sure.

"Why is it that things can go fine for months and the minute you come in there's trouble?"

"Is there?"

"Always."

"The sodbuster drew a gun on me. What did you expect me to do? Turn the other cheek?"

"You provoked him."

"He was cheating."

"I don't need any more trouble. The sheriff's been here twice already this week."

"Business or pleasure?"

"I'm serious, Jake. The town is up in arms again, wanting to shut me down. Every time there's trouble—"

"All right, I'm sorry."

She lifted her chin and laughed. "I doubt that. You either

stir up trouble at the gaming tables or cause a ruckus among my girls.''

"How's that?"

"They fight over you and you damn well know it," she snapped.

He turned to look at her then, grinning unabashedly. "Do they? Well, I'll be damned."

She assessed his good looks and that appealing arrogance he had acquired over the years. No longer a gauche boy, this was a man, a man both men and women had to reckon with. She tapped him on the chest with her feather fan. "You're bad for business."

Leaning down he whispered confidentially, "Then how come you're always so glad to see me?"

Priscilla's mouth tensed with vexation, but she succumbed to his ingratiating smile. "I've got better whiskey than that in my office." She laid a hand on his sleeve. "Come on."

Heads turned as the two crossed the room. There wasn't a man alive who could be impervious to Priscilla. She was attractive in a bawdy, lusty sort of way, and tales of what she was capable of doing to a man had made her a living legend. Even weighed against a man's bent to exaggerate when recounting his sexual exploits, stories about Priscilla Watkins were too wide-spread not to carry some credibility. Men didn't want their wives to have that sultry, brazen glint in their eyes, but they sure wanted their whores to.

Most of their desires were borne not of memories, but of curiosity and fantasy. Few had experienced those raunchy sessions with Priscilla firsthand. She was choosy. Even if they could afford the premium price she demanded, most wouldn't be selected to enter that inner chamber behind the door kept perpetually locked. It guarded enthralling secrets. Every man in the room envied Jake Langston at that moment.

But if the men looked at him jealously, the women looked at him with longing. The whores scattered around the room entertaining the early evening crowd were working women. They knew the value of a dollar. They had to be practical. Their time was money. So they practiced their seductive arts on their customers, but every one of them would have

traded the few dollars she would make for a free hour alone
with the cowboy Jake Langston.

He was slim-hipped and lanky, but moved with the feline
grace of a mountain cat and was just as tawny. Tight pants
fitted taut buttocks and long thighs like a second skin. The
gunbelt strapped low around his hips only emphasized his
manliness. Men respected his talent with his gun. To women,
his reputation with it only heightened the excitement of
being around him. It added an element of danger that few
respectable women would confess to finding stimulating.

His shoulders were broad, as was his chest, but not so
much that it detracted from his overall leanness. He didn't
merely walk. He sauntered. The girls who had had the good
fortune to entertain him in their rooms swore that he was as
bold about everything as he was with that swaggering walk
and that the rolling action of his hips wasn't a talent limited
to walking.

Priscilla drew a key from her low-dipping bodice and
unlocked the door to her private quarters. As soon as she
entered, she dropped her fan on a fashionably spindly chair
and crossed to a small table to pour Jake a drink from a
heavy crystal decanter. He closed the door behind them with
a definite click. Priscilla's eyes swung up to meet his. She
resented the accelerated beat of her heart.

Would tonight be the night?

The parlor could have belonged in any gracious hostess's
house, except for the nude of Priscilla painted by a customer
who had paid his bill by doing the portrait. He had no doubt
been her lover, having captured her on canvas in a pose of
indolent satiation. Unapologetically decadent, the portrait in
its gilded frame graced the wall behind the satin-covered
sofa, which was piled with pillows edged in silk fringe. The
draperies on the windows were moiré, but with no more
shirring than those found in most fine houses of the period.
Tables were draped with doilies as fine as spiderwebs. They
could have been crocheted by anyone's grandmother.

The oil lamps had large round globes with flowers painted
on them. Some dripped prisms that tinkled softly when a
whiff of air caught them. A thick carpet covered most of the

floor. There was a chest-high vase of peacock feathers standing in one corner. A seventeenth-century shepherdess, bare-breasted and saucy, was keeping an ardently admiring shepherd in perpetual distress on its china surface.

Jake surveyed the room slowly. He had been in here many times. It never ceased to fascinate him. Priscilla had moved up in the world from being the rebellious daughter of a dictatorial mother and a cowed father. Jake—then Bubba to everyone—had taken her in fallow fields and on muddy creekbeds. But when it came right down to it, the place didn't make any difference. A whore was a whore no matter where she practiced her trade.

Priscilla, unaware of his unflattering thoughts, went to him and handed him the whiskey. She plucked the cheroot from between his lips, carried it to her own and took a long draw, letting the smoke curl through her lungs before exhaling it in a long, slow stream. "Thanks. I don't let my girls smoke so I can't be a bad influence. Let's go into the bedroom. I have to change for the evening crowd."

He followed her into the next room. It was lacy, overtly feminine, and strangely unsuited to her. She was too hard a woman to be ensconced in this frilly, soft room, but Jake guessed that was part of the fantasy she provided for her customers.

"Help me, please, Jake." She offered him her back. He stuck the cheroot back in his mouth, clamping it with straight white teeth and squinting against the smoke. He set his drink aside. Deftly he unhooked the row of fasteners down her back. When he was done, she glanced over her bare shoulder, said a husky "Thank you, darling," and moved away.

Jake grinned as he flopped down on the brocaded chaise. He lifted his feet on it, disregarding the spurs, not to mention the caked mud, on his boots.

"What have you been up to lately?" Priscilla shimmied out of the low-cut dress with a move too effortless not to be rehearsed.

Jake blew a perfect smoke ring into the air and reached for his whiskey. "Working up in the Panhandle, stringing a fence from there to kingdom come."

Her brow arched eloquently as she kicked out of the purple slippers. She didn't bother to pick up after herself. Somehow dropping clothes where she took them off added to the wantonness of the act. Men preferred their women not to be too fussy about tidiness, especially when they were coming to bed. Such negligence made this paid sex seem more spontaneous. With mild derision she asked, "You've become a pliers man?"

That was a name given to cowboys who, after the decline of the long drives, found themselves hard pressed to find jobs. They often had to string the very barbed-wire fences that had closed the open ranges and put them out of work.

"Well, I've gotten accustomed to eating, things like that," Jake said easily. His eyes hadn't missed one seductive move she made.

Her corset was tightly laced. It pushed her bosom up and out until the sheer chemise beneath could barely contain it. She had always been well endowed. Jake remembered those large, firm breasts. Sweeping her petticoats aside, she sat down on a small round stool in front of a vanity table. It had mirrors hinged at the sides of the one she faced, so that she could adjust them and study herself from all angles. With a lamb's-wool puff, she dabbed powder on her neck, shoulders, and breasts.

"Are you on vacation?"

A low laugh rumbled out of Jake's chest. "Nope. I just got sick of seeing nothing but tumbleweeds and dust. I quit."

"What do you plan to do now?"

What did he plan to do now? Drift until a job turned up. The same thing he'd been doing for most of his adult life. He could earn some prize money in rodeos, enough to keep him and his horse alive, enough to enter a poker game now and then, enough to enjoy the recreation provided in places like Priscilla's Garden of Eden.

"How many drives did you make, Jake? I lost count of the times you came back to Fort Worth after going north."

"So did I. I went to Kansas City on several trips. Went all the way to Colorado once. Didn't like it. Pretty country, but too damn cold." He crossed his arms behind his head, enjoying the spectacle of her rouging her nipples. Her finger carried dollops of the colored salve from the tiny glass jar on the vanity to her breasts. She applied it soothingly, almost lovingly. "What about you, Priscilla? How long has it been that you've owned this place?"

"Five years."

"What did it cost you?"

Hours on my back, she wanted to say. Hours with sweating pudgy farmers who complained that their wives didn't want any more children and denied them their rights as husbands, and rough cowboys who brought the stink of the stockyards in with them.

She had worked in Jefferson first, the last stopping-off place on the frontier. But when the railroad bypassed that town, destroying it commercially, Priscilla had come to Fort Worth, where those tracks converged from all over the state. It was a raucous town full of cowboys who couldn't wait to spend the money they had made on the cattle drives.

Priscilla had seen to it that her reputation flourished. She gave her customers their money's worth in those days. Sometimes more than they paid for. She was popular. She saved her money. When she had enough, she went to one of her loyal customers, a banker, and had him secretly underwrite her purchase of the saloon. They bought out the former madam and converted it into a high-class pleasure palace that attracted not only the rowdy cowboys but the cattlemen who hired them. No expense was spared and the investment had been a wise one. She paid off the banker in two years. Except for the outrage of the "decent" community, her establishment, located in the area of town known as Hell's Half Acre, had given Priscilla little to worry about financially.

"If you need a job, you can always have one here dealing cards or acting as bouncer."

Jake laughed and set his empty glass on the table beside the chaise. "No thanks, Priscilla. I'm a cowboy. I don't like walls around me. Besides, according to you, if I were here constantly, your girls would stay all aflutter. We can't have that, can we?" he taunted.

Priscilla frowned as she pulled on a black satin dress. The

purple plume in her hair had been replaced by a shiny black
one anchored by a rhinestone clip. Jake Langston had gotten
too big for his britches. She smothered a smile as she
"corrected" her thought. Jake Langston had always been
too big for his britches. He certainly wasn't deficient when
it came to manly endowments.

She eyed him covertly as she pulled on the long black
lace gloves that encased her fingers and forearms. He had
matured to become too damned attractive. No wonder he
was conceited. He had been towheaded in his youth. Now
his hair had ripened, but marginally. Those white-blond
strands were like a beacon, drawing women to him like
moths to a lantern's flame.

His skin had been tanned like leather. Long hours of
exposure had turned it a coppery hue that intensified the
blue of his eyes. Fine lines were etched around his eyes and
down both corners of his mouth. But rather than detracting
from his appearance, that weather erosion added a new dimen-
sion to his attractiveness that hadn't been there in his youth.

He was rugged. Tough. Latently dangerous. He seemed
to have a secret lurking behind his lazy smile. The smile
hinted that the secret was naughty and that he was dying to
share it. And his cockiness made him a challenge no woman
could resist.

Priscilla remembered the boy she had sexually initiated.
Their tumbles had been hot and frequent, fierce and hard.
What would they be like now? For years he had wanted to
know.

"Will you be staying in Fort Worth for a while?"

"I'm on my way to east Texas tonight. I'm taking a late
train. Remember the Colemans? Their daughter is getting
married tomorrow."

"Coleman? The one from the wagon train? Ross, wasn't
it?" She knew well whom he was speaking about, but she
wanted to provoke him as much as he always wanted to
provoke her. It was a game they played every time they saw
each other. "And what was that woman's name? The one he
charitably married."

"Lydia," he said tightly.

"Oh, yes, Lydia. She didn't have a last name, did she? I always wondered what she was hiding." Taking the stopper out of a crystal perfume bottle, she dabbed it behind her ears, on her neck, her wrists, her breasts. "I hear they've done quite well for themselves with that horse ranch."

"They have. My mother lives on their land. So does my kid brother, Micah."

"That little toddler?"

"He's grown now. One of the best horsemen I've ever seen."

"What happened to Mr. Coleman's baby? The one Lydia wet-nursed before they got married."

Jake pondered a moment, looking for rancor from Priscilla. Finally he answered. "Lee. He and Micah are two of a kind. Always raising hell."

Priscilla contemplated her reflection in the mirror and patted her hair. "And they have a daughter old enough to get married?"

Jake smiled fondly. "Barely. Last time I saw her, she was still in braids, chasing Lee and Micah, begging to go along to round up a rogue stallion."

"A tomboy?" Priscilla asked, pleased. She remembered how Jake used to gaze at Lydia Coleman with calf eyes. All the men on the wagon train had been attracted to her, despite their wives' reluctance to accept her at first. If Lydia hadn't married Ross Coleman, Priscilla would have been insanely jealous of her. She liked to think of Lydia's daughter as an awkward, gangling girl, or a stringy tomboy.

"I guess if she's getting married, she must have changed some since I last saw her."

Priscilla picked up her fan and twirled around in front of him, preening. "Well?"

The bodice of the dress was tightly nipped in at her waist. The neckline was wide and low, barely covering her breasts with a lace as fine as that of her gloves. Its pattern didn't conceal the rouged nipples beneath. In front, the skirt rode the vamp of her black satin slippers and flowed into a short train in back. A modern bustle contributed to the hourglass shape of her figure.

Cynical blue eyes raked her insolently. "Very nice, but then I always did say you were the prettiest whore I ever knew." He watched the temper flare in her gray eyes. Laughing softly, he reached for her hand and yanked her down onto the chaise with him. Her fan flew out of her hand and landed softly on the floor. The plume in her hair was knocked awry, but Priscilla didn't object as Jake rolled her beneath him.

"You've been strutting your stuff for me all night, haven't you, Pris? Hm? Well, I reckon it's time I gave you what you've been asking for."

He slanted his mouth hard over hers.

Hungrily her lips opened for the intrusion of his tongue. Her girls hadn't exaggerated. He knew what he was doing. He summoned every feeling place in her body with that kiss and they all responded. His body was hard and rangy. She arched up against him as her fingers tangled in the thick blond hair at his nape.

With a practiced movement his hand found its way beneath her skirts and onto her thigh just above her lacy garter. He stroked the warm, quivering flesh. She raised her knee.

'Hm, yes, Jake, Jake,'' she whispered as her mouth moved over his.

He wedged his free hand between their bodies. She thought he was adjusting his clothing and looked up at him stupidly when he dangled a pocket watch in front of his eyes and checked the time. "Sorry, Pris." He made an insincere clucking sound with his mouth. "I've got a train to catch."

Furious, she threw him off her. "You bastard!"

Laughing, Jake rolled off the chaise. "Is that any way to talk to an old friend?"

Priscilla did something she rarely did. She lost her temper. "You stupid hillbilly! You dumb lout! Do you really think I wanted to make love to you?"

"Yeah, I really think you did." He winked at her and headed for the parlor. "Sorry to disappoint you."

"Aren't I good enough for you anymore?"

He spun around. "You're good enough. Too good. The best. That's why I don't want you. Because you're the best whore around."

"You sleep with whores all the time. That's all you ever sleep with."

"But if I don't know them, I can pretend it's something else. I can pretend that I'm the only one who's been there. You've been a whore since I've known you. Dozens of men have been in your bed. It kinda takes the romance out of it for me."

Her face went livid and Jake realized just how ugly she could be. "It's your brother, isn't it? You never got over being with me the day he died."

"Shut up."

He said it so emotionlessly that it terrified her. She took a step backward, but didn't relent completely. "You're still a dumb Tennessee hillbilly. Oh, you taught yourself to talk better. Your short temper has won you a reputation that men respect. You know how to please the ladies. But underneath you're still Bubba Langston, a stupid hick."

He stopped at the door. His eyes were no longer alight with mischief, but cold and hard. The skin over his face was stretched taut, the lines on the sides of his mouth more deeply engraved. "No, Priscilla. That boy Bubba vanished a long time ago."

Priscilla's fury subsided. Her eyes narrowed as she gazed up at him. "I'm going to prove to you that you still want me. That's a promise. One of these days you'll let yourself remember what it was like with us. We were just kid. Lusty, hot, dying for it. It could be that way again." Tilting her head back, she laid her hand on his chest. "I'll have you again, Jake."

Jake remembered too well the first time they had been together. That afternoon was indelibly imprinted on his mind. He removed her hand. "Don't count on it, Priscilla."

He closed the door to her private chamber behind him and stood there a moment meditatively. Business had picked up. The evening's diversions were in full swing. Scantily clad girls drifted through the parlors and gaming rooms, teasing, flirting, displaying their wares to the patrons. Several glanced at him expectantly, breathlessly.

He smiled but didn't offer them any encouragement. It

wasn't that he didn't have the urge. He had been several weeks without a woman. While he would never have taken Priscilla, he wasn't made of wood either. The sight of her unclothed, the scent of female flesh, had been a strong stimulant.

One more glass of whiskey? One more game of cards? One hour in one of the upstairs bedrooms, one moment of forgetfulness?

"Hiya, Jake."

One of the whores sidled up to him. "Hi, Sugar." Sugar Dalton had been in Priscilla's employ since Jake had been frequenting the place. "How're things?"

"Can't complain," she replied, smiling thinly through her lie. The lines tracking through her heavy makeup told him how bad things were and how much she hated her life. But she was pathetically resigned to it and anxious to please. Jake had always felt sorry for her. "I could make you feel good tonight, Jake," she said hopefully.

For her sake, he was almost tempted to take her upstairs. Instead he shook his head no. "But you can fetch my hat and saddlebag for me. Here's the ticket." He fished in his pocket for his claim check and she rushed off. When she came back, he tipped her fifty cents, much more than her errand, which he could just as easily have done for himself, was worth.

"Thanks, Sugar."

"Any time, Jake." She gazed at him with open invitation.

Should he be benevolent to her, kind to his starved body? No. Before he could change his mind he began making his way through the throng toward the front door. He had to catch that last train tonight. He was expected in Larsen tomorrow morning.

Banner Coleman was getting married.

ONE

It was Banner Coleman's wedding day.

She felt every bit a bride as she stood at the back of the church, out of sight behind a flower-bedecked screen, and gazed at the people who had given up a Saturday afternoon to come see her marry Grady Sheldon.

Just about everybody in Larsen had been invited. And it seemed, judging by the crowd that was rapidly filling the pews of the church, that all those who had received an invitation had dressed up in their Sunday finery and were in attendance.

Banner shifted her feet slightly, liking the rustling sound the silk gown made against her legs. The skirt was fashionably narrow and draped over matching satin pumps. The excess fabric was gathered into a soft bustle in the back, which cascaded into a short train. The tulle yoke, which opened high under her chin like the trumpet of a lily, was beaded with tiny pearls. It was sheer to where it met the underlying silk at the gentle slope of her breasts. It was a provocative design, especially since it so snugly fit Banner's shapely figure, but it was sweetly virginal too. The lace veil that modestly covered her dark hair and her face had been ordered by Larsen's finest seamstress all the way from New York.

Normally Banner liked vibrant colors, but the ivory wedding gown was a perfect contrast for her midnight black hair. Her complexion was the color of ripe apricots, not buttermilk pale, as was the vogue, because she preferred to stay out in the sun without what proper ladies considered the necessary protection of a parasol.

From her mother she had inherited a tendency to freckle across the bridge of her nose. These blemishes were lamented by the ladies in the sewing circles. "Such a pretty little thing, if only she would be more careful of our sun." Banner had come to terms with her face long ago. It wasn't classically pretty, but she rather liked its unconventionality. She couldn't be worried about anything as trivial as a few freckles. Besides, Mama had them. And Mama was beautiful.

From both parents she had gotten her eyes. Papa's were green. Mama's were the color of whiskey. Hers were somewhere in between—gold, shot through with green. "Cat eyes" some would say. But that wasn't quite accurate, for there was no gray in them, only that deep topaz gold swirling through the green.

The crowd was growing expectant and restless. The organist began to play. The pump organ wheezed only slightly. Happiness bubbled inside Banner and tinted her cheeks a peachy hue. She knew she looked lovely. She knew she was loved. She felt like a bride.

Every pew in the church was filled. From the center aisle ushers politely requested that people scoot close together to accommodate the crowd. Thankfully there was a southern breeze coming through the tall stately windows, six on each side of the church, and it gently fanned the wedding guests on this warm spring afternoon. The gentlemen squirmed and tugged on their uncomfortably tight collars. The ladies, their organdy ruffles fluttering, waved lacy fans and dainty handkerchiefs.

The scent of roses, cut fresh that very morning, filled the air. Dewdrops still clung to the velvety petals. Impartial to any one color, Banner had chosen to use every color of bloom available from ruby red to snowy white. Her three bridesmaids, standing in a small huddle only a few feet in front of her, were dressed in pastel gowns with wide sashes. They looked as fragile as the flowers decorating the church.

It was about the most perfect wedding Banner Coleman could imagine.

"Are you ready, Princess?"

She turned her head and looked through her veil at her father. She hadn't heard him moving to take his place beside her. "Papa, you look so handsome!"

Ross Coleman flashed her a smile that had stilled the hearts of scores of women. Maturity only heightened his attractiveness. There were now silver strands at his temples and in his wide, lavish mustache. At fifty-two, he was as tall and broad-shouldered as ever. Hard work had kept him trim and lean. Dressed in a dark suit and white shirt with a high collar, he was as handsome as a bride could wish her father to be.

"Thank you," he said, bowing slightly.

"It's no wonder Mama married you. Did you look this handsome on your wedding day?"

His eyes flickered away from her for a moment. "Best as I recollect, I didn't." It had rained that day. He recalled a soggy group of migrants gathered outside his wagon, a frightened Lydia looking like she was going to bolt at any moment, and himself resentful and angry. He had been roped into marrying her and he'd been furious. Little had he known that it would prove to be the best thing he'd ever done in his life. He had begun to change his mind about her when the preacher said, "You may now kiss your bride," and he had kissed her for the first time.

"You got married on the wagon train."

"Yes."

"I'll bet Mama didn't mind if you weren't so dressed up."

"I guess she didn't," he said with soft gruffness.

His eyes scanned the front of the church until they lighted on the woman who had been escorted to the front row just a few minutes before.

"She looks beautiful today," Banner said, following the direction of his gaze. Lydia was dressed in a beaded gown of honey-colored silk. Sunlight slanting through one of the windows caught the reddish glints in her hair.

"Yes, she does."

Banner nudged him teasingly with her elbow. "You always think she looks beautiful."

Ross's eyes came back to his daughter. "I always think you do too." He studied her carefully, taking in the gown and veil that made her somehow untouchable. She would soon belong to someone else. He would no longer be the most important man in her life.

It brought an ache to his throat to acknowledge that their relationship would forever change after today. He wanted her to be a little girl still, his princess. "You're a beautiful bride, Banner. Your mother and I love you. We don't give you up lightly, even to a fine young man like Grady."

"I know, Papa." Tears clouded her eyes. Coming up on her toes, she lifted the veil and kissed his hard cheek. "I love you too. You know how much I must love Grady if I'd leave you and Mama to marry him."

Her eyes sought the front of the church just as the door behind the choir loft opened. Their minister, Grady, and his three groomsmen solemnly filed out and took their places beneath the arch of garlands and flowers.

Her tears dried instantly and Banner's mouth widened in a smile of sheer gladness. Grady looked very handsome in his dark suit. His chestnut hair had been brushed until it gleamed. He stood straight and tall, if a bit rigid.

He had stood much like that the first time Banner ever saw him. It was at his father's funeral. She hadn't known the Sheldons. Grady's mother had died before they moved to Larsen and started their lumber business. Mr. Sheldon's death meant no more to Banner than an inconvenience when her parents had told her she had to accompany them to the funeral. That meant spending a day in a dress rather than the pants she wore around the ranch, and going to church rather than watching the cowboys break a frisky mare. She had been fourteen. Clearly she remembered being impressed by Grady, then twenty, who had stood so stoically at the grave site. He was all alone in the world now. To Banner, who was surrounded by people who loved her, such a thing was unthinkable. The worst that could happen to a person was to be alone and without love. In retrospect she thought she must have started loving Grady then for his courage.

Every chance she got, she accompanied Ross to the timber mill. It wasn't until about a year ago that Grady seemed to notice her. He did a double take the day she went into the lumberyard with Lee and Micah. At first mistaking her for a boy, since she was dressed like one, his mouth had fallen open in shock when she whisked her hat off and a mass of black hair had tumbled down around her shoulders and over breasts that gave shape to the otherwise shapeless cotton shirt.

Soon Grady was calling on her for Sunday afternoon rides in his buggy, asking her to dance at parties, and sitting beside her at church socials. He was one of many young men who vied for her attention, but it became distressingly clear to her other would-be suitors that he was the one she preferred.

The day he formally asked Ross if he could court her, she followed him from the house, riding Dusty down the lane as the mare had never been ridden before.

"Grady!" she cried, jumping from her saddle and shamelessly running toward him when he drew his buggy to a halt. As he climbed down, she launched herself into his arms, her eyes bright and her cheeks rosy with color. "What did he say?"

"He said yes!"

"Oh, Grady, Grady." She hugged him tightly. Then, realizing she wasn't being very ladylike, not to mention coy, she put space between them and glanced up at him through thick, sooty lashes. "I guess since we're officially courting now, you can kiss me if you like."

"I . . . is it all right? You're sure?"

Her black curls bounced as she eagerly nodded her head. In fact she thought she would die if he didn't kiss her. Everything inside her yearned for the feel of his lips against hers.

He lowered his head and kissed her chastely on the cheek. "Is that all?"

He pulled back and read the astonished disappointment on

her face. When she made no movement to separate herself
demurely from him, which was what he had expected, he
pressed his lips over hers.

It was nice, but still somewhat of a disappointment. This
wasn't the kind of kiss she had heard Lee and Micah
discussing in fervent whispers when they didn't know she
was around. The kisses they wistfully described in minute
detail were considerably more intimate. Tongues were
mentioned. Mama and Papa didn't kiss with tightly closed
lips, their bodies not even touching.

Banner, acting out of curiosity and impulse, wound her
arms around Grady's neck and arched her body against his.
He made a startled sound in his throat before his arms went
around her possessively. But he still didn't open his mouth.

Breathlessly, he pushed her away from him several reckless seconds later. "Lordy, Banner. What are you trying to
do to me?"

She blushed hotly. In fact, parts of her body she had
barely taken notice of before felt hot and feverish. She
wished they could be married that very afternoon, she
wished that slow fire would go on burning inside her
until . . . well, until *that*. "I'm sorry, Grady. That wasn't
very ladylike, I know. It's just that I love you so much."

"I love you too." He had kissed her chastely once more
before getting back into his buggy and saying goodbye.

Though she was mercilessly teased by Lee and Micah,
she began to spend less time outdoors around the corrals
with the hands and more time with Lydia and Ma in the
house. Ma Langston was teaching her to embroider. She
worked with painful concentration on pillowcases and cup
towels that she carefully ironed, folded, and placed in her
hope chest.

Housekeeping had always been a chore she dreaded and
avoided whenever possible. But she began helping Lydia,
even offering suggestions about rearranging furniture and
replacing curtains in the parlor.

The time she spent with Grady was enchanted and romantic. She was blissfully in love. When Grady asked Ross's

permission to have her hand in marriage, she had swirled in a cloud of happiness that still held her captive.

She looked at Grady now with the love that had brought her to the marriage altar. Her heart skittered at the thought of the night to come. With each day, it was becoming harder to suppress the longing their kisses inspired. Just a few nights ago when she had walked him to his buggy parked beneath the pecan tree in the front yard, the control Grady imposed on himself slipped.

With their arms locked around each other, they had swayed together. Her cheek rested on his heart, which she could hear beating as rapidly as hers. "Only five more nights and we don't have to say good night and separate. We can say good night in our own bed."

He groaned. "Banner, honey, don't talk like that."

"Why?" she asked, raising her head to look at him.

He brushed an errant strand of hair from her cheek. "Because it just makes me want you more."

"Do you, Grady?" There was no sense in pretending that she didn't know what he wanted. She hadn't grown up on a stud ranch without gaining a working knowledge of mating. Besides, such pretense was contrary to Banner's nature. It would never have occurred to her to feign ignorance.

"Yes," he sighed. "I want you." His mouth came down hard on hers. Her lips parted. He hesitated only a moment before he touched her open lips with his tongue.

"Oh, Grady."

"I'm sorry, I—"

"No. Don't stop. Kiss me like that some more."

He introduced her to a new way of kissing, one that made her breathless and giddy and warm. But rather than easing the aching in her body, it seemed to intensify it. She pressed herself against him.

"Banner," he groaned. His hand slid from her shoulder toward her waist, but on its descent it encountered the fullness of her breast. He paused, pressed.

The sensation that zephyred through her was rather more than she had bargained for. Frightened by its sizzling strength, she pushed away from him.

Grady's eyes narrowed for a split second, then his head fell forward and he stared down at his shoes, abjectly ashamed of himself. "Banner..." he began.

"Please don't apologize, Grady." Her soft tone brought his eyes back up to hers. "I wanted you to touch me. I still do. But I know girls aren't supposed to act like they enjoy the ... the baser aspects of married life. I don't want you to think badly of me. That's why I stopped you."

He clasped her hands in his, carried them to his lips and kissed them ardently. "I don't think badly of you. I love you."

She laughed, the throaty, husky laugh that had caused more than one cowboy in her father's employ to lose sleep at night thinking about what it would be like to tumble Banner Coleman. "You won't have a shy bride on your hands, Grady. You won't have to coax me into bed with you."

When she had gone into the house later, she overheard Ross and Lydia talking quietly in the parlor.

"Do you think she's ready for marriage? She's barely eighteen," Ross was saying.

Lydia laughed softly. "She's our daughter, Ross. All her life she's seen the way we love each other. I don't think married love holds any mysteries for her. She's ready. As for her age, most of her friends are married. Some already have babies."

"They're not my daughters," he growled.

"Come here and sit down. You're wearing out the rug with that pacing."

Banner could hear their movements as her father settled close to her mother on the sofa. She could picture him with his arm around Lydia, who would be cuddling against him familiarly. "Is it Grady you're worried about?"

"No," Ross said grudgingly. "I guess he's everything he appears, steadfast, ambitious. He seems to love Banner. God, he'd better do right by her, or he'll have me to answer to."

She could almost see her mother's soothing fingers running through Ross's hair. "If anything, Banner will lead him a merry chase. She's a headstrong young woman. Or haven't you noticed?''

''Wonder who she gets that from?'' Ross asked affectionately. There followed a silence. Banner knew they were embracing in a way that would have astounded most of her friends who had never even seen their parents touch. She could hear the whispering of their clothes as they settled more comfortably when the kiss ended.

Ross was the first to speak. ''I wanted so much for our children. Much more than you and I ever had as kids.''

''I don't remember anything beyond the day I met you.''

''Yes, you do,'' he countered softly. ''And so do I. I don't worry about Lee so much. He can take care of himself. But Banner.'' He sighed. ''I'd kill any man who hurt her. I guess I'm relieved that the worst of my fears hasn't come about.''

''What was that?''

''That some worthless cowboy would ride in here one day and sweep her off her feet.''

''She's not impressed by cowboys. She's been raised with them.''

''She's never been eighteen either and had that look in her eyes. It's been there since she was about sixteen.''

''What look?''

''Like the one you get every time I start unbuttoning my shirt.''

''Ross Coleman, you conceited—''

Her mother's harangue was cut short, and there was no doubt in Banner's mind that her father's lips were responsible.

''I don't have any kind of look,'' Lydia protested weakly a few moments later.

''Oh, yes, you do. In fact''—Ross's voice lowered—''you've got it right now. Come here, woman,'' he whispered, before another thick silence ensued.

Smiling, Banner turned out the lamp in the hall and made her way upstairs to her room. She gazed into the mirror over her dressing table, pressing her nose against the glass and peering deeply into her eyes.

Did she have ''that look''? Is that why Grady had dared

to touch her in one of those forbidden places she and her girlfriends whispered about? Was she bad to want to be touched? Was Grady bad because he wanted to touch her?

If it were hard on her to resist, what must it be like for poor Grady, who was a man and therefore whose physical urges were harder to control?

She had gone to bed and tried to sleep, her mind as disquieted with questions as her body was with the desire to experience the unknown.

Well, she didn't have much longer to wait, she thought as she watched her bridesmaids file down the central aisle of the church as had been rehearsed the day before.

"It's our turn next, Princess," Ross said. "Ready?"

"Yes, Papa."

She was ready. She was ready to be loved by a man, ready for the smoldering fires in her body to be ignited, then quenched. She was ready to belong to one man, to have someone to hold in the night, someone to hold her. She was tired of feeling guilty over stolen kisses and moments when passion threatened to overstep the bounds of propriety.

Ross led her around the screen. They started down the aisle as the organ music swelled after a dramatic pause. Everyone stood and faced her as she made that slow march. She was greeted by a sea of friendly faces, most of whom she had known all her life. Bankers, merchants, tradesmen, lawyers, neighboring ranchers and farmers, and their families had turned out for Banner Coleman's wedding day. With uncustomary boldness for a bride, Banner smiled back at them.

The Langstons were together in the row directly behind Lydia. First Ma, who was battling sentimental tears. Next were Anabeth, her husband, Hector Drummond, and their children, then Marynell. Micah stood between Marynell and Banner's half-brother, Lee.

Her tormentors.

Even now, as she cast them a sidelong glance, she could tell they were hard pressed not to burst into laughter unbefitting the occasion. Withering glances from both Ma and Ross were all that stood between them and hilarity.

The boys had become bosom buddies when Micah moved to River Bend with his mother. At first Banner had been vindictively jealous of Micah, who had robbed her of her sole playmate. He still reminded her of the time she had put a burr under his horse's saddle blanket. He had been thrown, but thankfully had escaped serious injury or death, which the six-year-old Banner had selfishly prayed for.

She had always tagged behind the boys, begging them to let her be a part of whatever mischief they were instigating. Often they let her participate, only to play the scapegoat when they got caught.

In spite of their squabbles, she loved both of them fiercely. They looked so handsome today standing together. Lee, with his dark hair and flashing brown eyes, which he had inherited from his mother, Victoria Gentry Coleman, and Micah, as fair as all the Langstons.

That brought Banner's eyes to the last man in the pew. He received the brightest of her smiles.

Jake.

Jake, whom she had adored as far back as her memory would go. She could vividly remember each of his rare visits. He would sweep her high over his head, holding her there, smiling up into her face, until she kicked and begged for mercy, hoping all the while that he would never let her go.

No one was as tall as Jake. No one as strong. No one as blond. No one as dashing. No one could push the swing higher. No one told better ghost stories.

He had been her hero, her knight in shining armor. The happiest days of her life had been when Jake came to River Bend, because his presence there made everyone else happy too. Ma, Lydia, Ross, Lee and Micah, old Moses before he had died, everybody looked forward to Jake's visits. The only bad thing about them was that they ended too quickly and were too infrequent.

As she got older and realized how seldom he came, the thought of his leaving often overshadowed the joy of having him there. She couldn't completely enjoy his visit because she knew he would ride out and it would be forever before she would see him again.

That's why near-chaos had broken out that morning when Micah and Lee came to the house for breakfast and Lee announced, "Looky here what we found sleeping in the barn this morning."

He pushed Jake forward through the back door. He was immediately surrounded by laughing, chattering people all talking at once.

"Jake!"

"Son!"

"Well, I'll be damned!"

"Ross, watch your language. The children."

"Why were you sleeping in the barn?"

"My horse got a rock under his shoe last night when we got off the train."

"We rode on the train, too, Uncle Jake!"

"Yeah, and she was scared, but I wasn't."

"I was not scared!"

"What time did you get in?"

"From where? Fort Worth?"

"Yeah, Fort Worth. It was late. I didn't want to disturb anybody."

"As if you could."

Ma hugged him tight, clasping him against her bulk, squeezing her eyes shut against the emotion that moistened them. Then, flustered, she immediately launched into a lecture about how thin he was. "Sit yourself down and I'll round you up some biscuits and gravy. Don't that rancher out there in the Panhandle feed his hands right? I've seen garter snakes fatter than you. Did you wash your hands? Marynell, git your nose out of that book and pour your big brother some coffee. Anabeth, quieten them young'uns down. They're makin' more racket than a bunch of loose rocks in a pail."

Jake had a young Drummond pulling on each leg like he was a wishbone. Another one had taken his hat and was trying it on for size. The one as yet unable to walk had crawled between his feet and was beating on the toe of his

boot with a spoon. Anabeth stepped around her children to
kiss her brother's cheek and murmur, ''Ma's been worried
sick about you,'' into his ear. After delivering that private
sisterly message, she hauled the children away from Jake
and shooed them outside, admonishing the oldest to keep an
eye on the baby.

Lydia walked into Jake's open arms and hugged him.
''I'm so glad you could come. We were worried you
wouldn't be able to.''

''I wouldn't have missed it,'' he said, his blue eyes
moving from one loved face to another. ''Hiya, Ross,'' he
said, reaching around Lydia to pump Ross's hand. ''How
are things?''

''Fine, fine. You, Bubba?''

Every once in a while the old nickname slipped out.
''Fair to middling, I guess.''

''How's the job?''

''Quit it.''

''Quit?'' Ma turned from the stove with a plate of hot
biscuits in her hands.

Jake shrugged, obviously not wanting to dampen the
festive mood by talking about his shiftlessness. ''I had to
come see the bride, didn't I? Where is she anyway?''

His eyes roamed over the group clustered around him,
deliberately overlooking Banner. She had hung back on
purpose, wanting his undivided attention when she greeted
him.

''Jake Langston, you know I'm the bride.'' She rushed
forward and flung herself into his arms, giving him a hard
hug. His arms encircled her waist and lifted her off the
ground. They spun two complete circles before he set her
back down.

Pushing her away, he said, ''Naw, you couldn't be the
bride. The Banner Coleman I know has braids and skinned
shins and holes in the knees of her drawers. Let me see your
drawers and I'll know for sure.'' He bent down to lift the
skirt of her robe. She screeched and swatted at his hands.

''You'll never see my drawers anymore, nor my shins,
skinned or not. I'm all grown up now, or haven't you

noticed?'' She struck an arrogant pose that all too clearly evidenced her maturity. She put one hand on her hip. The other she crooked behind her head, which she tilted drastically backward.

Lee guffawed. Micah whistled lecherously and clapped his hands. Jake assessed the Colemans' daughter, whom he had known from the cradle. "You surely are at that," he remarked seriously. "All grown up." He laid his hands on her shoulders and leaned down to kiss her cheek respectfully. Then, to her consternation, the open palm of his hand landed on her fanny with a resounding smack. "But you're still a snot-nosed kid to me. Find me a chair so I can eat these biscuits before they get cold."

She had been too happy to see him to take offense, even though everyone had laughed at her. Now her heart expanded an extra degree when she caught his eye as she glided down the aisle. She was so proud of him, so proud that this tall man with the white-blond hair and brilliant blue eyes belonged to her family. Well, practically.

He had traded his cowboy clothes for a white shirt and black leather vest. He had swapped the bandana he always wore for a narrow black necktie. But his gunbelt was still strapped around his hips. Banner supposed some habits were hard to break.

She reasoned that his behavior wouldn't bear too close a scrutiny. He had probably done some things the law was better off not knowing. She was certain he drank, gambled, and dallied with the kind of women she wasn't even supposed to know about. But none of that could stop her from loving him. His dashing and dangerous air only made him more appealing. No doubt the single girls at the wedding reception would demand an introduction.

One of those crystal-blue eyes, surrounded by sun-gilded lashes, closed, giving Banner a quick, secret wink. She winked back at him, remembering all the times he had told her secrets he swore he couldn't tell Lee and Micah. She had believed him because she had wanted to. The friendship between them was stingily guarded. Every word he had ever whispered to her was treasured. Where his attention was concerned, she was ferociously jealous.

Banner knew there was a bond between him and her parents, especially her mother, that was secret and sacred. They never spoke of it. It was a topic never discussed. But with the intuition of a child, Banner had always sensed that it was there. Whatever it was, she was glad of it, because it kept Jake in their lives.

She looked at her mother now as she and Ross came even with the first pew. "I love you, Mama," she whispered.

"I . . . *we* love you too," Lydia whispered back, including Ross in the endearment. Tears were standing in her eyes, but she was smiling.

Banner smiled on them both before facing the minister. Ross took his position between her and Grady.

"Who gives this woman in marriage?" the minister asked.

"Her mother and I."

Ross looked down into Banner's face. His green eyes were misty. He squeezed her hand, then slipped it into Grady's. He joined Lydia on the front pew.

Banner heard the shuffle of the crowd as everyone sat back down. She gazed into her groom's face, knowing that no woman in the world had ever been happier than she was at that moment. Grady was the man she had chosen to spend her life with. They would love each other the way Mama and Papa did. She would make him happy every day of his life, no matter what it took. She was just as certain of Grady's love as he looked down at her.

The minister began the ceremony. The poetic words took on new meaning for Banner. Yes, that phrase perfectly expressed what she felt for—

Crack!

The racket shattered the serene stillness in the church. The reverberation fell around Banner like pricking shards of glass.

Screams.

A rushing murmur rose from the congregation.

Banner whipped her head around.

Grady slumped against her.

A gaping wound bloomed red against his dark wedding suit.

TWO

"Grady!"

Beneath his sagging weight, Banner collapsed to the floor. He fell atop her. She struggled to a sitting position and gathered his head into her lap. Automatically she began loosening his necktie and collar. Small hiccupping sounds of pure terror stumbled from her throat. His eyes were opened and glazed with shock. He moved his lips uselessly but no words came out.

But he was still alive. Banner whimpered prayers of thankfulness as she covered the wound with her bare hand in an effort to stanch the flow of blood.

In the split second it all happened, Jake drew his pistol and whirled toward the man standing just outside the nearest window. He held a pistol aimed toward the front of the church.

"The bride gets it next." The warning was issued in a raspy, malevolent voice. It was underlined by a jabbing thrust of the pistol toward the altar.

Not only Jake but the River Bend hands attending the wedding had all drawn guns. They were trained on the man in the window. Frightened women leaned forward to bury their heads in their laps, covering them with their arms. Men were hunched down between the pews shielding their children from a threat that hadn't yet been determined or identified.

"Drop all them guns," the man shouted maniacally.

"Ross?" Jake said.

"Do as he says." At the first sound of gunfire, Ross had reflexively ducked and reached for his Colt, only to find it wasn't there. Who would have thought he would need his six-shooter at his daughter's wedding? He cursed viciously under his breath.

Jake regretfully tossed his pistol to the floor. The River Bend hands followed suit. Only then did the man at the tall window swing one leg over the low sill and step into the church. He pulled a young woman in behind him and shoved her forward with his palm in the small of her back.

"I'm Doggie Burns and this here is my precious girl, Wanda."

The two needed no introduction. Doggie Burns distilled the best moonshine in east Texas. He had customers who would travel miles for a supply of his West Virginia recipe. Few gave the man more than the time necessary to transact their business. He was shifty, wily, dangerous, downright mean, and anybody who had ever heard of him knew it.

He and the girl were filthy. Wanda's mousy brown hair hung lank and oily to her shoulders. The underarms of Doggie's shirt were ringed with generations of sweat stains. Their clothes were tattered and ineptly mended. They were a desecration to the pristine chapel, especially decorated as it was for the occasion. Like a fissure in an otherwise perfect diamond, they were all anyone could see and blotted out the beauty around them.

"Much as I hate to interrupt the proceedin's," Burns said sarcastically, tipping his hat to Lydia before clamping it back on his greasy hair, "it's my duty as a father to stop this here weddin' from takin' place."

Grady groaned in pain and clutched the wound in his shoulder. "Please, somebody," Banner cried. "Help him." She had swept back her veil. Her eyes looked huge in her face. Lydia passed her a handkerchief to blot at the bleeding hole in Grady's shoulder.

"He ain't gonna die, girlie," Burns said, shifting his nasty wad of tobacco from one side of his mouth to the other. Brown rivers of its juice stained the lines around his mouth. "If I'd've intended to kill him, he wouldn't've felt the bullet what hit him. All I done was to put a stop to the weddin' on account of what this bastard's done to my girl."

By now the congregation realized that the situation posed no threat to them. Tentatively heads were raised. Burns's coarse language set up a murmur of righteous protest and a number of fans to waving.

"What do you want?" the minister demanded. "How dare you offend the Lord in His own house?"

"Just hold your horses, preacher. You'll get to recite them purty words, but it ain't gonna be over the two of them."

Lydia had come to her feet with the bullet's blast. Ross had kept a protective arm around her. Now he withdrew it and stepped forward. "All right, Burns, you've got everyone's attention. What do you want?"

"See this here belly my gal's got on her?" He pointed the barrel of his pistol at the girl's swollen abdomen. "It's pumped full of Sheldon's kid."

"That's not true!" Grady croaked.

"Why are you doing this? I don't understand!" Banner exclaimed, suddenly becoming aware of what was going on around her. Until now, Grady, in his pain, had commanded her full attention. "Why would you come in here and ruin my wedding like this? *Why?*"

Everyone in the church was enthralled. This kind of drama never occurred in a small town like Larsen. It would be a tale to entertain gossip circles for decades. The audience clung to every word.

"Justice," Burns said, flashing a disgusting smile. "Ain't right and proper for you to be marryin' up with him when he's done put a kid on my Wanda, now is it?"

Grady stirred and, despite Banner's restraining hands, struggled to stand up. Reeling drunkenly with pain, he focused on the Burnses. "She's not pregnant by me."

That very word being spoken aloud sent another ripple of murmurs through the witnesses.

Banner came to her feet, took Grady's arm and defiantly faced the father and daughter who were doing their best to ruin her perfect wedding day, her perfect life, her perfect future. She didn't even notice that the front of her lovely gown was stained red with her fiancé's blood. Nor did she give heed to the speculative comments that were arising from the congregation.

Several men in the crowd had guiltily lowered their eyes. Lee was shifting uneasily from one foot to the other. He wouldn't meet the rabid eyes of Doggie Burns, or look at the sullen and silent Wanda. Micah was swallowing convulsively. Ma Langston was staring at him with an inquiring glower that would have made an archangel feel guilty.

"Well, Wanda says it's you, Sheldon," Doggie said sneeringly. "Don'tcha, Wanda?" He nudged her forward so everyone had a clearer view of her abdomen, distended by pregnancy.

There was no shame in the eyes that slyly moved over the crowd. Her mouth wore a smug pout. Those men in the room who were guilty of furthering Wanda's sluttish reputation rued the day they had touched her and only thanked the Lord it was Grady Sheldon who had been named. Numerous pledges of abstinence soared heavenward.

"It's his, all right," Wanda said sulkily. "He wouldn't stay away from me, kept comin' 'round when my daddy weren't home. Pesterin' me. He . . . he . . ."

"Go on, Wanda baby, tell 'em what he done."

She paused theatrically, then lowered her chin to her chest, picked at a piece of lint on her dress and mumbled, "He had his way with me."

"That's a damn lie!" Grady shouted over the furor that rose out of the pews.

Burns stepped forward, brandishing the pistol again. "You callin' my sweet daughter a liar?"

"If she says I forced her, yes."

Grady went white from more than blood loss and shock and pain. He realized in that instant that he had trapped himself. His eyes sliced first to Banner, who was as pale as her dress, then to Ross, who looked as dark as the devil himself. "I . . . uh . . . I mean . . ."

Ross lunged at him and grabbed his lapels, jerking him up so they met eye to eye. "Have you been keeping company with this slut while you were engaged to be married to my daughter?" he roared.

Jake had moved like quicksilver and was standing at Ross's elbow. When Grady began to moan with pain and sputter objections to Ross's rough treatment, Jake bent down and retrieved his pistol. Burns said nothing and made no move to stop him. The collective censorship had shifted. The congregation, assuming one personality, had turned their disparaging glances from the Burnses to Sheldon.

Jake cocked the Colt and shoved the long lethal barrel of it into the soft underside of Grady's chin. "Well, mister, we're waiting."

Grady threw both men a look of pure loathing. "Maybe I was with the girl a few times." Ross's knuckles turned white against Grady's dark coat. A feral growl rumbled in his chest. Grady stammered, "N-n-nearly every other man in town has bedded her. It could have been anybody."

"Every other man in town wasn't marrying my daughter," Ross snarled. He released Grady so abruptly the man almost buckled to the floor again.

"How could you?" Banner asked in the tense silence that followed.

Grady swallowed hard and staggered toward her. "Banner," he said, reaching out imploringly.

"Don't touch me." She actually recoiled. "I can't stand to think of you touching me with the same hands you . . ." She turned to look at Wanda Burns, who was standing with one hand on her outthrust hip, wearing a gloating expression.

Banner spun on her heel and marched down the aisle of the church. This time her carriage and tread were militant, haughty, proud. Her mother went behind her, equally as undaunted. The Langstons scrambled after them. The River Bend cowboys, like a small army, filed out and closed ranks around them in the churchyard while they mounted horses and climbed into rigs.

Still at the altar, Ross was so furious he was rocking on the balls on his feet, visibly quaking with fury. His eyes were molten with rage. In front of the whole town, the preacher, anyone within hearing distance, he warned, "If you ever come near my daughter again, I'll kill you. Understand? And before I finish it, you'll be begging to die."

He spun around and stalked from the church. Jake held Grady a captive of his icy cold stare for a small eternity. Gradually he lowered the pistol and replaced it in his holster. *"I'd* love to kill you right now." The ring of his spurs was the only sound in the church as he went down the aisle.

When he stepped outside, Banner was sitting in the buggy enveloped in her mother's comforting arms. Her weeping was heart-wrenching. Her supporters were subdued. No one was meeting anyone else's eyes.

Jake vaulted into the saddle of his borrowed horse. Since Ross's primary concern was for his daughter, Jake assumed the role of leader. "Micah, Lee, hang back. If anyone follows us, let me know. Everyone else fan out. Keep your eyes open." They followed his orders without question, forming a shield of feudal loyalty to protect the family.

Jake nudged his horse toward the buggy leading the others. Ross, his face as hard as granite, was handling the reins while Banner and Lydia sat huddled together, weeping quietly. Ross glanced at Jake as he pulled his horse alongside them.

"Thanks."

Jake nodded tersely. Words were unnecessary.

River Bend was decorated for the wedding reception that would never take place. The lane leading up from the river road to the main house was the first insult to Banner's sensibilities. Each whitewashed fence post was decorated with ribbons and flowers.

Her misery was intensified when she looked at the house. The railing encircling the front porch was draped with garlands of blooming honeysuckle. Sprigs of yellow forsythia had been used to decorate potted plants. Long tables had been set up in the front yard to accommodate all the food and drink that had been prepared days ahead of time for the multitude of guests who would never come. It was like looking at a nursery that had been lovingly prepared for a baby who had been stillborn.

Ross dropped to the ground from the buggy and assisted Lydia down. Jake dismounted and reached up for Banner's hand. She sat paralyzed, so benumbed by dismay that she didn't even notice Jake until he touched her arm and spoke her name softly. She glanced down and saw the sympathetic expression on his face. She smiled wanly as she accepted his hand. Laying her other hand on his shoulder, she let him swing her to the ground.

The cowboys rode toward the bunkhouse. A usually jovial, rowdy bunch, they were uncharacteristically glum. One of Anabeth's children was crankily complaining that he was thirsty. The baby was crying against his father's chest. Hector patted him, a little too hard. As silent and bleak as pallbearers, they trouped into the house.

Banner sustained another assault. Lydia had decorated the front parlor with baskets of flowers. Wedding presents that had been delivered, but were as yet unopened, were stacked on one of the several tables covered with lace cloths.

Banner shuddered on a sob. Ross came up behind her and placed his hands on her shoulders. "Princess, I—"

"Please, Papa," she said quickly, not wanting to submit to tears in front of them all, "I need to be alone."

She hitched her skirts up in a way that poignantly reminded them of her tomboyishness a few years earlier, and raced up the stairs. A few seconds later, they heard the door to her bedroom slam.

"Sonofabitch," Ross said under his breath. He whipped off his coat and wrestled with his necktie. "I should have killed that bastard with my bare hands."

Lydia didn't even reprimand him for his language. "I can't believe it of him, really I can't. Oh, Ross, that Banner's heart should be broken like this, I . . ." She went into her husband's arms and began to cry. Ross led her into the parlor.

Ma confronted the situation practically. "Anabeth, take

the young'uns into the kitchen and cut them a piece of that fancy cake the baker man brought out yesterday. No sense in it going to waste. You, Lee and Micah, take it out to the bunkhouse when Anabeth's done with it and tell the boys to polish it off.

"Marynell, you can start ladlin' up glasses of punch. I imagine everybody could use some. Hector, you sweat more than any man I ever did see. Take off that coat and tie before you melt."

Banner's wedding had provided an excuse for the Langstons to have a reunion. The family had traveled from Tennessee to Texas with Ross and Lydia. A friendship had developed between the Colemans and the Langstons that neither distance nor time had affected.

Ma Langston filled the role of grandmother to both Lee and Banner. Still tall and stout, she was an impressive woman, physically and spiritually strong, but gentle. Her scoldings were ear-blistering, but always love-inspired.

Zeke Langston had died so long ago Banner didn't even remember him. For a few years after his death, Ma had tried to work their homestead in the hill country west of Austin. During that time two of her children, Atlanta and Samuel, had died in a scarlet fever epidemic.

Fortuitously Anabeth, the eldest Langston daughter, had married a neighboring landowner and rancher, Hector Drummond. He was a widower with two young girls. They now had two boys of their own. He was managing the Langstons' land along with his. He had a small herd of beef cattle he was hoping to enlarge.

Marynell was somewhat of a bluestocking, having left home to attend school in Austin. She had worked as a Harvey House girl, waiting tables in the restaurant in the Santa Fe railroad depot to pay for her tuition. Now she was a teacher. She wasn't married and, if anyone asked, she declared she didn't intend to be.

Ross and Lydia had persuaded Ma to come live with them at River Bend when Hector took over the operation of her homestead. Ma hadn't agreed without laying down conditions. She refused to accept the Colemans' charity. She would work for her keep and so would Micah, the youngest Langston, who had been hired as a cowboy.

Ross had built Ma a small cabin. Behind it, in a field she cleared and cultivated herself, she grew and harvested all the vegetables eaten at River Bend. She also sewed for the family and ranch hands, as Lydia had never developed a talent with the needle.

The Langstons were as close as kin to the Colemans. Ma had no compunction about issuing orders whenever circumstances called for them. No one thought to question her instructions now and everyone scattered to obey them.

In the parlor, Jake was pouring Ross a tumbler of whiskey. He extended it to him wordlessly. Ross thanked him with his eyes. When the first rush of Lydia's tears had been dried, she lifted her head from her husband's shoulder. "I must go talk to her, but I don't know what to say."

"Hell if I do either," Ross grumbled, and tossed the whiskey down.

Lydia stood and smoothed her skirts. Before she left the room, she went to Jake and laid her hand along his cheek. "As always, we could count on your support."

He covered her hand, pressing. "Always," he said meaningfully.

It seemed fitting that her dress was covered with blood. She felt that her heart had been ripped out. Staring at her reflection in the mirror, she couldn't believe that only hours ago she had gazed at herself—happy, unsuspecting, innocent.

She couldn't stand the mockery of the wedding gown any longer. She thought she would scream if she didn't get out of it. Unwilling to wait for anyone to help her, she struggled with the row of hooks down her back, ripping them free when her frantic fingers couldn't unfasten them quickly enough.

At last, she flung the dress aside. Her bridal underthings were blood-stained too. She stripped until she was naked, then ruthlessly scrubbed herself from her washbowl. Long before she felt clean, tears were raining down her cheeks.

She pulled on a robe and fell across her bed in a torrent of tears.

How could he have done this to her? The pain of finding out was secondary. Knowing that he had taken another woman was the killing blow. How could he have gone to that trashy girl when he had professed his love for her? It was the cruelest, the most demeaning kind of betrayal. While Grady had been proclaiming his passion for her, he had been slaking it on Wanda Burns.

The thought of them together made her want to vomit.

She heard the door quietly open and close. She rolled to her side. Lydia moved toward the bed. Without speaking a word she sat down on the edge of it and gathered Banner against her breast.

They held each other for a long time, rocking slightly, until Banner's tears finally ran out. She burrowed her head down until it was resting in Lydia's lap. Lydia pulled her fingers through the hair that was as dark as Ross's, but which had the same volatile texture as hers. It was a mass of waves and curls that had a mind of their own and more often as not wouldn't yield to brushes or pins.

"You know that your father and I would have taken any pain on ourselves to spare you this."

"I know, Mama."

"And we'll do anything, *anything*, to help you through it."

"I know that too." She sniffed and wiped her nose on the back of her hand. "Why did he do it? How could he hurt me this way?"

"He didn't intend to hurt you, Banner. He's a man and—"

"And that makes what he did all right?"

"No, but—"

"I don't expect bridegrooms to be as virgin as their brides. I'm not that naïve. But when he's declared his love, asked a woman to marry him, isn't that a binding pledge of faithfulness?"

"I think so. Most women do. Men? I suppose most don't."

"Couldn't he have controlled his drives? Wasn't I worth waiting for?"

"He made no comparisons between you and that girl, Banner. That's obvious."

"I wanted that part of marriage just as much as he did! I told him so," she exclaimed.

Many mothers would have fainted to hear their daughters say as much. Lydia didn't flinch. She understood sexual desire and hoped her daughter would enjoy that aspect of life as much as she did. She didn't believe in making it something secretive and shameful.

"What if I'd gone to another man?" Banner demanded. "How would Grady have felt about that? Would I have been forgiven?"

Lydia sighed. "No. But that's the way of the world. Men are expected to have their . . . adventures. Grady got caught. He'll pay for it. But you'll pay too. That's unfair." She stroked Banner's cheek.

"Am I being petulant and intolerant? Should I forgive him? Did you have to forgive Papa any 'adventures'?" Banner sat up and looked directly into her mother's eyes. "Did Papa have other women after he met you?"

Lydia remembered the night Ross had helped a madam named LaRue and her covey of prostitutes with their wagon. He had stayed late and came back drunk and stinking of whores' perfume. He had sworn then and later that he had gone to the madam's wagon, but couldn't go through with the act. Lydia believed him. "Ross had many women before me, but after we met, no. I can understand how hurt you are."

"I guess Grady didn't love me like Papa loves you."

"But someone will, darling."

"I don't think so, Mama." This brought on another flood of tears.

When Lydia finally left her, Banner lay on her bed, gazing sightlessly at the ceiling. She had to face the truth about her emotions. Which did she feel more keenly? Hurt or anger?

Had her love for Grady disintegrated the moment she

realized his betrayal? She was furious with him for dragging not only her name, but that of her family, into disgrace. The people of Larsen wouldn't forget today for a long time. It was human nature to be absorbed by someone else's misfortune. It didn't matter that all the Colemans were blameless. Grady had stigmatized them just as he had himself.

She was angry. And it overrode her hurt. She didn't want Grady back, not in a million years. She ached more for her parents' suffering than she did for his. He had made his bed, let him lie in it. Never had the adage been truer.

So maybe she hadn't loved him as she thought she had. Still, if his deceit hadn't caught up with him today and revealed him for the weak character he was, she would have remained blissfully ignorant of that. She would have been his loving wife forever. Of that she was certain. Her anger could be absolved on that basis.

She lay there for a long while, not even noticing the passing hours until the room grew dark and she realized that the sun had gone down.

Coming off the bed suddenly, she vowed that she wasn't going to skulk around like she was the guilty party. She would be damned before she let Grady Sheldon and all the gossips in town defeat her.

She washed her face in cold water to relieve the puffiness around her eyes. Dressing in a simple gingham dress and smoothing back her hair, she descended the staircase. Everyone was gathered in the kitchen for supper. The conversation ceased abruptly when they noticed her standing in the doorway.

All eyes turned to her deferentially. Even Anabeth's children fell abnormally quiet. What had they expected? For her to retreat to her room for the rest of her life? Become an invalid? Hide behind gray, somber clothes? Develop a tendency to have vapors like a shriveled-up old maid?

"I'm hungry," she announced. "Is there anything left?"

They had all become still, captured like a painting on a Christmas card, when they saw her. Now everyone moved at once, shifting places to make room for her at the table, getting her a plate and silverware, passing bowls of food toward her. They were all talking in inordinately loud voices. Their smiles were too broad. Their eyes too bright.

"You were telling us about those new bulls of yours, Hector," Ross said in a booming voice that set Anabeth's baby to crying.

"Uh, yes, well, I, uh, I . . ."

Poor Mr. Drummond, Banner thought as she lowered her eyes to her plate. He was nervous enough without having to be put on the spot by making normal conversation. She didn't say much, but she refused to keep her eyes glued to her plate either. She wasn't really hungry, but forced herself to eat at least half the portion.

Someone, Ma probably, had seen to it that the house was relieved of its decorations. Not a trace of the wedding reception could be found save for the fruity punch they were drinking. Lydia had carried the defiled wedding gown from her bedroom. She hoped it had been burned. The baskets of flowers were gone. The yard had been cleared. Lydia had also told her not to worry about returning the gifts, that she would see to that painful chore. Banner supposed she had begun that process, for the gift-wrapped boxes were nowhere to be seen.

Except for the unusual number of people gathered around the table, it could have been any spring evening. Banner thought she was actually more at ease than the others. Frequently they glanced at her worriedly as though she might begin to tear at her hair at any moment.

When the children finished eating, Marynell offered to take them for a stroll outside. Lee and Micah left as soon as they were done, muttering something about a poker game in the bunkhouse. Ma began clearing the dishes.

"You stay where you're at," she ordered sternly as Lydia rose from her chair. "I'll get this done in two shakes."

Anabeth got up to help her. Hector and Ross were discussing ranching in general.

Lydia listened, gazing at Ross.

Jake quietly sipped his coffee, gazing at Lydia.

Banner thought nothing of that because that was normal.

"I think I'll go out on the porch," Banner said, scooting her chair back.

"Let's all go out there," Lydia said hastily. "It'll be cooler. Jake, Hector, bring your coffee if you're not finished."

When the kitchen chores were done, Marynell drove Ma to her cabin. Anabeth and Hector went with them to put the cantankerous children to bed. Banner let the desultory conversations flow around her. At last, she stepped off the porch into the yard.

"Banner?"

"I'm just going for a walk, Papa," she said over her shoulder, noticing the worry in his voice.

She went as far as the fence that served as a boundary for one of the pastures. A colt and his dam were playing chase in the lush spring undergrowth.

"Looks like a frisky one."

She turned to see Lee and Micah walking toward her. "He should be. Wasn't Spartan his sire?"

"Yep. He's one of the best. Don't you think, Micah?"

"Sure enough."

"Did you two come out here to discuss the breed stock? I thought there was a hot poker game going on."

"Got cleaned out," Micah said, and made a gesture of turning his pockets inside out. The moonlight made his hair look almost as light as Jake's. But not quite.

Banner put her hands on her hips. "Who was it just the other day who bragged he could beat anybody at cards?"

Micah cuffed her under the chin. "Don't you ever forget nothing?"

They were engaging in this familiar banter to try to alleviate the awkwardness. Making light conversation hadn't been easy on anyone since leaving the church.

"What did you really come out here for?" Banner asked them.

Lee glanced at Micah, who gave him an encouraging tilt of his head. "Well, we just wanted to, uh, talk to you about what happened in the church."

She crossed her arms on the top rail of the fence and leaned forward. "What about it?"

"Well, uh, Banner, Grady might not be the one at fault."

"What do you mean?"

Lee swallowed and looked to Micah for needed support. He was absorbed with the pony in the pasture and offered no help at all. "We mean that, uh, a lot of guys, you know, uh, have been with that little tart. She might very well be pointing the finger at the wrong man."

"Yeah," Micah suddenly chimed in. "It could've been any of fifty guys in town. But Sheldon, well, he'd be a fine catch for her to trap, seeing as he owns that sawmill and all. Ya see?"

"Just because he's been with her, that doesn't make it his kid. That's what we're trying to say," Lee finished lamely. "Maybe it'll make you feel better knowing that."

Banner's throat tightened with emotion. "What makes me feel better is knowing that the two of you care about me." She hugged first Lee, then Micah, who hugged her back awkwardly. He wasn't just another cowboy, but he wasn't legally family either.

He had teased Banner since she was old enough to have her braids tied in knots, but in the last few years he had come to notice the changes in her even if her brother hadn't.

Micah wasn't immune to them, but he was smart enough to keep his distance. He wasn't about to incur Ma's wrath, much less Ross's, or sacrifice his friendship with Lee by making a pass at Banner.

She was off limits to cowboys, and that included him. It was an indisputable fact that he had known for a long time. There were lots of girls in the world. Banner might be one of the prettiest, but no woman was worth sacrificing a buddy's friendship for, much less losing your life over.

"I appreciate what you're trying to do," she said softly. "Grady might not be that baby's father. But he *is* guilty of being with her. He as much as admitted that. Either way, he's betrayed me."

"Yeah, I reckon that's so," Micah conceded. He only knew that if he had been engaged to Banner Coleman he would have had the good sense not to risk losing her no matter how thick the front of his britches got. He had known plenty of fools, but this Sheldon was by far the biggest one he'd ever run across.

Lee plowed at the ground with the toe of his boot. "I feel sorry for the guy for getting caught doing what all of us . . . I mean, what so many others do. But at the same time, I'd like to pound his face to mush."

Banner laid a hand on his arm. "Don't do it, but thanks for the thought."

Lee lifted his head and smiled at his half-sister. "Say, Banner, they opened up a new dry-goods store in Tyler. It's supposed to be really something. Me and Micah were thinking of riding over there one of these Saturdays as soon as all the mares foal. Would you like to go with us?"

She knew then the extent of their love. She had always tagged behind them, begging to go along, only to get left in their trail dust. "Thanks, I'd like that," she said, including both of them in her smile.

They left her, melting into the darkness, their soft conversation audible long after the shadows swallowed them. She ambled back toward the house. Bracing her back against the trunk of the pecan tree, she took in the placid picture before her.

The frame house showed up whitely against the darkness. Oil lamps from inside made the windows glow golden, warm, and welcoming. Morning glory vines were just starting their summer climb up the six columns, three on each side of the porch. The first shoots of zinnias and larkspurs were greening the flowerbeds. Smoke still curled from the chimney in the kitchen. The setting was deceptive. It didn't look like a tragedy had just befallen the family who lived there.

When Ross and Lydia first came to the land, they had lived out of Moses's covered wagon. As soon as possible Ross had built a dog-trot house, having the kitchen and living area separated from the sleeping quarters by an open hallway. It was small and rough, but Lydia hadn't minded. She understood their priority was to establish the business first.

Banner was born in the dog-trot house and was ten before

the new house was built. Even by city standards it was
graciously constructed. There were four bedrooms upstairs,
though Lee most often slept in the bunkhouse. Downstairs
was a front parlor and an informal parlor, a dining room,
which was rarely used in preference to the eating area in the
large kitchen. At the back of the house adjacent to the
screened back porch was Ross's office.

Tears clouded Banner's eyes as she steeped herself in the
tranquillity of her home. She hadn't had any qualms about
leaving it to get married because she had thought she was
going into a home with even more love, hers and Grady's.
Her heart ached with what would never be.

Ross and Lydia were sitting together on the wicker glider.
Jake was standing in the corner of the porch, his shoulder
propped against the column. His cheroot was a glowing red
dot. Banner could smell its fragrant smoke from where she
stood beneath the tree. He looked so alone standing there,
apart from the couple on the glider.

Even as Banner watched, Ross cupped his hand around
Lydia's cheek and guided her head to his shoulder. He
leaned down and planted a soft kiss at her hairline. She
rested her hand on his thigh.

Twin tears escaped Banner's eyes. That's what she had
wanted, longed for, that kind of loving. It was comfortable,
peaceful. The touches. The speaking glances that excluded
the rest of the world. She had wanted to share that kind of
oneness with a man. Her disappointment was so profound
she ached from it.

Despair shackled her. Hopelessness smothered her like a
shroud. Hastily she left the protective shadows of the tree,
went up the steps of the porch, said a fleeting good night,
and climbed the stairs to her room.

She went to the valise in which she had packed part of
her trousseau and lifted out the nightgown that had been
specially made for her wedding night. It was self-punishment,
but it was something she felt compelled to do. The gown
was sheer white batiste with a scooped neck and long
sleeves banded at the wrists. The neckline was decorated
with embroidered yellow roses and a row of narrow lace.

Simple, elegant, and seductive. When she slipped it over her naked body, her figure was silhouetted within its sheer folds.

She went to bed alone, wallowing in the loss of what tonight should have been. She lay in her bed, feeling more alien and alone than she ever had in her life. Everyone had someone tonight. Ma Langston had her living children and her grandchildren gathered under her roof. Ross and Lydia had each other. Lee and Micah were bound by friendship. Even Marynell had her books for companions.

Only the bride was alone.

She heard her parents come upstairs and go to their room, closing the door behind them. Banner's heart twisted painfully. It wasn't fair! She had been cheated. Why couldn't Grady have loved her with the kind of love her parents shared? Was he the exception to the rule or were they?

Her body yearned for what she had mentally prepared it for. She longed for the warmth of another body beside hers. A man's body. A man's arms around her, touching tenderly. A man loving her. Her heart cried out for communion with another.

Restless, she threw off the light sheet and crossed to the window. The breeze cooled her cheeks, but not the raging inside her. The night was beautiful, bathed with the silvery glow of a half-moon. Stars winked. The clover in the pastures gave off its perfume. All her senses were atuned to the things of nature.

She saw movement. A red dot arced away from the porch and vanished like a firefly. Jake's cigar. Seconds later he stepped off the porch. His spurs jingled softly as he crossed the yard toward the oldest barn on the ranch where his injured horse was stabled.

Jake.

She wasn't the only one who was alone. Jake was. And it occurred to her then that he usually was. Even in the midst of Colemans and Langstons, there was a separateness about Jake. He talked and laughed like everybody else, but he was the loner.

Banner thought she knew the reason why, and it made her incredibly sad for him.

She watched him slip into the barn. Moments later the dim glow of a lantern shone through one of the dusty windows.

This was to have been her wedding night. She had been rejected. She had suffered the harshest insult inflicted on a woman. A bride, standing on the brink of a brilliant future, had been plunged into an abyss of dejection. She had been publicly humiliated.

Her confidence in herself as a woman must be restored. Tonight. Or it might never recover. She desperately needed someone to hold her, to tell her she was beautiful, to reassure her she was every bit as desirable as Wanda Burns. She needed love. Not parental love. Not sibling love.

She needed to be loved by a man.

Her heart began to pound. Her head throbbed with the thought that had taken root there. Like a seed, nestling itself in the earth, the idea had secured itself in her fertile brain. There was no stopping it from germinating and growing.

Whirling toward her dressing table, she gazed at her image in the mirror and tried to imagine how a man would see her, a man who was as alone and lonely and without love tonight as she.

Before she could change her mind, she yanked up a wrap and threw it around her shoulders. No one heard her as she crept down the stairs and let herself out the front door.

THREE

The old barn smelled of hay, horses, and leather. Banner liked those familiar smells. She filled her head with them as she slipped inside and soundlessly pulled the door closed behind her. The warm, musky air settled around her like a blanket. The atmosphere was still, yet teeming with hidden life. Mares, heavy with pregnancy, rested in their stalls. Crickets chirped from secret hideouts.

It wasn't all that unusual for her to be standing in the barn in her nightgown. Often she had been allowed to keep vigil through the night when a mare was in the throes of a difficult birth. But it was unusual to be in the barn in her nightgown and alone with a man, even a man who was a part of her memory as far back as it went.

She felt the first twinges of apprehension. What she was about to do was bold. Twenty-four hours ago, it would have been unthinkable. But twenty-four hours ago she hadn't known fate could take such cruel twists or that futures could be altered so drastically without one's consent.

The decision had been made. She had come this far. There would be no turning back.

Stalks of hay pricked her bare feet as she tiptoed toward the small pool of light in one of the back stalls. The stabled horses were so accustomed to her scent that they didn't even nicker as she moved down the row of stalls.

Jake's hat, wide-brimmed, flat-crowned, and black, was hanging on a nail on one of the support posts. She touched the felt brim, smiling at the dark streak her finger left behind by picking up dust.

She peered around the shoulder-high wall that separated the stalls. Jake was hunkered down at his mount's right front leg. He had bent it back and, with the hoof propped on his knee, was inspecting the bruise the stone had made.

Banner was glad she had this moment to study him without his knowing it. She had grown up seeing him in one light. Tonight she would consider him in a whole new way. He could no longer merely be her champion, her parents' trusted friend, or Lee and Micah's idol, or Ma's son. Banishing all her previous views of Jake Langston from her consciousness, Banner considered him strictly as a man, as though seeing him through a stranger's eyes.

What she saw pleased her mightily, and she honestly

didn't think that having loved him all her life in another way prejudiced her opinion as she gazed at him now.

Every fine strand of white-blond hair captured the lantern's glow. His hair was as vital as the rest of him, unruly, hard to control, lacking discipline. With his head bowed as it was, she could see that it grew from a whorl on the crown and fell about his head in wayward strands that arranged themselves attractively of their own free will. She couldn't imagine him ever plastering it to his head with pomade as Grady sometimes did his brown curls. No, Jake would never subject any part of himself to that much constraint.

He wore it long, whether from neglect or design, she didn't know. It brushed against the collar of his shirt when he moved. It was curled only slightly around well-shaped ears. Sideburns the color of ripened wheat grew down his cheek to the middle of his ear. Those hairs looked crisp, curlier. She wanted to touch them, to feel the contrast of them against the velvety softness of his earlobe. His eyebrows, which were now lowered in concentration, were that same incredible light shade of blond.

She analyzed the face she had known since childhood, what she could see of it as he bent over the injured hoof. His brow bone jutted slightly over his eyes and his cheekbones were prominent, his cheeks slightly concave. He was saved from appearing gaunt only by a discernible wiry strength.

His jaw was hard and definitely chiseled, with no softening contours to make it appear anything but determined. It seemed ready to issue a challenge to anyone, no matter how formidable. If allowed to grow, no doubt his facial hair would be blond, too, but its stubble now shadowed the lower part of his face.

She wondered what he would look like with a thick mustache like Papa's, but immediately dismissed the idea. His mouth was wide. The lower lip was a tad fuller than the upper, though the upper was nicely shaped. Staring at his mouth made her stomach feel funny. She decided it would be a crime to cover up such a beguiling mouth with a mustache.

She supposed he had changed out of his wedding clothes as soon as they returned to the house. He still had on what he had been wearing at supper, a soft cotton shirt in a muted blue. Denim pants. His boots were old and scuffed. There was a faded red bandana tied around his neck. He didn't have on the holster that carried his Colt, or a vest, or leather chaps which she had seen him wear.

The sleeves of his shirt had been rolled up to his elbows. Banner noticed how supple the muscles in his arms were when he moved them. His skin was deeply tanned and dusted with hairs so light they appeared white in the glow of the lantern.

His hands moved deftly but soothingly as they examined the horse's injury. The fingers were slender and long, but their strength was evident as he alternately squeezed and released them around the hoof. Watching that rhythmic massage, Banner's stomach took another unprecedented somersault.

She had never been aware of such maleness. Sheer maleness. Mature maleness. Packaged so compactly. And her curiosity in it was unwarranted because she had been around men all her life. Ross, Lee and Micah, the ranch hands. But she had never studied them as she did Jake now. Nor did she think she would have been as impressed if she had.

He was manly in a way that unnerved her.

She quailed against such raw masculinity.

But oddly, her femininity gravitated toward it too. It forced her to speak before she could talk herself into slipping from the barn unseen, to wonder forever what this night would have held for her if only she had had the courage to go through with it. She would have much to regret about this day on the calendar, but failure to act when she felt compelled to wasn't going to be one of them.

"How's your horse?"

Jake's head popped up. "Heavenly days, girl! Don't you know better than to sneak up on people? You almost spooked both me and Stormy." He took in her bare feet and the hem of her nightgown, which was all he could see beneath the deep fringe of her shawl. Her arms were crossed over her chest, wrapping her in the shawl like an Indian in his blanket. "What are you doing gallivanting around out here? I thought everybody had gone to bed."

His eyes really were incredibly blue. Why was it that she had never paid much attention to them before? Oh, if someone had asked, "Hey, what color are Jake Langston's eyes?" her automatic answer would have been "blue." But tonight they seemed to shine right through her as he looked up at her from his squatting position.

The colors were well demarcated. The whites were very white. The blue irises were as cerulean as the sky in late fall. The pupils were an ebony that reflected an image of herself. She noticed for the first time that his eyelashes were dark at their base and sun-bleached on the curling tips.

They were interesting eyes, and she wished she could stare at and assess them without his knowing it. She couldn't; he was looking at her expectantly, waiting for her to tell him why she wasn't safely tucked into her bed.

"I couldn't sleep." Suddenly shy, she ducked her head.

"Ah," Jake said, raising his body to its full height and patting Stormy's neck. He dipped his hands into a pail of water, washed and shook them off, then wiped them on a towel. "Well, that's understandable after what happened today."

Banner raised her head and looked up at him. Whatever he was about to say next was momentarily postponed, as though he had just taken a clip on the chin. "Uh..." he stalled. His gaze was riveted on her face. He removed it by force; he blinked. He noted her dishabille. "You could get in a heap of trouble fanning around out here in the dark dressed like that." His tone was a fraction cross.

"Could I?"

An expression of profound bewilderment flickered over Jake's lean face. His lips parted slightly. An instant later he drew them together in a stern line. "Yeah, you damn sure could. Come on, I'll walk you back to the house."

He reached to take her arm, but she sidestepped him and

ran her hand down Stormy's ribs. "You didn't tell me how Stormy is faring."

"Fine."

"Is he?"

"That hoof will be tender for a few days. That's all. Now come on—"

"Whatever happened to Apple Jack?"

"Apple Jack?" Jake repeated. His face broke into a spontaneous smile. "He was some cow pony, wasn't he? He knew before I even nudged him with my knees what I wanted him to do. I used to say that I could sleep all day in my saddle and Apple Jack wouldn't let one stray go by. He was a damn good horse. But he stepped in a prairie dog hole and broke his leg. I had to shoot him." He cocked his shining head to one side. "How come you remember Apple Jack?"

"I remember." She was still running her hand over Stormy's gleaming russet coat. Like all cowboys, Jake took better care of his horse than he did of himself.

For some reason, Jake couldn't take his eyes off her hand as it coasted over Stormy's broad back. The shawl slid back toward her elbow. The sleeve of her gown was sheer. Through it, he could see the shape of her arm.

"When I was about twelve you came to see us. You had been visiting for a few days, but you were leaving that afternoon. Mama had cooked black-eyed peas and cornbread for dinner, fried chicken, and apple pie. All my favorites. But I didn't eat anything. I was mad because you were going away again, even after Papa had asked you to stay. Papa told me to straighten up and act civil or leave the table. I went up to my room to pout and refused to say goodbye. From my bedroom window I watched you ride out of the yard."

She turned toward him then, leaning her head against the horse. "But I couldn't stand it. I bolted down the stairs and ran after you. I chased you down the river road, calling your name until you finally heard me and reined up. When I got even with you, you lifted me up onto Apple Jack with you and hugged me. You told me not to cry, that you would be coming back for Christmas.'' The eyes that had the warm glow of topaz and the liquid fire of emeralds gazed up at him accusingly. ''But you didn't.''

''I reckon something came up, Banner.''

''You didn't come back for two years.''

Only now did she realize the significance that day had had on her adolescence. Long after he had ridden away, she had lain in her bed and wept bitterly. Intuitively she had known it would be a long time before she saw him again and her young heart had been breaking over it.

She must have had a crush on him. He had been tall and good-looking. He was gallant and exciting and full of wonderful stories to tell. He had teased her, but not in the irritating way Lee and Micah did. His teasing had made her feel all grown up.

She rose and took a brave step closer to him, close enough for the hem of her nightgown to brush the toes of his boots. ''You let me ride to the gate with you on Apple Jack. That was a special goodbye because the rest of the family wasn't crowded around. I had you all to myself.'' She let her gaze lock with his. Her head tilted back and sent a dark cloud of hair down her shoulders and across her breasts. ''You kissed me.''

It had been one fraternal quick kiss on her cheek, but she had never forgotten it.

At those three whispered words, Jake jumped as though he had been shot. Roughly, he encircled her upper arm with his strong fingers and turned her toward the opening of the stall. ''It's time you got to bed. You need a good night's sleep.''

Purposefully she dragged her heels behind his hurried footsteps. ''Where are you going to sleep? In the bunkhouse?''

''No. I want to keep an eye on Stormy one more night. I'm going to bed down where I did last night. Here in the barn.''

''That couldn't have been too comfortable,'' she said, disengaging her arm from his grip.

''It was fine, Banner, now come—''

''Where were you sleeping? Did you have any padding?''

"Padding?" It was a near shout, but for the life of him, he couldn't pen down what was irritating him. "You're talking to a man who has spent more nights outdoors on the ground than indoors on a bed."

"Well, that doesn't mean you have to sleep like that when it's not necessary," she countered with an asperity that matched his.

Before he could stop her, she spun around and checked each stall until she found the one where his saddlebags and bedroll were.

Propping her hands on her hips she faced him. "Jake Langston, what would people think if they knew that the Colemans of River Bend let their guests sleep like saddle tramps?"

Her stance allowed the shawl to gape open over her breasts. She was revealing to him the scooped, rose-bordered neckline of her gown, not to mention what lay beneath it. She almost lost her nerve and gathered the shawl back across her breasts and ran, but she stood her ground, pretending to be vexed with him.

"It's fine, Banner," Jake said tightly. The muscles in his jaw looked like they were cramped and could barely move. "Now, if you'll get out of here I'll make use of this bed, such as it is."

"No, you won't. At least not before I make it more comfortable for you. Hand me a few of those spare horse blankets. They're clean. At least I can spread those beneath your blanket."

He ran an impatient hand through his hair before turning away to get the blankets. As he handed them to her he said tersely, "Hurry up. It's late and you shouldn't be out here."

Ignoring his deepening scowl and afraid to speculate on what it meant, she tossed aside his blanket and with more movement than necessary, flapped the first horse blanket in the air before letting it settle on the hay. She did three more like that before spreading his blanket over them and kneeling to smooth out the wrinkles. If she was aware that the shawl had slipped off one shoulder dragging the sleeve of her nightgown with it, she made no move to rectify it.

Her breasts moved beneath the sheer fabric of her gown. She could feel their swaying weight as she extended her arms to prepare his pallet. She felt the soft caress of the batiste on her nipples as her knees caught in the cloth and pulled it taut. The mellow light from the lantern was flattering to the tone of her skin. Was it creating a shadow in her cleavage? Had Jake noticed that she was no longer a twelve-year-old girl with a tear-streaked face? Garnering all her courage, she stood up and faced him.

"There, that's much better, isn't it?"

Jake wiped his palms on his pants legs. The lines running down the sides of his mouth had deepened considerably. A vein ticked in his temple. "Yeah, that's better. Now, good night, Banner."

He turned away abruptly and began arranging the items from his saddlebag on one of the slats that served as a shelf.

"But I'm not sleepy."

"Go to bed anyway."

"I don't want to."

"*I* want you to."

"Why?"

"Because you shouldn't be out here like . . . like this."

"Why?"

"Because."

His shoulders were hunched defensively. His motions were quick and clumsy. He was having a hard time getting his shaving mug to fit on the narrow shelf.

"Jake?" He grunted an acknowledgment. "Jake, look at me."

His hands stilled their needless activity. He even braced them for a moment on the top of the stall. Banner saw his shoulders lift and his ribcage expand with a heavy sigh. Then he turned around.

He didn't look at her, but stared into the near space just above her head. Her hands found each other at her waist and came together as through drawn by strong magnets. She stood straight and rigid, her legs pressed tightly together from groin to ankle. She wet her lips with her tongue.

"Jake, make love to me."

Seconds ticked by silently. The air was thick with tension, unspoken thoughts, labored heartbeats. Neither of them moved. Finally one of the stabled horses snuffled. Jake glanced in that direction. He looked down at his feet, rolling one back on its heel and inspecting the toe of his boot as though he'd never seen it before. He shoved his hands into the hip pockets of his pants, but removed them as though he'd touched something hot inside. He crossed his arms over his chest. He glanced down the row of stalls, up at the rafters, over at the flickering lantern.

At last his eyes came back to Banner. This time, he looked at her. "I think you would do well to leave right now and let's forget you ever said that."

She was shaking her head before he finished. "No. I've said it. It's what I want. That's why I came out here. Please, Jake. Make love to me."

He snorted a soft laugh, relaxing a bit and shaking his head. "Banner, sweetheart, honey, I don't want to laugh at you, but—"

"Don't you dare laugh at me." The words were brittle. "God knows that's what everyone else in town is doing tonight."

Jake cleared his face of all humor lest she mistake it for derision. "I would never laugh at you, Banner. But what you're suggesting is ridiculous and you know it."

"Why?"

"Why?" He winced when his shout startled several of the horses. He gave them time to settle down and lowered his voice to a hoarse whisper. "It's ridiculous. I'm . . . we're . . . you're . . . you're too young."

"I'm old enough to get married."

"But not to me! Banner, I'm twice your age."

She dismissed that argument. "I was supposed to be a bride tonight, Jake, to know a man's love. I've been cheated of that. Help me. I need you. Do this for me."

"I can't," he snapped.

"You can."

"I can't."

"You do it all the time!"

"That's a helluva thing for a young lady to say."

"But it's true, isn't it? I hear the men talking about your conquests."

He pointed a stern finger at her. "Now, Banner, you stop that dirty kind of talking right now. Go on to bed or I'll paddle your behind so hard—"

"Stop talking to me as though I were a child!"

"To me that's what you are."

She shrugged the shawl off. It landed on the hay with a soft whisper. "Look at me, Jake. I'm not a little girl anymore. I'm a woman."

Oh, Jesus.

His insides groaned. She was a woman all right. A beautiful, enticing woman. It was a fact he was trying his damnedest to ignore, but his body was making it tough. When had she stopped being darling little Banner? When had she stopped being the precious daughter of his best friends? When had she gone from all elbows and knees, long ungainly limbs and untidy braids, to soft womanhood? From coltish thinness to slender softness that curved voluptuously? Had the transformation taken place gradually over the years since he had seen her, or in the last ninety seconds?

Her hair was as black as midnight, a soft wreath of curls around her oval face. A man's hands could get lost in that hair. Jake could imagine it coiling around his fingers, feel it against his face, his lips, his belly.

He had acknowledged years ago that she was a pretty child, but this was no child gazing up at him with smoky eyes and a mouth that he suddenly thought he had to taste or die.

Her face was sensual and provocative. It should have belonged to a woman without morals, one who knew her way around a man and what to do to make him tick. That that face was worn by a sweet, innocent girl, one he had known from the cradle, was one of God's cruelest jokes.

Her eyes had too much fire to protect her purity from marauders. Framed as they were by arching dark brows and surrounded by spiky black lashes, they were too bold, too intriguing, too inviting for her own good. Her honesty and forthrightness were hazardous to her virtue. One look at that sensuous mouth was enough to drive a man right through the bounds of loyalty and allegiance. Who could think of old friendships with a temptation like that offering itself up to be sampled?

The smattering of freckles across the bridge of her nose was impudent. Her skin looked as soft as satin and as warm as fresh milk. Jake didn't dare imagine what it tasted like. She smelled like she had just washed with a soap scented with flowers. He wanted to bury his face in a bouquet of them.

She was naked beneath the sheer, virginal nightgown. To even think about Banner Coleman naked was a sin for sure. He had no doubt that Ross would shoot a man who even looked like he was thinking about Banner naked.

But what man with a beating heart and breathing lungs wouldn't fantasize about that slim body silhouetted against the soft fabric, wouldn't want it entwined with his own? What man would be blind to the fullness of her breasts which stirred the soft cloth covering them each time she drew a tremulous breath? And hell, if he could see the darker centers of them . . . ? Damn! Of the slender legs and that dusky shadow between her thighs he couldn't think at all or he would go stark, raving mad and do something he could be hanged for.

But her sexiness came from more than a provocative face and a seductive body. It was her spirit that first captured a man's imagination. There was a wildness about her that begged to be tamed by anyone with enough courage to try. Her fiery nature was a challenge any man worth his salt would love to tangle with, if not to break, then to bend to his will.

This tiny bundle of womanhood had walked up to him and, with a spunk he had to admire, asked him to take her virginity.

But no matter how appealing the thought, there was no way on God's green earth that Jake would touch her.

He loved her because of who she was. He wasn't about to

sacrifice a twenty-year friendship for twenty minutes' worth of pleasure. He cursed himself for not taking one of Priscilla's whores last night. Then his body wouldn't be so hungry. It would be easier to say no to Banner. He convinced himself that's why he had given the idea even this much thought.

His answer was never in question. He had to let her down. But gently. Without risking their affection for each other. Without dealing her pride another blow.

"I know you're a woman, Banner. Frankly I'm shocked to realize just how much of a woman you've become."

"Then make love to me."

"No. That would only make things worse. Tonight you're hurt, you feel rejected in favor of another woman. I understand. You're desperate. This is a natural reaction to what Sheldon did to you. You're trying to salve your wounded pride. That sonofabitch embarrassed you and you've got to get your pride back. But this isn't the way."

"It is," she argued earnestly.

He shook his head. Stepping forward, he laid his hands on her shoulders. That was a risky move, but one he felt he had to take. It was necessary to convince himself he could still touch her and think of her in the affectionate terms of an uncle. And he had to convince her that's how he felt toward her. "Banner, let's not talk about this anymore. Please go back to the house. In the morning things will look different. I promise. We'll go riding together and—"

"Jake, don't you want me?" she cried softly. "Aren't I desirable enough?"

"Banner," he groaned, pinching his eyes closed.

"If I were any other woman, would you want me?"

"But you're not."

"Does it matter that much?"

"It's all that matters. You're *Banner*, Ross and Lydia's baby girl. I remember when you were born, for godsakes."

Her heart thudding nervously, she laid her hands on his chest and gazed up into his face. "But if you didn't remember all that—"

"But I do." He shoved away and turned his back. His head fell forward and he ground at his eyesockets with the heels of his hands. If only he couldn't see, smell, feel. If only all his senses would stop operating. Instead they were clamoring, working furiously. His sex drive had always been his downfall, governing decisions when his brain should have governed.

He disgusted himself. It wasn't possible that he could have an erection for the little girl he used to push high in her swing until she squealed in glee. But he did. A helluva one. How? How could his body betray his conscience?

"You want a man tonight, Banner," he said roughly. "All right, I can sympathize and understand, though I still think that's no solution for heartbreak." He paused to draw a breath. "But I swear to you, I'm not the one you want. I'm a saddle tramp, a shiftless cowboy that farmers hide their daughters from. I've done things, witnessed things, that would make you cringe. I shirk responsibility. I'm a wanderer without a thing to my name except what I can pack in my saddlebags. When I do have a few dollars I spend them on whiskey, cards, and whores. And I've had plenty of them too. My hands aren't clean enough to touch you. Think about that."

"I love you, no matter what you are or what you've done. It doesn't matter. I've always loved you."

"I love you, too, Banner. But we're talking about something else entirely." He dropped his hands to his sides with a finality she couldn't misinterpret. "I'm not the man you want tonight, Banner."

"I'm not the woman you want either, Jake," she said harshly. "You want my mother."

He spun around sharply. "What did you say?" Gone was the weary defeat in his stance. The humility and self-deprecation had vanished. His face was hard. His brows were pulled down low over his eyes which were busily searching her face.

"I said that you want my mother," Banner replied clearly. He stared at her, hard and angrily. Her chin went up a notch. "You love her, Jake."

"You don't know what you're talking about."

"Deep down I guess I've always known it, but it only

occurred to me recently." His eyes continued staring at her in that penetrating relentless way. "I think Ma knows too. That's why she never presses you to stay on here, isn't it? That's why you never stay long, because you can't bear to see her and Papa together."

Emotion spasmed across his face. It shimmered off him like heat waves off the arid prairie in the summertime. "Ross is the finest man I've ever met. My best friend."

Banner softened and smiled. "I know that, Jake. You probably love Papa just as much as you love her, only in a different way. But don't insult me by denying you love Mama. I know you do."

He turned away from her again, but not completely, only a quarter-turn so that she saw him in profile. He drove his fingers through his hair, then laced them together and bounced them against each other. His face was ravaged by guilt and regret.

Banner's heart swelled with compassion. She had played her trump card and it had turned out to be a winning move, but there was no glory in her victory. She had always suspected the reason for Jake's self-imposed loneliness. Now her suspicion was confirmed. She stepped around him and pressed herself against him, locking her arms around his waist as she had when she was a child.

Only this time it was vastly different. It was surprising how good his body felt against hers. He was taller than Grady, harder, leaner. Something stirred inside her, something wonderful, something forbidden. Made more wonderful because of its forbidden nature.

"It's all right, Jake. I didn't say that to make you feel bad. Your mother and I are probably the only ones who have guessed, and we wouldn't tell anybody. You can't help loving her." She raised her head from his chest. "Since you can't have her tonight, take me."

Her hair fell away from her face to sift over her shoulders and down her back. Without thinking about it, Jake's arms went around her. He was still dazed by Banner's perception of the feelings he had harbored for Lydia all these years, ever since he first saw her lying near death in a rainy forest in Tennessee.

"You're alone, Jake, yearning for a woman you've loved for years. But she loves someone else, belongs to him and always will. I was supposed to become a woman tonight. I doubt I'll ever risk loving a man after the way Grady humiliated me. But I need to know I'm capable of winning a man's love. Give me my confidence back."

She raised her hands and touched his face. Her fingertips glided over it, acquainting her sense of touch with each rugged contour, each prominent bone. She indulged her curiosity and found the sideburns as coarse as she had suspected and the lobes of his ears as soft. She traced the stern lines curving down from the sides of his mouth.

"We're exactly what the other needs. Let's give each other comfort and love tonight, Jake."

Her gentle touches had roused him from his trance. They also served to give her words credence. His hands opened wide across her back and drew her close. He buried his face in her hair, hair so like Lydia's in texture. He moaned when her body naturally curved up to fit his. "We can't do this. Banner."

"We can."

"I'm the last thing you need."

"You're the only one I would consider asking to do this."

"You're a virgin."

"Yes."

"I'll hurt you."

"You couldn't."

"You'll suffer for this later."

"I'll suffer more if you don't." Her lips touched his throat where his shirt was opened. His skin was warm.

He sighed and nipped her shoulders lightly. "This is wrong."

"How could this be wrong? You used to kiss my scrapes and bruises to make them well. Kiss me now, Jake. Take away this terrible pain inside me. Even if you must pretend I'm my mother."

His mouth met hers even before she had finished speaking. A gentle brush of lips. An exchange of breath. Petal soft. But electric. Again. Longer this time. Then he pressed his mouth over hers. And stayed.

Her arms timidly went around his neck. He felt the peaks of her breasts against his chest and almost forgot to go slowly. His mouth moved over hers, hungrily now. He slanted it across hers until her lips parted. He swept her mouth with his tongue.

She reacted with a startled catch of her breath and a jolt of her body that straightened it and pulled it up hard and high against his, as though someone had tugged sharply on a string at the top of her head.

He got lost, irretrievably lost, in her taste and scent and softness.

Moments later, they fell to the bed on the hay. "Banner, Banner." His breathing was choppy. "Stop this. I can't now. And it's wrong."

"Please, Jake. Love me."

All the objections he had lined up in his mind were shot down like targets in a gallery as he slipped the gown off one shoulder and touched her throat with his open mouth. He reached between their bodies, adjusted their clothing.

Her bare skin caressing his. Her femininity cradling him. Soft and yielding woman flesh.

The road to hell was paved with silk.

"Oh, God, oh, God, help me not to do this," he prayed.

But God was otherwise occupied and didn't hear Jake Langston's fervent prayer.

He lay on his back, staring at the rafters and listening to her quiet weeping. He turned his head in her direction. He laid a hand on her shoulder. "Banner." The name rent his throat.

She lay on her side facing away from him. At his touch, she curled into a tighter ball and pressed her face deeper into her sheltering arm.

Jake rolled to a sitting position, glanced back down at her, and called himself every filthy name he could think of.

Coming to his feet, his rebuttoned his pants and stalked out of the barn, giving her the time alone he knew she needed.

Banner knew the moment he stepped outside. She turned on her back and wiped at her eyes until they stung. She sat up slowly, coming up first on her elbows, pausing to draw restorative breaths, then sitting up all the way.

Shaking hands smoothed her hair which was littered with hay. She picked up the shawl, shook it out and wrapped it around herself, then struggled to stand. Her hand stifled another series of sobs when she saw the bloodstain on his blanket. Mortification made her dizzy and for a moment she leaned against the wall of the stall in an attempt to regain her equilibrium before starting the long walk to the door of the barn.

The cool air outside relieved her skin of its fever. The relief was temporary. From the corner of her eye she saw movement and glanced in that direction. Jake was propped against the wall of the barn in the shadows. He pushed himself away from its support the instant he saw her and took a hesitant step forward.

"Banner?"

He stared forlornly into her shattered features, which the faint moonlight only emphasized. He saw the haunted expression in her eyes, the tears welling in them. The damp tracks down her pale cheeks testified that she hadn't been able to contain all of them. Her lips were swollen and beard-abraded. His plundering hands had wreaked havoc on her hair. She was pitiably clutching the shawl around her as though afraid he would snatch it away and take her again. Quickly she turned away from him and fled toward the house, disappearing into the shadows of the front porch.

Jake slumped against the wall of the barn. The back of his head thumped against the whitewashed planks as he grimaced ferally at the sky.

"Shit."

FOUR

Banner had thought yesterday was the worst day of her life. She had been wrong. Today was. Today she had not only Grady Sheldon to despise, but herself as well for the disgraceful thing she had done last night.

Hugging herself as though she had an excruciating pain in her middle, she lay on the bed and drew her knees up to her chest. What had possessed her to do it? Her motives had been pure. She had thought that taking such a drastic step would rid her of despair. Jake had been right. It had only compounded her shame.

Jake, Jake, Jake. What does he think of me?

He had always worshiped Lydia, keeping her on a pedestal above all other women. Intuitively Banner knew that was why he had never married, why he had never gotten close to a decent woman he would consider marrying. He wasn't being unfaithful to his love for Lydia when he took whores because his heart wasn't involved. He could be forgiven having to appease his flesh, but his soul had remained committed to Lydia.

He had loved Banner because she was Lydia's daughter. But now Jake would know she was no better than Wanda Burns. She had thrown herself at him and begged him to make love to her. The utter amazement on his face when she had first approached him haunted her even now. He had been shocked by her brazenness, probably repelled. If not so before, then certainly later when she had . . .

No, she couldn't think of the actual act. Shame bit into her too deeply when she did.

Her recollections skipped over those intense moments and picked up afterward, when she had rolled away from him to hide her face and treacherous body, from his sight. Her behavior had surely destroyed any affection or admiration he had previously held for her. He would hold her in no higher esteem than he did the whores he had been with. She would mean no more than another notch on his well-marked belt. She deserved no better regard because that's how she had acted.

"Banner?"

She sprang to a sitting position and wiped at her teary-bloated eyes. Frantically she smoothed her hair, even smoothed a hand down her chest. Did she look different? Would her mother be able to detect what she had done?

She leaped from the bed and pulled on a robe, as though her nightgown would give away her secret. "Yes, Mama?"

Lydia opened the door and came into the room. She had taken great care with this room for her daughter. Into it had gone everything Lydia had missed in adolescence and had always wanted.

The iron bed was painted an unspoiled white. Lydia and Ma had put hours into the colorful quilt that served as a bedspread. White ruffled eyelet curtains decorated the two windows. The window seats were piled with pillows made from fabric scraps and stuffed with goosedown. Braided rag rugs dotted the floor. Touches of a loving hand were everywhere. And as tomboyish as Banner had been, such femininity wasn't wasted on her.

Lydia's brow wrinkled in concern. Banner was standing in front of one of the windows. Her demeanor was proud, but it was apparent she had spent most of the night crying. Lydia closed the door behind her.

"We were getting worried about you. I could understand why you didn't come down for breakfast, but it's nearly noon. Are you coming down for dinner or would you like me to bring you a tray?"

Lydia's loving concern brought on a fresh batch of tears that Banner struggled to hold back. What would her parents think of her if they could have seen her moving beneath Jake? Shame washed through her like a scarlet tide. "I don't really want anything, Mama, but thank you. I think I'll just stay in my room today.''

Lydia took her hand and pressed it. ''You came down last night. Was it so terrible?'' She had hoped Banner would go right on living, climb right back into the saddle as the cowboys did after a bronco had thrown them.

''It's not that,'' Banner said evasively. ''I need to spend today thinking about what I'm going to do.''

Lydia drew her daughter into her arms and stroked her hair. ''I would never have said this to you yesterday. Your wounds were too fresh. But now I want to tell you something, and I want you to take it in the spirit it's given.'' She paused for a moment, carefully selecting her words. ''I'm relieved that you didn't marry Grady.''

Banner pushed herself away so she could better see her mother. ''Why? I thought you liked him.''

''I did. Very much. I always thought he was nice.'' Her amber eyes clouded. ''Maybe that was it. He was too nice. I don't trust a man who doesn't have some deficiencies, some minor flaws.''

Banner almost forgot her misery and laughed. ''Mama, you're such a contradiction. Any other mother would be glad that her daughter was marrying a flaw*less* young man like Grady.''

''It's not that I would have been unhappy. I just didn't think he had much substance. Not enough for you anyway.'' Grady had always struck Lydia as being too soft for Banner. He wasn't strong-willed enough for her daughter. She had feared that in time Banner would grow bored with him, and Lydia couldn't imagine anything more threatening to a marriage. She and Ross fought, they loved, they laughed. Boredom had certainly never been a part of her life with him and she hadn't wanted that kind of nonexistence for her daughter.

She touched Banner's cheek lovingly. ''I think you can do much better. I think there's someone absolutely wonderful waiting for you. I thought my life was over before I met Ross. He felt the same when Victoria died and left him with a newborn. We couldn't have predicted the second chance we got, and look at the marvelous life we've had together.''

Banner's throat knotted with emotion. She hugged her mother so she wouldn't see the guilt Banner knew must be obvious upon close inspection. If there were a wonderful man waiting for her, he wouldn't have her now. She was tainted. Not by Jake. By herself.

Jake was a man. A virile man. If she had harbored any doubts about that, they had been dispelled last night. She had provoked him beyond what a saint could withstand. He was blameless for what had happened. She wished she could transfer some of the burden of guilt to him, but she couldn't. She was fair, if nothing else. She had gotten exactly what she had asked for. It was she who must pay the price.

"Ross and I have been talking," Lydia said. "We thought you might like to get away for a while. Take a trip. Someplace really exciting. St. Louis or New Orleans. Whatever—"

"No, Mama," Banner said, shaking her head. "That's not for me. I'll never run away and hide. This is Grady's disgrace, not mine, and I refuse to let him drive me away from the people and the home I love." She drew a deep, shuddering breath. "I want to assume ownership of my land. I want to move across the river and start ranching just as we planned."

Dumbfounded, Lydia gazed at her daughter. "But, darling, that's what you were going to do with Grady when you married. You, a single woman, can't do it alone."

"I can and I intend to." Her voice carried conviction. It had come to Banner in the wee hours of the morning that there was only one way for her to save herself now and that was to exhaust herself with work, to pour herself into a project that would make demands on her physically and mentally, a project that would win her back her self-respect. "I must do this, Mama. You understand, don't you?"

Lydia sighed as she studied Banner's determined face. "I understand, but I'm not sure Ross will."

Banner clasped Lydia's hands. "Convince him, Mama. I can't sit here, idly waiting for another beau to materialize. I'm past that. I don't even want it. If I do nothing but continue being Ross and Lydia Coleman's poor unfortunate daughter whose wedding went awry, I'll wither and die. I *need* to do this.''

"I'll talk to him," Lydia assured her quietly. "You rest. Are you sure you feel all right? You look pale.''

"Yes, Mama, I'm fine. But tell Papa what I said. I'm anxious to make plans. The sooner I get busy, the better.''

Lydia kissed her forehead. "I'll see what I can do. But don't act too impulsively, Banner. Don't make any rash decisions.''

Why hadn't her mother cautioned her of that before last night? Would she have taken her advice? Banner honestly doubted it. "I know what I'm doing, Mama," she said softly, and only hoped it was true.

"I just don't want you to be too hard on yourself. Broken hearts take time to mend.''

Lydia was referring to Grady. After last night, memories of what had taken place in the church seemed blurred around the edges. What had happened between Jake and her had reduced the significance of Grady's duplicity.

When Lydia left, Banner went to her dresser, took off the robe, and let her nightgown slide down her body to the floor. She dipped a cloth in the cool water and bathed her face, pressing the cloth to her burning, gritty eyes. When she couldn't avoid it any longer, she looked at her image in the mirror. It was remarkably unchanged, though she felt she had been irrevocably altered. Everything inside her had been scooped out, rearranged, reassembled, and put back into the same mold. But nothing was the same.

She touched her lips, hesitantly, reminiscent of the first time Jake had touched them with his. She touched her neck. A faint bruise, so light her own mother hadn't noticed it, brought memories rushing back on beating wings as rapid as those of a hummingbird.

It wasn't possible. She was remembering it all wrong. Jake hadn't touched her, kissed her, possessed her the way she remembered. No.

But she was lying to herself. Her body told her so. Closing her eyes, she could still feel the steely pressure of him deep inside her, feel the soft soughing of his breath on her skin, feel the sweet persuasion of his lips on hers. No matter how hard she tried to forget, she couldn't. No matter how badly she wanted to block the memory from her mind, the fever in her blood wouldn't let her.

"Hey, Jake."

He entered the bunkhouse and made a beeline for the stove where a monstrous coffee pot was kept full and hot. "Yeah?" he growled as he poured the strong brew into a porcelain cup.

"Ross wants to see you as soon as you finish breakfast," one of the cowboys informed him. "He asked me to tell you."

The cup was halted on its way to Jake's lips. "Did he say what he wanted?"

"Nope."

"Thanks."

Jake wouldn't have been surprised to be greeted this morning by the barrel of Ross's pistol. It was a certainty that if Ross ever learned what happened in the barn last night, he would kill him, not even having any compunction about shooting him in the back.

Once, a few years ago, Lee had overheard one of the cowboys remarking on Banner's ripening figure. Lee had defended his sister's honor and the two had gotten into a scuffle. When Ross broke up the fight, the cowboy had been forced to repeat the crude comment. Ross was so furious he would have beaten the young man to death if Jake and several other hands hadn't pulled him off.

None of the women knew about the incident, but the men around River Bend never forgot it. They had always respected Ross as an employer and as a man, giving him wide berth when his temper flared. But after that day, they took pains not to look sideways at Banner no matter how tempting the sight. Those who had hired on since then were duly warned by their cohorts that the boss's daughter was sacred ground not to be trespassed upon.

Jake took a seat at the long trestle table and sipped the scalding coffee. He shook his head when Cookie offered him a plate of biscuits and bacon.

No, Ross didn't know about last night. If he did, Jake would already be dead. Not even his friendship with Ross would have protected him from a wrath incurred by his touching Banner.

But how in hell could he face the man? How? How did one face a friend when he had just violated his daughter?

He had defiled her, sweet little Banner.

Self-disgust almost sent the coffee he had swallowed back up.

"Heard you came through Fort Worth, Jake."

"Yep," he answered laconically.

"Visit Hell's Half Acre?" another of the wide-eyed cowboys asked.

Lee and Micah had furthered Jake's reputation with River Bend's hands and they considered him a legend. Most were too young to have gone on the long drives. The cowboys who had and were still around to tell about them were revered.

"I was there for a spell."

"How was it?"

"Rowdy."

"Yeah? You go to the Garden of Eden? Way I hear it, Madam Priscilla's got the finest whores in the state. Trained in New Orleans. Ain't that right?"

"New Orleans, huh?" Jake grinned at their gullibility. What was the sense of disillusioning them? "Yeah, I reckon a few of them were."

"Tumble any of 'em?"

"Hell, 'course he did," another said, scoffing at his friend. "Ever' single one of 'em. Jake's like a tonic to them gals. I heard that since he left, Madam Priscilla ain't been able to wipe the smiles off their faces. Look plumb sappy, they do, walking around grinnin' like possums."

Those around the table laughed. Jake only shrugged and took another drink of his coffee. His reputation as a womanizer wasn't one he was especially proud of, though he had done all he could to earn it. He was accustomed to being teased about his prowess in the bedroom.

This morning he was too worried about his forthcoming interview with Ross to pay much attention to the familiar banter. Sex, or the lack of it, was often the topic of conversation with lonely cowboys who were frequently without female companionship for months on end. There wasn't a vulgar story that Jake hadn't heard, a lewd joke he hadn't repeated himself around one campfire or another. They no longer impressed him as they did some of the younger men, who chose to take them at face value and believe them.

The mild insults and exaggerated compliments went in one ear and out the other until one cowboy said, "How do you handle an off night like last night, Jake? Or did you manage to sneak a woman into the barn?"

Jake came out of the chair, drawing his pistol from its holster so fast that laughter died in the throats of the other men. His gun was but an inch from the hapless cowboy's nose when Jake asked through clenched teeth, "What do you mean by that?"

The other man swallowed a goose egg of fear. He had heard that the easygoing Jake Langston could be mean when he wanted to be, that his temper matched that of a rattler, and that he was no man to trifle with. Now he knew that to be a fact, and he wished like hell he had stuffed his mouth with another of Cookie's biscuits instead of making the jibe that might cost him his life.

"N-nothin', Jake, nothin'. I was just funnin' with ya."

Jake could tell the man was telling the truth and he was suddenly embarrassed that he had lost his temper to the point of drawing a gun. Of course if the cowboy had breathed a word about seeing Banner going into the barn, Jake would have shot him before letting her reputation be compromised.

He eased the hammer of his pistol forward and returned it to the holster. "Sorry. Guess I'm not in a joking mood this morning." He grinned lopsidedly, but the former lightheartedness around the table couldn't be recaptured. Gradually the men carried their plates to Cookie, who managed the kitchen in the bunkhouse, and taking up hats, gloves, and ropes, left for the day's work.

Jake drank one more cup of coffee. When he couldn't put

it off any longer, he ambled toward the house. Anabeth and Lydia were sitting on the porch, watching the little Drummonds as they played in the yard.

"Morning," Jake said guardedly.

"Hi, Bubba," Anabeth said.

Lydia smiled up at him. "Good morning. We missed you at breakfast."

"I walked Stormy. He's still favoring that hoof."

"Have you eaten?"

He nodded, though it was a lie. "In the bunkhouse. Where is everybody?"

"Hector's helping Ma make a scarecrow to put in her corn," Anabeth said, smiling. "It was scaring the children so I brought them up here. Marynell's studying as usual."

Jake nodded without comment. His eyes roved toward the children who were playing leapfrog. "How... how's Banner?" It was a perfectly normal question. Everyone was concerned about her after yesterday. Neither his sister nor Lydia could read anything into it, unless they noted his tension as he asked.

"I went up to check on her awhile ago," Lydia said. "Her eyes are puffy. She must have cried all night." Lydia was looking at the youngest Drummond's efforts to scale his sister's back so she missed the quirk of regret that pinched one corner of Jake's lips. "We talked. I think with time she'll recover."

Guilt had a stranglehold on Jake and wouldn't let go. Banner might have recovered from Sheldon's shenanigans. But recover from last night? No. There was no getting over that. The damage he had inflicted on her was permanent. "Is Ross in the house? One of the men said he wanted to see me."

"He does," Lydia said, her eyes suddenly sparkling. "He's in his office."

Jake tipped his hat to the two women and sauntered across the porch and through the front door. "I'm worried about him," Anabeth said when he was out of hearing.

"Worried? Why?"

"Ever since Pa died and he ran off to sign up for that

cattle drive, he's been like a stranger. Look at the way he lives. From hand to mouth with no prospects for anything better. I wish he'd settle down with a wife, have some kids and stop roaming all over the place. He's a grown man. He should act like one.''

"Ma's worried about him too," Lydia remarked. "So am I.''

"You know what?" Anabeth continued. "I don't think he ever got over Luke's murder. I know that sounds crazy. It's been nearly twenty years, but he hasn't been the same since then. Maybe if we had found out who the killer was and had seen justice done, Jake wouldn't have taken it so hard."

Lydia lowered her eyes to her lap. Jake knew who killed his brother—her stepbrother Clancey Russell. And he had exacted his own punishment, a death sentence. He had been sixteen when he took vengeance on Luke's murderer. That's what he had never gotten over, the murder of his brother. Lydia was the only person in the world who shared that secret with him. It was a bond between them that would never be broken.

Jake went down the shadowed hallway toward the back of the house and tapped on the doorjamb. He felt as awkward as he had when he first met Ross. The passing years and Jake's inevitable maturity had closed the gap between their ages. But guilt was making him as jumpy as a boy about to get a thrashing.

"Ross."

Ross's dark head came up. He had been studying the pile of papers on his desk. "Come in, Jake, and have a seat. Thanks for coming over. Am I keeping you from anything?"

"No." He took the chair opposite the desk and tried to put on an air of normalcy by propping one ankle on the opposite knee. He took off his hat and sailed it onto the leather sofa against the wall. "I plan to spend most of the day with Ma."

"Good," Ross said solemnly. "She misses you."

"Yeah, I know." He sighed. It hadn't been fair, his leaving right after Pa died. But he couldn't take the farming life any longer. He would have gone crazy trying to scrape a decent crop out of that rocky ground that he had tried to convince both his parents was created for beef cattle. But all they had known was farming and there had been no changing their minds.

He felt guilty about having deserted his mother. He was the eldest son and therefore responsible for the family. Every time he got paid, he had sent money home, but he knew that she had needed him to be there with her more than she had needed his money.

He had wronged her. Now he met the eyes of the man whom he had wronged to an even greater degree. "What did you want to see me about, Ross?"

"The usual. The same thing I see you about every time you come to River Bend. A job."

"My answer is the same. No."

"Why, Jake?"

Jake shifted restlessly in his chair. Always before his reason had been Lydia. Banner had hit the nail right on the head last night. He couldn't stay long at River Bend because he loved her too much. Sooner or later it would become obvious and that would destroy the friendship he shared with both her and Ross. It wasn't worth the risk. But now he had a new reason. He could never face Banner again.

He was solely to blame. She had come to him, yes. She had lured him, yes. But he had responded. And truthfully without much effort on her part. He had responded, hard and hot and hungry.

He was the elder; he knew better. She had been hurt, heartbroken, needing comfort and reassurance. She had come to him seeking one thing, yet asking for another. Still, knowing all that, knowing it was wrong, knowing he was sacrificing his friendship with the Colemans, he had taken her anyway.

God, she must despise him this morning. When it was over, she had cowered fearfully from his touch. She would hardly look at him, and when she had it was with the eyes of a trapped animal. Had he hurt her that much? Was she still in pain? Couldn't he have shown a little more gentleness? Oh, no, not him. Not the prince of the pleasure palaces. He had gone at her savagely. Once he had entered her, he forgot that she was a virgin and untried.

Damn! She must think he was an animal. The sooner he was out of her life, the better. After he spent some time with Ma, he was clearing out. Today, if Stormy was up to leaving.

"I can't stay," he told Ross brusquely.

"I'd like to discuss it before you give me your final answer."

"Suit yourself. We're wasting your time, not mine."

"How 'bout some coffee?"

"No thanks."

"Whiskey?"

"No." Jake grinned. "What are you trying to do, bribe me?"

Ross grinned back. "If that's what it takes to get you to stay. You know I've wanted you to work with me since we parted company in Jefferson when the wagon train broke up."

"It was impossible then because of my folks. It's just as impossible now."

"Dammit, why?" Ross thumped the desktop with his fist. "Do you have another job waiting for you? You said you quit that one in the Panhandle."

"I did."

"So? What are you planning to do?"

"Find something else."

"Why, when I'm offering you a job right here? A damn good job."

Ross came out of his chair and circled the desk. Save for the silver hair threading through the dark strands, he was the man Jake Langston had always admired. Another spasm of disgust twisted his stomach. If Ross knew what he had done to Banner, he would be burying him instead of asking him to stay.

"I want you to be the foreman of Banner's ranch across the river."

Jake's head snapped up at the mention of her name. "Banner's ranch? What ranch?"

Ross was encouraged by Jake's sudden interest. "I set aside some acreage for each of them, her and Lee, several years ago. I acquired the land cheaply, a parcel here, a parcel there, over the years. For the most part, it's undeveloped. I was giving Banner and Grady her share for a wedding present." His green eyes hardened appreciably. "You can't know how much I wanted to kill that bastard yesterday."

"Yes, I can. I felt the same."

Jake had seen Ross mad. He knew enough of his past to know that he could be deadly... literally. He didn't doubt Ross was capable of murder and could only thank providence for interceding and preventing him from killing Sheldon. It would have served no purpose except to bring more hardship on the family.

"I would kill any man for hurting Banner," Ross was saying. "Sheldon didn't particularly overwhelm me as a husband for her, but I figured any father would feel that there wasn't a man alive good enough for his daughter. I couldn't fault Sheldon. I thought he was a safe choice. Since she got old enough to attract a man's attention, I've been afraid that some ne'er-do-well cowboy would come along and she would lose her head over him."

"You had every right to be afraid that might happen."

"He would marry her and give her nothing but children and misery while he spent my money on whores, gambling, and liquor."

Jake smiled grimly.

"At least Sheldon had a business, a standing in the community. I didn't worry about his morals." He cursed vilely. "I guess that shows what a rotten judge of character I am.

"Anyway," he continued, raking his fingers through his hair as though to wipe thoughts of Grady Sheldon from his mind, "we built a small house on this land for her and Grady to live in. Banner had already told him she didn't want to move into town. Now Lydia tells me that Banner wants to move there anyway, to start ranching as she planned. Without Grady. Without anybody."

Jake, caught up in Ross's explanation, responded honestly. "That's crazy. She can't do that."

Ross only grunted as though to say no one had better tell Banner she couldn't. "I had promised her a stud and a couple of mares to get started, but she also wants to try raising beef cattle in one of the less fertile pastures."

"What the hell does she know about beef cattle?"

"Not a damn thing. And neither do I except how I like my steak cooked." His eyes pierced into Jake. "But you do. It's a prime piece of property, Jake. You could do wonders with it."

At any other time Jake would have jumped at a chance like this. He would be in charge. He could run the ranch as he saw fit. Lord, what a temptation, what a ripe apple just waiting to be picked. But it was impossible for him to accept the offer, so there was no need even dwelling on it.

He left the chair and went to the window, sliding his hands, palms out, into the seat pockets of his jeans. "Sorry, Ross, I can't."

"Give me one damn good reason why."

"Banner," Jake said, turning around. She would raise billy hell if she could hear this discussion. He was sure she never wanted to see hide nor hair of him again, much less have her seducer running her ranch. "She'll want to hire her own foreman. I'm sure she has ideas of her own."

Ross chuckled affectionately. "I'm sure she does, too, but the fact remains that I retain control of the property. I didn't think she would want to fool with it on top of all that's happened. But Lydia says she is dead set on moving over there. But," he said, lifting an index finger and pointing it ceilingward, "she has another thing coming if she believes I'll let her live over there alone and run a ranch by herself. In the first place it would be physically impossible. Banner's a strong girl, but she's not up to doing the work that needs to be done. No woman could handle it."

"You can hire other hands."

Ross cocked a dark eyebrow at him. "Cowboys just itching to get their paws on my daughter?" Jake quickly turned back to the window. "Uh-uh. After everyone hears what happened yesterday, rumors are going to fly. You know how men talk about women. They'll assume Banner had Sheldon so keyed up he was driven to seek out somebody like that Burns bitch.''

"She's a beautiful young woman, Ross," Jake said quietly. "Maybe they're right."

"Maybe they are," Ross growled. "But Lydia and I raised her right. She didn't rouse him past the breaking point on purpose. I'd swear to that. And if he had any backbone, he could have bitten the bullet and lasted it out. In any event, I don't want a parade of lecherous cowboys applying for work just to get a glimpse of her.

"This thing will haunt her for a long time. Lydia and I are worried as hell about it. She's easy to hurt right now. She'll be desperate to restore her self-confidence. Some sorry cowboy could come riding in here and take advantage of her broken heart. I'd kill him on the spot, but such an alliance would ruin her for sure."

Her parents knew Banner well. Jake's hands balled into fists on the windowsill. He wanted to send them flying through the glass, to cause himself pain, to administer well-deserved punishment. Guilt tasted as bitter as bile in the back of his throat. It wouldn't leave him alone. It ate at him like a cancer. He was diseased with it.

Unwittingly Ross made it worse. "You're the only man Lydia and I would trust with her, Jake. Please do this for us. Take the job. It'll be the right thing for Banner and the right thing for you."

Jake kept his eyes closed, wishing he could close his ears as effectively. Finally he turned around slowly. He stared at the floor beneath his boots for a long time before he said, "I can't, Ross. I'm sorry."

"A hundred and fifty dollars a month."

It was a fortune. "It's not the money."

"Then what?"

"I can't stay in one place. I'm a drifter."

"That's bullshit."

Jake's smile was rueful. "Reckon it is. Reckon I'm full

of it. You don't want an ol' cowpoke like me running Banner's ranch.''

"The hell I don't. You're the best man I've ever seen astride a horse, second to me, of course.'' He flashed a boastful grin before becoming serious again. "Can't I change your mind?'' Jake shook his head. "At least think about it while you're here.''

Jake picked up his hat and headed for the door. He had already pulled it open when Ross stopped him. "Jake?''

"Yeah?''

"Even if I would take no for your answer, Lydia isn't going to. And you know what she's like when she makes up her mind about something.''

She found him on the riverbank that afternoon where he was fishing. Without a word, she plopped down on the grass beside him. "Catching anything?'' Obviously he wasn't. It was just as obvious he didn't care.

"Did you just happen by?'' he asked around the cheroot clamped between his teeth. They were at least a half-mile from the house.

She smiled up at him, looking exactly like the young woman of twenty who had first captured his adolescent heart. "Ma told me where you were.''

"And how did she know? Her knack for locating me when I don't want to be found is just plain strange. Once she found me dallying in a creek with Priscilla Watkins. I thought she was going to snatch me bald-headed. I was sixteen.'' He blew a cloud of blue smoke into the air. "Here I am thirty-six and she's still meddling into my affairs.''

"She loves you.''

"I know,'' he said, chagrined. "That's the hell of it. I went over to her cabin and ate dinner. All of us were there. Ma, Anabeth and her brood, Marynell, and Micah. But there are so many of us missing. Pa, the babies that never even made it through infancy, Atlanta and Samuel. Luke.'' He stared reflectively into the water. "I still miss him, Lydia.''

She laid a hand on his arm. "You always will, Bubba.''

He shook his head, laughing slightly. "So long ago. But sometimes I still imagine I hear him laughing. I catch myself looking around for him, you know?"

"I miss old Moses that way." The black man had joined forces with them when the wagon train broke up. His former employer, Winston Hill, had been killed. He had nowhere else to go.

Moses had been Lydia's friend and champion during those first awkward weeks of her marriage to Ross. As they settled on their land, Ross busy with building the first barn for his horses and her tending to Lee, Moses's help had been immeasurable. She still considered him one of her dearest friends.

"On the day we buried him I remembered how he carried Luke's body into that circle of wagons. That and the way he cried with such dignity when Winston was killed. He was one of the most compassionate men I've ever known."

Jake covered her hand where it rested on his arm. "That summer changed all of us, didn't it?"

"Certainly Ross and me." She stared at Jake's profile. The maturity there was still alien to her and never ceased to surprise her. When she looked at him, she expected him to be the towheaded boy with round blue eyes who had found her in the woods. "And you, Jake. I think it changed you most of all."

He had to concede that. His innocence had vanished that summer. More of life's adversity had been crammed into those months on the wagon train than a man ought to have to cope with in a lifetime. Bubba Langston had grown up fast. One didn't grow so rapidly without its leaving traces on him.

Lydia raised her knees, wrapped her skirts around her legs and propped her chin on her knees. "I spoke to Ross."

"And he told you my answer."

"I'm going to change your mind."

"Don't count on it, Lydia. Don't count on me for anything."

"I do. I count on your friendship."

"You've got that, but—"

"We need you now. Help us get Banner through this calamity."

"I'm not the man for the job."

"You are. You've got the experience the job requires."

"I'm not talking about the work. It's . . . it's Banner."

Lydia laughed. "I'll admit she's hard to handle at times. She's willful and impetuous. Volatile. She's a grown woman, but Ross and I can't just turn her loose to make mistakes she'll forever regret."

"I'm not a policeman," he snapped.

"I don't expect you to be. I expect you to be just what you've always been to her, a friend, an ally. We trust her with you."

Goddammit, he wished they would stop saying that! He felt like hell as it was. Did they have to keep reminding him of his betrayal?

"You'll find someone else just as capable and probably much more trustworthy. She'll have that ranch operating in no time."

"You don't understand, Jake. Ross won't permit her to do this unless you stay and run that ranch for her."

The blond head whipped around. "That's not fair. He'll be punishing Banner for my decision."

"He feels that strongly about it. He told me today after his talk with you that he wouldn't let her move onto the land if you don't stay."

"Damn." He surged to his feet and began pacing angrily. His cheroot died a sizzling death when he sent it plunging into the sluggish current of the river. He unplugged the cane fishing pole from where he had stuck it in the mud and tossed it aside.

"That's blackmail," he said. "Banner won't take kindly to it either. Ross must see how important this is to her. Especially now."

"He does. But he's as stubborn as a mule. If he doesn't think it's best for her, no amount of her tears and tantrums will change his mind."

Jake moved to the water's edge and stared into its murky depths. His shoulders moved restlessly beneath a shirt that suddenly seemed to have shrunk. He was being backed against a wall and he didn't like it. Not one damn bit. Maybe Banner could be coerced, but not him. He didn't like shackles. Wouldn't tolerate them.

To hell with it. What did he owe them?

Then his shoulders sagged and became still. He owed them everything after last night. He couldn't give them back Banner's chastity, but he could make amends by staying if that's what they required of him.

"You should stay here anyway, Jake," Lydia said. "Ma's getting old. I haven't wanted to worry you, but she's not as strong as she used to be. If you ride off and stay for years this time, you might never see her alive again."

His heels dug holes in the moist ground as he turned and fixed Lydia with an accusatory blue stare. She lowered her eyes guiltily. "Ma's as strong as a horse," he said. "You're blackmailing me, too, Lydia."

She came to her feet with an agility and grace that belied her age. Moving close to him, she tilted her head back and met his gaze squarely. "All right. I'm not fighting fair. But I'm fighting for my daughter's life, and where she's concerned I have no pride. She needs you. We all do. I'm asking you, please, Jake, stay this time. Don't leave us."

He gazed down into the face that was never far from his conscious mind. He had loved it for so long he barely remembered a time when he didn't. He felt his defenses weakening, unraveling like an old rope.

When Lydia asked anything of him, could he refuse her? He had killed for her once, rid her of the stepbrother who had brought her nothing but disgrace and misery. That Clancey had been Luke's murderer had been a convenient coincidence. He would gladly have eliminated Clancey Russell from Lydia's life anyway.

"Don't give me an answer now," she said gently, taking his hand and squeezing it. "Sleep on it tonight. Tell us tomorrow."

She climbed the knoll that sloped to the river and disappeared over its crest. Jake paced along the bank. The grass beneath his boots was deep and green. The trees overhead were lush with new leaves. The air was scented with wildflowers. He didn't notice.

What should he do?

He owed this to Ross and Lydia for being his steadfast friends for so long, but if he worked for them every day of his life from now on, he wouldn't be able to atone for last night.

They were sincere when they said they considered him the best qualified to handle the job. Hell, he could do the job. He had no qualms about that. But could he face Banner day after day?

His mother needed him. He had let her down. She would never ask him to stay, but she would be pleased to have him settled in one place.

And Banner. It always came back to her. She would need a strong back. She would need protection. Ross's argument was sound. Every yokel with an itchy prick would be panting after her now. Jake would do his damnedest to protect her. No man would touch her without having to kill him first.

He was surprised at the depth of his jealousy and the intensity of his possessiveness. He supposed it stemmed from her being Lydia's daughter, and convinced himself it had nothing to do with how responsive her mouth was, how sweetly she moved in his embrace, how good it had felt to be surrounded by her. Tight and warm and . . .

Damn. Will you get your mind off that and back to the point?

If he didn't stay, Banner wouldn't get her land. Ross could be just that bullheaded and still convince himself that he was acting in Banner's best interest.

Having robbed her of her virginity, could he rob her of her land as well? Eventually Ross would come around, but when? Banner needed this ranch now to take her mind off Sheldon.

Was that his answer then?

He would stay. Just until she got on her feet and things were running smoothly.

She wouldn't like it. There would be hell to pay. He'd

witnessed several of her tantrums and knew that she had
inherited temper from both her parents. Of course he would
make it clear from the beginning that they had to put last
night out of their minds, pretend that it had never happened.

He would convince her he was staying for her own good.
Whether she liked it or not, he would be her foreman.

Miss Banner Coleman would just have to get used to the
idea of having Jake Langston around.

FIVE

"What?"

Just as Jake had thought, there was going to be hell to
pay.

"What did you say?"

"I said that Jake has hired on to be your foreman."

As the words fell from Ross's lips, Banner's cheeks
paled, then blushed a vibrant shade of pink. Her hands
balled into fists and her back went rigid. Her hair seemed to
crackle with indignation.

She had been summoned to her father's office soon after
breakfast. Always before she had been able to wrap Ross
around her little finger. This morning, with her future riding
on his decision, she had approached the office door with
anxiety.

It had been even more disconcerting to find that Jake was
there too. He was standing with his back to the room,
staring out the window. Smoke from his thin cigar curled
around his head.

Banner went weak at the sight of him.

Did her parents know? Had Jake confessed? Oh, God,
please no. The parents who loved her would be so disillu-

sioned if they knew what she had done. Surely Jake hadn't told them. Their expressions were concerned, not censorious.

Lydia had smiled encouragingly. "Is that one of your new culottes? I like it. And the shirtwaist is a perfect fit."

"Good morning, Princess." Ross had stepped toward her and affectionately kissed her cheek. "You're still looking pale. Why don't you get outside today? Give Dusty some exercise." He led her toward the leather sofa and sat her down as though she were made of priceless crystal.

"Please stop fussing over me," she told them, showing some of her former spirit. "I'll survive."

She was so profoundly relieved that they didn't know about Jake that she could afford to be a trifle petulant.

But Jake was still in the room, a brooding presence. She was sharing space with him, fighting for every breath she drew. It was the first time she had seen him since . . . then.

She noticed things she never had before, like how his tight pants shaped his buttocks, dividing and defining. Had his shoulders always been that broad? His stance that indolent? His thighs that muscled?

He looked long and lean and lanky silhouetted against the window. She could remember every wiry inch of his frame and how it felt pressing against her.

She was recalling things only a lover would know and her thoughts made her feel hot all over, though she was shivering. If he looked in her direction, she thought she might faint.

"We don't mean to fuss over you, Banner," Lydia said diplomatically. "We just thought an outing—"

"I'll ride across the river today," Banner had interrupted breathlessly. Jake's long fingers were twirling the cheroot near his mouth. He rolled his fingers back and forth, first one way, then another. She looked away quickly as though caught watching an intimate act.

"That's what I wanted to talk to you about this morning," Ross had said. "Your mother tells me you want to move to your property and start ranching."

"Yes, Papa, I do."

Ross looked at Lydia, then back at his daughter. He hoped he was doing the right thing. She looked so frail, so distraught. His thoughts turned murderous toward Sheldon. He wouldn't let that sonofabitch ruin his daughter's life. Maybe Lydia was right. Maybe Banner did need this chance to get her life back on track. She was a willful, energetic young woman. She would never tolerate idleness. Already their cosseting irritated her. "All right. You have our permission."

Banner's eyes had filled with tears of gratitude. She had thought she loved Grady above everything else. Now she knew she hadn't loved him nearly as much as she loved this land. Losing it would have been a much greater loss than losing Grady. "Thank you, Papa."

"Jake has consented to be your foreman."

It was at that point that Banner had sprung off the sofa as though something had popped out of the cushions and bitten her. She demanded that Ross repeat what he had just said.

When the hateful words sank in, she whirled toward the man who was still standing silently at the window. He hadn't moved. He could be deaf and blind for all the reaction he showed to what was going on behind him.

Banner faced her parents again. "I don't need a foreman."

"Of course you do," Ross said reasonably. "You can't manage that place alone."

"I can!"

"You can't. Even if you could, I wouldn't let you live over there by yourself."

"It's only a few miles."

"I know how far it is," Ross said, raising his voice a notch. "Now, that's an end to it."

"No, it's not, Papa." Banner matched her volume to his. "That land is mind. You gave it to me. I'll make the decisions."

"The land is yours with this condition."

"That's not fair!"

"Maybe not, but that's the way it is."

"Will the two of you please calm down," Lydia interrupted sternly. "Listen to yourselves."

Banner and Ross subsided, but their identical tempers still

simmered on the surface. Banner met Ross's flashing green eyes with a pair just as fiery and a chin just as stubborn.

Acting as placater, Lydia said, "Banner, we thought you'd be pleased. Isn't this what you wanted? You can't be objecting to Jake. You've always loved him and begged him to stay each time he left."

Banner cast a hasty glance toward Jake. He was still gazing out the window, as though he were impervious to their conversation.

"It isn't that I have anything against Jake. Of course that's not the reason." Banner nervously wet her lips and pressed on. "It's just that I don't need anybody watching over me. I'm not a child. Don't you think I'm capable of doing a good job?"

"Your mother and I have every confidence in you," Ross said.

"Then let me run the ranch the way I want to."

"Jake's not going to go against anything you say," Ross said. "Jake, we haven't heard from you. Do you plan to do anything over there that's not to Banner's liking?"

Jake turned slowly to face the room, but Banner didn't see. Her gaze had dropped quickly to the floor. Only by an act of will did she keep her hands from damply gripping each other in consternation.

"I know what has to be done," Jake said in clipped tones. "So does Banner. I imagine we'll work together fine. But I won't take the job unless she wants me to." He paused significantly. "How about it, Banner?"

She simply couldn't. She couldn't look into those eyes and see his ridicule. But she had no choice. Her parents were watching her, waiting for her answer. Slowly she raised her head and looked at Jake.

His face was implacable. His eyes were cool, neither accusing nor smug. They looked hollow, as empty as she had felt the last two days. She wanted to go on staring, trying to discern the thoughts behind that impenetrable mask, but she was required to speak.

"It's my ranch," she said huskily. "I should be allowed to choose my own foreman."

Jake's lip twitched and his eyes blinked rapidly, once, as though a shooting pain had crossed his face. "Don't you think I'm qualified?"

Suddenly she was furious with him. If he hadn't been so damned obliging to Ross and Lydia, she wouldn't have been placed in this position. His defensive tone only aggravated her further. "Yes. I know you're qualified. But you've been handpicked by my parents to be a mammy to me. I don't need a watchdog!"

"Mammy!" Jake exclaimed, taking several belligerent steps forward until they were almost chin to chin. "You think I'm going to spend my time over there spoon-feeding you? Guess again, young lady. Do you know how hard it is to build corrals, string barbed wire, haul hay? You ask Ross what kind of backbreaking, gut-wrenching work it takes to make a place like this. You don't remember the blood, sweat, and effort he and Lydia put into River Bend, but I do."

Her eyes flashed dangerously. "I'm not a fool, Jake Langston, and I'll ask you not to talk to me as though I were."

"All right, then, so stop suggesting that I'm going to be sitting on my rump entertaining you all day, because that's not how it'll be."

"Entertain . . . you . . ." she sputtered.

Ross crossed his ankles, folded his arms over his chest, and leaned against the desk. He was enjoying the spectacle. Jake had been responsible for spoiling Banner as much as anybody. It was high time he saw the contrary side of her nature. Rather than her haughtiness changing his mind about accepting the job, Ross thought it would goad him into it.

Lydia quietly took a seat on the sofa and spread her skirt around her feet, looking for all the world as though she were enjoying a matinee in a playhouse. Banner's usual willfulness was manifesting itself. She wasn't the weepy, jilted bride any longer. The reversal delighted her mother.

"I don't expect anybody to entertain me."

"Well, good. Just so that's understood."

"I intend to do my share of the work." Banner swept her hair over her shoulder with an impatient motion of her hand.

"You're damn right you will." Jake punctuated his statement by wagging his finger at the tip of her nose.

She swatted it aside. "So we're agreed on that point. And stop shouting at me."

"I just don't want you to get faint of heart once we get over there."

"I've never been faint of heart in my life."

"Because not only will there be the ranching to take care of," he went on as though she hadn't spoken, "there'll be the everyday chores to take care of, like cooking and pumping water and carrying firewood."

"I'll manage to keep myself fed, Mr. Langston, but don't think I'm going to waste time puttering over a hot stove when I could be outside."

"But, Banner, you'll have to cook Jake's meals."

Banner's gaze sought her mother's face. Her mouth opened, but no words came out. She was too stunned to speak. "But . . . but won't he eat in the bunkhouse with all the other hands?"

"That would be damned inconvenient," Ross said. "He'll be staying over there with you. We figured he could sleep in that tack room at the back of the barn."

Banner's eyes bounced between her parents in disbelief. At last, she looked at Jake. "You agreed to sleep . . . to live there?"

The question carried enormous meaning for Banner and Jake. They had almost come to terms with working together on the ranch. Their respective jobs would be specialized. There wouldn't be too many occasions for them to get in each other's way. But his staying there each night, sleeping so close to the house, taking his meals with her, was something else again.

"That was part of the job." The words seemed to have a hard time finding their way out of his stiffly held mouth.

Banner turned away. Possibly, *possibly*, she could have accepted the condition of having him manage her ranch. But to live so close to him, knowing that every time he looked at her he would remember that night? Never.

She looked at Ross and tilted her head to a proud angle. "I don't accept your condition. As I said earlier, I want my independence. I won't be watched over like a child."

"Then this conversation has been a waste of time," Ross said firmly, "because you're not going to live over there by yourself."

Banner smiled the smile that had never failed to coax him out of one more candy stick. "You'll change your mind, Papa."

"Not this time, Banner. If you don't take Jake along with the property, you'll have to do without it for the time being."

She shuddered at his resolute tone of voice. "You don't mean that."

"Yes, he does." Jake spoke with enough quiet emphasis to bring Banner's eyes back to him. "At first I turned down the job. I didn't want it any more than you want me. But he's not going to give you that place at all unless you do it his way." Seconds ticked by while they stared at each other. Banner was the first to look away.

"Mama?"

"I can't argue with Ross's reasoning, Banner. It's for your own good. You'll need Jake's protection."

The irony of that struck Banner as funny, but she dared not laugh. She was afraid that if she started she would never stop. Wasn't she due a spell of hysteria? What a luxury that would be, to scream, to cry, to lose her control. But she couldn't risk giving it free rein or she might never recapture it.

Jake's eyes were blank. What was he thinking? What lurked in the depths of his eyes? Pity? Heaven forbid. Was he taking the job out of pity for her? Why? Because she had been made a fool of in front of the whole town or because she had made a fool of herself trying to seduce him? Had she been that amateurish?

Her chin went up another degree. She sure as hell wouldn't accept any largesse from a saddle bum like Jake

Langston and bitterly resented his offering it. "I'll think about it and let you know," she said loftily. With her head held high, she sailed from the room.

As soon as the door closed behind her, Jake cursed expansively. "Dammit, I told both of you she wouldn't cotton to the idea. Let's call the whole thing off right now."

Ross chuckled. "She'll come around, Jake. She wants that land too badly. Right now she's just being stubborn. What she needs is a good paddling to teach her some humility. She's spoiled rotten and accustomed to getting her own way. Lydia wasn't strict enough with her."

"Me!" Lydia faced her husband with both hands on her hips. "You're a fine one to talk, Ross Coleman. You've always been putty in her hands. Besides that she inherited her stubbornness from you, not to mention her temper."

He reached out and grabbed her by the waistband of her skirt, jerking her against his chest. "And her feistiness from you," he growled, searching for her lips with his.

"Ross, stop it. I mean it now. It's almost dinnertime and I have to get—"

He clamped his mouth over hers in a possessive kiss. She struggled no longer than a heartbeat before she locked her arms around his neck and angled her head to deepen the kiss.

"I need to give Stormy a little bit of a workout," Jake mumbled, taking his hat off the hook near the door and slapping it on his head. He slammed the door behind him when he left, but Lydia and Ross didn't notice.

After everyone had eaten the noon meal together, the Drummonds left for home. Marynell was going with them as far as Austin. Amid the confusion of their leavetaking, goodbyes were said and hugs and kisses exchanged. Banner tried to avoid looking at Jake. She wasn't very successful. But if he was worried about the decision she would make, he didn't show it. He played with his nieces and nephews, talked earnestly to Hector about the price of feed, and teased Marynell about her spinsterhood until she whacked him on the head with a tin measuring cup.

As soon as Banner had waved the company off, she pleaded a headache and retreated to her room. Jake's seeming indifference piqued her, especially since her mind was in turmoil.

If her papa had appointed anybody else but Jake—

The thought brought her whirring mind to a standstill. Who else but Jake? If she could roll back the clock forty-eight hours and erase that hour in the barn from her past, she would be ecstatic that Jake had consented to be her foreman.

As it was, her own guilt made the situation untenable.

What did he see when he looked at her?

Did he see her in a plain white shirtwaist and split navy skirt? Or was she forever imprinted on his mind wearing that sheer nightgown, which had been no deterrent for his knowing caresses?

Did he remember the instant she recovered from the shock of feeling his tongue in her mouth and had actually opened her lips wider to receive it? She would certainly never forget the wet, darting movements of his tongue, nor the slow sensuous ones that penetrated and stroked.

Oh, Lord, she groaned. Did he recall her hands acting of their own accord and grasping handfuls of his hair? And when his body had begun to pump rhythmically into hers, did he remember that she had shamelessly chanted his name like some ritualistic, supplicating prayer?

Of course he remembered. If her recollections were vivid enough to make her heart pound and her body respond as though it were all happening again, weren't Jake's likely to be the same?

She covered her face with her hands. Would she have to sacrifice her dream of having her own ranch because of one night's folly? Wasn't that paying dearly for pride?

She had made a mistake, and the consequences must be met. But she couldn't wear a hair shirt for the rest of her life. Jake was obviously willing to put what had happened behind them and go on with his life. Didn't she have as much courage as he? Would she cower in front of him forever? Damned if she would give him that satisfaction!

She stamped to the window seat and flung herself against its cushions, her face working with emotion. Through the window she could barely see the trail dust of the wagon bearing Anabeth's family and Marynell to the depot in town. Banner had been distracted throughout their visit and hadn't fully enjoyed having them at River Bend. She thought of them wistfully and with affection. They were family, though not kin.

While growing up she had wondered why she didn't have cousins, grandparents. When she first went to school and discovered through other children this lack in her own life, she had asked her parents about it. Where were her grandparents, aunts and uncles, cousins? Why didn't she have any—as other children had?

The answers she got were vague and unsatisfactory. When she was old enough to realize that Ross and Lydia were being deliberately evasive, she tactfully stopped asking. They seemed to have no past beyond the day they arrived in Texas. Even the details of their time together on the wagon train were sketchy.

This vacancy in her heritage had always gnawed at Banner. Did Ross and Lydia share a secret? Was that why they often smiled at each other in a way that closed everyone else out? There was a privacy about them that even Lee and she had never been able to violate.

She didn't know why she felt compelled to have her questions answered. But she was driven to discover who her parents were, where they had come from, what quirk of fate had brought them together.

If anyone could provide clues, it was Jake. They would be seeing a great deal of each other. Such daily contact made for familiarity. Perhaps he would open up and talk to her. Inadvertently he might slip her information that would supply the missing pieces of the puzzle. Gaining enlightenment on her parents' past would be worth any price, wouldn't it?

The pluses outweighed the minuses. Aside from its being awkward to face Jake day after day, everything pointed to the advantages of having him as her foreman. It wouldn't be easy, but in the last two days she had learned to cope with adversity. And wasn't that lesson long overdue? For the first eighteen years of her life she had been blissfully unaware that the world was anything but rosy and full of love. Innocence couldn't last indefinitely. It was time she became acquainted with the harsh realities of life.

Banner waited until suppertime to go downstairs, perversely wanting to make Jake sweat over her decision. The kitchen seemed large and empty without the Langstons and the Drummonds. Lee was eating in the bunkhouse. Jake wasn't there, and his whereabouts weren't mentioned. Only Ross and Lydia sat at the table with Banner.

She didn't even broach the subject of the ranch until after the dishes had been carried from the table to the dry sink. Ross, seemingly without anything noteworthy on his mind, was sipping his after-dinner coffee.

"I've decided to move to my ranch as soon as possible," Banner announced abruptly. Ross arched one inquiring brow. Banner swallowed the last of her pride and added, "and to take Jake with me as my foreman."

She didn't miss the satisfied look that passed between her parents, but they didn't gloat. Ross only said, "Good," before taking another nonchalant sip of coffee. "You'll have two studs and five mares to start with. That's one horse more than your mother and I had."

"And a little money for operating capital," Lydia added. She was at the sink, drying her hands on a cup towel.

Her husband's eyes sliced to her. "Operating capital?" he said.

Lydia met his familiar scowl levelly. It had ceased to intimidate her years ago. "Yes, operating capital."

Ross's mouth thinned beneath his mustache while his green eyes glared. A silent contest of wills ensued. Finally he was heard to mutter, "And some operating capital," before he again drank from his coffee cup.

"Thank you, Papa. And I'll pay back whatever money you advance me within a year, with interest." Banner stood up, holding herself regally, as though he were the one who had come around and not she. "Please tell Jake that—"

"Uh-uh. You tell him. He's your foreman. You're the one who insisted on this period of time to think it over. Otherwise it would have been settled this morning. Since you've delayed him from making any plans one way or another, I think you should be the one to give him the good news."

"But—" She bit back her objection because both of them were staring at her curiously. She didn't want them to wonder why she was reluctant to speak to Jake alone. Besides, she might just as well jump in feet first and get used to facing him on a regular basis. "All right."

The heels of her shoes tapped smartly as she left the kitchen. Her back was straight. Her head was held high. On the inside, she was jelly.

She paused in the hall to check her reflection in the mirror. Her hair had been brushed earlier, but the spring humidity had caused it to curl and wave whimsically. She looked pale after having spent the last two days inside. A brisk pinching on each cheek remedied that somewhat. She smoothed her hands over her linen shirtwaist, which was slightly wrinkled. She sighed. "Well, I'll have to do."

She pushed open the front door and crossed the porch with all the enthusiasm of a convict going to the gallows. What did they expect her to do, march up to the door of the bunkhouse and ask for him? She would be teased unmercifully. Besides, the bunkhouse was the one place on the ranch that was off limits to her.

Should she try the barn first? Would he be tending to Stormy? Her footsteps faltered. She didn't think she could ever go into that barn again. The memories of what had happened there were still too fresh.

Indecisively she stood in the yard. As it turned out, fortune smiled on her. She saw Jake sitting on the top rail of the fence bordering the grazing pasture nearest the house. The heels of his boots were hooked over the next lowest rail. His back was slightly bowed. He sat staring out over the pasture, perfectly still. In the gathering twilight he was cast in profile. He held a cheroot between his lips.

Banner approached him soundlessly. He didn't hear her until she was almost even with him. Then his head snapped around abruptly. Foolishly, she jumped back. One hand went flying up to her chest as if to capture her heart before it leaped from her body.

She cursed herself for acting like a witless ninny. "I . . . I need to talk to you, Jake."

He swung down from the fence railing and swept his hat from his head in one fluid motion. Then, as though realizing how ridiculous he must look, he replaced it and nudged it to the back of his head with his thumb. His shoulders found the railing he had just been sitting on and he leaned against the fence with an attitude of indifference. If only Banner had known that his heart was pounding as fitfully as hers, she might not have been so nervous. As it was, he looked in full control, unmoved, unapproachable, aloof, cool.

Her bravery evaporated as quickly and as surely as her breath mingled with the sultry night air. She turned her head to gaze in the direction his eyes had held only moments before. Her profile was cleanly etched against the darkening violet sky. The breeze that had come up from the south was flirting with her hair, puffing ebony curls against her cheek, then lifting them away.

She wet her lips with her tongue. Jake's eyes caught the unconscious movement. So innocent, yet so provocative. He closed his eyes to ward off the spear of desire that pierced through him. He opened them just in time to meet her gaze when she finally looked up at him.

"I'd like for you to be my foreman."

"*Like* for me to be?"

She made an impatient gesture with her hands. "I have no choice."

"Yes, you do, Banner. Tell me to pack and leave and you'll never see me again."

"What kind of choice is that?" she demanded. "They would assume that we had quarreled. They would know that something wasn't right between us because I had driven you away instead of begging you to stay the way I always have before. Then where would we be? You'd be gone and I'd be left behind to make the explanations.'' She ended on a flurry of emotion and quickly turned away. She laid her forehead on her hands which were stacked on the top rail of the fence.

She heard the jingle of his spurs and knew that he had moved closer. But her ears weren't the only sensors making her aware of him. She could feel the heat of his body as it spread over her back when he came nearer. He had ground out his cheroot, but the scent of tobacco still clung to him. And leather. And man. Her insides felt weightless, then unbearably heavy as they seemed to flow toward and concentrate in the valley between her thighs.

''Banner?'' he asked softly. ''Are you all right?''

She raised her head and looked at him. ''What do you mean?''

His eyes delved into hers, stripping away all the pretense between them, painful though it was. ''I meant exactly what I said. Are you all right? Did you have any . . . ill effects, any pain?''

Suddenly she wanted to punish him. She wanted to throw herself against his chest and pummel it with her fists. She wanted to tell him that she had bled and suffered excruciating agony after what he had done to her.

But she couldn't. Because it hadn't been that way. Jake hadn't done anything she hadn't begged him to. She shook her head before once again letting her gaze drift away. ''No.''

She felt him sag with relief. It wasn't an overt movement, just an immediate lessening of the tension in his body, as though he had been holding his breath for a long time.

''God, I've been sick with worry. I wanted to ask you this morning, but . . . well, there really hasn't been a chance for us to talk.'' Her failure to respond urged him on. He was desperate to make things right. He wanted her to tell him not to worry about it anymore. He wanted to hear her say that she was fine and well and that she had forgiven him. ''I told you it would hurt, Banner.''

''I expected it to.''

''Then it did?''

"A little."

"I should have been gentler."

"It's all right."

"I didn't want to hurt you."

"Please, Jake," she whispered. Her chin buried itself against her chest and she closed her hands over her ears so she wouldn't hear his reminders. Unfortunately it didn't serve to close off the words that reverberated in her head.

I don't want to hurt you, Banner.

I'll hurt you.

Oh, God, you're sweet.

Then a gasp had torn through her whole body. It echoed again and again. Even now she relived that instant of glorious pain, that moment when she had known his full possession.

Jake stared down at her, feeling helpless and angry with himself. She looked so tiny and defenseless. The row of buttons on the back of her shirtwaist only emphasized the graceful curve of her spine. He wanted to lay his hands on her, give her comfort, but he couldn't bring himself to touch her.

Before, he would have thought nothing of making physical contact with Banner. He had touched her frequently, given her bear hugs that made her squeal in mock pain, tugged on wayward strands of hair. Hadn't it been on the very morning of her wedding that he had swatted her bottom? He couldn't imagine doing such a thing now. They had robbed themselves of such playfulness.

"I don't want to talk about it," Banner said gruffly, withdrawing her hands from her ears.

"We have to talk about it. We can't see each other every day with something like this festering between us. We'd be crazy in a week."

She faced him angrily. "Why didn't you think of that sooner, Jake? Why did you put me in the position of choosing? Why didn't you just refuse the job and leave?"

"I tried to. I couldn't."

"Why?"

No longer ashamed, no longer meek, she was a firebrand

again. Her whole body was vibrating with pent-up frustration. Jake was just as agitated.

How could he want her again? How, when he would do anything, give anything on earth, to take back what had already happened, how could he want to crush that dainty body against his and taste her sweet mouth one more time? Just once more.

The memories wouldn't desert his mind. They stayed there in the forefront to torment him like waving red flags in front of a bull. Now he knew just how alive her hair felt when it curled around his fingers. He knew the taste of her skin and the texture of her earlobe. Against his will his eyes lowered to her breasts which were trembling with anger. Had his hands really reshaped them, or did he just want to remember it that way?

He yanked his eyes back to her face and targeted in on her mouth. He had defiled it, scoured it, raped it with his tongue. Some low-class whores wouldn't even let you kiss them with such intimacy. He had hated himself afterward and wondered why Banner hadn't put a stop to it then. But now, all he could think about was doing it again. He wanted a second taste of the sweetness that lay just beyond her lips.

And he hated himself all over again.

He turned away suddenly and braced his elbows on the top rung of the fence. Clasping his fingers together tightly, he tapped at his front teeth with his thumbnails. The lines of his jaw were rigid.

"I felt like I owed it to you to stay."

"Owed it to me?" she ground out.

"Yes, owed it to you. This is my way of paying you back for what I took."

"Don't do me any self-sacrificing favors. You didn't take anything I didn't offer."

The muscles in his arms bunched tighter. "You offered it, but I should have patted you on the head and sent you back to the safety of the house." His eyes flickered down her body. "I didn't. I owe it to you to see that this ranch of yours gets off to a good start. Then maybe I can leave with a clear conscience."

"I don't want your pity!"

His head came around and she recoiled from the cold glinting light in his eyes. "I didn't pity you the other night, did I? Compassion damn sure wasn't one of the reasons I did what I did." He took a step forward and seized her shoulders. "I wanted you. Pure and simple, I wanted you. You got me hard, Banner. So hard I couldn't help myself. But if I were going to do it, why couldn't I have taken it slow, not come at you like some—"

Later, he could never say what stopped the flow of words. Suddenly, his lips fell silent and his mind went blank. Banner was gazing up at him. Her eyes were limpid. Her lips were slightly parted. He stared back, mesmerized by the mellow expression on her face.

In that transference of thoughts, they relived those moments of fierce possession when they had been one. The memory of it refused to be sealed away in the crypts of their minds like something dead. It was very much alive. It seethed between them, a living thing, almost tangible. It swirled around them, an invisible, soundless tempest that shook the foundations of their souls, just as Jake had trembled at the moment of climax.

Then it was over.

Banner was the first to look away. Jake let his hands slide away from her shoulders. The silence stretched out interminably. They were both embarrassed. Banner fervently hoped that Jake didn't know she still ached for something unknown, something just beyond her grasp. Jake wondered if Banner knew how badly he wanted to embed himself inside her again.

"Why did you stay?"

"I needed the job."

They spoke in hushed tones. They didn't look at each other. This was something that had to be said. It had to be settled now or it would ferment and become sour.

"You could always find work as a cowboy."

"Yeah, but that's no life. Not for someone as old as me. I need to do this, Banner."

"I see." And she did. "That's the only reason?"

"I need to stay close to Ma." He was using the same lame argument on Banner that Lydia had used on him. But Ma *was* old. And who knew when her time would come?

"I can understand that."

"But I still refused Ross's first offer. I want you to know that."

"Why?"

"Because I knew how you'd feel having me around after... after the other night."

"What changed your mind?"

"Ross's stubbornness. He wasn't going to give you what you wanted unless it was an arrangement that included me."

"You and I both know that I could have changed his mind eventually." She looked at him now. She hated the question she needed to ask, but she had to know. "Why did you stay, Jake?"

He met her gaze honestly. "Because Lydia asked me to."

Banner nodded silently. She turned and waded through the grass toward the house. Well, she had asked. And he had told her.

She was surprised, and a little frightened, that it hurt so much to know.

SIX

"Is this all?"

Wanda Burns, slatternly as always, dug her fists into her hips and confronted her new husband. She had riffled through the boxes he had carried into the shack she shared with her father. Garments and hats, shoes and gloves were scattered over the bare ticking of the shuck mattress.

"All?" Grady growled. "Isn't it enough? You can't wear any of it until your brat gets here anyway."

He looked at her with patent disgust. She was dirty. Her face was bloated. Her hands and ankles were swollen. Her body was obscenely burdened with a baby he still wasn't convinced was his. Why she had insisted that he provide her with a new wardrobe, he couldn't imagine. Except that it was just another way to put her claws into him, to eliminate any doubts that she was truly Mrs. Grady Sheldon.

"I wanna be dressed like a proper lady when I go into town with you," she had said.

Grady knew he would as soon die as go anywhere in her company, especially into town where the whispered taunts followed him like shadows every time he passed down the street.

He had laughed at her demand for the new clothes. But Doggie's leering grin as he stroked the barrel of his shotgun had changed his mind. Dutifully Grady had promised to bring some things back the next time he came to their cabin deep in the piney woods. It wasn't distance alone that made it seem apart from civilization.

The Burnses had made a fool of him and he didn't like it. He was going to have to do something about it. Soon. But what? And when?

"Them things look right purty, Wanda," Doggie said from the doorway. He stamped in carrying two dead squirrels, which he tossed down on the rough table in spite of the fact they were still bleeding. "Is this here husband doin' right by you, honey?"

"I guess so, Daddy," she said sullenly. "But he still won't let me move into that fancy house of his in town." She pouted up at Grady and he wondered how in hell he had ever found that sulky mouth attractive enough to kiss.

That first night he saw her she had looked pretty enough. He had ridden out to buy moonshine and found not Doggie, but Wanda, taking care of business. The evening had been lit by an autumn moon that hung low and large over the treetops. The air had been crisp and cool.

Having just come from taking a bath in the nearby

stream, Wanda was clean, at least comparatively so. Her tight, threadbare dress clung to her damp skin and let him know right away that she wore nothing under it. She had done everything in her power to make him aware of her lush body, moving with sinuous motions, brushing against him.

She had spoken in whispers, as though they already shared a delicious secret. He had had to stand close in order to hear her, bending his head down on a level with hers. But the effort had been worth it. His conceit had been stroked by her every word.

He was so tall.

She loved curly hair.

She had even feigned a weakness with one of the barrels and cooed appreciatively when he hoisted it to his shoulders and carried it for her.

What a sap he had been. And it was all Banner's fault. If she hadn't stirred his blood so, he wouldn't have been randy for a female. If Banner's innocent kisses hadn't promised so much passion, he wouldn't have been aching to taste Wanda's mouth. Once he had kissed Wanda and felt the hot welcome her body offered, there was no stopping him. Her body had been pliant and generous.

Afterward he had felt wonderful. Wanda had screamed her pleasure like a female panther. She had told him he was handsome, that no man equaled him as a lover.

She said everything he needed to hear. It vexed him that a man of Ross Coleman's stature would be his father-in-law. He was jealous of Coleman. But he was willing to pay the price of living in Coleman's shadow in order to have Banner and all that being married to her would benefit him. That timberland, for instance. Still, each time he came away from River Bend, his pride had taken a beating. He would never measure up to Ross Coleman, not in the eyes of the community, not even in Banner's eyes.

Wanda Burns had given Grady his self-confidence back. She had used her body like a silver platter to serve it up to him. After that first night, he came back often. Each time they made love it was raunchy and nasty and wild. Physically she wore him out. But he took pride in the fact that he was virile enough to satisfy a woman with her sexual appetite.

He had been talking with some of the men in town. He wasn't ignorant of Wanda's reputation. That's what made her safe. He was having what many others considered their due when their wives were indisposed. Hell, he didn't see why he couldn't keep seeing Wanda even after he and Banner were married.

Oh, he liked Banner well enough. She was a damn good-looking woman and no doubt her body was as alive as it hinted at being. Their marriage bed wouldn't be sterile. But Grady was too pragmatic to entertain any notions about love, though he had paid lip service to loving her.

Banner was convenient. It would elevate his standing in the community to have her as his wife because the Colemans were so well respected. That she was pretty and popular with hostesses in town were added bonuses. Not to mention the property she would bring to the marriage.

She had shared her dreams of a ranch with him. He knew all about the horses she wanted to breed and the beef cattle she wanted to raise. He had listened, pretending interest and enthusiasm, all the while bored to tears.

Because *his* ideas about what to do with that land were different from Banner's. He'd let her breed a few horses, even a few cows if that would keep her content, but he wanted that acreage because it bordered one of the state's thickest forests. He had planned to build a sawmill there, an annex to the one in town. He could triple his production in a year.

Of course he hadn't mentioned that to Banner. After the honeymoon would have been soon enough. But there hadn't been a honeymoon. All because of the slut who stood before him now, strutting around under one of the parasols he had brought her. She had insisted on a parasol.

Now he addressed the topic she had brought up moments earlier. "I've explained why you can't move into the house in town. It's for sale. I put it on the market when Banner and I became engaged. She wanted to live on her ranch."

Wanda laughed gustily. "I'll never forget the look on her

face. That prissy Miss Coleman," she said, imitating a mincing walk, "always sashaying around town with her nose in the air."

As ridiculous as the imitation was, Grady took a perverse delight in it. He had thought for a long time that the Colemans were a bit too sure of themselves and needed to be taken down a peg or two. Especially Ross. Damn the man for making a fool of him at the wedding. How dare he threaten his life! Grady would never forget or forgive that.

"They got theirs the day of the weddin', didn't they, honey?" Wanda sidled up to him and ran her hand down the front of his trousers. He shoved her away. "All them Colemans will remember the Burnses, won't they, Grady, honey? Them and that tall blond-headed man that poked a gun in your gullet." She giggled when Grady's face went red with indignation. "What'd you say his name was?"

"Langston. Jake Langston." He went to the table and despite the sickening squirrels, tilted the jug standing next to them to his lips and swallowed a long draft of Doggie's burning moonshine.

"Jake Langston," Wanda repeated dreamily. She languidly ran her tongue around her lips, staring at Grady through slitted eyes. "Mmm. He may be a friend of the Colemans, but I'd like a taste of that cowboy."

Doggie lunged toward her and slapped her so hard her head went flying back. "Shut up that sluttish talk. You're a wife now and you'll stop those whoring ways of yours or I'll rearrange that face you take such pride in."

She cowered, dabbing at the blood that trickled from her lip. "I didn't mean nothin', Daddy."

"I'm hungry. Git started on them squirrels. Grady, you're stayin' for supper."

"I can't, I—"

"I said you're stayin'." Doggie spoke softly, but that raspy voice promised more menace that a shout would have. His eyes were beady beneath the bushy brows, and they glowed maniacally. His lips drooled tobacco juice as he smiled maliciously. He thrust the jug toward Grady. "Have another drink while you tell me why Wanda can't go live with you in town.''

Grady slumped into the rickety chair, furious and frustrated. "There's a family who wants to buy it. I can't move her in only to move her out if the purchase goes through.''

"Don't sell it," Doggie said, wiping his mouth on a gritty fist after swilling from the jug.

"It's not that simple.''

Doggie slammed the jug back onto the table into a puddle of sticky, congealing blood left by the squirrels. Wanda had taken the carcasses out on the collapsing front porch to skin. She was slinging their entrails to a pack of mangy hounds that fought viciously over the meat.

Grady swallowed his nausea. There was no way in hell he would live with these scum. He hadn't had a choice but to marry Wanda. The preacher had been there and Doggie's shotgun had been figuratively, if not literally, tickling his spine. He had stalled them about moving her into his house and that excuse was wearing out.

He had to do something before they robbed him of his sanity as well as everything else. He was a desperate man willing to take desperate measures to rid himself of this blight.

Once her decision was made, Banner acted upon it. The next day, she and Lydia packed everything they could think of that was necessary for setting up a household. The boxes were loaded on a wagon for transport across the river.

"These aren't doing me any good packed away," Banner said, dropping the pile of pillowcases and cup towels she had painstakingly embroidered and stored in her hope chest. "I might just as well put them to use.''

"Banner, how do you feel about Grady now?" Lydia asked. "You know he was forced into marrying that Burns girl. That was the talk going around town when Ross rode in yesterday.''

Banner sighed and sank onto the floor alongside her mother, where she was packing the lavender-scented linens into a box. She toyed with the decorated hem of a pillowcase.

"I don't feel anything, Mama. Isn't that strange? I thought I loved him. I guess I still do in a way. I'm sorry for him for ruining his life. At first I was angry. Now, I just feel an emptiness inside me."

Lydia squeezed her hand. "You're doing the right thing. You're not pining away over something that was none of your fault. I'm proud that you're my daughter."

"Oh, Mama." Banner stared into her mother's face. It was no mystery why Lydia had the love of two men. She wasn't pretty in the classical sense. Her beauty was uniquely her own. Her coloring was flamboyant, her figure provocative. Long before Banner understood why, she had seen cowboys stop their work and stare after her mother when she crossed the yard. If Banner could have chosen, she wouldn't have selected as her mother one of the refined ladies in town who seemed bloodless when compared with Lydia. She would have chosen the one whom she had been blessed with.

She leaned forward and kissed her mother's cheek. "I'm glad you're my mother too. I've always been proud of you."

Lydia sniffed away her mounting emotion. "Before we get sentimental, we'd better get back to work."

They worked diligently throughout the day and into the evening so that by the time Banner climbed the stairs to bed, she was exhausted and weary enough to fall asleep without any haunting memories to keep her awake.

She woke up refreshed and rested early the next morning. Ross and Lydia were already in the kitchen with Lee when she joined them.

"Well, I guess this is our last morning together," Lee said.

"Lee!" Lydia wailed. "Don't make it sound so final."

"Please don't." Ross groaned. "She cried half the night."

"So did you," Lydia retorted. Ross swatted her fanny as she walked past him on a trip to the stove.

"Did you, Papa?" Banner asked, smiling at him.

"You're my princess, aren't you?"

"Always."

Ross winked at her. "Eat your breakfast. I've told everyone to gather in the yard at eight."

An hour later, Banner took one last glance around her room to see if she had left anything vital behind. She had a momentary attack of homesickness, but pushed it down as soon as it formed. It was up to her to make her own home. This is what she wanted. Staunchly she marched down the stairs and out the door.

Ma was seated atop the wagon with the reins in her hands. "You're going with us, Ma?" Banner asked in delight.

"Hmph!" she grunted. "I reckon I have to go and see that things is done right."

"You'll come see me often, won't you?"

"Am I invited?"

"Of course."

Ma smiled. "Then I'll come."

Lydia came bustling out the front door with a basket on her arm. "I brought along some sandwiches." She joined Ma on the wagon seat.

Ross, Lee, and Jake rode into the yard. Trailing them were three of River Bend's hands. Ross introduced the cowboys to Jake.

"Peter, Jim, and Randy. Good men. I picked them out for you myself. Boys, your new foreman, Jake Langston. I'm sure you know him."

The three men nodded and Jake said laconically, "Glad to have you."

Last night Ross had given him the names of the men who would be working with him. Jake had privately sought out Micah. "What do you know about them?"

"Pete's the older guy with the gray hair. He doesn't say much. Good worker though, tough as nails. Wouldn't want to get on his bad side, but I've never seen him lose his temper.

"Jim is the one with the scar on his face. He said backlashing barbed wire nearly took half his mouth off. Reckon that's so, but I've heard others say it ain't. They say he got that scar in a knife fight with a half-breed Comanche. Ugly cuss, but friendly enough. Best roper I've ever seen.

"Randy only came here a few months ago, but he ain't given anybody problems. Likes whiskey but saves his drinking for Saturday nights when he gets skunk drunk. Cheats at poker, but only laughs when he gets caught. And, uh, Jake, I'd keep an eye on him around Banner."

Jake had listened to the recital without comment. At that comment, though, he'd turned his head slightly, his blond brows scowling. "Why's that?"

"They say the name Randy fits him."

Jake pondered that for a minute. "What do *you* say?" Jake could tell Micah didn't want to disparage the cowboy whom he considered a friend, but he didn't relent. "Well?"

Micah gnawed on his bottom lip. "I'd say they're probably right," he replied reluctantly. "He's popular around town. Smilin' all the time. Ain't ever had a problem gettin' a woman, know what I mean?"

"Yeah, Jake had said, slowly coming to his feet and tossing aside the straw he'd been chewing. "I know what you mean."

Now Jake eyed the men from beneath the wide brim of his black hat, deciding they looked like good cowboys. As long as they worked during the week, he didn't care if they got drunk on Saturdays or in knife fights with half-breeds. But they damn sure better stay away from Banner.

"Are we all ready to go?" Ross called out. When everybody chorused "Yes," he nudged his mount toward the gate.

Lee followed. Ma clicked her tongue to the roof of her mouth and flicked the reins over the horses pulling the wagon. Banner walked toward Dusty. The spirited gelding was tied to the hitching post at the porch.

Jake hadn't looked directly at her yet, though he had been aware of her. Now that her back was turned, he treated himself. Her hair reflected the morning sun like a dark mirror before she covered it with her flat-brimmed hat. Her shirt was a startling white contrast to the black split skirt she wore. It was belted with black leather trimmed with silver.

Ross had brought her that belt from Mexico when he made a trip down there several years ago to buy horses. Jake remembered her proudly showing it to him on one of his trips to River Bend.

It hugged her waist tightly. That cinched waist emphasized the feminine curve of her hips. The culotte fit snugly across her derriere before it flared out and fell just below the knees. The black leather riding boots were smooth and supple and clung to the muscles of her calves, defining their shape.

He watched as she placed her left foot in the stirrup and reached up for the pommel of her saddle. The raised knee only served to display her rounded bottom as it pulled the fabric of her skirt tight. She swung into the saddle and positioned herself as she had been taught to almost before she could walk. That impeccable posture was partly responsible for the heart-stopping, mouth-drying, palm-moistening, loin-teasing display of her breasts. But not solely. They didn't need much help. Jake knew they were high and round and . . .

"Dammit," he muttered, and jerked on Stormy's reins to turn him around. Stormy came nose to nose with Randy's mount. The cowboy was leaning forward in his saddle. His glazed eyes were trained on Banner, just as Jake's had been only moments before.

"What are you gawking at?" Jake's question carried with it a threat that the answer had better be to his liking.

"N-nothing. Nothing, Jake, sir."

"Then get goin'. It'll take all three of you to drive those horses across the bridge."

Randy tipped his hat and spurred his horse to catch the others. Banner pulled Dusty up beside Jake. "Randy looks like the devil's got ahold of his horse's tail. What's the matter with him?"

"Don't you have anything else to wear?" Jake asked crossly.

She looked at him in bewilderment. "What?"

"Wear, you know, clothes, the things you dress in," he said impatiently. She glanced down at herself in perplexity, having no idea what he was talking about. He wasn't sure he knew himself and that made him even madder. "Oh, hell, never mind. Just get one thing straight right now, Banner. I don't want any trouble brewing among these men. There will be enough for me to worry about without having to break up fistfights. Stay away from them."

Her eyes flashed angrily. "The only person I'm going to concentrate on staying away from is *you*." With a nudge of her knees, Dusty vaulted away. His hooves thundered over the pebbles in the lane, but rather than riding through the gate, Banner jumped the fence.

"Spoiled brat," Jake said, clamping a cheroot between his teeth. Then, grim-lipped and frowning, he spurred Stormy forward to join the caravan.

"Reckon that's everything," Ma said. She folded the cup towel and carefully laid it on the drainboard.

Jake's eyes roved around the kitchen. "Everything looks nice. I know Banner appreciates you helping her to get unpacked."

"I started supper," she said, cocking her head toward the shiny black iron stove in the corner.

"Smells good."

Ma eyed her eldest shrewdly. He hadn't really seen her handiwork in the kitchen any more than he had smelled the beans and ham hock cooking. He had something on his mind. She could always tell when something was bothering Jake. He withdrew deep into himself and, as though that caused him to itch, he fidgeted, as he was doing now with his glove.

Even when he was a little boy, he would lurk around her until he got her attention. After that it usually didn't take much prodding on her part to get him to say what was bothering him. Most often it was a confession of some small sin that he was just dying to make.

She remembered one occasion distinctly. He had returned from his second trail drive to Kansas and come home for a visit. After supper, he had lingered at the table. She had picked up the hint and invented reasons for everyone else to leave the room until she and Jake were alone.

She inquired about his life as a cowboy. His answers were desultory. Finally she asked bluntly, "Have you done somethin' you ought to be ashamed of?"

His eyes had met hers then and she realized that her Bubba was no longer a boy. He was a man and carried the weight of the world on his shoulders. "I've done something that was *necessary*, Ma."

She had gathered him against her bosom and he had cried like a baby. She had never asked what that "necessary" something was because she thought she was better off not knowing. But she mourned for the boy who had grown into a man and whose growing process had been so painful.

He had that same look about him now. A bleak, hopeless look that meant he wanted to tell her something he couldn't quite bring himself to talk about.

Of course she had always known he loved Lydia Coleman. She suffered with him for that too. She suspected that Lydia also knew. They had shared secrets and innermost thoughts with each other for years, but that was one subject that was never broached. It was as though they were afraid if they ever spoke of it aloud, things would never be the same between them. And they were right.

Jake lifted his eyes from the glove he had been fiddling with. Ma had poured him a cup of coffee. It sat cooling near his hand, untasted. "You haven't said anything about me staying on here."

Ma sat down in the chair across from him. "You haven't asked me."

"I'm asking now."

She drew a deep breath that expanded her massive chest even more. "I'm glad you're settlin' down somewhere. I didn't like goin' to bed every night wonderin' where you were. It's selfish I reckon, but I'd like to have each and every one of you gathered around me all the time."

He smiled sadly. "You've had to give up so many of us."

She wiggled her nose dismissively. "Lots of women have buried their husband and children. I ain't no different."

He had tossed the glove aside and had taken up twirling the coffee mug round and round in an endless pattern. Ma knew he wasn't finished talking yet. Whatever was pricking his conscience was still there.

"Do you think it'll work out, me and Banner working here together?"

Ma's mind snapped closed around his words like a steel trap on a baited animal. Banner. *Banner?* Could it be? She watched Jake closely without his knowing. He was squirming in his chair like there were ants in his britches; his fingers moved restlessly around the cup as though it were hot. He showed all the symptoms. Yep, that was it. Something having to do with Banner.

The girl was a lot like her mother. Attractive in a lusty sort of way men couldn't ignore. But Jake and Banner? That would take some getting used to. Their age difference alone ... seventeen, no, eighteen years. He'd always treated her like a kid sister. Still, stranger things had happened.

"I reckon it will," Ma said offhandedly. "She'll be a handful, make no mistake." She hauled herself up to stir the beans bubbling on the stove. "That gal's been spoiled all her life by everybody at River Bend, includin' me. She's had a disappointment, the first big one in her life. I didn't cotton much to that Sheldon feller. If you ask me, this is the best thing that could have happened to her. She had to learn sometime that life ain't gonna cater to Miss Banner Coleman's every wish. That might sound mean, but you know I love that young'un like she was my own.

"Still, I know she's stubborn and headstrong. She's like a keg of dynamite ready to be set off. And the man who does that will either regret for the rest of his days that he sparked that fuse, or be damned glad. That'll depend on the man."

She saw his Adam's apple take a plunge before working itself back up to its rightful position. It was Banner, all right. Ma turned her back and salted the beans.

"How do you know it'll be a man that, uh, sets her off?"

Ma laughed. " 'Cause she's her mama's daughter, that's why. And her papa's. And she's grown up feeling that heat between the two of them. The ways of men and women ain't foreign to her. You know what I think?''

''What?'' Jake asked in a voice that sounded like it didn't belong to him.

''I don't think she was itchin' to marry that Grady Sheldon as much as she was itchin' to *marry*. No 'ifs,' 'ands,' or 'buts' about it.''

''I don't know anything about that.'' Jake stood up suddenly and carried his coffee cup to the sink, pumping water over it and rinsing it out. He glanced out the window. Banner was bidding her family goodbye. Lee bent down and kissed her cheek. She slapped him lightly. He socked her in the stomach. They laughed together. Ross and Lydia, their arms linked around each other's waists, smiled on lovingly.

''But I'll tell you one thing,'' Jake said sternly, spinning around and surprising his mother with his vehemence. ''Ross has given me a job to do. It's a damn good job and I'm glad to have it, but it's going to involve a lot of hard work. I'm not going to put up with any shenanigans from Banner. I'm damn sure not going to stand for any of her tantrums. And the sooner she gets that through her head, the better.'' With that, he yanked up his hat and pushed through the back door.

''Well,'' Ma huffed. Then she smiled and went to join the others outside. It was time they left.

''Was the cornbread all right?''

''Yeah. It was fine.''

''Well, you could have said something.''

''I just did! I said it was fine.''

''Thank you.'' Banner virtually jerked his plate out from under him and whisked it away.

Jake's hands balled into fists where they rested on the table edge while he slowly counted to ten. His eyes were squeezed tightly shut as he tried to get a grip on his temper. This was their first evening meal together. The first of many to come. The Colemans and Ma had left. The cowboys followed soon afterward. They wouldn't be back until sunup the next morning. Until then he and Banner would be alone.

How this first night went might determine how the others would go. If they survived tonight, maybe they would have a chance of making this work.

When he opened his eyes she was standing at the sink washing dishes with her back to him. She had changed clothes at some point during the day. Instead of the culottes and shirt, she was wearing a calico print dress. It camouflaged her figure more, but it was softer and made her look more touchable.

But he couldn't touch her. So he might just as well get that thought right out of his mind. He pushed his chair back and carried the serving dishes to the sink.

"You don't have to," she said, when he set them on the drainboard.

"I know I don't have to. You don't have to cook my supper either, but that was part of the deal. I want to help you, so let's not argue over it."

He used the cajoling tone he had used on her when she was a little girl. It had never failed to draw her out of a pouting mood. But it wasn't a little girl's face that turned up to his. It was a woman's. Soft in the lamplight. Damp from having her hands in hot dishwater. Rosy and freckled from hours spent outside today.

Her eyes were remarkable. He had always thought Lydia's were, but Banner's were even rarer. He could see his reflection in their green and gold depths and could almost laugh at the stupefied look on his face. He wore the duped expression of a man who had just walked into an invisible wall.

But he couldn't have conjured up a laugh if his life had depended on it. Any more than he could conjure up the willpower to look away.

The walls of the house closed around them like a gentle fist. It was a small house, having only a front room, a bedroom on one side and this kitchen on the other. It had been designed and built with plans to add on later. But now its miniature size seemed to squeeze them closer together. The pervading silence contributed to the intimacy.

"You're as touchy as a rattler, Banner," he whispered. Did he fear he would break the spell if he spoke out loud?

"So are you."

"I guess I am."

"You take offense at everything I say."

"We can't tease each other anymore, can we?"

"No."

"I can't go back to treating you the way I did before."

She sucked in a tremulous little sigh. "I know. Things will never go back to how they were before."

"Are you sorry for that?"

"Yes, aren't you?" He nodded. "I should have thought of that before I asked you to . . ." She caught her bottom lip between her teeth and held it there before she went on. "That night will be a barrier between us from now on. We'll always remember it."

Lord, he remembered it. He remembered it with every masculine cell in his body. His eyes, flagrantly disobeying the commands of his brain, dwelled on the perfect shape of her lips. If only he couldn't remember those catchy little gasps she had made as his tongue sampled her mouth for the first time. If only he couldn't remember her awakening when her mouth had learned to respond.

Inadvertently he inclined toward her until his body heat melded with hers and they became indistinguishable. He spotted the fluttering of her pulse at the base of her throat where his lips had pressed, and pressed again. The taste still lingered on his tongue.

Her breasts drew his eyes downward. Her nipples were puckered beneath the cloth of her dress. He saw them and yearned.

An involuntary groaning sound vibrated through his chest and up his throat. Beneath the fly of his pants he was high and rock hard. Lifting his eyes, he scanned her face, the black cloud of undisciplined hair that wreathed it, and he ached to have her.

"Banner . . . ?"

"Yes?"

Suddenly he realized that he was about to kiss her again.

And if he did ... If he did, he wouldn't stop there. He would dip his head and kiss her breasts through her dress. He would sip those sweet peaks between his lips. He would cup her hips with his hands and draw them close, as he had done before, lifting her against his rigid manhood. He would do the unthinkable again.

Before he yielded to the temptation, he stepped away from her. "Nothing. I'll see you in the morning. If you need anything, yell."

"Where are you going?" It was too early to go to bed.

"Out to check on that temporary corral we put up today. Randy can't drive a straight nail."

"I thought he was doing all right for the first day."

Her taking up for the cowboy was the only catalyst he needed to explode. He vented his frustration through his temper. "Well, he didn't impress me as being so wonderful. If he doesn't live up to the job, he's gone." With that, he slammed out the back door.

SEVEN

The night was incredibly dark. Banner hadn't realized how remote her small house was until darkness closed in around it.

From the day she was born she had slept in a house with other people. Tonight she was alone, completely alone, for the first time in her life.

Sleep wouldn't come to eliminate the loneliness. Her ears were sensitive to every sound. The noises of a settling house had never alarmed her. At River Bend, in her upstairs bedroom with the window seats and eyelet curtains, those sounds had been familiar and reassuring. She recognized the shape of each shadow outside her window.

But tonight each whisper of leaves was sinister. The groaning of new lumber sounded like a lament. The shadows weren't friendly.

Had she made a mistake by leaving her home and family? She had never understood how Ma Langston could live alone in her cabin. Often Lydia and Ross had urged her to move into their house and use one of the upstairs bedrooms. She had always adamantly refused. Banner couldn't imagine preferring solitude to being surrounded by people you loved and who loved you.

It was awful, this solitude. Maybe she had acted rashly by moving here alone. What if she had to live out her days without anyone for a companion in the night? What if she grew old living here by herself? What reward would there be in making it a profitably working ranch if she had no one to share it with?

Irritated with herself for harboring such gloomy thoughts, she kicked off her covers and went to the window. At least the moon offered a pale illumination. Her gaze traveled to the barn. It looked new, almost artificial in its newness. It had none of the rustic flavor of the oldest barn at River Bend in which she had played hide and seek with Lee when they were children. This barn looked alien.

But from one of its windows emanated a feeble light made by a lantern turned down low. Jake was there, not too far away, within shouting distance if the shrouding darkness and stark loneliness got to be too much for her.

She took comfort in his presence and was able to fall asleep when she returned to bed. As soon as dawn broke, she got up and dressed in work clothes.

Pearly sunlight filtered through the windows of her kitchen as Banner started breakfast. The butter-colored glow lent the room a homier aspect and lifted her spirits considerably from what they had been in the dark, lonely hours of the night. She even began to hum as she sliced bacon and laid the thick slices in a skillet.

But her humming ceased when she saw Jake emerge from

the barn. Indeed, all of her went completely still. A slice of bacon dangled limply from her fingers. Her lips parted slightly.

He came out scratching his head and combing his fingers through the hair that looked like tangled spun gold when the rosy sunlight fell on it. He yawned broadly, revealing straight white teeth. Well, the bottom row was slightly crooked in front, but the imperfection was barely noticeable.

Linking his fingers together and turning them inside out, he raised his hands high above his head and stretched with the sinuous leisureliness of a mountain cat.

The slice of bacon slipped heedlessly from lifeless fingers.

He had pulled on his pants and boots, but . . . the pants hadn't yet been buttoned. And it wasn't so much what she could see that intrigued Banner, as what she *couldn't* see.

As he stretched with unself-conscious luxury, his feet wide apart, his back arched, Banner was treated to an unrestricted view of his muscular torso. Her mouth went dry, but another part of her body reacted just the opposite. It wasn't that she had never seen a man shirtless before. She had, many times. Her father, Lee, Micah. But she had never seen Jake without a shirt. Even keeping her opinion as fairly unbiased as possible, she thought he was spectacular to look at.

His shoulders were broad. The muscles of his upper arms curved and cupped into them smoothly. Soft nests of light brown hair lined his armpits. His chest was covered with a network of crisp golden hair, light against the coppery hue of his skin. Almost hidden in that fair pelt were flat brown nipples that were pebbling under the kiss of cool morning air.

Banner swallowed and pressed her knees tightly together.

The muscles of Jake's chest could have been the handiwork of a sculptor's fingers. He was lean, but every rippling cord was clearly defined.

His chest tapered down to a hard flat stomach and an even trimmer abdomen. A sleek line of hair connected that forest on his chest with the thatch that swirled around his navel. It grew darker and denser there. Banner's eyes tracked it until it disappeared into the V made by his opened waistband. Her curiosity went wild. Why had he hitched his pants up quite so high?

Strange, she thought, that she had lain with this man, yet this was the first time she had seen him any way but fully clothed. Pride welled inside her. He was magnificent. Beautiful. Golden and lean. At least she didn't have to be humiliated by the fact that her first, and possibly only, lover had been someone undesirable.

Jake lowered his arms and shook them out to restore circulation. Going to the water pump in the yard between the house and the barn, he bent down and let the water splash over his head and neck as he pumped. When he raised up, he covered his face with his hands and shivered. Gradually he lowered his hands and shook his head to rid it of dripping water. It flew out around him like a shower of diamonds, each prism catching the sunlight.

He went back into the barn only long enough to retrieve a shirt. When he came out again, he was pulling it on. He walked around the back of the barn until he disappeared from Banner's sight.

For several moments she stared at the spot where she had last seen him. Then, as if coming out of a trance, she blinked her eyes and drew a deep, ragged breath. One by one her muscles relaxed and the tension ebbed from her limbs. She was amazed to find that a slice of bacon had wastefully been dropped to the floor.

Her equilibrium was none too steady, but she forced herself to finish preparing breakfast. Any moment now Jake would come in expecting scalding coffee and a hot meal.

Were her cheeks flushing as warmly as she thought they were?

Would he know she had been spying on him?

But so what if he had? she thought, suddenly angry. He had no business parading around half naked like that! She certainly hadn't *wanted* to look at him; it had been an accident. Nor did she crave to touch . . . anything. And that vague twinge of disappointment she felt in the pit of her stomach wasn't because he had been wearing a shirt that night they made love. Certainly not! It probably wouldn't have felt good anyway, all that hair and hard muscle against her breasts.

She coughed to relieve her throat of a sudden congestion.

When he knocked on the back door, she jumped like a frightened rabbit and whirled around just in time to see him coming in.

He noticed her agitation instantly and asked, "What's the matter?"

"Nothing," she said with breathless rapidity.

"You sure?"

"Yes. Of course. What could be the matter?"

"I don't know, that's why I asked."

She turned her back on him. "Sit down. Breakfast is ready."

He gave her an odd look, but did as she said, pulling a chair back from the table and dropping into it. She crossed to the table quickly, bringing the coffee pot with her. She reached over his shoulder to pour him a cup. "Sleep well?" he asked.

He turned his head to glance up at her. They froze.

Leaning forward as she was, with her arms extended, her breast was on a level with his face. They were so close if he had puckered his lips they would have touched her. She even felt his indrawn breath against her nipple, which was tight, unaccountably so since it surely wasn't cool in the kitchen. Indeed, Banner had never been so uncomfortably warm in her life.

She sloshed the coffee into the mug and pulled back quickly. "Yes, I slept fine. You?"

"Fine, fine." His teeth were grinding together and he was rocking slightly in his chair. But he was facing forward now and looked like he intended to stay that way forever. Lesson number one: Never, *never* turn your head when Banner is serving you. He cleared his throat. "That room is cozy enough." Liar. He hadn't snatched but minutes of sleep at a time. He had tossed and turned, thinking of her in the house, worrying if she had remembered to lock the doors, if she was cold, if she was hot, if she was hungry, if she was scared. He had tried a thousand times to convince himself that he ought to check on her, knowing damn good and well that he shouldn't.

"It won't be too hot in there this summer, will it?" She felt it was necessary to make idle conversation to cover her own nervousness as she carried the serving dishes to the table.

"If it is I can sleep outside. I've done it often enough."

He had referred to his sleeping habits that night in the barn. Why the hell had he repeated it now to act as a reminder? Maybe she wouldn't remember. But when his gaze slid up to meet hers, he knew she did. Her cheeks deepened a shade pinker and she turned away hurriedly.

It was then that the pants registered with him.

She was outfitted in pants. They had either been a pair of Lee's sized down or tailor-made to fit her because they gloved that cute little butt in a sanity-threatening way.

Hell! How did she expect him to swallow bites of scrambled eggs—cooked just the way he liked, by the way—when she was sashaying around the kitchen, fetching and carrying, in those damn tight britches?

They should have been outlawed. Because if he had speculated on the shape of her thighs before, they held no mystery for him now. They were long and trim and designed to make a man's mouth water. Jake had seen dance hall girls perform in scandalously sheer tights and none had been as provocative as Banner wearing form-fitting faded denim. Only days ago, he had teasingly swatted her on the bottom and thought nothing of it. Well, he thought about it now. He thought about it so hard his palms began to tingle. If his hand ever landed on that sweetly rounded flesh again, it wouldn't be for a playful spanking, but a caress.

When everything had been carried to the table, she sat down across from him. Jake breathed a sigh of relief. But his relief was short-lived. Her front acted like a magnet for his eyes. She was wearing a simple cotton shirt, nothing fancy, one you could find on any cowhand. But Banner altered its shape considerably. She couldn't have put anything into the pockets if she had wanted to. They were already filled with her breasts.

"Gravy?"

"What?" He jerked his eyes from her chest to her inquiring face.

"You haven't sampled my gravy yet. Scared?" Banner cocked her head to one side. The taunt was a valiant attempt to put things back on an even keel. Jake was acting as strangely as she was. He was probably still upset over their argument last night and that was the reason for the tension around his mouth.

She longed for the days when they had been good friends and confidants. Hadn't he pressed her head against his chest once when she was crying over a lost kitten? She hadn't had this warm, curling flurry in her stomach then. Why couldn't they recapture that kind of camaraderie?

What a senseless question to ask herself. She knew why. Things would never be the same between them, but maybe they could *pretend* that the night in the barn had never happened. At least she was going to try. "Don't you think I can cook?"

He chuckled and ladled a generous amount of thick, steaming gravy over the biscuit he had broken apart. "I have a stomach made of iron or I never would have survived eating out of chuck wagons. I imagine I'll be able to choke down your cooking." He took a bite, closed his eyes and savored it as he chewed. Only after he had swallowed with comical exaggeration did he open his eyes. He smacked his lips and said, "Delicious."

She grinned at him and felt much more at ease. "I've been thinking about a name for the ranch."

"I thought it already had a name."

She sipped her coffee and shook her head. "I don't want it to be just an extension of River Bend. I want it to have a name of its own. Any suggestions?"

"Hmm. I hadn't thought about it."

She laid her fork on her plate, clasped her fingers, and leaned forward on her elbows. "What do you think of Plum Creek?"

"Plum Creek?"

"That's the name of the creek that runs through the forested edge of the property, the creek that channels into the river."

"Plum Creek Ranch?" he mused aloud, his brow furrowed. "Sounds sort of . . . uh . . ." He searched for the right word. "Feminine."

She had wanted his face to light up with shared enthusiasm for the name and it irked her that it hadn't. "Well, *I'm* feminine."

His eyes snapped up to look into hers, then immediately dropped to her breasts again. This time they were softly billowing with indignation. His hands itched to experience that trembling agitation. And he damn sure couldn't dispute the fact that she was feminine.

Frustrated to the breaking point, he said sharply, after he lifted his gaze back to her face, "It's your ranch, name it anything you please."

"Thanks so much for your permission." Her voice dripped sarcasm as thick as honey. She scraped back her chair and stood, clanging dishes together as she stacked them.

Jake rose from his chair too. "I don't think the hands are going to like working on a ranch with such a prissy name."

"It was only a suggestion. I haven't made up my mind yet."

A knife slid from one of the plates she was carrying to the sink. She bent down and picked it up, sending her rear in the air. Oh, hell, Jake groaned. Was she driving him mad on purpose? He turned toward the door. "The hands will be here soon. I've got to get to work."

"What are you going to do today?"

"Start building the permanent corral."

"I'll come out and check on things later."

In those pants, with her hair wild and free, she would be a distraction to a eunuch. That's all he needed, a bunch of randy cowboys who wouldn't get a lick of work done for ogling Banner.

"Well, before you do, get rid of those britches."

"What?"

"You heard me."

"Why?"

"Because it'll make my job of protecting you a helluva lot easier if you're not prancing around in tight pants."

"Prancing!"

"They're . . . they're indecent."

She slammed a dish onto the drainboard. "Indecent!" she cried, enraged.

But Jake was already stalking across the yard.

"Oh . . . Priscilla . . . honey."

Dub Abernathy's eyes were glazed with desire. His forehead was damp with perspiration. The sparse gray hair, each strand of which he valued highly, was plastered to his moist scalp. His fingers worked frantically at the buttons of his vest. He had discarded his coat as soon as he came in. He always did that before accepting a glass of the madam's finest whiskey.

The woman and the whiskey were forbidden pleasures he indulged in every Tuesday and Thursday afternoon and sometimes on Saturday mornings if Priscilla was willing and he could arrange his schedule.

"Hmm." He moaned as he shrugged out of his vest and tossed it to the floor. He grabbed for the glass at his elbow on the small, three-legged table and gulped. "Go on, finish."

Priscilla stood before him in corset and camisole, stockings and high-heeled shoes. The corset forced her breasts up and out, pinched her waist to a drastic narrowness and exaggerated the natural flair of her hips. The garters that ribboned down her thighs held up black sheer stockings that were a shocking contrast to the ivory fairness of her skin.

Priscilla delighted in teasing Dub to his limit. His desire for her was so obvious. He was so shamelessly licentious and without morals in bed. That's why she liked him. He was unabashed by his passion, having learned and admitted long ago it had nothing to do with love. He wasn't duped by man-made ideals. Human beings were incapable of loving anyone but themselves. But they could give each other pleasure. That's just what she and Dub did. This slow striptease was one of the erotic games they played for entertainment.

For the last several years Dub Abernathy had been one of Priscilla's regular customers and among the few she handled herself. None of their standing appointments had ever been canceled. She enjoyed their romps, because Dub was adventuresome. Unselfishly he gave her pleasure too. He was a valuable friend to have for several reasons, not the least of which was his standing in the community.

Abernathy might be one of the Garden of Eden's staunchest supporters, but he was also a respected businessman in Fort Worth. He served on the board of directors of one of the city's banks, he was chairman of the deacons at the First Baptist Church, he was active on the City Council.

He was a fraud.

That's another reason Priscilla liked him. He lived the life of a sterling citizen, but was decadent. She adored corrupting such pillars of the community.

Slowly Priscilla raised her arms and pulled the pins from her hair. One shining long coil, as though trained to do so, fell over her shoulder to curl beguilingly on her breast.

The same lips that called on the Lord in prayer on Sunday mornings spoke his name now blasphemously. Priscilla smiled with feline smugness.

She threw her head back and rolled it from side to side, knowing Dub liked to watch her hair sweep the naked skin of her back.

"Touch yourself," he whispered raspily. She laid her hands on her chest and lightly skimmed them down until each covered a breast. "Oh God, oh God, oh God," Dub panted. He unfastened the buttons of his trousers and spread them open. Rooted in the banker's conservative gray pinstripes was his rampant desire. Priscilla gloated.

She pressed her hands over her breasts, rubbed slowly in a circular motion, closed her eyes, and swayed sensuously. Dub's breathing accelerated. To reward him for wanting her so much, Priscilla peeled down the camisole and bared her breasts.

"Make them hard for me," Dub said hoarsely.

This was routine, too, but it never failed to excite Priscilla. She had this man virtually apoplectic for want of her. He might sway City Council votes and expound on the terrors of hell in the Sunday school class he taught, but when he came into this room, she had him in her power. And power was the strongest aphrodisiac.

Her fingers fanned her nipples, slowly at first and then faster in rhythm to Dub's uneven breathing. She pinched them between her thumbs and fingers, enjoying his groaning sighs.

At last he said, "Bring them to me now."

She walked forward with an undulating sway that hypnotized him. When she was still several feet from him, he lunged from the chair, clasped her around the waist and hauled her against him as he fell back. His mouth covered one breast hotly. Priscilla locked her hands around his head as she knew he liked. The pads of her thumbs pressed into his temples. She straddled his lap and impaled herself on him.

His mouth moved feverishly from one lush breast to the other while she knowledgeably milked him. He lashed at her nipples with his tongue, bit her hard enough to hurt. She slipped her hands into his collar. Her nails dug savagely into the sides of his neck as her pumping movements became more frenzied.

Then the businessman who owned controlling stock in numerous enterprises, who eloquently presided over board meetings, who would never think of offending his wife, squealed like an animal in its dying throes and spent himself between the thighs of Texas's most notorious whore.

Because he had brought her to climax, too, Priscilla forgave him the slack mouth that now drooled over her breasts.

Gracefully she stood up and retired behind a screen to wash and repair herself. When she joined Dub again, he was lying naked on her bed awaiting the ablutions that always followed. She bathed his now naked body with a warm towel.

"Another drink?" she asked soothingly.

He toyed with her breast. "No. Better not. I have a meeting this afternoon."

She laid the towel aside. Joining him on the bed, she propped herself on a pile of pillows and drew his head to her breast, as was their ritual. This was the most valuable part of their liaison. She enjoyed the sex, but the information she gleaned in the aftermath couldn't be obtained anywhere else.

"How is my railroad stock doing?"

"You've already doubled your investment," he mumbled between kisses to her neck. "Just as I said. That steel company is doing well too. Would you like to invest in a race horse?"

"Sounds like fun."

"I'll keep an eye on his training and let you know." He raised himself up slightly to see her better. A stubby finger drew circles around one breast. "Speaking of horses, didn't you tell me once that you knew the Colemans of River Bend over in Larson County?"

Her fingers, which had been lightly scratching his back, became still. "Yes. What about them?"

"I heard some gossip the other day. Seems they have a daughter."

"I knew that. She just got married."

Dub chuckled. "She was *supposed* to. But the wedding got interrupted by a white trash moonshiner. He dragged his pregnant daughter into the church and declared that the bridegroom was the baby's father."

Priscilla's eyes lit up, her mind conjuring up the unpleasant scene. "No!"

"I swear that's the story going around. One of my clients was invited to the wedding. He told me, and he has no reason to lie."

"What happened?"

Dub filled her in on the facts as he knew them. "This fellow she was marrying, Grady or Brady Sheldon I think was his name, was forced into marrying the moonshiner's daughter instead of the Coleman girl."

"What did the Colemans do?"

"Struck off for home surrounded by their friends and allies."

Jake Langston, Priscilla thought. She hated to think of him resting in the bosom of the Colemans, but it gave her secret satisfaction to know that Lydia's daughter hadn't been able to hold her man.

"Thanks for telling me," she cooed to Dub. To compensate him, she ran her hand down between their bodies.

"Jesus, girl, are you trying to kill me?" he asked on a gasping breath when her fingers enfolded him.

"You don't like it?" Her tongue lapped his ear.

He liked it very much and it didn't take her long to coax back his desire. This time he was stronger and more potent than before. He slumped atop her, but he was jubilant. It did his self-image a supreme amount of good each time he took Priscilla. His wife, so prim and proper, had no inkling that humans could perform the acts he and Priscilla engaged in. Mrs. Abernathy had never given him satisfaction, and he had only sired one less-than-enchanting daughter out of her.

Wasn't a man deserving of such pleasures as Priscilla afforded when he worked as hard as he did? He justified his sport, but it worked to salve what little conscience Dub Abernathy retained.

Priscilla was helping him with his coat when he brought up a subject of interest to them both. "Sweetheart, I must caution you to beware."

"Of what?"

"The Women's Society is organizing a new movement to have Hell's Half Acre wiped off the map."

Priscilla picked up a hairbrush and pulled it through her hair. "They've tried before," she said airily. "They always fail."

Dub looked grim. "Maybe not this time. They've got the backing of our new hellfire and brimstone preacher."

She laid the brush aside and spun around. "I thought you were going to keep him from coming here."

He shrugged. "I tried. I was outvoted." He laid his hands on her shoulders. "He means business, Priscilla. He's a fanatic and he's getting a lot of backing. People are siding with him.''

"Maybe farmers and stupid—''

"No. Businessmen."

She squirmed away from his hands and began to pace. "But dammit, we're good for Fort Worth's business community. If they shut us down the whole economy would feel the effect. The cowboys would stop coming here to spend their money. The saloons aren't the only places that profit from their patronage, you know. Every business in town enjoys the traffic we bring through here."

She picked up a fan, drew her finger along the silk and tossed it back down on her vanity. She was vexed. There was no mistaking that. "They preach and rant and rave about us, but it's been understood for years that their protests are all for show. They like having us here."

Dub was impatient with her refusal to see things as they were. "They have been before, but business is good without the cowboys. More and more families are moving in. They want to make this a safe city for respectable folks." Priscilla made a rude sound, but Dub pressed home his point. "Fort Worth is no longer just a cowboy's playground, a place for him to gamble away his money, get roaring drunk, and catch a dose of the clap."

She faced him. "Do something, Dub. Calm them down. Make some grandstanding gesture to satisfy them the way you have in the past. Remember the picket lines last year? Nearly every sign carrier was a customer of mine. They organized that protest to placate their wives, and it worked. It'll work again."

He hadn't intended to get her so riled. He could see the writing on the wall, whether Priscilla could or not. The days were numbered for the Garden of Eden. Priscilla would still be a rich woman. She had enough well-paying business interests to be well off for the rest of her life. But Dub knew she loved being the best-known madam in the state. It was a matter of pride with her. No one would take that title from her without a fight.

He hugged her and stroked her back. "I didn't mean to

worry you. Just be aware of what's happening. Things might get hot.''

"But they always cool down eventually." She slid her hands beneath his coat and pressed him closer. "As long as I have friends like you on my side, I'm protected. Right?"

"Right." He kissed her swiftly before she could see his duplicity.

For a long time after he had gone Priscilla sat and pondered her future. She hated not being in control.

EIGHT

They had survived the first two weeks without either of them committing murder. In view of their dispositions and the number of shouting matches they had had, that was a major feat. Banner mentally congratulated both of them for that accomplishment as she guided the wagon over the bumpy ground.

It was noon. The sun was hot. Jake and the three hands were stringing a barbed-wire fence to enclose some of the acreage designated as pastureland. Banner, restless and bored in the house, had made a jug of lemonade and was taking it out to the work site along with a basket of sandwiches and cookies.

Her labor of love would win her nothing but a scowl from Jake. He scowled frequently. In fact every time he looked at her, his brows were drawn into a frown of disapproval. Since that first morning when he had ordered her to exchange the pants for something else, she had defied him by wearing them every day, even in the evenings when he came to the house for supper.

Some rebellious demon inside her prompted her to provoke Jake. Why, she couldn't say. He was like a thunderstorm about to happen. She was ready for it. She couldn't stand that dark, turbulent, sulfurous atmosphere between them any longer. Better to have the storm erupt and clear the air than for it to keep brewing.

She flicked the reins over the horse's rump. The journey over the rough ground couldn't be any harder on him than it was on her. It jarred her teeth each time the wagon wheel ground over a rock. She would much rather be on horseback, exercising one of the breed horses. The trip to the work site would have been accomplished in a third of the time. But she had needed the lemonade and the cookies and sandwiches as her excuse to trespass where Jake had specifically told her not to go. And to carry them, she had to bring the wagon.

She had wanted to work on stringing the fence herself, or at least supervise. Jake would have none of it. He had shaken his head adamantly. "It's hard work."

"I'm used to hard work."

"Not this kind."

"Every kind."

"It's dangerous. You could get hurt."

"I won't."

"That's right, you won't because you won't be anywhere around. Busy yourself with things in the house and let me run the ranch."

That had earned him a defiant stance and a tiger-eyed glare. "I've been involved in ranch work all my life. I'm bored with the house. There's nothing to do in there. I have it arranged like I want it. I get through with my chores by ten in the morning and have nothing to do all day."

"Ride Dusty."

"Where? Around the yard? You told me not to venture off."

"So take up a hobby. But stay away from me and the men!"

As with most of their encounters, he had stalked away, muttering under his breath.

Well, today she wouldn't stay inside. It was the first day

that truly felt like summer and she wanted to be outside to enjoy it.

She drew the wagon to a halt beneath a shade tree at a point where the meadow began to blend into the forest. Upon seeing her, the three hands stopped to mop their brows with the backs of their sleeves. A terse word from Jake, which Banner couldn't hear, called their attention immediately back to the fence.

She hopped down from the wagon, took the jug and basket from the back and set out to cover the remaining distance on foot. "I thought you all deserved a rest," she called out cheerfully. Her gaiety was a deliberate taunt to the thunderous look Jake was giving her. She ignored him and beamed upon the other three men. "Lemonade, sandwiches, and cookies."

"That's a regular picnic," Randy drawled, whipping off his hat and bowing gallantly.

Banner's giggle went through Jake's gut like a serrated blade. *Just look at her*, he thought, *flaunting herself in those damn pants*. He hated them.

No, he liked them. A lot.

But so did the other men and that's what he couldn't tolerate. He knew she only wore them to aggravate him. That he could stand. It was the way the men looked at Banner when she wore the pants that set his teeth on edge.

"That's right nice of you." Jim's scarred mouth fashioned itself into a facsimile of a smile. Pete didn't say anything, but he eyed the basket appreciatively.

Without even consulting him, the men began to dig into the lunch she had brought and to pass around the jug of lemonade. They exchanged pleasantries with Banner like this was a Sunday social instead of a workday. None of them thought to ask if it was all right if they took this break. He *was* their foreman, wasn't he? But Miss Coleman was the owner of the ranch. As much as he would like to reprimand her as a family friend for flirting dangerously with women-hungry men, and as a foreman for jeopardizing his authority, he didn't say a word. Instead he turned away and began stretching the wire around the post they had just driven into the ground.

"Jake, don't you want any?" Banner asked.

Her hair was iridescent in the bright sunlight, as sleek as a raven's wing. It seemed a living thing with its riot of waves and curls that she didn't have the decency to bind up or hide under a modest bonnet. Her cheeks were flushed with color. He could barely see her eyes through the forest of dark lashes as she squinted up at him, but he knew they were mocking.

He wanted nothing more than to kiss that smirk right off her lips.

"No thanks."

"Suit yourself." She turned her back on him and gave her full attention to Randy, whose voice had turned to the consistency of melting butter.

The cowboy had a real knack for making her laugh, for making her throw back her head, sending that ebony wealth of hair shimmering down her back. When she did, her throat was exposed, not to mention that V of chest between the collar of the ordinary work shirt. Was it Jake's imagination or did it fit tighter across her breasts today?

He picked up a hammer, drove a nail into the fence post, and managed to catch his thumbnail between the two. His elaborate profanity brought a momentary halt to the joviality going on only a few yards from him, but it resumed when Banner asked Randy to tell her about the last rodeo he had entered.

Jake had won numerous purses in rodeos. Had she ever asked him about his prizes? No.

She then engaged the men in a spontaneous roping contest. When Randy succeeded in lassoing the fence post for the third straight time and Banner laid her hand on his arm in worshipful awe, Jake went over the edge.

"Party time's over," he barked. He tossed down his hammer and confronted them as though daring anyone to contradict him. He threatened them all with the glacial stare that had intimidated many a brawny cowboy.

Jim and Pete thanked Banner and humbly went back to

their tasks. They had better sense than to tangle with Jake. He was a fair foreman. He didn't demand more of them than he gave himself. But they had sensed that where the girl was concerned he was as ornery as a mama bear.

Randy wasn't so perceptive. "Let me carry these things back to the wagon for you, Banner."

"Why, thank you, Randy."

Since when were they on a first name basis? Jake wondered.

He couldn't object to Randy's offer to help her without looking like a cad. So he gritted his teeth when Banner smiled up at him and said, "You're doing a fine job here, Jake," as though he was no more to her than a lowly hired hand.

Jake watched her walking away with Randy, her face tilted up at him coquettishly. His jaw bunched. Ross had entrusted him to protect her from just that sort of infatuation. But how in hell was he supposed to do that when she looked the way she did and used every female wile she possessed to keep those cowboys' blood stirred up?

Banner's mind wasn't on the jolly conversation she was having with Randy. She was looking into his face with its lazy smile, but she was seeing Jake, his cold eyes and the hateful way he looked at her. Did he despise her that much?

She and Randy arrived at the wagon and he stored the basket and jug in the back. She was just about to hoist herself onto the seat when he forestalled her.

"Ooops, ooops, Banner. Hold real still, honey." He grasped her around the waist.

"What is it?"

"A caterpillar on your collar. He must have dropped on you from one of the trees."

The thought of anything so creepy-crawly on her person sent her into a typically female panic. "Where? Where? Get it off! Hurry!"

"Hold on, hold—Aw, damn. He fell inside your collar."

She screamed and began to dance around frantically. "Get him, Randy. Oh, I feel him. Get him, get him."

"All right, I will, but you'll have to calm down and hold still." He finally succeeded in anchoring her back against his front with one arm across her middle. The other hand plunged down the back of her shirt in search of the caterpillar.

"Oh, Randy, no—"

"Hush now. Quit wiggling."

"Randy, please."

"Let her go!"

The words were as hard and cold as the steel barrel of the pistol that was pointed at Randy. The two who were locked in the bizarre embrace froze. Four wide eyes riveted on Jake, who had come running at Banner's first scream and was now standing not three yards from them, his gun arm extended at shoulder level.

"I said take your hands off her." He pushed the words through clenched teeth.

Randy wet his lips but otherwise remained motionless. "Easy with that gun, Jake."

"Get away from her," he roared.

Randy moved slowly, precisely, not wanting the man with the frigid eyes to mistake any movement he made. His arm around Banner's waist was withdrawn first. Then he gradually pulled his hand from the back of her shirt. Finally he stepped away. Banner put more space between them, mutely staring at Jake.

Randy opened his fist where Jake could see it. The furry caterpillar crawled across his palm. "I was only getting this off her back." Randy shook his hand and the caterpillar fell to the ground.

Jake stared at Randy's hand. Any other time, he would have laughed, joked at having made an ass of himself. But he was still too shaken by seeing another man's hands on Banner to find any humor in the situation. He holstered his gun and jerked his head in the direction of Jim and Pete, who were standing by the fence post where they had been working, sadly shaking their heads at how foolish men could behave when a woman was in the picture.

"You have work to do." That was all Jake needed to say. Quickly Randy tipped his hat to Banner and loped off, glad to be escaping with his life. "Get in the wagon," Jake said to Banner.

She was too humiliated and furious to argue. She vaulted onto the seat and slapped the reins on the horse's rump. Jake whistled through his teeth, and Stormy appeared from out of the trees where he had been grazing in the shade.

He caught up with Banner and rode beside her while she kept her eyes trained forward, not deigning to look at him, much less speak.

When she pulled the wagon into the yard in front of the house, she alighted and starchily made her way toward the porch. Jake came off Stormy with remarkable agility and went after her, catching her just as she reached for the front door knob. He dug his hand into the waistband of her pants and yanked her to a halt.

"I want to talk to you."

She rounded on him, as enraged as she had ever been in her eighteen years. "Well, I don't want to talk to you. At least not until I calm down. Otherwise I'm afraid I'll say something that would be better left unsaid."

"Like what?" He thrust his face toward hers.

"Like you're a bossy, bullying, bad-tempered—"

"Me? Bad-tempered?"

"Yes, you."

"Your temper ain't anything to brag about, Miss Coleman."

"Well, I've had just cause to lose mine. Plenty of times in fact, from having to put up with you these last two weeks. Nothing I do pleases you. You criticize my clothes, my hair, everything. You're cross and grouchy when you come to breakfast and dinner. I'm tired of you grumbling into your plate and passing it off as mealtime conversation."

"Anything else?" he growled in just the manner she was speaking of.

"Yes. I'll kindly ask you to stay out of my personal affairs, which are none of your business!" She turned on her heel and marched haughtily through the door.

Jake was right behind her, kicking open the door she tried to slam in his face. It crashed against the wall, but went unheeded.

"It damn sure is my affair when a cowboy like Randy paws you. I promised Ross that—"

"*Paws* me? He was getting a caterpillar out of my shirt."

"And taking a helluva long time to do it!" he shouted. "What were you screaming about?"

"I was frightened."

"Well, you scared the hell out of me. I didn't know what he was doing to you. What was I supposed to think?"

"That's my point. You weren't supposed to think anything."

"So if you start screaming in the middle of the night, I'm to roll over and go back to sleep, is that it? Assume that you don't need help."

Her look was one of undiluted condescension for his obtuseness. "I had a caterpillar down my back."

"So why scream? I remember when you used to play with caterpillars and mice and worms, and God knows what else."

She was fighting her temper for all she was worth. She paused to draw in several deep breaths. They might have restored her, but they did nothing to calm Jake down. He stared at the expanding front of her shirt. "I've changed since I played with caterpillars."

With his eyes still preoccupied with her breasts, he could grant her that. But he was still too furious to be reasonable. "Well, next time you get any caterpillars down your back, you just call me and I'll get them out."

"What makes you any different from Randy or any of the others?"

"I don't go around with my tongue lolling out every time you come in sight, that's what."

She stared at him as though he had gone daft. "That's *crazy*," she said incredulously. "They don't do that."

"Don't they?" He pointed an imperious finger at her. "I warned you about wearing those tight pants and flaunting yourself in front of the men."

"Flaunting!" She slapped his accusing finger aside.

"Yes, flaunting." He peeled off his leather work gloves and threw them to the floor in the medieval tradition of throwing down a gauntlet as a challenge. His hat went the way of the gloves. "You strut around here like a queen, enticing them until—"

"I do not strut." She said each word precisely. "And I don't entice anybody."

"The hell you don't."

"I wear pants because they're the most comfortable, practical thing to do ranch work in and that's the only reason."

He leaned toward her and whispered, "But doesn't it give you a thrill to know all the men around here want you?"

She recoiled as though he had struck her. Her face drained of color. Is that what he thought? Did he think that since she had so shamelessly asked him to make love to her, that she would do it again with another man? "No!" she exclaimed softly, on the verge of tears.

"No?"

"No."

"Well, then, you had better mend your ways and start acting more ladylike. The next time I might not be around to stop Randy from giving you what you were asking for."

"And what was that, Jake Langston? What was I asking for?"

"This."

He reached for her and pulled her against him with an impetus that drove the air from their lungs when their bodies collided. His mouth came down hard on hers, cruelly, punishingly.

Emotions that had been riding just below the surface gushed forth, but not as anger, as passion. He buried his hands in her hair. His fingers tangled in the curly mass. He roughly angled her head to one side and slanted his mouth over hers. His tongue breached the barrier of her lips and plundered.

Banner's first reaction was livid anger. Then swamping confusion. How should she respond? Fight him? And by fighting convince him that she wasn't hungry for a man's touch as he had accused her. Or surrender? Surrender to the sweet violation of his tongue.

That's what she wanted to do. She wanted to lose herself in the uncompromising possession of his embrace, to savor the taste of his kiss, to relish the sensations that were flooding her body like swollen streams after spring rains.

The choice was taken from her. Mindlessly, she merely responded. Her arms went around his waist and her hands splayed wide on his back. All ten fingers sank into the muscled flesh beneath his shirt and vest.

Jake groaned and his tongue, tempered with tenderness now, delved deeper into her mouth. One hand moved from her hair to her back, sliding up and down its slender suppleness until it slipped below her waist. His hand covered the curve of her derriere, which had tantalized him for days. He pressed, drawing her against him.

Banner felt his hard desire and murmured deep in her throat. Rather than being repelled, she moved against his body. She was immune to shame now. The splendor of their kiss had washed it from her being, eradicated it, as though she had never been acquainted with it. Her arms curled up under his until her hands came from behind to cup his shoulders and pull him closer to her.

Jake was equally lost. The red mist of rage that had burned in him only moments before had mellowed to the golden haze of desire. He was obsessed with it. His pores oozed it.

Her mouth. Oh, God, her mouth. It tasted even better than he remembered. Again and again his tongue dipped into its delicious mystery, but no matter the number of honey-gathering forays, he couldn't get enough of it.

Her breasts were full and ripe against his chest. Yes, yes, he remembered how they felt beneath his hands. Even in repose they had filled his palms, overflowed them. The soft cloth of her bridal nightgown had slid over her skin as he massaged. His thumbs had skated over her nipples. And they had responded, sweet and hard and small.

But he hadn't dared to remove her nightgown. He hadn't seen her breasts as he had wanted to. He hadn't tasted her. That's all he could think about now as his tongue rolled over the tip of hers. What did she look like? What did she taste like? How would she feel against his tongue?

A low humming started in the pit of his body and worked

its way outward. He ground his hips against her middle in a vain effort to get closer. God, what he would give to bury himself again in that silken channel that had gloved him so tightly, so rightly.

Moaning, he tore his mouth free and nuzzled his face in the hollow of her neck, hugging her hard. He prayed that the memory would vanish, that he would find the willpower to release her and never even think the thoughts his body wanted him to act on.

He vividly recalled the instant her virginal shield had given way. He regretted the pain it had cost her, but even that hadn't diminished the wonder and the feeling of utter helplessness that had come over him the moment her body enveloped his. He had a sense of inevitability, of having crossed a long elusive finish line.

She had been fashioned for loving, at least for his loving. Never had a woman fit him better. He had hesitated to move. It would have satisfied her if he had left her then. She wouldn't have known the difference and he wouldn't have had to live with the guilt of not only doing what he had done, but of enjoying it so much.

As it was, no power on heaven or earth could have forced him to leave her then. He had begun to move, slowly, conscious of her body, rigid with shock, beneath him. But soon she had relaxed and it had become easier. He had thrust, stroked, until that dam inside him had burst more explosively than ever before.

He had come away from her weak, depleted. But recalling it now made him want to experience that small death again. Sweat broke out over his body. He gnashed his teeth in an effort to conquer the desire that coursed through him and gathered painfully in his loins.

At last, he pushed her away and turned his back. He breathed deeply, but it did little good. He shook as though with ague. Glancing at her quickly over his shoulder and getting only a vague impression of her pale face—God, she was probably terrified of him now—he pushed through the door and called back to her, "I'm going into town this afternoon for supplies. Don't wait supper on me."

* * *

She gazed up through the leafy branches of the pecan tree. She had always been a champion tree climber. Her shins had been scraped by rough bark in her efforts to best Lee and Micah more times than she could count. She hadn't outgrown her penchant for climbing as high as she could, seeking solace in being suspended between heaven and earth. Up here, she could think clearly, as though the problems attached to the ground could no longer reach her.

The afternoon had dragged by sluggishly. The house had been too confining to bear. She was depressed and dismayed and disturbed. All her problems revolved around one source.

Jake Langston. What was she going to do about Jake?

He was an issue in her life and there was no getting around it. That night in the barn *had* happened. Wishing that it hadn't or regretting that it had were exercises in futility. It had forever changed her relationship with Jake. There was no going back to the way things had been. These facts she had reconciled.

What she couldn't reconcile was the present. She and Jake couldn't go on living as they were, fighting like ravenous scavengers over a carcass. They were both too stubborn, too headstrong, too temperamental, and too guilty over that night to stay as they were without destroying each other. They would bring Plum Creek's prospects for the future right down with them.

And she *was* going to name her ranch Plum Creek whether he liked it or not!

She almost smiled. She argued with him in her mind even when he wasn't around. But the smile didn't quite materialize. After that kiss this afternoon, she had a whole new set of worries to keep a smile off her face.

She had liked it. Very much. Far more than she should have. Far more than was proper. And far too much to hope that she would forget it any time soon.

What had provoked it? One minute he had been shouting at her, looking as though he could easily wring her neck. The next he had held her captivated in an embrace from which there was no escaping. His mouth had been stamped possessively over hers in a way that even recollecting it made her insides churn with warm sensations.

What happened to her when Jake touched her? What chemistry between them ignited feelings she had never experienced and which made her a stranger to herself? Why was she yearning to experience those feelings again?

She shifted her position on the tree limb and rested her cheek against the bark. Idly she shredded a leaf, let the remnants float to the ground below, and plucked another.

The thought that had taken hold in her mind simply wouldn't let go. It was bold and unthinkable, but she had done bold and unthinkable things in the recent past and knew that bold and unthinkable actions had never deterred her before. The idea endlessly circled in her mind like the blades of a windmill.

She and Jake could marry.

There, she had voiced the idea to herself and the world hadn't come to an end. She hadn't been struck by lightning. The earth hadn't opened up and swallowed her.

Well, why was it such a preposterous idea?

It made sense. She needed him to run her ranch. He needed the ranch. Plum Creek promised him a sound future. For years he had been wandering, wasting his talent and spending his youth in aimless pursuits. An opportunity like this wouldn't come around again. Why wouldn't he want to seize it?

Apparently he didn't have anyone else in mind to marry. Banner knew whom he really loved. But Lydia was unavailable and always would be. That didn't make Jake less of a man. He needed a woman, often, and if the kiss this afternoon and that night in the barn were any indication, he didn't find Banner lacking.

They would have no problems sharing a marriage bed. Sharing it intimately. There was no doubt about that. Besides, they would both want children.

Her whole body went hot with the thought of sleeping with Jake night after night. All right. So she wasn't above feeling passion. Was that anything to be ashamed of? Her parents had taught that it wasn't. But they had also taught her that passion should be limited to "the confines of marriage."

It would be silly to pretend she hadn't enjoyed Jake's kiss. Well, slightly more than enjoyed. She hadn't wanted him to stop. If he had led her into the bedroom, she would have gone gladly and there was no sense trying to convince herself that she wouldn't have, despite the lessons on morality she had been taught from the cradle.

Instinctively she knew that something had lain just beyond her reach that first time. It was frustrating, wondering what had caused Jake's body to tremble violently before becoming so weak with contentment he could barely move. She had been left feeling hot, and restless, and anxious for something she couldn't even name. If for no other reason, she would have followed Jake to bed today to discover what that something was.

She wasn't in love with him. Was she? He wasn't the one she would have originally chosen for a husband, but she had always loved him another way. The transference of one set of feelings to another was what she was having to grapple with.

That and the loneliness of her life. She wasn't adjusting to solitude well. Each night when Jake retired to the barn, leaving her alone in the house, despair settled in. She had envisioned Jake sharing the living room with her, smoking his cheroots while she mended his shirts. Granted, the picture was farcically domesticated, but it illustrated the closeness she craved with a man. Jake couldn't be any less lonely than she.

She knew she was vulnerable where other men were concerned. If it wasn't Randy trying to seduce her—and she knew, though she had denied it to Jake, that the cowboy had been flirting with her before the caterpillar incident—it would be another.

Eventually, out of loneliness, she might succumb. Another man wouldn't be as caring for her reputation as Jake. Another man would brag until her father got wind of it and ended up having to kill him. She would be blamed for dragging her whole family into disgrace and lawlessness.

Or, if she were lucky enough to find someone she loved enough to marry, he would discover that she hadn't come to him pure. Such disillusionment would be a disastrous way to start a marriage. No, she couldn't marry anyone else.

Finally, she was afraid that one of these days they would have a shouting match that would culminate in Jake's leaving. That painted a frightfully dismal picture in her mind. She didn't want to care that much, but she did. She could see herself chasing down the road after him as she had done as a child, tears streaming down her face, begging him not to go.

That didn't bear thinking about either.

So if she didn't want him completely out of her life and if she couldn't go on living with him as they were, fighting both their guilt over what had happened and their desire that it happen again, what was the only alternative?

She shimmied down to the lowest branch of the tree and jumped from there to the ground. She dusted her hands on the seat of her pants as the answer impressed itself upon her.

"I'll get Jake to marry me."

She couldn't hand down an ultimatum. He would run in the opposite direction. It had to appear to be his idea. If she started acting more wifely, he might come to think of her in those terms. She must stop losing her temper and be soft and approachable, the way men liked their ladies to be. At least the ladies they married.

Never one to leave things to chance, Banner made her plans. She didn't believe in fate. If one wanted something, one had to go after it. One made one's future what she wanted it to be.

With her former doldrums vanquished, she cooked a mouthwatering meal. She bathed out of the washbowl in her bedroom, not wanting to take the time to heat water and fill the tub. Everything had to be ready by the time he returned home. She had until sundown. He wouldn't leave her alone after the cowboys returned to River Bend.

When Jake drew the wagon into the yard, Banner stepped from the front door. The lamplight spilling through the windows made a halo of her hair, which she had secured into a loose knot on the top of her head, leaving beguiling wisps lying on her neck and cheeks.

"Hello, Jake," she said softly.

"Hello."

"Did you get your errands run? Buy everything you need?"

"Yep. I ran up quite a bill." He swung down from the wagon. He wouldn't quite meet her eyes, so she took a few more steps that brought her to the edge of the porch. If he noticed her dress in place of the hated pants, he didn't comment.

"You don't have to unload tonight, do you?"

"I should." At last he raised his eyes to the porch.

She could have sworn they widened in delighted surprise, but it might have been a trick of the faint light in the gathering dusk. She clasped her hands together. "Later, then. I've kept supper warm for you."

"I told you not to wait it on me," he said crossly.

At that point, her temper almost slipped. But she held it in check, physically trapping it inside by biting her lower lip. When it was safely subdued, she asked, "Did you eat in town?"

He shrugged. "I had something."

"But you could stand some more? Steak and potatoes?"

He shifted his shoulders self-consciously and hitched his thumbs in his belt. "I reckon I could eat a little something."

"Come on in then."

She gave him her back and took those long, agonizing steps toward the front door. Only when she heard the tread of his boots and the jingle of his spurs on the porch behind her did she allow her breath to seep out in a long, relieved sigh.

NINE

Jake followed Banner into the living room. He trod lightly, like a convict who had just been granted a stay of execution. She seemed tranquil enough, but he didn't trust her mood. He had meddled in her business when she had made it plain his interference into her personal life was unwelcome. If she wanted to dally with Randy, who was he to stop her?

Then he had kissed her. What had possessed him to kiss her like that this afternoon? He had been mad enough to strangle her, but he had sought another outlet for his emotions, one even more damaging. He wouldn't have been surprised if she had opened fire on him the minute he drove into the yard. Instead she was treating him like a king just returned to the castle.

"Hang your hat on the rack, Jake," she said. "And I don't think you'll need that gunbelt any more tonight."

"Banner, about this afternoon—"

"Never mind about that."

"Let me apologize."

"If you must, apologize to Randy. He hadn't done anything to warrant you pulling a gun on him."

"I intend to apologize to him tomorrow. I don't know what got into me." He spread his hands wide in a helpless gesture. "It's just that Ross told me to protect you, and when I heard you screaming—"

"I understand."

"And about the other—"

"Are you sorry you kissed me, Jake?"

Her face commanded all his attention. It shone pale and

149

creamy in the golden lamplight, surrounded by the dark cloud of her hair. Her eyes were wide with inquiry, as though how he answered her question was of the utmost importance. Her lips were as tremulous and moist as if he had just kissed them.

His answer was no. But he couldn't admit it out loud, so he said nothing.

She relieved them of the ponderous moment. "Come on in the kitchen."

"I haven't washed up yet."

"You can wash in here. I have warm water waiting."

Turning, she seemed to glide from the room, her full skirt swishing behind her. It was a simple cotton broadcloth dress she was wearing, but nothing would look simple on Banner. It was green, trimmed in lace the color of cream. Both colors enhanced her complexion. The ruffled apron looked more for show than utility. Its sash was tied in a perky bow at her waist in back. It bounced slightly each time her heels struck the floor. It was a beguiling sight, that bow.

She turned toward him and caught his stare. For a moment their eyes locked and held before she said, "You can wash at the sink while I serve up the dinner."

He nodded dumbly.

There was a vase of wildflowers standing in the center of the table. It had already been set. To Jake, who had eaten many meals out of a tin plate behind a chuck wagon, the table looked as fancy as the dining room in the Ellis Hotel in Fort Worth with its linen cloth and napkins folded into neat triangles. The aromas wafting from the stove were delectable. The lamps had been turned down so that barely a flame flickered off their oil-soaked wicks.

If he didn't know better, he would think Banner Coleman was up to no good.

"I've been cooking this steak real slow all day with onions to flavor it," she said from the stove.

Standing at the sink, he unbuttoned his shirt sleeves and rolled them to his elbows. "It sure smells good." As promised, there was a basin of warm water waiting for him. He dipped his hands into it and began lathering them with bar soap. "I had ham and eggs at Mabel's Café in town, but they weren't any good."

Banner made a scoffing sound. "That's no dinner for a hardworking man."

She smiled at him over her shoulder and his gut knotted. He scrubbed his hands mercilessly, as though to wash his conscience off them. He was shaking them dry when she said, "There. Everything's ready. Come sit down, Jake."

He unrolled his sleeves and rebuttoned his cuffs as he crossed to the table and took his seat. He gazed at the steaming platters of food, the scalding mug of coffee at his place setting, the flowers. It was all too good. He could get accustomed to this kind of royal treatment real fast. That kind of thinking was dangerous. It was best to put things in their proper perspective right now. "You've done yourself proud, brat."

Her eyes flashed with irritation. That wasn't what she had wanted to hear. And that made Jake all the more glad he had said it. If Banner had any mischief up her sleeve, he damn sure needed to know about it beforehand.

She recovered quickly and smiled. "If you don't get busy on it, I'll probably gobble it all up myself. I'm starving."

While she filled his plate, she asked him about the supplies he had bought. They conversed about ranch business as they ate. The food was delicious. Banner never let his plate get empty, but waited on him constantly. She was her saucy self, teasing and gay, but there was a new element to her that intrigued him. She was softer and more obviously feminine.

Jake found himself mesmerized by her mouth as she ate. Her hands moved gracefully when she lifted her napkin to her lips and blotted, then spread it again in her lap. Green and gold lights flickered in her eyes with each slight waver of the wicks in the lamps. One raven curl lay flirtatiously against the side of her neck.

The wide yoke on her dress extended from the point of each shoulder, across her shoulder blades in the back, and over the curves of her breasts in front. The seam was bordered by an inch-wide strip of cotton lace which fluttered each time she moved.

Jake couldn't seem to take his eyes off that lace. Or off
the shape of her lips, or the color of her eyes, or the curve
of her cheek, or the texture of her hair. She was totally
captivating.

It was the pleasantest meal they had shared together, just
about the pleasantest one of Jake's life. He regretted that it
would soon come to an end. She was just so damn good to
look at. He figured that he enjoyed watching her so much
because she reminded him of Lydia. And yet—

"Are you finished, Jake?"

He laid his hands over his stomach. "I couldn't hold
another bite."

"Another cup of coffee maybe?"

He grinned. "Maybe half of one."

She carried their plates to the sink, then came back with
the coffee pot. She filled his cup, smiling at him when he
said, "Whoa!"

"You might be thirstier than you think."

He broke his own cardinal rule and raised his eyes to her.
She was looking down at him. Could it be his imagination,
or was she keeping her arms held at that awkward angle
longer than she normally did? It provided him an unrestricted
view of her breasts. They amply filled the bodice of her
dress.

Damn! His sex began to stir and swell beneath his belt.
He lowered his eyes quickly.

When she rejoined him across the table and sipped her
coffee, he kept his eyes resolutely away from her. Silently
they drank their coffee. Then Banner set her elbows on the
table and propped her chin on her hands in a way that
framed her face between them as though she were offering it
up to him.

"You're so lucky, Jake, to have such a large family."

He was surprised by the topic of her conversation, but
relieved as well. That heavy silence was getting to him, but
he didn't want for them to talk about themselves. Or to
argue after all the trouble she'd gone to to fix him this
supper. "Yeah, I am. But you know I've lost several
brothers and sisters as well as Pa."

"I know." She sighed and smiled at him sadly. "Ma has told me stories about each one of them, the pranks they used to pull on the wagon train. That's where you first met my folks."

"Yep." He sipped his coffee.

"Tell me about it."

He set his cup down. "About what?"

"About how you came to be such good friends with Mama and Papa."

"Well, Ross hired me to help him take care of his horses. He had five mares and that stallion, Lucky. That was the prettiest horse I've ever seen."

"I remember him. He had to be shot when I was about five. Mama cried for days afterward. Most of the horses at River Bend are Lucky's descendants." She folded and refolded her napkin, shaping it to the edge of the table. "And Mama? When did you meet her?"

What was she after? Jake wondered. Why this sudden interest in the past? He knew Ross and Lydia had guarded some aspects of their past from their children, and he sure as hell wasn't going to be the one to divulge any secrets.

He responded with carefully selected words. "My brother Luke and I found her in the woods. She was lost. We brought her back to Ma. About that time Ross's wife died delivering Lee. Ma took Lydia to his wagon to . . . uh . . ."

Did Banner know that Lydia had wet-nursed Lee? Did she know her mother had just given birth to a stillborn baby when he and Luke found her? He didn't think so, and he wasn't going to tell her.

". . . to help him take care of Lee," he finished.

"But what was she doing lost in the woods? Where had she come from? Didn't she have a family?"

Clancey Russell, Jake thought, his face going hard and his fists clenching as he thought about the man who had murdered his brother without motive or provocation, but out of sheer viciousness. "No," he said curtly. "No family that I know of."

Banner pondered that and looked at him suspiciously, as

though she knew he was lying. "I wish we had a larger family, with grandparents and cousins to play with."

"You're surrounded by Langstons," he said jovially, in an effort to turn the conversation.

"Yes, and I'm glad. But it's not quite the same as having blood relatives. No one has ever said, 'Banner reminds me of Aunt so and so,' or 'How is Cousin so and so's gout?' "

"I don't think Ross or Lydia either one had family to speak of."

"That's just it. They've *never* spoken of it," Banner exclaimed. "They've never even mentioned relatives who have died. It's as though they didn't exist until they met each other. That's always bothered me."

"Why?"

"I don't know," she said, flinging her hands aside in frustration. "I feel like there's some terrible secret that's going to come out some day and bring ruination to us all."

Jake had his own secrets to hide. He didn't know if she was better off not knowing and being frustrated, or knowing and having to cope with the ghosts of the past. "It doesn't matter, Banner."

She gave him a wry look. "That's what old Moses used to tell me."

Jake smiled. "He was devoted to your parents. You should have known you couldn't pry secrets out of him."

"I loved him so much," she said, her mood turning sentimental again. "He was one of my first friends. He would pay attention to me when Mama and Papa were busy and Lee was ignoring me. He used to take me fishing with him. He taught me how to whittle. I never could get the knack of it, but some of the first toys I played with, he made for me. I was the one who found him the day he died."

Jake watched her eyes cloud with tears. Instinctively, he reached across the table and covered her hand with his. "I didn't know that."

She nodded her head. "I went to his cabin early one morning. We had planned to pick berries that day. He was sitting on the porch of his cabin." Suddenly she sat up straighter and her tone changed. "You know he never would let Papa do anything for him. He said he had been a slave once and wasn't going to depend on anybody to take care of him again. He built his own cabin down there by the creek." Jake nodded.

"Anyway," she continued, "he was sitting on his porch. When I got closer I noticed he was holding his head funny. I called his name, but he didn't move. I knew he must be dead. I started crying and ran back to the house."

Jake's thumb rubbed commiserating circles into the back of her hand. "Did you know Winston Hill, the man Moses came to Texas with?" she asked at last, blotting at her eyes with her napkin.

"Yeah. He was a Southern gentleman, very mannerly. He was sickly."

"Moses told me he died on the way."

But not how he died, Jake thought. Hill had been shot in the chest while protecting Lydia from her stepbrother. No one knew that but Jake. He had overheard Clancey bragging to Lydia about murdering Winston Hill and Luke. Clancey hadn't lived long after that.

Jake had been only sixteen, but he would go to his grave remembering that blank stare on Clancey Russell's face the instant Luke's knife was plunged into his belly and he knew he was going to die.

Jake realized his hand was squeezing the life out of Banner's and he released it immediately. When he raised his eyes to hers, she was looking at him strangely. He didn't want her to know that he harbored his own secrets. He forced himself to take a nonchalant sip of coffee.

"Nothing I remember of that summer bears repeating," he said sharply. Luke. Luke. He would love to talk to her about Luke, but he could never bring himself to empty his soul about that. Even after all these years, the pain was still too raw.

"I've tried to get Mama and Papa to tell me stories about the wagon train, but they never do. Or if they do, they stop talking when I start asking questions."

"It was a long time ago. Maybe they don't remember that

far back." She shot him a scathing look and he chuckled. "I mean it. Maybe when you were born they were so dazzled to have such a daughter, they forgot everything that had happened to them before then." He leaned across the table and whispered, "You know, I think you were started on that wagon train."

She clamped her upper teeth over her bottom lip and hunched her shoulders as she smiled mischievously. "I think so too," she whispered back. "My birthday comes barely nine months after they reached Texas."

Jake laughed and sat back. "A proper young lady shouldn't be discussing such things with a man. You shouldn't even know about them."

Her eyes became hazy. They wandered slowly over his face, down his chest, and back up to meet his. "I know about them, Jake."

That struck too close to home. Whatever she knew about what men and women do together she had learned on a horse blanket spread on a pile of hay in a barn and had been taught by a man who had had no right to teach her.

Jake reached in his pocket and took out a cigar. Then he crammed it back in and mumbled, "Sorry."

"About what?"

"The cigar. Most ladies don't want their houses stinking of cigar smoke."

"I like the way your cigar smells. Smoke if you want to."

Knowing he should leave now before their conversation veered toward the personal again, he nonetheless took the cheroot out of his pocket and bit off the end. He carefully placed the tip on the saucer beneath his coffee cup. Holding the cigar between his teeth, his hands went on a fruitless search through his pockets for a match.

"Here, I'll get one for you." Before he could object, Banner had flown from her chair toward the stove where she picked up a box of matches. When she came back, he held out his hand for the box, but she shook her head and opened it herself. Striking the match, she held it at the tip of the cheroot until it glowed red. Jake puffed and a cloud of smoke rose between them.

Through that blue-gray vapor, Jake looked up at her. Banner, her eyes never leaving his, puckered her lips delicately and blew on the match until it was extinguished.

Jake's reaction was profound. He almost choked on the smoke he sucked in. An arrow of desire shot through him and found its target. His loins ached with the accuracy of its striking force. He lowered his eyes away from her, afraid that if he looked one second longer into that provocative face he would toss the cigar to the floor and, disobeying every vow he had made to himself as he drove into town that afternoon, drag her onto his throbbing lap.

Banner retreated to her chair. She propped her chin on her hands again as she unabashedly watched him smoke. "Does it taste as good as it smells?"

"Sometimes, like now, it does."

"Let me try." Filled with inspiration, she sat bolt upright and sent the lace that dangled over her breasts to quivering.

"No!"

"Please."

"What are you thinking of, girl?"

"I want to try it."

"No. Your parents would kill me."

"Please, Jake. They won't find out."

"They might."

"Would you tell them?"

"No."

"Neither would I. Please. What's wrong with it?"

"Ladies don't smoke."

"Some ladies do."

"Then they aren't ladies."

"You know some women who smoke?" she asked, her eyes rounding. It had only been a wild guess on her part that such a thing was possible.

"A few."

"Who?"

"Nobody you'd know."

"Whores?"

Jake coughed and his eyes teared. "Where'd you hear that word?"

"It's in the Bible." When his eyes narrowed skeptically she confessed. "From Lee and Micah."

"They talk to you about whores?" Jake asked, flabbergasted.

"Not exactly," she said defensively. "But I can't keep from overhearing them sometimes."

Jake roared with laughter then. "Why, you little eavesdropper. You'd better be careful of that," he said, pointing the cheroot at her. "You might hear something you'd rather not."

"I'm not a baby. I don't just know the word, I know what it means. Now, tell me about just one woman who smokes. She's a whore, I'll bet. Priscilla Watkins?"

For the second time in sixty seconds she had shocked him. "Where did you hear that name?"

"Lee and—"

"Micah," he finished. "My God, they're wellsprings of information, aren't they?"

Banner's eyelids fanned downward. "They say you know her, this Watkins woman who's so famous."

He could see her watching him from beneath that seductive screen of lashes. For the life of him at that moment, he couldn't recall Priscilla's face. Or the face of any other woman for that matter. He saw only Banner, but he was careful to keep his expression impassive. "Yeah, I know her."

"They say she's a friend of yours."

He shrugged. "Maybe you could call her that."

"But she *is* a whore."

He chuckled and twirled the tip of the cheroot on the rim of the saucer until part of the ash fell off. "Definitely a whore."

"Do you visit her?"

"Sometimes."

"In her bawdy house?"

"Yes."

"Do you . . ." Her voice lowered to a husky whisper

"Do you share her bed?" She met his gaze steadily, with bold, burning eyes that defied him to lie to her.

"No." He spoke so quietly, yet so precisely and honestly, that Banner knew he was telling the truth.

"Oh," she said in a small voice.

Jake watched her closely. He could have sworn she was jealous. His male vanity wondered what she would have done had he confessed to being Priscilla's lover. He had behaved like a man possessed this afternoon when he saw Randy's hands on Banner. She was obviously jealous of Priscilla. Jealousy between them was dangerous. And he knew it. And the sooner he called an end to this cozy evening, the better. He shoved his chair back and stood. "I need to be getting—"

"No, wait." She came out of her chair like a coiled spring and took two rapid steps forward. When he looked at her as though she had taken leave of her senses, she fell back a step. Catching her hands at her waist, she said quickly, "I have a favor to ask. If you ... if you have the time."

"What is it?"

"In the living room. I have a picture to hang and I wondered if you could help me with it."

He glanced over his shoulder toward the center room. One small lamp was burning in the corner. The room was cast in shadows, as intimate as those in the barn had been. The parlor was also the scene of the kiss that afternoon. Jake was better off not being reminded of that at all.

"I'm not much good at picture hanging," he hedged.

"Oh, well." She made a dismissive little wave with her hand. "You've put in a full day already and it isn't the foreman's job to hang pictures, I suppose."

Hell. Now she thought he didn't want to help her. She looked crestfallen, disappointed that she wouldn't get her picture hung and embarrassed for having asked his help and being turned down.

"I guess it wouldn't take too long, would it?"

"No, no," she said, lifting her head eagerly. "I have everything ready." She brushed past him on her way into the parlor. "I got the hammer and a nail from the barn this afternoon while you were gone. I tried to hang it myself, but couldn't tell if I was getting it in the right spot or not."

She was chattering breathlessly. Jake thought she might be as nervous as he about returning to this room. But she made no effort to turn up the lamp or light another one. Instead she made a beeline for the far wall.

Was this her way of telling him that she had forgiven his behavior that afternoon, that she wasn't afraid to be in an empty house with him long after the sun had gone down? Had everything she had done tonight been a peacemaking gesture? If so, he was grateful to her. They couldn't have gone on much longer without killing each other or...

The "or" he would do well not to think about. Especially since she was facing him again.

"I thought I'd hang it on this wall, about here," she said, pointing her finger and cocking her head to one side.

"That would be nice." He felt about as qualified to give advice on hanging a picture as he would be to choose a chapeau in a milliner's shop.

"About eye level?"

"Whose eye level? Yours or mine?"

She laughed. "I see what you mean." She scraped the top of her head with her palm and slid it horizontally until it bumped against his breastbone. "I only come to here on you, don't I?"

When she glanced up at him, his breath caught somewhere between his lungs and his throat. How could he have ever considered this creature with the bewitching eyes and teasing smile a child? He had been with whores who prided themselves on knowing all there was to know about getting a man's blood to the boiling point. But no woman had ever had an impact on him the way this one did. Except perhaps Lydia those months they were together on the wagon train.

His love for her had mellowed since then. He no longer experienced rushes of passionate desire every time he saw her. That summer traveling between Tennessee and Texas, he had been perpetually randy. Desire for Lydia, desire for Priscilla, desire for women, period.

He had been sixteen, the sap of youth flowing sweetly, but painfully, through his body. But that's what he felt like every time he looked at Banner. He felt sixteen again and with no more control over his body than he had then.

Her skirt was rustling against his pants. Her breasts were achingly close to his chest. She smelled too good for it to be legal. He could practically taste her breath as it softly struck his chin. Before he drowned in the swirling depths of her eyes, he said, "Maybe we'd better—"

"Oh, yes," she said briskly. Taking a three-legged stool from in front of an easy chair, she placed it near the wall and, raising her skirt above her ankles, stepped up on it. "The picture is there on the table. Hand it to me, please, then step back and tell me when it looks right."

He picked up the framed picture. "This is pretty."

It was a pastoral scene of horses grazing in a verdant pasture. "I thought it looked like Plum Creek." She glared at him, daring him to say anything derogatory about the name she had selected.

"I didn't say anything."

"No, but I know what you're thinking," she said accusingly. He only smiled benignly and passed her the picture.

She turned her back, raised her arms and positioned the picture. "How does that look?"

"A little lower maybe."

"There?"

"That's about right."

Keeping the picture flat against the wall, she craned her head around. "Are you really judging or are you just trying to get this over with?"

"I'm doing the best I can," he said, acting offended. "If you don't appreciate my help, you can always ask somebody else."

"Like Randy?"

Her taunt was intended as a joke, but Jake took it seriously. His brows gathered into a V above his nose as he took in the picture *she* made perched on that stool, leaning toward the wall with her arms raised. There was a good two inches of lacy petticoat showing above her trim ankles. Her rear end was sticking out. The apron's bow, topping that cute rounded bottom, was a tease no man could resist. The way her breasts poked out in front clearly defined their shape. No, not Randy. Not anybody if Jake could help it.

He considered the placement of the picture with more care this time. "A little to the left if you want it centered." She moved it accordingly. "There. That's perfect."

"All right. The nail will have to go in about six inches higher because of the cord it hangs by. Bring it and the hammer. You can drive it in while I hold the frame."

He did as he was told, straddling the stool and leaning around her. He tried to avoid touching her, adjusting his arms in several positions, none of them satisfactory.

"Just reach up between my arms with one hand and go over the top with the other."

He swallowed and held his breath, trying not to notice her breasts as his hand snaked up between them. He held the nail in place with the other, though that was no small task because he was shaking on the inside.

This was ridiculous! How many women had he tumbled? Stop acting like a goddamn kid and just get the job done so you can get the hell out of here! he shouted inwardly.

Carefully he drew the hand holding the hammer back. But not carefully enough. His elbow pressed against her side. One of his knees bumped the back of hers. The backs of his knuckles sank into the plumpness of her breasts.

"Excuse me," he muttered.

"That's all right."

He struck the nail, praying it would go into the wall with only one blow. It didn't. He moved his hand back and struck it again, and again, until he could see progress. Then, in rapid succession, he hit it viciously several times.

"That's good enough," he said gruffly, and withdrew his arms.

"Yes, I think so." Her voice sounded as unsteady as his.

She draped the silken cord around the head of the nail and leaned as far back as she could while still maintaining her balance on the stool.

"How's that?"

"Fine, fine." He laid the hammer on the nearest table and ran his sleeve over his perspiring forehead.

"Is it straight?"

"A little lower on the left."

"There?"

"Not quite."

"There?"

Damn, he cursed silently. He had to get out of here or he was going to explode. He strode forward, wanting to straighten the picture quickly so he could leave and get some much needed air to clear his head. But in his haste, the toe of his boot caught on one of the stool's three legs and it rocked perilously.

Banner squeaked in alarm and flailed her arms.

Life on the trail for so many years had given Jake reflexes as quick as summer lightning. His arms went around her faster than the blink of an eye and anchored her against him. When the stool clattered onto its side, Banner was being held several inches off the floor.

One of Jake's arms was around her waist, the other hand was flattened against her chest. Rather than letting her slide down, he lowered her. His back rounded slightly as he followed her down, bending over her.

But once her feet were safely on the floor, he didn't release her. Jake had spread his legs wide to break her fall. Now Banner's hips were tucked snugly in the notch between his thighs.

His cheek was lying along hers and when her nearness and her warmth and her scent got to be too much for him to resist, he turned his head and nuzzled her ear with his nose. His arms automatically tightened around her. He groaned her name.

How could anything that felt so right be so wrong? Lord, he wanted her. Knowing in his deepest self that what had happened that other time was an abomination against decency, he wanted her again. There was no use lying to himself that he didn't. He had hurt her once. He had sworn never to again. He had betrayed a friendship that meant more to him than anything in the world.

Yet such arguments were burned away like fog in a noonday sun as his lips moved in her hair and his nose breathed in the fragrance of the cologne that had been dabbed on that softest of spots behind her ear.

"Banner, tell me to leave you alone."

"I can't."

She moved her head to one side, giving him access. His lips touched her neck.

"Don't let this happen again."

"I want you to hold me."

"I want to, I want to."

He moved his hand from her chest up to her neck, then her chin, until his hand lightly covered her face. Through parted lips her breath was hot and quick on his palm.

Like a blind man, he charted each feature of her face with callused fingertips suddenly sensitized to capture each nuance. He smoothed her brows, which he knew to be raven black and beautifully arched. His fingers coasted over her cheekbones. They were freckled. He had come to adore every single freckle. Her nose was perfect, if a bit impudent.

Her mouth.

His fingers brushed back and forth over her lips. They were incredibly soft. The warm breaths filtering through them left his fingers moist.

He pressed his mouth to her cheek, her ear, into her hair.

The hand at her waist opened wide over her midriff. He curled his fingers against the taut flesh. She whimpered. He argued with himself, but there was no stopping his hand from gliding up the corrugated perfection of her ribs and covering her breast. Their moans complemented each other.

Her ripe fullness filled his hand, and against his revolving thumb, the center of her breast tightened into a bead of arousal.

"Jake—"

"Sweet, so sweet."

"This happens sometimes."

"What?"

"That," she answered on a puff of air as his fingers

closed around her nipple. "They get that way sometimes . . . when I look at you."

"Good God, Banner, don't tell me that."

"What does it mean?"

"It means I never should have stayed."

"And they won't go down. Not for the longest time. They stay like that, kind of itchy and tingling—"

"Oh, hush."

"—and that's when I wish—"

"What?"

"—that we were in the barn again and you were—"

"Don't say it."

"—inside me."

"Jesus, Banner, stop."

He made a cradle of his palm and laid it along her cheek, gradually turning her head to face him. And as her head turned, so did her body. The fabric of her clothes dragged against his like the tide on the seashore, separate, yet bound.

When their eyes met and locked hungrily, he lowered his mouth to hers. He thrust his tongue deep into her mouth as he pressed her hips against his swollen front. She cradled his hardness between her thighs.

He tore his mouth free. "No, Banner. I hurt you before, remember?"

"Yes, but that wasn't why I was crying."

"Then why?"

"Because it began to feel good and I . . . I thought you'd hate me for the way I was acting."

"No, no," he whispered fervently into her hair.

"You were so . . . big."

"I'm sorry."

"I just didn't expect it to be so . . . and . . . and so . . ."

"Did it feel good to you at all, Banner?"

"Yes, yes. But it was over too soon."

He laid his hard cheek against hers. His breathing was labored, otherwise he didn't move. "Too soon?"

"I felt like something was about to happen, but it didn't."

Jake was stunned. Could it be? He knew whores faked it. He didn't have any experience with decent women. Certainly not with virgins. Never with a virgin. He had never taken anyone he could feel tenderness for.

But tenderness for Banner enveloped him now. He cupped her face between his hands and went searching in her eyes for the truth. He saw no fear there, only a keen desire that matched his own. Making a growling sound deep in his throat, he lowered his head again.

"Hello!" a cheerful voice called out. "Anyone at home?"

Only then did they become aware of the jingle of harnesses and the unmistakable sounds of a wagon being pulled to a halt outside.

"Banner? Where are you?"

It was Lydia.

TEN

Banner watched the dawn sunlight turn from pink to gold as it weakly filtered through her bedroom window. She lay with her cheek pressed against her pillow. Frequently a tear would spill over her lower eyelid and roll down her cheek. It was absorbed into the soft pillowcase as all the others before it had been.

Her thoughts were on last night. She couldn't believe the turn it had taken. Before Lydia's untimely arrival, things had gone according to plan. Jake had been swept into the romantic mood she had created.

Never having had to lure a man before—that one night in the barn didn't count—she had tried to remember the lures and schemes her girlfriends had sworn by to snare a husband. A good meal, soft lighting, flowers, a pretty dress, and a sweet disposition, everything to appeal to a man's senses and make him think that it would be marvelous to have that kind of tender loving care all the time.

Banner had always thought such machinations were beneath her dignity, compromising to her integrity, and downright ridiculous. To the disbelief of her friends, she had even declared that she wouldn't want a man who could be so easily manipulated.

But there must be something to such female schemes because everything had gone so well. Until Lydia knocked on the front door.

Jake had jumped like he had been shot. He tripped over the stool still lying on its side. Only a miracle and some deft footwork had saved him from sprawling on the floor.

Banner had smoothed her hair, pressed her hands to flaming cheeks, and rested her pounding forehead on the doorjamb for a few precious seconds before swinging open the door and saying, "Mama! What a nice surprise."

"Hello, dear."

Lydia breezed in carrying with her crisp night smells that seemed to cling to her hair and clothes the way one sprig of honeysuckle makes a whole house smell good.

Banner's heart sank.

Lydia looked beautiful in a plain ecru shirtwaist and brown skirt. She would still turn any man's head with her whiskey-colored eyes and hair the reddish-brown shade of cinnamon. Her figure was trim, but her breasts and hips were womanly full. What man wouldn't want to rest his head on her maternal breast and stay for the rest of the night? Lydia looked comfortable, as though she was all a man would need to make him happy and self-satisfied.

"Hello, Jake." She smiled at him and Banner's heart slipped down another notch toward the bottom of her soul. Lydia's smile was guileless, open, friendly, but could he help himself from melting beneath it?

Jake looked like he had just swallowed something distasteful and was about to vomit. "Lydia." One brisk nod of his blond-white head was all the greeting she got and Banner had known it was because he didn't trust himself to

speak yet. He had been about to kiss one woman, and in
had walked the one he really wanted. That was enough to
rattle even the staunchest of men.

An awkward silence stretched out until Banner seized the
moment and stepped forward with her hand pointing toward
the picture. "What do you think, Mama? Jake was just
helping me hang it when we heard your wagon pull up."

"I wondered what was taking you so long to answer the
door," she replied absently as she studied the picture. "I
like it." She pivoted slowly on her heels, taking in the
entire parlor. "You've done wonders with the room, Banner. Everything looks just right and . . . homey."

"Thank you."

"Maybe you need another lamp," Lydia said, laying her
finger along her cheek ponderingly. "It's a trifle dark in
here."

Banner wished the floor would open up and swallow her,
but since it didn't she asked, "Would you like some
coffee?" She desperately needed something else to do with
her hands besides wringing them damply together.

"No. It's too hot."

"Something else?"

"A seat?" Lydia asked, teasingly.

Banner's hand flew to her chest. "I'm sorry, Mama. Of
course, sit down. Jake . . . ?" She turned to him, indicating
another chair.

"I've got to get that wagon unloaded," he said awkwardly,
and made for the rack by the door where his hat and gunbelt
were hanging.

"Sit down, Jake, for heaven's sake," Lydia said with
some exasperation. "This isn't a formal call. What's the
matter with you two?"

"Nothing." The word virtually tripped over Banner's lips
on its rush out. She glanced toward Jake for support, but he
had slumped into a chair and was staring at the floor. "Jake
is just sulking. He didn't appreciate me asking him to hang
the picture."

"Ross is the same way. He hates doing 'piddling things in
the house' as he calls it."

Banner took courage from her mother's familiar smile. "I'm glad you came to see me, Mama."

"You two have been strangers to River Bend. We were wondering if we had done something to offend you." She was still smiling, but there was a hint of inquiry in her eyes.

"No," Banner said, laughing falsely. "We've just been so busy. You can't imagine all the work we've been doing around the place."

"That's what we hear from the hands," Lydia replied. "Are they working out well for you, Jake?"

He raised his eyes to Lydia and pulled himself up straighter in his chair. He looked like a boy who had just been called on in school. "Yeah, they're fine."

"Frankly I was worried about that younger one, Randy," Lydia said.

Jake's eyes flickered to Banner for only a heartbeat before he said, "He's rowdy, all right, but I've managed to keep him in line. How's Ma?"

"Fine. A little put out with you for not riding over to see her."

"I've got to get around to that soon."

"That's why I rode over this evening," Lydia said. "I was going to wait until tomorrow, but Ross and Lee got involved in one of their endless checkers tournaments and it was such a nice evening, I decided to drive on over now." She paused and drew a deep breath. "We're giving a party Saturday night."

"A party?" Banner asked, surprised. "What for?"

"To show people that our lives, and especially yours, aren't over because of what happened at your wedding."

Banner went cold on the inside. For long moments she remained unmoving. Then she came to her feet and began to stamp around the room, straightening this, rearranging that, whisking away imaginary dust motes.

"Is that what everyone thinks?" she asked tartly. "That my life is over, that I'm pining?"

"Please don't take this the wrong way, Banner. Your father and I don't give a hoot what people think or say. We learned a long time ago that you can't keep them from thinking or saying what they please. But we both know how labels hurt. Once you get one, you're stuck with it.''

"What do you mean?"

Lydia glanced at Jake, but his face remained stony and gave away nothing. "It only means that we don't want people to get the wrong impression of you, because it might be a lasting one. Ross went into town a few days ago. He said people asked about you like you had a fatal disease that might claim you at any moment. Lee and Micah said the gossip going around is that you've moved out here to hibernate."

"That's not true!" Banner shouted. Her cheeks were flushed now for an entirely different reason. She was vexed and her posture showed it as she pulled herself up regally. "I feel more alive and vital now that I'm working on my own place than I ever have in my life."

"That's why we're holding the party. We want folks to see you as your old self and put these rumors to a stop before they get out of hand."

"But a party." Dispiritedly Banner sank back into her chair, suddenly quelled by the thought of everyone gawking at her. "Is that necessary? I haven't been into town since the wedding. Couldn't I start with that . . . be seen there by folks?"

Lydia shook her head. "You know how people are. They wouldn't come up to you. They'd gossip behind their fans and make up their own minds. This way they'll be forced to talk to you, and there will be no mistaking that you're perfectly fine. It won't be formal. Just a barbecue outside. What do you think?"

"I suppose so." Her eyes went to Jake. He refused to look at her and that hurt. When he held her, had he only been slaking a natural hunger for a woman? Would any woman have done? Had she merely been convenient tonight? And did he hate her and himself now because he had defiled his feelings for Lydia?

She had planned to seduce him into the idea of marrying her. How foolish she had been. Other men might fall for such feminine wiles, but never Jake. Had he known what she was up to and merely played along for his own amusement? In any event, she had had her chance, and it had ended disastrously.

"I guess I do need to start seeing people again." By people she meant men. Apparently that was the idea behind the party.

Lydia stood up briskly, as though her mission were accomplished. "Wonderful. Of course you'll come too, Jake." Without waiting for his answer to her nonquestion, she went to Banner and drew her into a tight embrace. "Ross and I miss you terribly, but we're so proud of what you're doing here. Is everything all right?"

"Yes, Mama, fine. I'll come see you more often." She kissed Lydia's cheek. "Do you have to leave so soon?"

"Yes. I promised Ross I wouldn't be long. Good night," she said, kissing Banner's temple. "We'll see you Saturday."

"I'll walk you out," Jake said, taking his hat and gunbelt from the rack. "I was on my way out when you came in. Thanks for dinner, Banner."

And she had stood there alone in the doorway while they walked across the porch and down the steps together, Jake's hand solicitously under Lydia's arm. Their heads were close.

"Is she truly all right, Jake? We're so worried about her," Banner overheard her mother whisper.

"She's fine."

"Ross and I would go out of our minds with worry if we didn't have you to look after her."

"I'm doing my best." He helped her into the wagon. "What's Ross thinking of, letting you drive over here after dark by yourself?"

"Why, Jake Langston, I can take care of myself, thank you," Lydia said haughtily, swatting him playfully on the arm.

"Do you have a gun?"

"Yes," she said wearily. "Ross wouldn't let me go anywhere without one. You two, I swear! You'd think I was helpless and had to be cared for."

"Be careful driving over that bridge. It looks rickety in

places. As soon as I catch up with some of the work around here, I'm going to shore it up.''

"Don't worry about me. I'll be fine. Good night. See you around seven on Saturday. Did I tell Banner the time?''

"I'll pass it along. You get home before it gets any later.''

"Good night, Jake,'' she said, clicking her tongue to the horse who pulled the wagon.

" 'Night, Lydia.''

Long after she had ridden off, Jake stood there in the yard gazing after her. Banner watched him watching after her mother, sending her back to her husband, loving her.

Tears flooded her eyes now as they had periodically throughout the night. What a fool she had made of herself! How could she have thought to tempt Jake into loving her, just a little, when his eyes and head and heart were so full of Lydia? It had rent her heart in two to see him walk back into the barn, his shoulders slumped dejectedly.

How could she face him after throwing herself at him last night? After talking to him about—

Lord, had she truly revealed how she had felt about that other time, spoken aloud the thoughts she had harbored for weeks, thoughts that she had been ashamed even to contemplate? Had she returned his passionate kisses measure for measure? Little good it had done her except to make herself more contemptible in his eyes.

She had failed on two accounts. First, she had thrown herself at him and been rejected. He hadn't come back in to pick up where they left off after Lydia left. And, when she had probed him, he hadn't been forthcoming with any information into her parents' past. He had clammed up just like everyone else when she baited him.

Something didn't mesh. Why had Lydia mentioned the labels placed on people? When had anyone labeled Lydia anything but an ideal rancher's wife and mother? There was something in their past that her parents didn't want Lee and her to know, and everyone who loved them was keeping their secret intact.

Added to her humiliation concerning Jake and anguish

over her heritage, was dread at the party Saturday night. If it were only herself involved, she would thumb her nose at everybody in Larsen County. Let them talk. Let them think what they liked.

But Mama and Papa were involved. They had always wanted the best life possible for her. The way the rest of the world saw the Colemans was important to them. Papa had to do business with the men in town. Those men had wives who gossiped. Mama was right. They needed to show everyone that the Colemans were far from suffering defeat at the hands of Grady Sheldon.

But how she was going to survive the week with that blasted party hanging over her head, she didn't know.

The water in the tub had grown tepid, but still Banner lay immersed in it. Earlier that afternoon she had washed her hair in rainwater which she had been collecting in a barrel outside the back door. She had pinned it up on her head before stepping into her bath. The tub was stationed in the middle of the kitchen floor. It had been filled from the pump in the sink and kettles of heated water off the stove.

Ordinarily she would have looked forward to the party all week. But getting ready for it held no joy for her today. Jake had been as cranky as a hungry wolf. They hadn't exchanged a private word that wasn't necessary. Indeed, he had avoided her as much as possible. He had bolted down his meals as through the devil had given him a time limit. He didn't stay to linger over a cup of coffee or smoke a cheroot, but left by way of the back door after saying a terse, "Thanks."

For the most part, Banner had stayed indoors after exercising the horses each morning. Studiously she kept her distance from the cowboys, not wanting to provoke Jake's anger.

As for the ranch, it had been a productive week. They had finished the barbed-wire fence around the pasture. Banner had whitewashed the boards of the corral, working on it after the men had ridden away for the day.

But it had been a tense week in which the hands sensed

the prevailing mood. Thinking it was a leftover from the incident with the caterpillar, they walked on eggshells around Jake. For the past several days Plum Creek hadn't been a happy place to be.

Banner had used the hot bath to soothe her nerves and ease some of the tension from her muscles. But if she wanted plenty of time to dress, she had to get out now. She stepped from the tub just as someone tapped on the back door.

"Banner?"

Jake! "Just a minute." She snatched up her robe and wrapped it around her, sloshing water on the floor as she went to the back door and opened it.

His face went perfectly blank when he saw her. "What are you doing?"

"Taking a bath," she replied candidly.

"Christ!" he hissed through his teeth, and glanced toward the three cowboys who were mounted and waiting for word from him. "I just came to tell you that I'm skipping that party tonight. I'm riding back with the boys now. I'll send Lee after you. And for godsakes get some clothes on."

"No."

"No?" he asked under his breath.

"No, you're not skipping the party tonight."

"I'll do as I damn well please on a Saturday night."

She could hear the snuffling of horses just beyond the door, so she, too, was keeping her voice low and tense. "I don't care what you do with any of your other Saturday nights, but tonight you're going to that party."

"Why should I?"

"Because it'll look strange if you're not there, and I don't want anyone to think there's something wrong between us, that's why."

He stared at her long and hard, irritation making his mouth a straight, narrow line. Over his shoulder he said, "You all go on ahead. Banner's got some business she needs to discuss with me."

The three men muttered goodbyes. Jake waited until they

were safely out of the yard before he turned back to Banner. "There *is* something wrong between us."

Her gaze slid from his face to the bandana tied around his neck. He was never without it, no cowboy was, but it looked so good on Jake, even coated with dust as it was now. "You're talking about the other night," she said softly.

"I'm talking about all of it. That first time in the barn *and* the other night *and* all the times in between when we—"

He broke off and she raised her eyes back to his. "When we what?"

Now it was Jake's turn to look away. For days he had cursed himself anew for flirting with something so dangerous. He was dancing around a keg of dynamite with torches in his hands, daring it to blow up in his face.

What would Lydia have thought if she had found her daughter in his arms, Banner's mouth beneath his? That question had haunted him all week. She would have thrown up her hands in horror. Oh, he knew Lydia loved him like a brother, would give anything he asked for that was in her power to give. She would have done that for any Langston.

But she didn't love him like a son-in-law. He was all right being her friend and Ross's friend, but as a mate for their daughter? Uh-uh. Jake knew better than to deceive himself. Banner was their princess and he was about as far from a prince as a man could get.

If Ross had ever seen him about to kiss Banner, Lydia's outrage would have been mild by comparison. Ross would kill him on the spot. He knew Jake's reputation with women. Hell, he'd even told Ross about some of his wilder exploits. They had laughed at his escapades with the opposite sex over whiskey and cigars in the middle of the night. The tipsier they got, the bawdier the tales became.

"That fine pecker you're so proud of is going to fall off if you don't give it a rest," Ross had said one night, wiping tears of mirth from his eyes.

"God grant me death from exhaustion," Jake had replied, a sappy grin on his face.

Ross had thought it all highly amusing then, but his

opinion of Jake's reputation would change drastically if applied to Banner. Would he want Jake's whore-tainted hands on his daughter? Hell no. He'd be crazy or stupid if he *didn't* shoot Jake.

The smart thing to do would be to make a clean break, say his goodbyes, saddle Stormy, and ride out never to return until he heard that Banner was safely married.

But he couldn't bring himself to do that.

This place was already under his skin. He loved every drop of sweat it had cost him. He had visions of this ranch becoming as grand as River Bend. He wanted to be a part of that. His life needed to account for something. He didn't want to leave the job unfinished.

Since killing Clancey Russell, he had run away from responsibility. But that was no way for a man to live, shirking duty and keeping himself apart from anything meaningful. He had been given a chance, perhaps his last one, to prove to himself that something in his life could work out right. He simply had to do this.

But how could he stay away from the girl? Especially when she gazed up at him, as now, with those eyes that shot sparks of green and gold alternately. Her skin was moist and fragrant from her bath. Lord o'mercy, didn't she know that her robe was clinging damply, revealing the proud, firm shape of her breasts and their pointed tips, revealing the columns of her thighs, the delta between them, revealing everything that should be concealed at all costs? Did she have any idea how alluring her hair was, haphazardly pinned up, with more escaping than remaining confined? Did she know how goddamned kissable her mouth was?

"Jake, where are you? What are you thinking about? You said 'all the times in between when we' and then you stopped and I want to know just *what* you have in mind."

Jake drew himself out of his befuddlement and said harshly, "We put more stock into what happened between us than we should."

"Speak for yourself," she cried. "I got what I wanted that night. I don't regret it."

"Well, good!" he said furiously. Would anybody she

happened to find in the barn have served just as well? Someone younger? Better looking? Randy? "Then you should be looking forward to the party tonight." He sneered. "It'll give you a chance to dance and flirt with all the young bucks in town who would like to tumble Banner Coleman."

"Oh, you can be so crude."

"Well, that's what parties are for, isn't it?"

"For what?"

"For you to get all gussied up and strut your stuff in front of all the eligible men. To flirt and giggle and compare dance cards with the other young ladies from around these parts who aren't married."

She closed her eyes and counted to ten slowly, in a vain attempt to curb her temper. "Are we back to that again?"

"Back to what?"

"To you speaking to me as though I were a child."

"Compared to me, you are."

She placed her hands on her hips, an unwise move since it drew the damp cloth tight over her straining breasts. She tilted her head back, again unwise because it caused her hair to tumble down and exposed her throat. But she was unconscious of all that. She was caught up in their argument.

"Oh, yes. Poor ol' Jake Langston. You're virtually decrepit. Ancient. I'll bet Mama wanted you at her party so you could act as chaperone for all us *young* folks."

He ground his teeth. "I ain't going." He stressed each word as though learning to speak it for the first time. His nose came dangerously close to touching hers as he leaned forward for emphasis.

"Then neither am I," she said airily. As she spun around, she slammed the door in his face. It remained closed only a fraction of a second before it was almost ripped off its hinges. Jake came barreling through, reached out, grabbed her arm and twirled her around. "What's that supposed to mean?"

"Just what I said. If you don't go, neither will I." She thumped his chest with her index finger. "And *you* can make our excuses."

He released her and sailed his hat toward the hooks by the

door. It missed them all and fell into the puddle of water her wet feet had left. He cursed expansively, raking his hands through his hair and mumbling deprecations about spoiled brats who made life hell for everyone around them.

"All right, Banner," he said finally, pointing a finger at her. "But this is the last time you're getting your way. I mean that now. And you stay away from me over there, you hear? If I've got to go to that goddamn party, I plan on having a rip-roaring time, you understand me?"

She batted her eyelashes. "Why, of course, Jake," she said on a sugary drawl. "That's what I intend to do too. Didn't you say that's what parties are for?"

He had a powerful urge to toss her over his knee and whip the daylights out of her. But that would have entailed touching her. And he couldn't touch her, not without any more protection between them than that cotton wrapper. She was naked beneath it. He didn't need an encyclopedia to tell him that. Her skin was rosy. No doubt it would be warm and . . .

Damn! He whirled toward the door. "I'll pick you up—"

"Wouldn't you like a bath?"

He stopped dead in his tracks and came around slowly. "What?"

"A bath. I'll warm up this water."

"I was going to the creek."

She wrinkled her nose, calling attention to her freckles. "That won't be the same as a nice, relaxing, warm bath."

Without waiting for his acceptance, she began preparing another bath. She tested the kettles on the stove and found they still had boiling water in them. Humming under her breath, she dipped some of the water in the tub into a pail and emptied it out the back door. That made room for the fresh steaming water she poured in. She wiggled her fingers in it.

"There. That's just right." She turned to face him, having ignored him as she went about busily getting the water ready. "You *are* going to use it, aren't you?"

He gnawed on the inside of his cheek. He had stood there like a damn fool while she wrapped him around her little finger. But he had been so captivated by the way her body looked in that clinging robe he couldn't move. It had stuck to her hip as she bent over the tub, outlining the gentle curves for his avid eyes. It had gaped when she emptied the pail, giving him a glimpse of the creamy flesh of her breast.

In contrast, the rest of her looked vulnerable. Strands of ebony hair clung to her damp cheeks. Her bare feet looked too small for an adult. He wanted to examine them closely. When she moved past him, she seemed incredibly small and in need of protection.

Knowing he should run as hard and fast as he could, he heard himself say, "I guess I'll have to, since you went to all the trouble to fix it."

"I'll get you a towel while you fetch some clean clothes from the barn."

He hadn't returned when Banner came back to the kitchen. She peered out the window anxiously. Only when she saw him emerge from the building carrying his clothes did she breathe. By the time he opened the back door, she was fussily arranging a towel and washcloth and soap on the table within his reach.

"I'll give you some privacy now," she said softly.

"Thanks."

"You're welcome."

She closed the door between the kitchen and parlor and left him. She went into her bedroom. She didn't close the door behind her. Something inside her, a naughtiness she had never known was there, prevented her from shutting the door. When she peeled out of her robe, she faced the door to the kitchen, wishing Jake would open it and see her.

But he wasn't going to. Already she could hear the water splashing. He was in the tub. With that thought came hot, coiling sensations that ribboned around her thighs, between them, up her middle, through her breasts. Her nipples pouted.

Hesitantly, she lifted her hand to one. She was vividly reminded of Jake's hands touching her, teaching her things about herself she hadn't known. Her flesh was receptive.

She trembled. Between her thighs she felt a liquid heat forming.

She dropped her hand quickly, afraid she would be struck dead by God's wrath for being so wicked.

But the image of Jake in the tub wouldn't go away. Having grown up with a brother, she wasn't completely ignorant of the male anatomy as most of her peers were. But she had never seen a grown man naked and was made to understand from a few married friends who would dare broach such a forbidden subject that *that* was a fearsome sight to behold.

She couldn't imagine it being anything but beautiful. The rest of Jake was beautiful, why not that? She wouldn't be shocked. She had grown up on a stud farm and knew what happened to male animals when they were aroused.

Besides, she had experienced it. It had been frightening, his first hard thrust into her body, but the pain had been temporary. She had felt him, his silky length and steely hardness. But she had never seen him and was consumed with curiosity about the way he looked.

Maybe she should offer to wash his back.

But even as she took steps in the direction of the door, she rejected that idea as too obvious.

She supposed she was terribly wanton, but that didn't stop her from hoping that one day she and Jake would do that again and that the next time they would be naked. As she pulled on her clothes, she was aware of every inch of skin on her body. Cool cloth whispered across each fevered surface.

She chose a dress of vivid green. It had a scooped neckline and fit snugly at her midriff. The skirt was only full enough to sway gently when she walked. The dress buttoned down the back, and therein lay her problem. She couldn't reach the top few buttons because the bodice fit too well.

She glanced at the kitchen door. It was still closed, but she hadn't heard any splashing sounds in the last few minutes. She crossed the parlor and knocked on the door. "Jake?"

"Yeah?"

"May I come in?"

"It's your house."

She pushed the door open. He was dragging the tub across the floor. At the back door, he tilted it forward and let the water drain out over the steps.

Banner stood entranced. He had pulled on only a clean pair of black trousers. He was barefooted and shirtless. The muscles of his chest and arms and back held her attention captive as he lifted the empty tub and placed it back in the closet. When he turned to face her, her breath caught in her throat.

Up close his chest was even more magnificent than seen from afar. The bronze disks of his nipples, nestled in swirls of golden hair, intrigued her. If touched, caressed, did they react as hers did?

She followed the satiny strip of hair that arrowed down the middle of his torso until it met that which whorled around his navel just above the button on his pants. The black cloth cupped his sex. The snug fit left little room for imagination. Her recent thoughts came washing over her like a scalding tidal wave and made her dizzy.

She dragged her eyes back up to his. "I need some help with my buttons." Her voice was raspy, inadvertently intimate. She went toward him and turned her back. Her hand swept her hair up off her neck.

He managed the buttons with more alacrity than she wished. How many other buttons had he been asked to do up? Or undo? The thought was unsettling. Had she measured up to the other women he had known? If she hadn't she would! No one would be as good for Jake as she was. She would see to that. She couldn't give up now.

Keeping her hair swept aside, she turned around and looked up at him from beneath her lashes. "Sharing bath water, you buttoning me up. By all appearances we could be married, couldn't we?"

His face was hard, immobile. The blue of his eyes had gone almost colorless. "Hardly, Banner. If we were married and you met me at the door dressed in no more than a damp robe, I'd have already had you in bed, with your skirts over your head, fucking you till your ears rang."

Her mouth dropped open. The air left her body in one disbelieving gust. She fell back a step and raised her hand to her breast as though he had struck her. The skin on her face went pale and stretched taut.

Then she spun around and fled the kitchen. He heard the bedroom door slam behind her.

Jake slumped against the doorjamb. His fists were balled at his sides so tightly his knuckles were white. "I'm sorry, Banner, I'm sorry," he whispered to the ceiling.

He wasn't sure when it had hit him. Maybe it had been sneaking up on him all week. Maybe it had occurred to him like a bolt out of the blue. But somewhere between the house and the barn when he had left to get his fresh clothes, he had known.

Banner was trying to seduce him, not into bed, but into marriage.

That's what the other night had been about. The kindnesses, the perfect dinner, the considerate attention, the silent promise that if he had wanted to share her bed, he could have. What a blind idiot he had been!

It had almost worked. If Lydia hadn't chosen that time to come visiting, he would have obeyed the will of his body and made love to Banner. One time, at her request, might, *might* be forgivable. But twice? Never. He would have had to marry her.

He didn't blame Banner. She was still just a kid, a high-strung young woman whose pride had been dealt a deathblow. Practically speaking, their marrying made sense. Had he turned over the idea in some hidden corner of his mind?

If not, why, when Lydia drove out of the yard, had he not yearned for her as always? Why had he yearned much more to return to the house and continue what he and Banner had started? It had saddened him that he hadn't felt that familiar tugging around his heart when Lydia left him to return to Ross. She had looked beautiful, just as she always did. But she was no longer the most beautiful. When had Banner become the standard by which he judged all other women? He was supposed to love Lydia. Just what in hell was happening here?

He and Banner were getting too familiar, that was all. Too intimate. They were isolated, and as lonely people do, they were reaching out to whomever was available. Well, it had to be stopped. He had to put an end to these intimacies before she got any more fool notions about them being to each other any more than they were.

He had resolved that he had no choice but to wound her. So when he returned for his bath and saw the hungry way she was looking at him, when he felt his own body betraying his good intentions, he had said that horrible thing.

He had hurt her. And he would go on hurting her. There was no other way. She had to be made to see that anything between them simply could not be.

And while he was convincing her, he hoped to God he could convince himself.

ELEVEN

Grady Sheldon heard the screams long before he rode his horse into the clearing and tied it to the lower branches of a sad pine.

That Doggie Burns was beating Wanda to within an inch of her life was his first guess as to what was wrong. But, as he dismounted, he saw Doggie sitting on the sagging front porch. A hound was parked at each foot, one was stretched across his lap. The moonshiner lifted a jug of his own brew to his flaccid lips, through which he mumbled incoherently. It was Grady's guess that it wasn't Doggie's first drink of the day.

Another high-pitched wail that could have originated in the dungeons of hell rose from the cabin. Grady, without haste, walked toward the derelict dwelling. One of the mangy hounds came tearing toward him, growling and snapping at his heels. He kicked it in the head and sent it skulking and whimpering back beneath the porch.

Doggie's bleary eyes came around to his son-in-law. "What's going on in there?" Grady asked him.

"Your young'un's 'bout to be borned, that's what."

Another scream rent the air, followed by hard, harsh panting sounds that made Grady's stomach churn. "That," Doggie said, hitching his head toward the door and wiping his mouth after taking a long pull at the spout of the jug, "has been goin' on all day and I'm gittin' sick to death of it. Screamin', yellin', disturbin' a man's peace like she was the only woman what ever birthed a babe. Silly damned bitch."

The thought of birth made Grady queasy and unaccountably nervous. He gazed into the dim void of the yawning front door which welcomed insects, beasts, varmints of any kind to venture inside. "Has she . . . did you try to get the doctor?"

Doggie looked up at him through eyes hazy from alcohol consumption. "Hell, man, you think I'm crazy? Why would she need a doc to whelp a brat? Damned quacks. Good for nothing but stealin' a man's hard-earned money. Nope. Wanda's ma borned her in a bed no better'n that one, and she done all right. All that cryin' and screamin's just for show, boy. Don't let it fool you none."

The next scream ended on a trailing wail that curdled Grady's blood. "She, uh, she sounds like she's really in pain."

Doggie crackled a laugh. "Reckon she is, reckon she is. It's God's punishment for her whorin' ways. He's punished every whore since Eve for their wicked ways. Shut up in there," he bellowed, loud enough to disturb the hounds surrounding him. They raised their soulful eyes, then returned to their naps. "Git on in there," Doggie said to Grady. "She's your wife. And for the love of Jesus shut her up. I can't stand that screamin' no more."

Grady entered the dim, smoky, stuffy room. The smells were hideous, an insult to human nostrils. He tried holding his breath for long moments at a time. When he did breathe, the air was thick with filth and squalor.

Wanda lay on the bed amid soiled linens. Grady swallowed the scalding bile that filled his throat. The rough sheets were stained pink from the water that had flowed from her womb and precipitated her labor.

Her knees were bent and raised and opened wide. Her face was gray and puckered. The lips through which passed those gasping sounds were bruised and cracked where she had obviously gnawed them in an effort to stifle her screams. Her hair was matted with sweat. Her eyes were closed. A scanty shift had been raised as high as her breasts, leaving her lower half bare.

Grady was thoroughly disgusted by the sight of her. So disgusted that he wanted to vomit. The breasts that had once enticed him were now bloated with milk, the nipples large and dark. She evoked no pity in him, even though he could see her body twisting, garnering energy for the next painful assault.

Her shoulders left the mattress and she clutched her knees, drawing them toward her chest, as she grunted and strained until her face was beet-red and swollen with the effort. When she fell back and opened her eyes, she saw Grady watching her.

"So you finally put in an appearance," she said in shallow, rapid breaths. "Look what you done to me, you sonofabitch. You brought me to this."

"Are you sure it was me, Wanda?" Grady taunted.

"You or some other bastard who thought he was too good to speak to me on the streets of town but who sneaked out here when he wanted a good tumble." She gnashed her teeth and groaned in agony. But she couldn't contain her anguish and released it on another scream that pierced the ramshackle walls of the cabin.

"You're bothering your daddy. He sent me in here to stop your screams."

"Goddamn him. And goddamn you."

"Charming as ever, Wanda. Motherhood becomes you." His eyes slid down her puffy body. She was opened, stretched wide. The baby's head was emerging. His gorge rose again.

Wanda, screaming, propped herself on her elbows and pushed with all her might. She tucked her chin against her chest as she made low, guttural, animal noises that were repulsive to Grady's ears. Then she threw her head back and screamed until her voice cracked.

"I told you to shut her up," Doggie yelled from the outside. "Goddamn women," he muttered as he staggered off the porch, sending the hounds scuttling in every direction. "I'm goin' to git me another jug." He ambled away into the gathering twilight.

When Grady's eyes swung back to Wanda, she was in the throes of another contraction.

"Help me, Grady, help me." She was pleading now, all arrogance gone. Pain had reduced her to a pathetic being. "The babe won't be borned. It won't be. Help me. Do something!" she screamed when he just stood there looking at her.

"Your daddy told me to keep you quiet." His voice was as devoid of expression as his face.

"I can't help the screaming. It hurts." Again she collapsed onto the sweat-stained pillow. Then her body convulsed with another pain and her throat opened up and she wailed loud and long.

The baby's shoulders had pushed their way through. In a moment it would be born. Grady Sheldon, young, handsome businessman, would be saddled with yet another Burns. The thought that he could have sired a brat out of Wanda Burns made him even more sick to his stomach than the sights and smells around him. That he might have to support this clan of white trash all his life was unthinkable.

For weeks he had debated about what he should do. He had come to a conclusion, though that, too, had been unthinkable. But he was desperate. And desperation urged men to do things that would ordinarily be unthinkable.

"Doggie told me to keep you from screaming. I think I

should." He picked up the extra pillow on the bed. "Don't scream anymore, Wanda."

She looked up at him through glassy eyes, filled now not only with agony but fear. "What are you doing? Huh? Oh, God." She gritted her teeth as another spasm seized her. "Oh, God, oh, Jesus," she chanted while her body strained to dispel the life in her womb.

"Don't scream," Grady warned menacingly.

"I can't . . . can't help . . ." Her mouth opened wide and she let loose a scream that championed its predecessors. It split her throat just as her body split open and the child was expelled.

Grady acted.

He closed the pillow over her face, pressed her back onto the mattress, and held her there. She struggled but briefly. Hours of agonizing labor had left her weak. Grady didn't remove the pillow until long after her limbs had become still.

When he lifted it away, sweat was rolling down his body in cold rivers. He didn't look at Wanda, but lowered his eyes to the mewling baby lying between her thighs. He didn't even turn it over to see it if was a boy or a girl. No use wasting energy on that. It wouldn't live long. Not if his plan worked. And it had to.

He whirled around when he heard Doggie's shuffling walk. He tiptoed to the door, peeked out, and saw the man weaving his unsteady way back to the cabin. About every third step, he hauled the jug to his shoulder, tilted his head back and took a long draft of the moonshine whiskey.

When Doggie reached the cabin, his alcohol-befuddled brain discerned that something was amiss. "What's 'is?" he muttered. He started forward, staggered, and almost fell over one of his hounds. Cursing it, he stumbled up on the porch, grasped one of the rough cedar posts to keep himself from falling and called out, "What's goin' on in yonder, huh? Wanda? Sheldon? Is the young'un borned yet?" He took a lurching step forward. "Why ain't there no noise? Huh? Why—"

He never saw the piece of oak firewood that came

crunching down on his skull the minute he cleared the doorway. Heavily he dropped to the floor.

After having held his breath for the past several minutes, Grady stepped from the shadows and leaned over Doggie. The man didn't move. Grady wiped his sweating face on his sleeve.

It was their fate to die like this, Grady convinced himself. They were trash, not fit to live on the same planet with decent folks. Who would miss Doggie Burns and his sluttish daughter? He had done the world a favor by ridding it of them. He had only helped fate out a little bit, that's all.

He went to the apple crate that served as a bedside table and casually tipped the kerosene lantern over, making sure its globe broke against the plank floor and that the fuel spread in a wide pool.

No one could blame him for this. Fate hadn't been too kind to him lately. He had lost Banner, a chunk of prized real estate, and the backing and endorsement of the Colemans, which went a long way in Larsen County. He had been humiliated in public and shunned in town by people who used to suck up to him. He'd been laughed at. He'd taken about all a man could take, hadn't he? From now on, he intended fate to decide things in his favor.

He struck a match and lit the end of a cigar he had had the good fortune to bring along. See? Fate was already turning the tide. He sauntered out of the cabin and drew the tobacco smoke into his lungs, releasing it on a long, slow exhalation.

Everybody knew the Burnses lived like pigs, that Doggie was constantly drunk. Wanda too. No one had seen him leave town. Even if they had, who was to say he had come out here? He would circle around, ride back into town from the opposite direction and make sure he waved to several people who would remember it later if the sheriff got suspicious about the fire at the Burns place.

Grady tossed his cigar into the open doorway of the shack. He didn't even wait to see if it caught.

Fate was on his side now.

*   *   *

The party was already in full swing by the time Banner and Jake arrived. They were late.

It was an indisputable fact that the Colemans knew how to throw a shindig. Lanterns covered with gaily colored paper were hanging from the lowest branches of the trees. Tables, lined up end to end in the yard, were laden with food. The barbecue pits emitted the delicious aroma of mesquite-smoked meat. Kegs of beer had been set up. Ma kept the punch bowls brimming with lemonade for the ladies.

The music was toe-tapping and loud. Two fiddles, a banjo, a harmonica, and an accordion played one lively tune after another. Their musicians' repertoire was as limited as their skill, but they made up for both with their enthusiasm.

When Lydia and Ross saw the familiar wagon pull into the yard, they rushed toward it to greet their daughter and Jake. Ross lifted Banner off the wagon seat and twirled her around.

"I almost forgot how pretty you are, Princess. Ranching hasn't made you ugly, by any means."

"Papa." Banner hugged him tight when he set her back on the ground. She hadn't realized how much she had missed him until now. He felt so safe and strong. She wanted to stay in his protective embrace for a long time. But that would be out of the ordinary, and she had to make things seem ordinary, even though her heart was breaking and she could think of a hundred places she would rather be than at a party.

She and Jake hadn't spoken since he had said that dreadful thing to her. Of course, she was unfamiliar with the word, but in context and given the brittle quality of Jake's eyes when he had said it, she could imagine how unspeakably foul it was.

When she had finished dressing, she had come out onto the front porch. He had been sitting in the wagon, smoking a cheroot. He barely glanced at her, but got out of the wagon and came around to assist her. She disdained his extended hand and pulled herself onto the seat. He had merely shrugged and returned to his place, taken up the reins, and driven in silence across the river.

Banner had sat stonily still, hoping that he could sense the undiluted loathing of him that flowed through her veins with every beat of her heart.

Again she had made a fool of herself, but that was the last time. He wouldn't have an occasion to humiliate her again. Friendliness between them would cease. She would speak to him only about ranching matters and only when necessary. He wouldn't eat in her kitchen again. She would leave a tray out on the front porch for him. She would feed him as one did a pet, making the food available, but not sharing it.

"Jake, how are you?" Her father's hearty welcome snapped her back into the present. Ross was heartily pumping Jake's hand. "There's beer over there or something stronger inside in my office."

"I'll take something stronger," Jake said, his mouth grim.

Ross smiled beneath his mustache. "Figured you would. I want to talk to you about something anyway."

"Ross," Lydia moaned, "don't talk business tonight. You'll miss the party."

He reached for her, drew her to him and kissed her soundly on her startled mouth. "Wanna bet? I have a party planned for you and me later."

"Ross, keep your voice down and let me go. Everybody's watching," she protested, but her cheeks were rosy and her eyes were filled with an excitement that matched her husband's. After another quick kiss, he released her.

"Come on, Jake," Ross said, slapping the younger man between the shoulder blades and keeping his hand there companionably as they made their way through the crowd in the yard toward the house.

"*Men!*" Lydia turned an exasperated face toward her daughter, but it immediately converted into a smile. "You look beautiful, Banner."

"Thanks, Mama." It was good to hear it. Jake certainly hadn't complimented her on how she looked. His indifference piqued her more than she could imagine, and that in itself was an irritant. "Everything looks wonderful. You've gone to too much trouble as usual."

"I had lots of help. Ma and the boys."

"The boys" was Lydia's collective term for Lee and Micah. "Where are they anyway? I miss those two, though why I do, I can't imagine."

Lydia smiled and touched Banner's hair which was perfectly coiffed. She had piled it high, but left wisps to coil against her cheeks and neck. A green satin ribbon that matched her dress had been wound though the dark strands. "They wouldn't admit it in a million years, but they miss you too."

"They have no one to torment."

"All of your friends are here," Lydia said softly, knowing how difficult it would be for Banner to face them the first time. "They're clustered under the pecan tree."

"I'll go see them now." Banner squeezed her mother's hand in reassurance.

"Have a good time."

Banner nodded and wended her way through the crowd. She went out of her way to speak to everyone, smiling brightly, tossing her head, letting everyone know that she hadn't fallen to pieces after what Grady had done to her. The shame was his, not hers. She intended for everyone to know that and held her head proudly.

"Georgia, Bea, Dovie, hello," she called out as she reached the group of young women. They were all dressed in summer pastels. As Banner approached them, decked out in the bright leaf green, they all faded to blandness by comparison.

"Banner!" they chorused, and gathered around her.

They exchanged pleasantries and gossip about mutual acquaintances. Since she hadn't seen them for several weeks, she was behind on current events. When they asked Banner if it were true that she was ranching, she answered in the affirmative and then went on to describe her life much more colorfully than it warranted.

But their interest in fences and corrals and crossbreeding

quickly waned and the talk turned to engagements and weddings and tea parties and babies and china patterns. It didn't take long for Banner to become very bored, and she wondered if she had ever been as shallow and shortsighted as they.

Excusing herself, she wandered off. She came up behind Lee and Micah, who had their shoulders propped against a tree. Unaware that she was within hearing distance, their conversation was much more interesting than that of her girlfriends.

"You think she does?"

"Hell yes. You can tell by her eyes. Their eyes always give them away."

"What about Lulu Bishop?"

"Hmm. I don't know. Probably not. Too scared of her mama."

"Yeah, but I hear she opens her mouth when she kisses."

"Who told you?"

"The fellow who works in her daddy's feed store."

"The one from Indian territory?"

"Yep. Think he was lying?"

"Might have been."

"Now Bonnie Jones . . ."

"Nice on top, huh? Big and ripe as melons." Micah's elbow found Lee's side and they chuckled together. "Bet they taste just as juicy too."

"I touched 'em once," Lee bragged.

"The hell you say," Micah scoffed, straightening and facing his friend in challenge.

"Swear to God."

"When?"

"About two years ago. Even then they were bo-da-cious. We were at the Fourth of July celebration the church gave for all the young folks."

"The church!" Micah said beneath his breath. "Are you lying?"

"No! You should have come."

"I had the trots and Ma wouldn't let me. What happened with Bonnie?"

"We sneaked off from the others. You know that place in the river where the rapids are. She leaned out over the rocks, lost her balance, and nearly fell in the water. When I reached out to catch her, that's what I caught."

"Liar."

"I swear."

"What'd she do?"

"Oh, she blushed and straightened her dress. She said, 'Lee Coleman, you best watch where your hands are touching.'"

"I said, 'I'm watchin' 'em, Bonnie honey, I'm watching 'em.' I was looking right down on 'em, ya see."

Micah snickered. "Then what happened?"

Lee's face fell. "Then the Sunday school teacher came thrashing through the woods, rounding all of us up for fireworks. Hell, if I'd had Bonnie alone for another sixty seconds, there would have been some fireworks all right." He tossed down a piece of bark he'd peeled off the tree. "Heard she's marrying a guy from Tyler. Tell you what, he's in for a real treat on their wedding night."

"You two are positively disgusting." Banner stepped from the shadows and nudged her way between them. She glared at them with an air of superiority.

"Hellfire, Banner," Lee said angrily, "we didn't know you were there."

"Obviously."

"Up to your old tricks again?" Micah asked, smiling. "Spying on us?"

Banner's good nature won out and she giggled. "You're more entertaining than anyone else at this party. But, Lee, how dare you talk about one of my friends that way? Bonnie Jones is a nice girl and if you touched any part of her anatomy, I'm certain she was mortified and highly offended."

"You shouldn't have been listening," he defended himself. "This is the kind of thing men discuss."

"And how would you know what *men* discuss?" He frowned threateningly, but she wasn't in the least intimidated. "What would you do if someone discussed me like that?"

Both of them all but growled with an instinct to protect. "I'd tear the hair off their heads," Lee said.

"Well, if Bonnie had a brother... Who invited *her?*" Banner stopped midsentence to comment on the arrival of another young woman who joined the group still gathered under the pecan tree.

"Who?" Micah asked, his eyes scanning the crowd. More people were dancing now and it was difficult to distinguish faces.

"Dora Lee Denney. I can't stand her."

The boys cast knowing glances at each other. "How come?"

"She's sneaky and snooty and snide."

"She's right pretty though," Micah observed.

"Hmph!" Banner had always thought the blue-eyed blonde was tacky. Her hair was too elaborately styled, her clothes too fussy, her perfume too strong. What Banner disliked most was the way Dora Lee ingratiated herself with men and women alike. She dominated every conversation and her favorite topic was herself. She always spoke in syrupy tones that Banner knew were false. Often Banner had wanted to punch Dora Lee in her petulant mouth just to get one honest reaction out of her.

"I'd better go back and see what she's saying. It would be just like her to tell everybody that I had attempted suicide after the wedding."

She left them. Micah stared after her, watching as she insinuated herself into the circle of young women again. "What do you think?"

Lee's eyes were focused in the same direction as Micah's. "I don't care if my sister likes Dora Lee or not. I'd like a chance to sample some of that. How about you?"

"I was thinking the same thing. Nothing serious, you understand. Just a nice, quick roll in the hay."

"Yeah," Lee agreed, his eyes narrow and hazy. "Reckon she does?"

"Wouldn't surprise me. You can tell by—"

"Their eyes," Lee finished.

"What can you tell by their eyes?" Jake struck a match

against the tree and both boys jumped guiltily. He laughed at their confounded expression.

He had stepped out on the porch after his visit with Ross, wishing he didn't have to endure this party. He should ride into town and raise hell, blow off steam. What he needed was some good whiskey, some bad woman, some hard gambling. Maybe then the images of Banner would be blotted from his mind and he could go on with his life as he had before that cursed night in the barn.

Pictures of her were flashing through his mind so vividly he had expected Ross to know what he was thinking about. Banner in her bridal nightgown, Banner in the tight britches, Banner serving him dinner, Banner lighting his cigar, Banner standing on the stool with her back turned and her fanny in the air, Banner just out of the bath. Banner, Banner, Banner. She had a monopoly on his thoughts. He wouldn't have been surprised if Ross had cursed him, lunged out of his chair with a pistol drawn, and put a bullet right between his eyes. And for what Jake was thinking about his daughter, Ross would have been vindicated.

But Ross had treated him as he always had, and that had make Jake feel even worse. He'd been glad when Lydia called their visit to a halt by sticking her head around the office door and demanding that Ross come out to greet the mayor of Larsen who had just arrived.

The moment Jake stepped out on the porch, he spotted Banner. She was laughing with her friends. He was glad she was laughing. She had looked so stark and wounded after what he had said to her that afternoon. But it had been necessary to hurt her. He had felt compelled to insult her in the cruelest, crudest way. She would be better off seeing his true nature right now so she would get any romantic notions out of her head.

Seeking diversion from his tumultuous thoughts, Jake had ambled toward Lee and Micah, whose heads were bent together like conspirators. He had guessed they were up to no good and he had guessed right, if their guilty expressions were any indication.

"How come all the girls are over there and the two of you are lurking in the dark over here? Did they scare you off?"

"Naw," Micah told his older brother. "We were just discussing women in general and one in particular."

"Which one in particular?"

They pointed out Dora Lee. "What about her?" Jake asked with mild interest.

"We were just speculating on whether the rumors we've heard about her are true," Lee said.

"What are the rumors?" Jake's analytical eyes hadn't left the girl who was chatting with much hand gesturing and eyelash batting. He could tell even from this distance that Dora Lee was the kind of woman he despised. She thought too highly of herself and of her appeal, just as Priscilla Watkins always had. She was smug about her prettiness and her motions were calculated.

But that was just the kind of woman he needed tonight, one he had absolutely no tender feelings for.

"The rumor is that she, you know . . ." Micah finished with a wink.

Jake's smile was slow and lazy. "Oh, yeah? Well, maybe I can settle the matter here and now." He stepped away from them and they were left to admire him with awe.

"Jake," Micah whispered after him, "watch it. She's the mayor's daughter."

Jake grinned another of those heart-stopping, but dangerous, smiles. "That's the best kind." He winked at the boys who poked at each other's ribs punishingly.

"Mama and Papa wanted me to go to that new girls' school in Waco, but I—"

Dora Lee suspended her boasting recital and stared at the man who was walking through the dancers. In the lantern light, his hair shone white, though his skin was dark. Even from afar she could tell that his eyes were intensely blue. "Who is that?" she whispered.

Banner followed her gaze and spotted Jake coming through the crowd of bobbing dancers. His hips rolled as he walked in a loose-boned cowboy stagger that somehow called attention to the place where his gunbelt bisected his middle. If she had noticed the decisive evidence of his sex earlier, she was sure that the lascivious Dora Lee did now.

Nor could the breadth of his shoulders be disguised beneath the white cotton shirt stretched taut over their width, and the black leather vest that looked as soft as butter. The red bandana tied around his throat lent him a rakish air. He looked as cunning as a tomcat that had just caught a mouse, and as dangerous as a mountain lion on the prowl.

Jake stopped, took the cheroot from his mouth, dropped it in the dirt and ground it beneath the toe of his boot. Every movement was sensuous, slow, deliberate.

"That's Jake Langston," Banner said. "He's my foreman."

Dora Lee had bitterly regretted missing Banner's wedding. She had missed it on purpose, going to Galveston for an extended visit with a cousin so she wouldn't have to celebrate "Banner Coleman Day," as she had scathingly called it. She never liked sharing the spotlight with anyone, especially Banner, who outclassed her on every point.

But when Dora Lee returned from her trip and learned what had transpired, she had been furious with herself for missing what she considered a much deserved comeuppance for Banner. She had also heard talk of the cowboy who had rallied to the Colemans' defense. She had thought the accounts of him were exaggerated, but obviously they weren't.

Jake kept up that predatory gait until he stood within a few feet of the gape-mouthed Dora Lee. "Dance?" That was all he said. It was enough. For once having nothing to say, Dora Lee glided toward him and allowed herself to be swept into his arms and away from the group of envious young ladies.

Banner felt something die inside herself. He hadn't even looked at her. His eyes had been trained on the girl she thought to be blowsy and loud and obnoxious and thoroughly unlikable.

Good! Let him have her! They deserved each other.

"Why are we all standing around here?" she said with forced gaiety. "Let's coax these gentlemen to dance."

She began circulating and flashing the smile that had tripped many a hopeful heart before she became promised to Grady Sheldon. Within seconds she had a partner, then another, then another. She whirled in time to the music, laughing gaily, smiling, convincing the young men she danced with that there was hope of winning her heart yet, and convincing her parents that she had come through a terrible ordeal unscathed.

But Banner cataloged every move Dora Lee and Jake made. She knew when his arms tightened and pulled her closer to him, and she knew when Dora Lee submitted and allowed it. She also knew the moment they disappeared behind the barn.

Within minutes Jake was cursing himself for coaxing Dora Lee into the shadows. She was stupid and vain and silly, but he had known that when he went after her. Her predictability was wearisome. She pretended coyness, but surrendered with a notable lack of resistance.

The conquest had been too easy, and there was no thrill to what he found when he peeled her bodice back and bared her breasts to moonlight and his eyes.

"I don't usually let a man—"

"Yes, you do." He kissed her neck, then raised his head to test her reaction to his lack of chivalry.

She gazed up at him with vacuous eyes. She wet her lips and tried again. "But I really like you, Jake."

"Then show me," he whispered raspily.

Her tongue whipped around his mouth like a striking snake. She tasted disagreeably like dill pickles. He wanted none of her, but forced himself to fill his hand with her generous breast. His body responded to the touch of female flesh, but from the waist up, there was not a whit of desire to be found in him. He could have her, possibly slake a longing that had been building in him for weeks. But the relief would be temporary. The hunger would come back tomorrow, because it was for someone else.

He wasn't being fair to this girl, silly and self-centered though she was. Since when had the heartbreaker Jake Langston started worrying about fairness? Since the night in the barn. He was getting soft and sentimental in his old age. Ordinarily he would have taken a tart like Dora Lee without a moment's hesitation.

Instead he kindly pushed her away. "We'd better get back." Anxious now to be rid of her, he fumbled with the buttons on her dress. He saw that she was about to object and rushed to add, "I don't want your pa to come looking for you."

To save face, Dora Lee pretended that she had called a halt to things and restored her hair with swift, trembling hands. "I don't want you to get the wrong idea about me. I guess I lost my head there for a moment when I let you touch me. I . . . want your respect." She prattled on until they returned to the party.

Immediately Jake excused himself from her and went to get a beer. He took a long drink just as Lee and Micah came rushing up to him, breathless and wide-eyed. "Well?"

He smiled sadly at their innocence and wished for a moment he had his back. "Dora Lee definitely does. Good luck."

The party wound down. Jake spent some time with Ma, whom he had sorely neglected to visit. She rested in a rocker on the porch, fanning herself. He tried to keep his mind on their conversation, but his eyes continually strayed to Banner. She danced with every man there, young and old.

And she had a damn good time doing it too. Did she have to hold her head at just that angle, baring her throat to that yokel who looked like he wanted to take a bite of it? Wasn't that jackass holding her too tight and didn't she care? Who was she waving at? Who was that brilliant smile for? And if Randy asked her to dance one more time, Jake was going to have to do something about that stud once and for all. Castration came to mind.

He whipped himself into a fine froth. By the time the guests had left and Jake made his way to their waiting wagon, his gut was coiled so tight he was ready to hit something.

They made their goodbyes.

"Wonder what that is?" Ross asked. He gazed toward the northeastern horizon. It was tinted a dull red.

"Fire," Jake replied, following Ross's gaze.

Micah whistled through his teeth. "Must be a helluva fire to light up the sky like that."

"I wonder what it could be. It's a good distance from town," Lydia said.

"Brush maybe," Ross said reflectively. "We need rain something bad. It's been a dry spring."

That seemed to satisfy everyone's curiosity about the fire. But it wasn't burning nearly as brightly as the green jealousy in Banner's eyes.

TWELVE

"Ross, this is—"

"Be quiet, woman, and kiss me."

"But—"

Ross covered Lydia's mouth with his, stopping her insincere protests. Knowing he enjoyed the chase, she sometimes gave him one. But her responding kiss was just as hungry as his.

He pulled her down onto the blanket in the hay and rolled her beneath him, heedless of the havoc he wreaked on the dress she had worn to their party. The guests had departed, the musicians had packed up their instruments and left for home, Ross had sent Ma to her cabin without letting her start the clean-up, everyone at River Bend had retired. They were left blissfully alone.

As his tongue went on darting, teasing forays into her mouth, his hands pillaged her hair, seeking out pins with nimble fingers and pulling them free.

"Shame on you," she breathed, when at last he released her mouth to nuzzle her neck.

"I had about all I could stand of manners and respectability for one night." He chuckled. "I needed some good ol' vice, a reminder of my wicked youth."

"So that's why you dragged me up to the hayloft rather than into our nice, respectable bedroom."

"There's something naughty about making love in a haystack, isn't there?"

"You ought to know," she said with mock primness. "You've brought me up here on more than one occasion in the middle of the day. I was always afraid the children would catch us while they were playing hide and seek."

Ross laughed as his hands worked free the buttons on her bodice. "That threat only added to the excitement."

She plowed her finger through his dark hair and lifted his head to see his face. "I don't need anything to add to the excitement. Every time I've made love with you has been exciting."

"That kind of talk can get you in a heap of trouble, lady," he warned in a low, vibrating voice.

"I like this wildness in you," she whispered. "That streak of Sonny Clark is still there if anybody but me knew to look for it. You're my outlaw and I love you, no matter what name you live under."

His eyes rained emerald fire down on her. The emotions that shimmered from her face were as untamed as his own. "I love you, Lydia."

"I know. I love you too."

They kissed with a heat that hadn't cooled in twenty years of living together. Hasty hands tore at clothes they couldn't be rid of fast enough. He reached beneath her skirt and petticoats and unfastened her drawers. When she was free of them he lifted her on top of him to straddle his hips. Their hands engaged in frantic combat over the buttons of his trousers.

Cries of ecstasy echoed in the still, quiet barn when they came together. As passionately in love with him as ever, Lydia's head fell back and she rode his hard body. She allowed him liberties with her breasts. He primed them with hands that knew just what to do to give her the most pleasure, then took them into his mouth to love.

"Ross, Ross, Ross!" She collapsed onto his chest when the climax came.

He reached high into her at the instant of his release. As always, he died a little, only to be renewed, refreshed, and reborn. Lydia always returned as much as she gave.

They lay together quietly, breathing rapidly, listening to the song of the cicadas in the trees outside. She unbuttoned his shirt and sifted chest hairs through her fingers. They murmured love words, they kissed—the intensely private exchanges of lovers who are familiar and devoted. Finally, they drifted into more meaningful conversation.

"Banner seems to be fine, don't you think?"

Ross sighed, shifting to draw Lydia closer. "I think so. She's intelligent. She's as stubborn as another female I could name." He pinched her bottom lightly. "It would take someone with bigger balls than Grady Sheldon's to defeat Banner."

Lydia snickered and tweaked a chest hair. "But weren't you worried about her? For a while? Just a little?"

"Yes. I was worried. You knew it all along, didn't you?" She nodded, rubbing her smooth cheek against his nipple. "I can't quite get used to the idea that our baby girl isn't a baby anymore. Banner is a woman and has to stand on her own two feet. She'll be held accountable for any decisions she makes from now on and that frightens me. She's so damn impulsive. It's easier to leave Lee to his own devices, I guess because he's a boy. But I want to go on protecting Banner." He ground his chin against the top of Lydia's head. "I love both our children so much, sometimes I'm afraid for them."

Lydia squeezed her eyes closed. She knew the kind of parental panic he was talking about. Each time Lee or Banner left her sight, a desperate feeling of finality clutched at her heart. She was always afraid that might be the last time she would see them. Such notions were foolish, but every parent had them.

Lifting herself slightly to gaze down at Ross, she said, "Maybe we wouldn't feel that way if we . . . if *I* had been able to have more children."

That again, Ross thought.

He turned his head to gaze up at her. He still thought hers was the most beautiful face he had ever seen. It wasn't traditionally pretty as Victoria Gentry's had been. But it had much more life, vitality, character, spirit. Her sherry-colored eyes glowed with the personality of the woman inside. Ross took in each lively feature, the cascade of tumbled hair and the well-kissed fullness of her mouth.

"Lydia, you have made me happier in the last twenty years than I ever knew was possible. I told you that the number of children we had wasn't important to me."

She lowered her eyes self-consciously. "I know that's what you've *told* me. I just hope it's so."

"It is. I wouldn't change anything about our lives since the day we left Jefferson with Moses and the baby."

"I'm so glad you already had Lee. And I'll be grateful to God for the rest of my life for giving us Banner. I only wish I had been able to have more of your children. I'll always regret that, Ross."

This had been an issue between them for a long time. She couldn't accept the fact that she hadn't conceived after Banner was born. He had assured her a thousand times that he didn't feel shortchanged. He loved Lee. His son may have been born of another woman, but Lydia had nourished him. And Banner. Banner, the child he had created with Lydia, was very special.

He wanted to take that sad expression off her face forever. But he knew it would recur. All he could do was go on reassuring her. His hand found her breast warm and full. He cupped it lovingly and finessed the nipple with his thumb until it beaded.

"There's nothing to regret, Lydia," he whispered softly. "You have done nothing but please me. Ever." He raised his head and pressed his lips against her breast. She watched as his mustache surrounded her nipple. His lips enfolded it. His mouth sucked it. Then he stroked it with his tongue.

Her eyes closed. She breathed his name repeatedly and wondered if God would punish her for loving Ross more than she loved Him. Ross rolled her on her back and covered her body with his. He was hard again and she was dewy with need. He drew back and in one long, slow plunge gave her his love.

Lydia's thoughts, those both happy and sad, scattered as the winds of passion rushed through her once more.

Banner tore the pins from her hair and flung them into the darkness. She struggled with each one. They had secured themselves in her hair with the tenacity of fish hooks. As soon as she worked one free, she flicked it from her fingers over the wagon's edge before she could scream. She was in a tizzy.

"What the hell are you doing?"

"Taking down my hair."

"Why?"

"Because I can't stand it up any longer."

"What's the matter with it?"

She shook her head, sending her hair flying in every direction. When a silken coil slapped Jake in the face, he brushed it away.

"Stop that!"

"It's hurting my head and I like to feel the wind blowing through it. Not that it's any of your business."

Jake made a grunting sound and kept his eyes trained on the rump of the horse pulling the wagon. "Well, be still. You might fall off the wagon and break your neck."

Banner was fuming. She was restless and couldn't sit still. Like a kettle about to come to a boil, she seethed. She was virtually bristling with pent-up anger. As a kid, she had butted her head into Lee's stomach to start a brawl when she was furious with him. That's the way she felt now. She was spoiling for a fight and would seize any excuse Jake gave her to have one.

But he did nothing but drive the wagon and smoke that damned cheroot. No doubt his thoughts were concentrated on that little snot Dora Lee. Banner couldn't dismiss from her mind their images as they strolled back into the thick of the party.

Dora Lee had cast a gloating, telling glance toward her. Jake had whispered something to Lee and Micah that caused them to laugh. No doubt he had said something thoroughly revolting and indecent. Banner had wanted to slap them all as hard as she could.

Instead she had danced and laughed, pretending to have the time of her life, when in fact she had never been so angry and miserable. Every time her mind conjured up a picture of Jake kissing Dora Lee the way he had her, darts poisoned with jealousy speared through her. It oozed through her system, making her soul black and oily with it.

Even before Jake had returned for her wedding, she had been jealous of the time he spent with other people. Now her feelings of possessiveness had doubled. The jealousy was unreasonable, but she couldn't help feeling it.

"Did you enjoy the party?" she asked crisply. If she didn't break the tense silence, she would crack in two like a walnut shell.

"Uh-huh," he answered laconically, keeping his eyes straight ahead.

"Of course you did. I could tell you were having a good time by the way you strutted around in front of all the ladies." Banner tossed her head back. She arched her throat to look at the stars overhead and give an appearance of nonchalance. "I had a delightful time. I love to dance. My feet will probably be sore tomorrow, I danced so much." She wanted to remind him that she hadn't lacked plenty of partners.

"You can soak them if they are."

"I will." Damn that cool tone of his! "I suppose Dora Lee will have to soak hers too."

"You reckon?"

Banner laughed mirthlessly, a short, huffing laugh that barely said "Ha!" with a lot of force behind it. "She doesn't care who she danced with as long as he's male."

"'S that a fact?" He rolled the cigar from one side of his mouth to the other without using his hands. Banner had a good mind to jerk it out of his mouth and send it the way of the hairpins, but she didn't quite dare.

"Everybody in town knows her reputation with men."

"Hmm," Jake said musingly, "I thought she was kinda cute."

"Cute! I'll just bet you did."

"I did."

"Aren't you sorry you had to bring me home? I'm sure you'd much rather be escorting Dora Lee to her house."

He said nothing, only shrugged in a manner that fueled Banner's temper. "I saw you two sneaking off together. Is her trampy reputation well earned?" She didn't give him room to answer. "I'm sure it is. I saw the simpering, stupid expression on her face when you came back. Shameful." She shook her head and shuddered.

"I suppose you kissed her. And no telling what else. Did you touch her too? I've heard she lets . . . well, I can't even bring myself to say it." She tossed her head again. "She's so obscenely chesty. And so proud of it. Hmph! All her bosom is baby fat that never went away. I guess you were impressed with her figure. Did she show it off for you?"

Jake inhaled on his cigar, let the smoke slowly curl out of his mouth, then tossed the cheroot into the river as the wagon rolled over the bridge. "I never kiss and tell, Banner." He turned his head and pierced her with his light blue eyes. "And you, especially, should be glad I don't."

If he had slapped her, she couldn't have been more stunned. Or offended. Or hurt. She stared back at him blankly. The vituperative chatter ceased abruptly. She couldn't even draw a breath. All the air had been sucked from her body. And with it had gone her fighting spirit. She whipped her head around, unable to look at him any longer.

Jake cursed silently. He had been in a fit of jealous rage too. But he had sensed Banner's mood immediately. And since the wagon would have likely ignited if they'd both lost their tempers, he had squelched his own and given her room. He hated himself for what he was having to do. He was being cruel to be kind.

But maybe he was being *too* cruel. Maybe he should put

his arm around her and apologize. Maybe if he just held her...

No, Jake, he told himself. *If you put your arm around her, all your good intentions will be shot to hell.*

Her hair was too dark and seductive in the night. He had liked the feel of it against his face too much. Her scent was becoming something he missed when she wasn't around. She looked too delectable in that dress. Her breasts, swelling from the bodice, were too tempting with the moonlight, silvery and soft, spilling over them.

He tried telling himself that the tender spots forming on his heart for her were those of an uncle for his niece. But that argument was no good. He was experiencing about the most unhealthy feelings for a niece that an uncle could have. Add incest to his sins.

No, Jake. Don't touch her. You've acted the fool more than once and both of you are paying for those lapses in judgment now. Don't act the fool again.

When he pulled the wagon into the yard, she almost fell out of it in her haste to get away from him. It broke his heart to watch her marching proudly toward her front door, head high, back straight, when he knew she was humiliated beyond endurance. He couldn't let her leave him without saying something.

"Banner."

She stopped. Her head fell forward for a heartbeat, then snapped up before she turned around and faced him defiantly. "Yes?"

"I shouldn't have said that."

"But it's true, isn't it?"

His eyes skittered from one object to another to keep from looking at her, to keep from feeling her suffering and knowing that in order to be safe, he couldn't do anything to alleviate it. But he could postpone saying good night. "Ross told me about a cattle broker in Fort Worth. He thinks this man could put together a small herd for us at a fair price. What do you think?"

She didn't want to talk about cattle. She wanted to ask why he was being so hateful to her. Did he hate her? Did he hold her in contempt for what she had done with him? Did he ridicule her clumsy attempts to lure him back and into marriage?

"Whatever you think, Jake. You're my foreman."

"Yeah, well," he said awkwardly, fingering the leather reins in his fingers. "I guess I ought to to go Fort Worth soon and see him."

"If you think that's best."

He nodded. "Well, good night," *Please, Banner, don't look at me like that. I want to hold you, but I can't.*

"Good night." *Jake, why are you punishing me for a sin that belonged to both of us? Don't hate me for it.*

"Lock up good now, hear?" *I remember how sweet you were, Banner, and I want you again. But I can't, I can't . . .*

"I will. Good night." *You were so sweet to me that night, so tender and caring. Why are you being so mean to me now?*

She went into the dark house alone and closed the door behind her. He waited until he saw the lamp's glow in her bedroom before he pulled the wagon into the barn.

"Oh, my Lord."

The three logs of firewood rolled from Banner's arms and thudded to the ground. One hand flew to her lips to trap a small scream. The other flattened over her lurching stomach. "What are you doing here?"

Grady Sheldon stepped out of the shade on the porch and took a hesitant step toward her. "How are you, Banner?" he asked humbly.

Banner recovered from her shock at seeing him, though it had been alarming. Jake and the cowboys were working far beyond the house, clearing a pasture of post oaks and scrub brush. She was alone at the house and had just gone to the woodpile on the far side of the barn. It would have startled her to see any man waiting on her porch, much less this one.

But now that her initial fear had subsided, she was consumed with fury at his gall. She bent down to retrieve the logs. When she straightened, her eyes drilled through him as though he wasn't there. "I'll tell you how I am,

Grady. I'm amazed you have the nerve to face me. And if you aren't gone in ten seconds, I'll shoot you."

She stalked past him, making her way to the front door. But he caught her arm and forced her to a halt. "Banner, please. I need to talk to you."

"Well, I don't need to talk to you. Now let go of me and get away from here. Don't come back."

"You heard about my . . . my wife?"

She dropped the wood on the porch and faced him squarely. The fire that had killed Wanda and Doggie Burns had been the big news in town the day after the party. Jake had told her about it when he returned after a trip into Larsen. That had been two weeks ago.

"I was sorry to hear about that, Grady. Her death was tragic, but it has nothing to do with me."

"It does, Banner," he said anxiously. "I want to talk to you, explain things. I never got a chance to explain. That's not fair, is it?"

"What you did wasn't fair either, Grady. Excuse me now. I have to get dinner started." She went through the door and turned to close it. Before she did, she said, "I don't want to see you anymore. Don't come back."

He had reined his horse on the other side of the corral. That's why she hadn't noticed it as she crossed the yard. Now she watched from the parlor window as he rode out of sight. Only then did she realize that she was trembling. Wiping her damp hands on her pants legs, she went into the kitchen to prepare supper.

She decided not to mention Grady's visit to Jake. It would only make him angry. They had been civil to each other since the night of the party, civil and constrained. She hadn't stuck to her vow to feed him from a tray left on the porch, but as soon as he finished eating each night, he rode into town. She didn't want to think about where he went. To the saloon? To see Dora Lee? She never fell asleep until he returned.

They were at least coexisting peacefully. Grady's appearance wasn't worth sparking Jake's ire, and there was no reason to tell him. She was certain Grady wouldn't have the gumption to come back.

But he did. The next day, in fact. At about the same time. She wondered later if he had planned his visit when he knew she would be alone while the men were working away from the house. This time, he knocked on the back door. He was holding out a bouquet of flowers when she opened it.

She stared at the flowers, but didn't reach for them. "I told you not to come back."

"May I come in?"

"No. Go away, Grady. I thought I made it plain to you—"

"Please, Banner. Please."

She eyed him closely. He had changed. His face no longer looked boyishly handsome, squeaky clean, open and honest. There was a weariness about his mouth and eyes that she had never seen before. He looked haggard. The changes were subtle, but obvious nonetheless.

Pity tugged at her heart. Had he suffered as much as she? Impossible. Men came away from these scandals unaffected. Lydia had said so.

It might have been pity, or it might have been a determination that she appear unafraid of him that compelled her to let him inside. Timidly he stepped over the threshold. She didn't offer him a chair. He awkwardly held the flowers, then leaned forward and laid them on the table.

"Banner, I know you must hate me."

"I don't hate you. I have no feelings for you one way or another. Whatever emotion I felt for you died the instant I knew you had been unfaithful to me."

He stared down at his shoes. Damn her. He hated playing a meek and mild toady, coming to her like some penitent. For a little of nothing he would tell all the Colemans to take the next train straight to hell. But he might need them later on. The last two weeks had been the worst of his life.

First he had had to pretend shock, if not anguish, over the fire that had destroyed the Burns place and taken the lives of his wife and father-in-law. Then there was the ordeal of the inquest. It had turned out just as he had hoped it would. The fire and deaths were ruled accidental, but he hadn't liked the sidelong glances the sheriff and everybody else in town gave him.

He needed an alliance with the high and mighty Colemans. If he were reinstated with them the town would accept him again. His business was still sound and prospering because his was the only timber mill and lumberyard around, but people no longer treated him with respect. He could read the disdain in their eyes.

And, dammit, he wanted all those acres of timberland that Banner Coleman now owned. To get that, he had to eat humble pie in front of her. He had to appear a broken man. Women loved to be in a position to forgive a man something. They couldn't resist having that superiority over him. Banner wouldn't be the exception. He would bet on that.

"Banner, what happened in the church was ghastly. I hated it for you more than for me because I knew what you must be going through, what you were thinking about me."

"You embarrassed me and my family in front of the whole county."

"I know."

"That isn't something I'll likely forgive and forget any time soon, Grady."

"But I hope you will in time," he said earnestly. "After I've had a chance to explain about Wanda."

"I don't want explanations. Just say goodbye and leave."

"Please, Banner. Please listen to me." He wet his lips and took an anxious step forward, his hands extended suppliantly. "I felt terrible about the way she died, and the baby and all. But . . . but I feel like someone who had been sentenced to life imprisonment and just got released. Surely you must know that a girl like Wanda meant nothing to me."

"You made love with her!" she cried.

He hung his head. "I know, I know. Believe me, I've regretted it with every breath I've drawn since then. I was with her just one time, Banner. I swear that. Only one time," he lied. "And it's not like . . . well, it's not 'making love' with a girl like that. It's something else altogether. I don't think I was that baby's father—I pray to God I wasn't—but there was no way to prove it.''

"None of that matters. The point is you betrayed me and the love you claimed to have for me.''

"I know it's hard for you, as a woman, as a lady, to understand that kind of passion.'' His eyes were still downcast so he didn't see Banner suddenly pale. "It just happens that way sometimes, Banner. Before you know what's happened, you've done something to regret.''

When he risked raising his head to gauge the effect of his confession, she was no longer looking at him, but staring out the window over the sink.

"It happened so fast,'' he rushed on, taking her silence for pensiveness. "I went out there to buy some whiskey. She was alone. She . . . she . . . well, you can imagine how immodest she was. I had just been with you. I wanted you so badly. And when Wanda . . . well . . . I pretended for just a few minutes that it was you I was kissing. Only she wouldn't stop, Banner. She kept on and on, touching me. I shouldn't be talking to you about such things, I know. But she touched me, in private places, you know, and said things to me that—''

"Please,'' Banner whispered, gripping the rim of the drainboard so hard her fingers ached. "Stop.''

Like a taunting litany, she could hear herself begging Jake to take her. She had pleaded, cajoled, connived, using every argument she could think of, even going so far as to remind him of his love for her mother. Scalding tears blinded her. Lord, no wonder he held her in such contempt. Just as Grady did his whore.

"You would have to be a man to understand, Banner. But when it gets past a certain point, there's no going back. A man loses control. I hated myself afterward, couldn't believe I had done it. I swear I didn't touch her or another woman after that. I wanted only you. I love you.''

She wiped at her tears and Grady's spirits lifted, thinking they were for him. When she turned to him she asked, "What do you want from me? Why did you come here?''

"I want you back. I want us to be married.''

"That's impossible."

He shook his head stubbornly. "No, it isn't. Not if you forgive me. Banner, I appeal to you. I made one mistake. One unfortunate mistake. It came at the worst possible time in my life. Please don't make me pay for it forever. Say you'll think about taking me back. I can't live without you. I love you so much."

She marveled over how empty the words sounded. Only weeks ago she had thought she loved him as he professed to love her. But had she loved him? What did she feel now? Only sadness for him. But love? More and more she was coming to believe that the word was meaningless. It was applied to a variety of emotions for lack of any other word so encompassing.

Who was she to judge Grady for his fall from grace when hers had been just as hard and just as far? He had betrayed her love, yes, but hadn't she betrayed those who loved her? Her parents? Ma and Lee and Micah? Jake himself?

Jake. She was in love with him. There, she admitted it.

She had loved him all her life and it had been a happy, bubbling feeling inside her that welled to the surface and overflowed every time she saw him. It had been a wholesome love, one she could openly express.

But *this* love, this love was different. It had brought her nothing but misery. It was swathed in secrecy. It couldn't be celebrated. It couldn't *be*.

Grady offered her a safe way out. If she married him she would live, if not happily, then at least contentedly. She would be free of this strife that made her want to tear her heart out to keep it from breaking. But she had reservations about Grady's proposal. He wasn't the same dapper young man, sure of himself and his future. The stigma of his indiscretion would haunt him for a long time. His apologies seemed sincere enough, but could she ever trust him again?

As though reading her mind, he said, "I know you might not believe me. But everything I've said is true, Banner. I adore you. You're all I've ever wanted."

She wondered if he would be quite so ready to claim her as his bride if he knew she was no longer a virgin. If Grady had changed, she had changed more. The bright and bouncy Banner Coleman he had first proposed to no longer existed.

"I don't think we can ever go back—"

He held up his hand. "Don't give me an answer today. Just think about it."

Banner was suddenly tired, fatigued to the point of collapsing. She just wanted him to leave. "I'll think about it. I need time."

"I understand." He garnered enough courage to reach for her hand and carry it to his lips. He kissed it tenderly before releasing it. It fell listlessly back to her side, dangling limply from her arm. "I won't give up, Banner, until you say yes."

He turned on his heel and went out the door.

Banner sank into a chair, buried her face between her hands and wept. For weeks, since the party and that horrid afternoon prior to it, she had kept her tears damned behind a stubborn will. Now they gushed from her eyes in hot, salty streams.

How simple life would have been if the wedding had gone off as planned. She would have been blissfully happy never to know about Grady's dalliance with Wanda Burns or anybody else. She and Jake would still be friends. There wouldn't be this animosity between them. How had she ever convinced herself that going to him in the barn that night would be an answer to her problems? How?

She jerked her head around when she heard the tread of Jake's boots at the back door. He swung the door open after one swift knock and called her name. She averted her head, but not before he saw the streaks of her tears. "What's the matter? What's happened?"

"Nothing."

"Have you been crying?" He crossed the floor, his spurs ringing, and crouched down beside her chair.

"No."

"You have too. Don't lie to me."

He pushed his hat back and a lock of blond hair fell over his brow. As her heart twisted with love, her face crumpled. "Oh, Jake."

Suddenly his arms were around her and her face was buried in the crook between his neck and shoulder. Tears drenched his collar. Her hands clenched and unclenched against the muscles of his back.

He rubbed his face in her hair. His hands spread wide over her narrow back, drawing her closer, making her as much a part of him as possible. He didn't push her away until she had cried herself out and her sobs were reduced to soft hiccups absorbed by his bandana.

Only then did he clasp her upper arms and lift her from his chest to peer down into her face. "Do you want to tell me what's wrong?"

"Would you believe hayfever?"

He looked at the flowers. "You never had it as a kid."

"How do you know? You weren't here. You were always going off and leaving me."

His eyes came to rest on her chastising mouth and stayed. Even when he raised one hand to his mouth and pulled off the leather glove with his strong white teeth, his eyes didn't stray from her lips. He laid his thumb against them vertically. He glidingly moved it to one corner, slowly returned to the center, then slid it to the other side. "I'm sorry. For every time I left you, for every time I hurt you in any way, I'm sorry, Banner."

He laid the ungloved hand along her cheek. The other hand went around her waist and pulled her forward until her breasts were crushed against his chest again. Then he lowered his head and pressed his lips to hers.

A tremble of emotion rippled through her, a slight aftershock from her eruption of tears. Her arms curled up under his. Her hands met at his spine and her fingers intertwined across that ridged column.

"Who taught you to kiss, Banner?" he asked moments later against her mouth.

"You."

"This isn't the way I taught you. Open your mouth."

"I don't want you to think I'm a whore like that Watkins woman or a flirt like Dora Lee Denney."

"Oh, for Christ's sake." He sighed. "Kiss me right, will ya?"

He didn't exactly leave the choice up to her. His tongue probed the seam of her lips with such delicious persuasion that they parted. He tilted her head to one side with meager pressure of his hand on her cheek. Then his tongue probed deep, prowling and penetrating and pumping. It swirled to touch the roof of her mouth, the back of her teeth, the slick lining of her lips. It stroked evocatively, delving deeper into her mouth with each magic thrust.

He wasn't finished when he released her mouth. She sagged against him weakly, trustingly. He sipped the lingering tears from her eyelashes, touched the tip of her nose with the tip of his tongue, dropped light random kisses over her tear-stained cheeks. They nuzzled. And it was peaceful. And turbulent. And wonderful.

"Why were you crying, Banner?"

She smiled against his hard lean cheekbone. "I told you. Hayfever."

He sank his fingers into her hair, lifted it and caught her earlobe between his teeth. She gasped and he smiled. "Don't you know better than to pick flowers when you've got hayfever?"

"I didn't pick them."

"Where'd they come from then?"

"Grady brought them to me."

Jake's head snapped back. Seconds ticked by ponderously while he stared at her. Slowly he straightened his knees and rose to his full height. He took off his hat, which had somehow managed to stay atop his head during their embrace, and slapped it against his chap-covered thigh, creating a cloud of dust.

"I hope I heard you wrong."

"Grady brought them to me," she repeated, disliking the tight expression on his face.

"Grady Sheldon?" His lighthearted, pleasant tone was belied by the tension emanating from him.

Banner came out of the chair. "Yes, Grady Sheldon."

Jake's temper flared. He slapped his hat against the rack

near the door. Luckily it caught one of the pegs on the first pass. He faced Banner with his fists digging into his hips. "And you let him come in?"

His stance, his inflection, his expression clearly told her he thought she was stupid beyond belief. That did Banner's temper no good. "Why not?" She went to the sink for lack of anything better to do and needlessly, but viciously, began to pump water into it.

"Why not?" Jake's roar rattled the panes of glass in the window.

"Yes, why not? I was once engaged to marry him, remember?"

"Yeah, I remember," he said, advancing toward the sink. He peeled off his remaining glove and tossed it down on the table beside the other one. "I also remember him getting a hole shot in his shoulder the day of your wedding for putting a kid in some white trash girl."

She spun around. "You have such a quaint way of putting things," she said sarcastically.

"What were you thinking of to let him come in here with you alone?"

Now that Jake pointed that out to her, she realized how foolhardy she had been. Lee had told her later that Ross had threatened Grady's life in the church. A man as proud as Grady couldn't have taken that lightly. What if he had come here today seeking revenge instead of forgiveness? But he hadn't. Even if she had any qualms about letting Grady in now, she wasn't going to admit them to Jake. She faced him with cool detachment. "He's sorry for what happened. He's asked me to marry him."

Jake stared at her in mute incredulity. Finally he shook his head and laughed mirthlessly. "I hope you're not considering it."

"I might be."

Jake's eyes narrowed dangerously. He didn't trust Sheldon any further than he could throw him. To Jake's way of thinking the fire that had killed Wanda and her father smacked too much of coincidence. How it had started was still unexplained. He had hated the sonofabitch from the moment he saw him in the church. Jake had known immediately that Sheldon wasn't man enough for Banner. He had always detested shifty, sneaky, ambitious bastards like Sheldon.

"Did that little runt threaten you?"

"No!"

"Then what did he say?"

"That's my business."

"Don't get smart with me, Miss Coleman. Ross would kill Sheldon on sight if he knew he had come anywhere near you."

"And I suppose you'll blaze a trail right over to River Bend and report it."

Disgust showed in every weather-beaten feature of his face. "I'm not a tattletale, Banner, and you're not a child."

"That's right. I'm not. And I'm at liberty to accept flowers from any man I choose to. You're the foreman of Plum Creek. I defer to your judgment on business decisions, but until I ask your advice on my personal life, kindly keep it to yourself."

He didn't know whether to throttle her or kiss her again. But he was too mad to do either. He grabbed up his gloves, snatched his hat from the rack, and slammed out the door. His spurs spun crazily as his heels struck the hard-packed earth. He cursed in tune to them.

Spoiled rotten brat. She didn't know what was good for her. She wouldn't recognize good fortune if it came up and kicked her in the butt. She didn't know he was only trying to protect her from weasels like Sheldon and seducers like Randy.

And goddamned if she hadn't been kissing him with Sheldon's friggin' flowers lying right there on the table!

Why the hell he should care he didn't know. He had promised Ross he'd look after her. All right, he would. But he wouldn't be blamed if she got hooked up again with some no-account like Sheldon. Hell no, he wouldn't. If she got herself in a fix, it would be no more than she deserved.

Still, he knew as well as he knew the sun would come up tomorrow that he would kill Grady Sheldon before he would let the man touch her.

THIRTEEN

Cool gray eyes scanned the column of figures in the ledger and were pleased with the tally at the bottom. It showed a considerable profit. Let the church groups march with their silly signs that promised condemnation and God's wrath. Let the preachers warn of hellfire and brimstone. Inside the Garden of Eden, things couldn't be better.

A knock sounded on the door. Priscilla checked the small gold clock on her desk. It was time for Dub Abernathy's appointment. "Come in." Meticulously she locked the ledger in the bottom drawer of her desk. She was wealthy. No one knew quite how wealthy, and she intended to keep it that way.

Dub always blustered in, as swift and sudden as the first norther of the season. He did so today, but turned to close the door softly behind him so as not to wake the sleeping whores upstairs.

He had often wondered how Priscilla bore up under the hours she kept. She was up until the wee hours of the morning when the Garden of Eden closed. While her card dealers and prostitutes slept well into the afternoon in preparation for the evening to come, she worked in her office and entertained personal clients. He knew he wasn't the only one, though the number of that favored few was limited.

It was not surprising that Priscilla's saloon was the most profitable in town. Dedication such as hers went hand in hand with success. Dub was a Trojan himself, never satisfied with what he had, always hungry for more. He recognized that kind of greed in someone else.

"Priscilla, dear." He laid his bowler hat and cane on the satin-covered chair by the door and advanced into the room.

Priscilla's greeting was noticeably cooler than usual. "Hello, Dub." He crossed the room to take her into his arms and kiss her long and hard. Today, she avoided his embrace, going to the sideboard instead and pouring a shot of whiskey into a tumbler. "Drink?"

"Of course." He sensed her reserve, knew the reason for it, and cursed to himself. This liaison was becoming complicated. He enjoyed Priscilla and tremendously liked what they did in bed together. But soon he might have to make other arrangements.

A very attractive widow had recently joined his church. She lived alone in a quiet part of town in a comfortable house surrounded by a white picket fence. Only yesterday she had come into the bank seeking his advice about her finances. There was a definite possibility there. She might not have Priscilla's sexual expertise, but she could be coached. And weren't widows starved for affection? An affair of that sort wouldn't be subject to these complications. That was a big plus in the widow's favor.

Priscilla handed Dub the glass of whiskey and poured one for herself. She drifted into the bedroom beyond the office. Dub followed her like a faithful puppy. "You missed your appointment last week," she said idly, checking her appearance in the mirror of her dresser.

"I'm sorry, sweetheart. An emergency board meeting was called. I had no choice but to attend and there wasn't time to notify you. I hope you didn't worry."

"I didn't," she said to his reflection in the mirror. "I merely added the usual fee to your bill." She smiled, but the warmth didn't reach her eyes.

Dub squelched his irritation just in time to ask repentantly, "Are you angry with me?"

She turned to face him. Her hair was loose around her shoulders. She was dressed in a blue satin robe. Its long bell sleeves fell over her wrists in cascades of pearl-gray lace. The satin conformed to the lush figure beneath. One smooth thigh peeped through the folds of the robe in front.

"Not angry, Dub. Disappointed. The last time you were here, you promised to keep these religious fanatics out of my hair."

"I didn't promise."

"As good as promised. I thought you could sway public opinion."

"One man can only do so much against a growing mob."

"Mobs are just like sheep. They go where they're led. Put them onto some other cause. Get their attention off Hell's Half Acre."

"How do you propose I do that?"

"I don't care." She was pacing now, angrily tossing her head back and forth. "I've never asked you for favors, Dub. I don't now. All I want to do is run my business like any other citizen. What makes me any different from the butcher, baker, and candlestick maker? No one is raising hell about them." She pointed a finger at him. "And I'd bet next week's profits that they're not as honest in their business dealings as I am."

Dub sank wearily onto the chaise longue and rubbed his thumb and second finger into his eyesockets. He didn't need this today. He had escaped the pressures at the bank for a good frisky romp in Priscilla's bed and a few glasses of her Tennessee whiskey, that's all. No arguments. No scenes. He could have that in the boardrooms.

He lowered his hand and looked up at her. She was mad. Anger radiated off her in waves. Her eyes shone hard and cold. He had never noticed those unflattering lines around her mouth before. When had they gotten there?

"You hardly provide the same service as a baker, Priscilla," he said dryly. "How do you expect me to call off the dogs when this part of town is in constant turmoil? This past weekend one of your own girls was murdered."

Priscilla sat down on the padded stool in front of her vanity. She picked up a powder puff and dusted it across her palm and up the inside of her arm. "That's a hazard of this business and every girl who takes a paying customer into a bedroom knows that. She might be unfortunate enough to get a farmer whose wife found this life more exciting than

milking and gathering eggs, or a jealous lover, or a do-
gooder who takes a whore to bed, then sees it as his duty to
God to punish her for leading him astray.'' She shrugged her
shoulders eloquently. ''It happens all the time. 'Another
Fallen Dove Slain.' '' She quoted the familiar headline.

''There was a gunfight in the streets last week. Three
cowboys shot it out after a poker game. Two of them died.''

''That didn't happen in my place.''

''Still, decent folks don't—''

''Decent folks!'' she cried. She left her seat on the stool
and began pacing again. ''I'm sick up to here with decent
folks. What makes them decent? They're trying to ruin my
business. Is that decent? Is that what that preacher of theirs
tells them is the *decent* thing to do?'' She whirled on Dub.
''Do something about him.''

''I can't. He's got a following and it's growing. I warned
you about him, Priscilla. He's putting pressure on the
sheriff. Sooner or later the sheriff is going to sit up and pay
attention. That preacher's got voters on his side, lots of
voters, and this is an election year. If it takes closing down
Hell's Half Acre and boarding up the businesses in this part
of town, he'll do it to win next fall. The sheriff's ambitious.''

''He's a fraud. He's in here nearly every night right along
with the men he throws in jail.''

''I know that,'' Dub said patiently. ''And you know it.
But they''—he tilted his head in the direction of downtown—
''don't. Or if they do, they don't care so long as he keeps
the peace.''

''Shit,'' Priscilla muttered under her breath. She flounced
down on the stool again and crossed her legs. The robe
separated to accommodate her thighs. Her blue satin, high-
heeled mule with the egret feathers on the toe whisked back
and forth like an angry pendulum.

Dub was entranced by the length and shape of her leg. He
was growing bored with the conversation. It wasn't what he
had taken time out from his busy schedule for. His eyes
ventured up her leg to her lap, then to her breasts which
were trembling with agitation. Her nipples were hard and

pointed. The thickening in his groin became more pronounced by the second.

"Baby," he said in a conciliatory tone, "I know you're upset."

"Damn right I am."

"I'm doing what I can."

"It isn't enough."

"So I'll do better," he snapped. He was losing patience. How dare a whore have the gall to speak to him, Dub Abernathy, with no more deference that Priscilla did? That pretty widow lady had been as meek as a lamb in his office yesterday, speaking softly, weeping quietly, looking at him with limpid eyes that were filled with timorous respect. "Come on, Priscilla. Are you going to waste my hour away from the bank arguing?" He pouted at her like a little boy.

His theatrics didn't impress Priscilla. Dub was shrewd and manipulative and she knew it. She also knew that if it came down to protecting her or protecting himself, there would be no choice in his mind. Such selfish disloyalty only went to prove that a girl had to look out for herself. If she had a good time along the way, she was damned lucky.

She came to her feet slowly. Her fingers caught the ends of the robe's sash and pulled until the belt fell away and the satin parted. She was completely naked underneath. A sensuous shimmy of her shoulders sent the robe slithering down her body to pool around her feet.

"I don't ever want to argue with you, Dub. But your point is well taken. Your visits to me are too precious and too short for us to waste time discussing business." She ran her hands down her sides, skimming her thighs, trailing her fingers through the thatch of hair between them. "Maybe I should start coming to the bank for our business meetings."

He dragged his eyes up from her pelvis. Priscilla delighted in the sudden paling of his beefy cheeks. He gave a nervous little laugh and shifted uncomfortably on the chaise. "We both know you can't do that." He smiled sickly, not sure if she were joking or serious.

She took baby steps forward. "Then I suggest you get busy and get this preacher off my back so we won't have so many business-related things to talk about while you're here." By now, she was standing directly in front of him. He reached out to fondle her breasts, belly, and thighs. "What do you say, Dub? Will you do that for me?"

"Sure, Priscilla, sure. You can count on me to take care of it. I always have, haven't I?"

"Always. Don't disappoint me this time."

"I won't, I won't," he mumbled against her stomach as his hand slipped up between her thighs.

She drew him to his feet and kissed him wantonly while she lowered her hand to the fly of his trousers. "I depend on you," she whispered as the buttons were released with dispatch. She hissed in feigned surprise when her fingers closed around him. "You're so strong. So strong."

Eyes squeezed shut, teeth bared and clenched, Dub muttered incoherently. His arguments and his promises were massaged away by a deft hand. He was stroked straight to heaven by one of Satan's most illustrious angels.

"Lee! Micah!"

Banner joyfully rushed to hug them in greeting. They had followed Jake through the back door into the kitchen. "I didn't expect to see you two tonight."

"Have enough supper for us?"

"We'll make do." She was glad to see them. Their long, angular bodies seemed to shrink her kitchen, but she welcomed the racket and confusion that followed them in. Lately her house had been far too quiet.

"We decided to ride over before dark so we could look around," Lee said, after kissing her cheek.

Micah arrogantly flopped down in a chair. "We've got to give this place our stamp of approval, don'tcha know?"

She lunged toward him and tried to kick the back legs of his chair out from under him. He was too fast for her and let the front legs hit the floor before she could unbalance him. "Make yourself at home, Micah," she teased.

"Oh, I intend to, I intend to." He casually draped an arm over the top rung of the ladderback chair and gazed around.

"Have a seat, Lee." Suddenly Banner felt shy and

nervous. She had never cooked a whole meal for anyone but Jake. Would they make fun of her? "You, too, Jake, sit down," she said, meeting his eyes squarely for the first time since he had entered the house. "Supper's ready."

"Thanks."

"Let's see, I need to set two extra places." Quickly she turned away to get the extra place settings from the cabinet. She and Jake hadn't had much to say to one another since the day Grady had come to see her. It hadn't gone unnoticed that he stayed closer to the house, doing jobs that would constantly keep him in sight.

He had meant what he said. He intended to keep her away from Grady. She was both resentful and grateful, resentful of his unflagging vigilance and grateful that she didn't have to confront Grady again any time soon. No matter what she had said to Jake, or to Grady, she didn't want to marry him and hoped to put off giving him that answer as long as possible.

"It's just beef stew," she said apologetically as she approached the table with a china tureen and began ladling the aromatic stew onto their plates. "But it's Ma's recipe and we all know that nobody can make beef stew taste like ambrosia the way Ma can."

Lee shoved a huge spoonful into his mouth and after shifting it around, making huffing noises and fanning his mouth in front of his lips because it was so hot, he said, "It's good, kid."

"Not bad." Micah strengthened his comment with a wink.

Jake said nothing, but began to eat mechanically.

Banner brought cornbread to the table, glad that it had risen just right. It was golden and crunchy on the outside, light and grainy on the inside, not doughy. Ma had promised that it was a no-fail recipe.

Banner joined them at the table but could barely eat between bouts of laughter. Lee and Micah were as full of incredible stories and partial truths as ever. They regaled her with tales they swore were true, but which she seriously doubted.

It felt so good to laugh. Most evenings now, Jake was taciturn. They held desultory conversations about the ranch. That was all. He no longer went into town after dark, but she knew that was because he didn't want Grady to visit her in his absence.

Nor were there any more tender kisses like the one after her crying jag. That kiss might never have happened. They were extremely careful not to touch each other.

"I don't have any dessert except some of last year's blackberry jam for your cornbread."

"Sounds all right to me," Micah said, slicing himself another hunk of cornbread.

"Me too."

"If you'd let a lady know you were coming to supper instead of just dropping in," Banner said with mock annoyance, "she'd be better prepared."

"That was my fault." Jake pushed his place aside and scooted back his chair. "I met the boys at the river today and told them to come on over tonight. It'll be easier to get off in the morning if they're already here."

Banner returned from the pantry with the jar of blackberry jam. "Get off to where?"

"We're going to Fort Worth to bring those cattle home," Lee said excitedly. "Didn't Jake tell you?"

Her eyes turned toward Jake. "I guess he failed to mention it."

"I told you the night of the party."

"But not when."

"Tomorrow's the big day!" Micah slapped a spoonful of jam on his cornbread. "We're gonna raise he—"

"Micah!" Lee rolled his eyes warningly toward Banner.

"Gonna raise hell?" she asked sweetly.

Micah swallowed the cornbread without chewing it. "I only meant—"

"Oh, I know what you meant, Micah. I'm not stupid. Maybe Jake will introduce you to his friend Priscilla."

Lee dropped his spoon just short of the jam jar. It clattered to the table noisily as he gaped at his sister. "You know about *her?*"

Banner looked blandly at Jake, whose white brows were drawn into a glower. "Jake's told me quite a lot about her. She smokes cigars."

Both boys turned their heads toward Jake for confirmation. He made a negligent gesture with his hand. "She's guessing."

Banner only laughed. "Well, maybe I'll be able to meet the famous Priscilla Watkins myself. How long are we staying?"

Without moving another muscle in his body, Jake's eyes slid to her. "Micah, Lee, and I are staying for several days."

"What about me?"

"You aren't going."

Banner carefully blotted her mouth with her napkin, refolded it, and placed it beside her plate. When she lifted her eyes they were just as resolved as the blue ones they clashed with. "Yes, I am."

A muscle ticked in Jake's jaw. Otherwise he remained perfectly still. "Not this time, Banner."

"This time and every other time I choose to go." Her voice had a definite edge to it.

"Well, uh, we, uh, we gotta be goin'," Micah said. He came out of his chair too quickly and sent it crashing to the floor. Cursing, he bent to right it.

"Yeah. We got things to do," Lee said. "Come on, Micah, let's get busy." Together they bumbled and stumbled their way to the door.

"I've got to shake out my saddle blanket real good and . . ."

"And . . . uh, oh, yeah, what else were we gonna do, Lee?"

Lee pushed Micah through the door. "We'll just bed down in the barn. See ya in the morning," he called over his shoulder.

The comedy act had escaped Banner and Jake, who were still staring at each other like prize fighters from opposing corners of the ring.

"I'm going."

"You are not."

"Watch and see."

"I'm not taking a woman to Fort Worth to buy cows and that's that, Banner."

She shot out of her chair as straight as an arrow. "This is *my* ranch. Don't you think I should be consulted before you go off and buy cattle for it?"

Jake came out of his chair likewise. "I did consult you."

"You didn't go into any details."

"I don't know any. Since the night of the party Ross has been in contact with the broker. He made the appointment for me for this Friday. There. Those are the details, but you're still not going."

"You'll need help."

"I asked Lee and Micah to go because I don't want to take Jim and Pete and Randy away from the work that needs to be done here."

The taunt jumped into her mind like an imp doing acrobatics. She thought better of speaking it aloud, but couldn't resist. "Aren't you worried that Randy will try to take advantage of me while my 'Mammy' is away?"

Jake took a menacing step toward her, his face fierce. "You're not staying here alone. You're going to stay at River Bend while I'm gone. I arranged it all with Ross and Lydia."

"Well, you can just *re*arrange it, Mr. Langston. Because I'm going to Fort Worth."

"I've already bought the train tickets."

"I'm perfectly capable of buying a train ticket." She thrust her chin out.

He could see that arguing with her was futile. A fight only made her more stubborn, if that were possible. So he appealed to her reason. "It's a rough town, Banner."

"I've been there."

"When?"

"A few years ago. With Mama and Papa."

"This will be different. You won't like it. It isn't safe for a woman alone."

"I won't be alone. You and Micah and Lee will be with me."

"Not all the time!" he shouted.

She squinted at him suspiciously. "Why are you so against me going? What's the real reason? I won't care what you do once you get there. If you think I plan on interfering with your drinking and gambling and whoring, you've got another thing coming."

"Damn right you won't interfere."

"So why are you shouting?"

"You're shouting too."

"Why do you need to go all the way to Fort Worth to indulge your vices? Haven't we got all that right here in Larsen? Isn't that why you were going into town every night?"

"Yeah, that's why I was going," he said stepping around a chair and shoving it away. "But I ain't been lately, and what Larsen's got to offer isn't quite sordid enough for my tastes."

"I can't believe that!" They faced each other belligerently, chests heaving so hard they almost touched. Finally Banner said adamantly, "I'm going."

Jake was ready to explode, but he knew that short of hog-tying her, he couldn't stop her. "We're leaving early," he ground out.

"I'll be ready."

Without another word, he slammed out the back door.

Banner saw to it that they didn't have to wait on her in the morning. She was ready early, sitting primly in the wagon even before Jake led Stormy from the barn. She was going to drive the wagon into town to carry what little luggage they were taking.

Jake took one scornful look at her ensemble, including the matching veiled hat on her head, and turned away without saying so much as a good morning. But Banner was too excited to let his foul mood dampen her spirits. She wasn't even daunted when the three hands reported for work. When she announced she was going to Fort Worth,

Pete glanced worriedly at Jake. "She is?" he asked around a wad of tobacco. His dubious tone spoke volumes.

Jake merely shrugged and pulled himself into his saddle. Their horses would be left at the livery stable in Larsen. They would need them to drive the cattle home when they returned by train.

Micah and Lee were ebullient and their gaiety was infectious. They rode on both sides of the wagon and kept Banner laughing at their antics. Only Jake seemed to have his mind on the more serious aspects of the trip.

The depot was deserted at that hour of the morning. Jake swung down from Stormy. "I'll go buy Banner's ticket and check to see if the trains are on time. Then we'll take the horses and wagon to the livery and walk back."

As Lee and Micah discussed all they were going to do once they reached Fort Worth, Banner watched Jake's retreating back. He really was an impressive-looking man, with his broad shoulders and narrow hips and that loose-jointed cowboy walk. He had folded his best suit of clothes into his saddlebag for his meeting with the cattle broker, but for the trip he was dressed in his normal cowboy garb, chaps, spurs, and all. His clothes were clean and his hat had been brushed. As he entered the depot, he whipped it off. The sun's warm rays found a home in his white-blond hair.

Banner didn't want to think he was the handsomest man she had ever seen. She was still mad at him for even thinking of leaving her at home. And he was so hateful!

He could have said something about her dress. It was to have been her going-away suit and was the most stylish, the finest outfit she owned. The bodice fit her breasts and waist snugly. The apricot silk flattered her complexion and the matching gloves and hat made her feel feminine and beautiful. But Jake had only given her a derisive look more cutting than a verbal insult.

She tugged on the lace around the hem of her glove. Would he really slip off to see his friend Priscilla while they were in Fort Worth? What could she do to prevent it? And how would she live through the heartache if he did?

The thought of him with another woman made her sick to

her stomach. Would he caress another woman as he did her? Kiss her with the same passion? Pictures of him making love with some nameless, faceless woman flashed across her brain. She closed her eyes tight against them.

She didn't see him emerge from the building, swearing and clapping his hat on his head, but the younger men did. "What the hell's wrong with him?" Lee asked.

"Don't know, but I hope I'm not responsible," Micah said beneath his breath as Jake approached them.

"The sonofabitching train's not running."

"Not running?" they all asked together before Banner added, "Why?"

"Strike. Labor strike. Workers have got the tracks blocked at several points from here to Dallas. The railroad's trying to avoid violence and there's no way to get the strikers off the tracks short of shooting them. So they've stopped service until negotiations get this business all straightened out. Dammit!" He kicked up a shower of gravel with the toe of his boot.

"What will we do?" Banner asked hesitantly.

"Damned if I know."

"Your appointment with Mr. . . . Mr. . . . ."

"Culpepper," Jake supplied.

"With Mr. Culpepper is Friday, isn't it?"

"Yes. We've got several days, but—" Suddenly Jake's head swung around with a new thought. "We'll go by horseback. Boys, do you mind camping out?" He consulted Lee and Micah, who had remained crestfallen and silent, thinking their dream trip would be canceled.

"Fine with us. Right, Lee?" Micah said eagerly.

"Right!"

"Okay then," Jake said, nodding decisively. "You two head over to the store and buy only what we'll need. Cans of beans, a pound or two of bacon, some coffee, and a small bag of flour. A box of bullets. Oh, and a skillet or two and a cheap coffee pot. We won't need blankets if you can sleep on your saddle blankets." They nodded. "All right, git. I'll meet you there in ten minutes to load up. I think we ought to take a spare horse, so I'll go to the livery."

The boys scampered away. They didn't think to call a goodbye to Banner. Jake seemed to have forgotten her, too, until he spun around and nearly collided with her. He caught her by the shoulders with his gloved hands. "Banner! Honey, I almost forgot about you. Can you make it back to River Bend alone?"

"Of course."

"Fine. Tell your folks what happened. I'll get a refund on the tickets to cover the expenses at the store. We might be gone a few days longer than we planned. Maybe the trains will be running by the time we need to come back. The stationmaster said the strike wouldn't last long. Goodbye."

He pulled her to him and kissed her quickly and soundly on the mouth. But she knew he never realized he had. He mounted Stormy and urged him in the direction of the livery stable at the other end of Main Street without a backward glance.

"... then by Friday evening, all the business should be taken care of and you can start having fun." Jake's teeth shone in the firelight as his mouth split into a wide grin. "How does that sound?"

Micah did a backward somersault in the grass. Lee whooped, his eyes wide. "Can we stay over Saturday night too?"

"Suuuure," Jake said, stretching back to rest himself against his saddle which served as his pillow. He granted the request as though it were the whim of benevolent royalty. "I promised you a good time, didn't I?"

"I can't wait till—"

"Shhh!"

"What?" Lee asked, lowering his voice.

"Shhh." Micah waved a hand at him.

"What is it?"

"I thought I heard somebody over there by the horses," Micah whispered across the campfire to his older brother. Jake was no longer indolent, but alert to every sound.

He eased his hand to his holster and drew out the Colt six-shooter. "Stay still," he mouthed. The three, ears strained for any sound other than the soughing of the wind through the trees and the popping of dry firewood, remained perfectly still.

Then they heard the unmistakable crunch of boots grinding over twigs as the intruder came forward. Three pairs of eyes penetrated the darkness, all discerning at once the young cowboy who stepped into the circle of light made by their fire. Shadows cast by the flickering flames danced around him. He was dressed as they were, in denim pants and a work shirt, a vest and a bandana, but he was a scrawny, skinny son of a gun. His wide-brimmed hat kept the features of his face a mystery.

As they watched, a pale slender hand came up to sweep the hat off. A cloud of hair as dark as the night settled around a pair of shoulders too narrow to belong to a boy of any age. A familiar voice, sultry, feminine, and tinged with humor, reached them from across the clearing.

"Good evening, gentlemen."

FOURTEEN

Jake leaped to his feet. "What the hell are you doing here?"

Banner ignored him and moved closer to the fire. She squatted down in front of it. "Hmm. That coffee smells good."

Jake's hand closed around the plump part of her biceps and hauled her to her feet. "I almost shot you!" he yelled directly into her face. "Don't you know better than to sneak up on somebody that way?"

"I didn't sneak!" She wrenched her arm free. "I've been

following you all day. It's a good thing I'm not a robber or a renegade Comanche or something. You'd all be dead.''

Micah and Lee couldn't hide their disappointment. They liked Banner's company, but they treasured Jake's. He was their idol. They had looked forward to his introducing them to the raunchier night life in Fort Worth. Banner's unexpected appearance would no doubt stymie Jake's party mood. He hadn't wanted her along in the first place.

Still, Lee admired his sister's spunk. No other girl he knew would venture out on her own and ride horseback all day the way Banner had. "When did you make up your mind to follow us?" he asked.

Banner dropped her saddlebag on the ground and, after glaring at Jake, knelt to rummage a tin coffee cup out of it. "My mind was already made up. You scattered in three different directions before I had a chance to tell you that I had no intention of canceling my trip just because of a little inconvenience.'' She sipped at the coffee she had poured herself. It was scalding and thoroughly unpalatable. But she acted as though it were nectar.

"A little inconvenience?" Jake shouted. His temper wasn't extinguished by any means, only simmering. Like an active volcano that belches smoke frequently, he released it in spurts. "You don't know the half of it."

Banner patently ignored him. "I watched you ride out of town, then I bought some clothes more suitable for camping. I left the wagon at the livery and took my suitcases, along with a note to Mama and Papa, to the post office. They'll get them when they pick up the mail. I caught up with you within an hour.''

She had addressed her story to Lee and Micah, but Jake responded. "You think you're pretty smart, don't you?"

"I made it here all right."

"Don't try to act like your butt's not as sore as hell, because I know better."

"You know nothing of the sort."

"Tomorrow it'll have blisters on it and—"

"And they will be no concern of yours,'' she shot back.

"I'm fine. I've wanted to camp out all my life but wasn't allowed to simply because I was a girl."

"Which ought to tell you something," Jake said scathingly. "Why are you always trying to be like a man? It's no wonder your fiancé climbed into another woman's bed."

"Jake!" Micah had never thought his brother could say something so cruel.

"Well, why isn't she home cooking and sewing and knitting like other women? She's no good at being a woman, that's why. She...oh...*hell!*" he finished furiously, and stamped off toward where the horses were tied up.

Lee and Micah looked commiseratingly at each other, then turned their sympathy toward Banner. She had sunk to the ground when Jake left. Her weariness showed in every sagging muscle. Lee patted her back as Micah handed her a plate of scorched beans. "He'll sleep on it and feel better in the morning."

But in the morning Jake looked as mean and foreboding as a thundercloud. Like a surly general, he issued orders to break camp, barely giving them time to bolt down the cold biscuits left over from the night before and to drink one cup of the horrible, reheated coffee.

He was right about one thing. Banner's butt was as sore as hell, but she didn't give its condition away as she swung up into her saddle.

"Where did you get the horse?" Jake asked, riding up beside her a few moments later.

"I borrowed him from Mr. Davies at the livery stable." She leaned forward and patted the gelding's neck.

"Borrowed him?" Jake growled. "I had to buy the extra one."

She cast him a radiant smile. Her malice only showed in her sugary tone. "Then I'm good at one womanly thing, aren't I?"

If she had looked at Davies the way she was looking at him now, Jake wouldn't have been surprised if the old coot had *given* her the horse.

It irritated him that she looked so fresh and well rested. He had hoped she would wake up with stiff joints and puffy eyes shadowed with dark circles. Instead, the eyes that glared at him steadily were as brilliant as usual and her cheeks were blooming with color. And she should know better than to sit on horseback quite so erect. It taxed the buttons of her shirt to hold her breasts inside. Damn!

"If you don't keep up, you'll get left," he warned. With that he spurred Stormy forward, making her eat his dust.

Jake's black mood didn't lighten with the passing hours. They rode the horses hard, stopping briefly at noon to water them in a creek and to take greedy drinks from their own canteens. It was a hot and dusty ride, but Banner didn't complain. She would have cut her tongue out first. Her muscles ached. Her hair was matted with sweat beneath the hat she wore to protect her face from the sun. She knew freckles must be sprouting like popcorn kernels in a hot skillet.

Later in the afternoon, as they rode west, the sun unmercifully beat against their faces. Banner prayed for one cloud, a small one, just large enough to blot out that fiery disk, but there was no relief from it.

Even the boys, who would have ridden straight into hell if Jake asked them to, became wilted and restless in their saddles.

"Hey, Jake," Micah called out.

"Yeah?"

"There's a house over there on that rise."

"What about it?"

"Well, I was thinking how good a nice cold drink of well water would taste."

Banner could have kissed him. She wouldn't have confessed that her canteen was empty if she had been tortured. For hours her mouth and throat had felt gritty.

Jake pulled up on Stormy's reins. Through squinting eyes he scanned the farmhouse on the crest of the hill. "All right. We'll stop and see how neighborly they are."

The boys spurred their horses into a gallop. When Jake glanced at Banner, she shrugged as if it were a matter of supreme indifference to her and slowly walked her gelding up the hill.

The farmer was splitting firewood. It was a modest place, but well maintained. There was a barn, only large enough to accommodate a few milk cows, a plow mule, and one horse. Chickens were kept behind a wire fence. A sow grunted from her pen. The well-plotted garden boasted rows of tall corn, beanstalks, onions, turnips, squash, and potatoes. Near the house, heavy green tomatoes bent the stems of their dusty plants.

The farmer laid his ax aside when he saw them, took a handkerchief from the back pocket of his overalls and ran it around his face. He took off his hat, mopped his balding forehead, then replaced it.

These were all slowly executed moves and on the surface seemed casual. But Jake was quick to note the shotgun propped against the wall of the barn not three feet from the farmer's hand. Jake didn't blame him. It was a man's duty to protect his home and family. These days, with out-of-work cowboys prowling the countryside, bands of train robbers, and endless labor disputes, one couldn't take any chances. He tried to ease the farmer's mind.

"Hello."

"Howdy," the farmer said. He didn't come forward, but let them ride closer to him until they reined up only a few feet away.

"Could you spare us a drink of water?" Jake asked with friendly politeness.

The farmer gauged them carefully. Jake kept his hands on the pommel of his saddle as the man's eyes noted his gunbelt and rifle scabbard. Micah and Lee imitated Jake. They didn't move. When the farmer peered closely at Banner, his eyes widened slightly, then they came back to Jake.

"Where're you folks from?"

"Larsen County." Jake had learned a long time ago not to divulge more information than was necessary. Most men on the trail were reticent for one reason or another. That was the best policy. The less one man knew about another, the better. "We're headed to Fort Worth to buy cattle. The railroaders are on strike. The trains aren't running."

The farmer nodded, satisfied. He had heard about the strike that morning when one of his neighbors rode by. "Help yourself." He indicated the water trough for the horses and the well nearer the house.

They dismounted. Banner was careful not to grimace when her sore muscles were required to get her off the horse. While Jake was leading Stormy to the trough, she surreptitiously rubbed her aching behind.

"How're you doing, Banner?" Lee asked. "He's pushing us—"

He broke off suddenly, his eyes bugging. Banner glanced over her shoulder to see a young woman about her age coming from the house. Lee whipped his head around, cleared his throat loudly to attract Micah's attention, then, with unnatural movements of his eyes, indicated the girl.

"Hello," she said shyly as she ventured toward them. "My name's Norma. Ya'll want a drink of well water?"

Lee and Micah stumbled forward. "That would taste mighty good, Norma," Micah said with an engaging grin.

"You must've read my mind, Norma."

Banner gazed at the young men in unconcealed exasperation and wondered if Lee had any idea how goosey that expression on his face looked to the rest of the world. So, Norma had big brown eyes, a voice as smooth as honey, and a well-formed chest beneath her calico dress. So what? Was that any reason to gawk?

The girl gave Banner one cursory look and dismissed her. She led Lee and Micah toward the well. Jake was talking horseflesh with the farmer, who had admired Stormy. With one booted foot propped on the side of the trough and his hat pushed to the back of his head, Jake leaned forward slightly to rest his forearms on his raised thigh.

When Banner turned toward the well and caught Norma's speculative eyes on him, she shot her a quelling look.

"Whose wife is she?" Norma asked the boys, who were emptying the ladles of water as thirstily as they were gazing at Norma.

"Nobody's," Micah guffawed.

"She's my sister." Lee's eyes weren't on Banner, but on

Norma's impressive bosom as she leaned forward to lower the bucket into the well again. His gaze met Micah's across the well and they nodded at each other, two assessing males coming to the same conclusion.

"Mind if I have a drink too?" Banner asked crossly. She been standing at the well for a full minute and no one had taken notice. Norma, with a marked lack of graciousness, handed Banner a cup of water.

"Who does he belong to?" Norma's eyes slid to Jake, who was making sure the horses didn't drink too much.

"Me."

At Banner's terse answer, Lee and Micah looked at her sharply. Her eyes were narrowed on Norma.

"He's my brother," Micah said uneasily.

"Oh." Norma looked at Banner in a smug way that infuriated her. She was suddenly aware of how untidy she was while every hair on Norma's soft brown head was tucked neatly into a crown of braids. Norma smelled like homemade bread. Banner knew she smelled like salty sweat and horses.

"Isn't your husband awfully *old?*" Banner asked.

Norma's cheeks flared. "He's my pa."

"Oh." She repeated Norma's noncommittal response out of sheer perversity. "May I have another drink, please?"

"Why, of course."

After Norma had refilled the cup, Banner stalked off with it. She carried it to Jake. As she approached him, she smiled beguilingly. "Here, Jake. I thought you might like some cold water too." Banner hoped Norma was watching.

Jake, eyeing her suspiciously, took the cup from her hand. "Thanks."

"You're welcome." She flashed him a brilliant smile. After all, Norma didn't know what they had said to each other.

But apparently Banner was competing for Norma's attention. Just then a giggle came from the direction of the well. The farmer's eyes took on a hard glint as he saw his daughter being entertained by the two young men. "What's going on over yonder, Norma?" he called out.

"Nothing, Pa."

"Time to go," Jake said quickly.

Nothing on earth could compare to the wrath of a farmer who felt his daughter's virtue was in jeopardy. From south Texas to Colorado, cowboys, especially Texas cowboys, were the scourge of every parent with a marriageable daughter. They were to be protected against cowboys at all costs. There was even a song about it. Jake remembered the lyrics. "Don't you wed with them Texas boys."

He tossed down the rest of the water and handed Banner the cup. "Take it back to the young lady and then mount up. Lee, Micah, let's go. *Now.*"

His tone left no room for discussion and elicited immediate action. The boys doffed their hats to Norma just as Banner thrust the cup into her hand. Banner smiled at her cattily, a look that said, "I get to ride off with them, but you have to stay in this dreary life with a mean ol' pa."

Jake thanked the farmer once more before swinging into his saddle. He let the others ride out in front of him. Only when they were well on their way again did Jake breathe easier. He didn't want any trouble on this trip, especially with Banner along. Last night he had been ready to kill her. It wasn't that he hadn't been glad to see her. Before his fury took over, his heart had betrayed him and tripped with joy when he saw her standing in the circle of firelight.

But when he thought of her impulsiveness, his blood ran cold. There were a thousand hazards on the trail, and she, a young woman, was vulnerable to them all. He intended to avoid towns. She would attract the attention of all the young bucks like a lightning rod.

Banner was headstrong. She acted on the spur of the moment and thought about the consequences later. It was a wonder trouble hadn't caught up with her before now. But he damned sure didn't want it to find her on this trip.

He looked at her as she rode ahead of him. His eyes went unerringly to her bottom. He knew it must be killing her, but she hadn't made a murmur of complaint. Stubborn little cuss. In spite of himself he smiled as he watched her hips bounce on the saddle. She had the cutest—. . .

He pushed the thought aside instantly. What the hell was he doing? He spurred Stormy forward and called out, "As soon as we locate a creek with enough fresh water, we'll camp." From now on, he would make it a point to ride in front of Banner, not behind.

Before long they sighted a copse of willows in the distance. Riding toward it, they were delighted to find a gurgling creek. The season had been so dry that water was scarce. Banner offered to make the coffee, recalling the viscous brew the men had made the night before. She also volunteered to cook the meal if they would gather the wood, build the fire, and clean up afterward. No one argued.

After they had eaten, they gathered around the fire, but not too close. It was a warm evening. Jake settled back against his saddle to smoke a cheroot. Lee went into the brush to answer a call of nature.

Jake probably wouldn't have even noticed Micah if the younger man hadn't been sitting so still. As it was, that stillness and the blank expression on his face caught Jake's attention. He followed the direction of Micah's rapt gaze to find Banner at the end of it.

She was sitting with her back to the fire. She had taken off her shirt. Her camisole showed up whitely against the darkness. She was pulling a hairbrush through her thick, dark hair.

As Jake watched, she lifted the heavy strands off her neck, bent her head slightly and let the faint breeze blow against her neck. Her skin looked golden and pale in the firelight. The reflection of the flames caught on the raven strands of hair that were gradually sifting back onto her shoulders.

She sighed tiredly, stretching her spine in the process and casting the profile of her breast into sharp relief against the velvety blackness of the night.

Jake's manhood reacted throbbingly. Irritated with his response, he turned away only to notice Micah's entrancement again. He nudged him with his boot. "You can catch flies with your mouth gaping open like that," he whispered.

Micah jumped guiltily. He cast one more furtive glance at Banner. "She's sure pretty though, ain't she?"

Jake, too, took another forbidden peep. "Yeah, she's pretty. Now mind your own business."

Micah sensed his brother's displeasure. "I didn't mean nothing by looking at her, Jake."

"Well, look someplace else." He came to his feet just as Lee returned. "I'm going down by the creek to cool off. I suggest you all get some sleep. We've got another hard day's ride ahead of us tomorrow."

Banner watched his retreating figure until the darkness obliterated it. He was still in a bad mood and couldn't say anything without sounding grumpy. All day she had been an exemplary traveler, making trouble for no one. Had he shown her an iota of approval? No. He was so stubborn!

Sighing, she replaced her hairbrush in the saddlebag. She felt a little better, having bathed her face and neck in a pail of water Lee had fetched from the creek. She would have given her last nickel for a bath. *Tomorrow night*, she thought wistfully, *in the hotel. I'll treat myself to a bath.* She lay down on her blanket.

The boys were talking together softly. "What are you two whispering about?"

"Nothing," Lee said quickly, too quickly not to arouse her suspicions.

"We, uh, thought we'd go for a ride," Micah said.

"A ride?" Such an idea was beyond her comprehension. "You've been riding all day."

"Yeah, well, we, uh—"

"To cool off," Micah said.

"Yeah! To cool off," Lee agreed, and stood up. "You tell Jake that's what we're doing, riding to cool off."

Before she could offer any more arguments, they saddled their mounts and quietly led them from camp. Banner flopped down on her blanket. If they wanted to go galivanting off in the middle of the night like fools, it was none of her concern.

Jake didn't take their desertion quite so calmly. "And you just let them ride off without stopping them!" he exclaimed when he returned to the fire and she told him what had happened in his absence.

She sprang upright. "What was I supposed to do? They're grown men."

"You could have called me."

"It was none of my business."

"How long have they been gone?"

"About a half-hour," she replied.

Cursing, Jake sat down on his own bedroll. "I can't track them in the dark. I guess the only thing to do is wait for them to come back."

Banner rolled to her side and propped herself up by one elbow to see him better. "You know what I think?"

"What?" Why hadn't she put on another shirt? If she thought the night was providing her any modest covering, she was wrong. That flimsy camisole was hardly adequate to contain her breasts, especially in the position she had assumed. The uppermost breast was swelling over the lacy border of the garment, dangerously close to spilling out.

"I think they're going back to see that girl."

"What girl?" Jake pried his eyes from her chest. "That farmer's daughter?"

"Norma," Banner said sweetly. "Didn't you see the way they were ogling her?"

"I saw it," Jake muttered, turning away. He was doing his fair share of ogling lately. "Her daddy saw it too. Surely those boys wouldn't do anything stupid." His blue eyes pierced the night.

"They're girl crazy. That's all they talk about, think about. It's so silly." Banner lay back down and folded her arms over her stomach.

Jake chuckled. "Silly? What do girls talk about? Hmm? Men."

"Some do. Not me."

"Oh, no?"

"No."

"Why, Banner Coleman, I do believe you're lying. I'll bet—"

He stopped midsentence when popping sounds echoed in

the still air. Banner sat up again. "What was that?" It only took another volley to convince Jake what it was.

"Gunfire. A shotgun if I'm not mistaken."

He had already jumped to his feet and was running toward Stormy, toting the heavy saddle in one hand and his rifle in the other. Banner kicked free of her light blanket and went after him. "Do you think that farmer is shooting at Lee and Micah?"

"That's a distinct possibility that's crossed my mind," Jake said through grim lips. He buckled the cinch belt and flopped the stirrup down. Taking his pistol from its holster, he spun the chamber, checking to see that it was loaded. He unfastened the rifle's scabbard and made certain he had ammunition for it. Banner watched his calculated, practiced moves with frightened eyes.

"Wait, I'm coming with you," she said, when he placed his boot in the stirrup and pushed himself up into the saddle.

"No, you aren't, young lady. And I mean it this time, Banner," he said sternly. "You are to stay here and not to move. Do you understand?" He gave Stormy's reins a vicious yank and rode off into the night.

The well-trained animal ate up the ground surefootedly. Jake had only to keep his mind on staying in the saddle and counting the gunshots that split the night air with alarming frequency. They were too close to be coming from the farmhouse. Could he have been wrong? Was this a wild goose chase? He hoped to God it was.

But he knew better.

He spotted flashes of light in the darkness long before he crested a hill and looked down on the dry ravine they had crossed that afternoon. He remembered it. It was a gully about twelve feet deep and forty feet across. There was a narrow bridge spanning it. He drew Stormy to a halt and pulled the rifle from the scabbard.

It was Lee and Micah all right. He could see them cowering behind a clump of pampas grass while the farmer fired his shotgun at them from across the ravine. Thankfully he was a sorry marksman.

Their horses had run out of range. Jake spotted them in a

grove of wild plum trees. He crept up to them, quieted them, and secured their reins in the lower branches of the trees.

Running back to Stormy, he pulled himself back into the saddle, laid the rifle across his lap, and took his pistol from its holster. If he rode back and forth along the rim of the ravine, he could cover the boys by firing over the farmer's head while they ran for their horses. As soon as he knew they were out of range, he'd hightail it after them. He doubted the farmer would chase them. He had the girl with him. Jake could hear her pleas as he rode closer.

"Pa, I swear, we weren't doing nothing."

"You call sneaking off to meet two randy cowboys nothing?" Another blast of the shotgun rent the air.

"You don't let me have any fun."

"You ain't supposed to have fun. I promised your ma I'd raise you up proper."

"I am proper. They only wanted to talk to me."

"I know what they wanted. And it appears to me I was just in time to keep them from getting it. I found one of the bastards kissing you."

"One kiss. I swear it."

"Shut up. I'll get to you later."

If it hadn't been so serious, it would have been hilarious. But not so much as a shadow of a grin curved Jake's lips as he gave a Rebel yell that would have curdled the blood of the most ruthless savage and spurred Stormy into a gallop that defied gravity. His powerful thighs gripped the stallion's back. He thundered along the edge of the ravine, firing both the pistol and the rifle. He aimed well above the heads of Norma and her irate father.

Lee and Micah didn't waste any time. Once they had assured themselves that the nightrider was Jake and not some demon from hell, they scrambled from their cover and ran toward their horses. The farmer wasn't so easily cowed. They weren't out of range when he started shooting again, cursing virulently.

Jake wheeled Stormy around and began riding back in the opposite direction. He was almost even with the farmer when he nearly ran head-on into another rider. "What the—"

He didn't have time to finish his exclamation before Banner streaked past him like a flash of lighting. Only a shell from the farmer's shotgun whistling past his head too close for comfort caused him to bend over his saddle and continue riding forward. He drew Stormy to a stop and turned him. Without having to think about it from so much practice, Jake reloaded his pistol.

He could see Banner turning her mount around and riding toward him again. The fool! And why hadn't she put a shirt on? Her white camisole was making her a perfect target, but she was peppering the air across the ravine with bullets. When they passed each other again, she shouted over the racket of the farmer's shotgun, "Are they to their horses yet?"

Jake whirled his head around and saw that Lee and Micah had just reached the copse of trees. "Let's get the hell out of here." He wheeled Stormy in that direction, twisting in his saddle to fire across the ravine a few more times for good measure. Banner was right behind him.

When they rode past the plum trees, Lee and Micah joined them. "Thanks, Jake," they shouted over the thundering hoofbeats.

"Keep riding!" he yelled at them. The horses kicked up more dust than a cyclone, but they didn't slacken their speed. They raced toward their campsite. Jake looked over his shoulder once to see if they were being pursued, but all he could see behind them was a ghostly cloud of dust.

When they reined in, he slid from his saddle with one lithe movement. As soon as Micah's feet touched the ground, he caught Jake's flying fist on the chin. His head snapped back and it was a miracle to him that it kept its post on his shoulders.

"What the hell did you think you were doing? Trying to get us killed? Huh?" Jake was enraged. "Keep your pants buttoned up until we get to Fort Worth, understand? Then I don't care if you diddle every whore in Hell's Half Acre. But stay away from nice girls."

Micah's head wobbled in agreement.

"Yes, sir," Lee said, wetting his lips with a dry, dusty tongue and praying to God Jake wouldn't send a bone-cracking fist at *his* chin. The only man he respected as much as he did his father was Jake. He feared his temper just as much too.

"Now douse that campfire. That sodbuster might come after us yet. Get your horses rubbed down. Then get to your bedrolls. Banner, you—"

He looked around, but saw only Lee's and Micah's properly chastised countenances gazing back at him. "Where'd she go?"

Stupefied from the blow he had sustained, Micah wasn't certain he'd ever heard of anybody named Banner. Lee's eyes glanced around the camp. He was anxious to please and redeem himself, but he couldn't produce Banner. "She was right behind you, I thought."

"Banner!" Jake shouted into the darkness. A squeezing fist of fear got hold of his heart. "Banner!" Nothing answered him but unrelenting darkness and his own pounding heart. "Either one of you see her?"

They shook their heads. Lee said, "I saw her riding right behind you just as I got on my horse. By the time I rode out to meet you, I wasn't looking anywhere but straight ahead."

Jake vaulted onto Stormy's back. "Stay here." He rode out into the night again.

Jake never panicked. He had been called cold and heart-less. Men he had ridden with had seen him bury friends and not show one trace of emotion in those blue eyes. Nerves of steel. Ice water in his veins. That's how his peers would have described Jake Langston.

But not if they could have seen him riding back toward the ravine that night. His face was a mask of fear.

What if that goddamned farmer had got off one lucky shot? What if Banner had caught it? No, she couldn't have. She had ridden back with them. Hadn't she? Hadn't there been four horses racing back to the camp? God, with the dust and the noise, he couldn't swear to it now. If she had gotten back safely, where was she?

He came to the ravine and slowed Stormy to a trot. The horse's sides were bellowing; his coat was lathered. For once Jake didn't notice his mount's distress. His eyes scanned the darkened landscape. Bile filled his throat when he realized he was looking for her body, Banner's body, lying lifeless and bleeding in the dust, that sweet frilly camisole soaked with blood.

He wiped the image from his mind and rode in closer. All was quiet on the opposite side. He rode along the ravine, back again. Several times he made that ride, but saw nothing, not Banner, not the borrowed gelding.

He had no choice but to return to camp. Maybe she had just gone into the bushes to relieve herself and hadn't heard him call her. That was probably it. He had gone off half-cocked and hadn't given her time to come back. They were probably all in camp laughing at him.

But when he arrived,, the gelding wasn't with the other horses. Lee and Micah had obediently curled up in their bedrolls. Lee raised his head.

"Find her?"

"Not yet. But I will. She's bound to be around here somewhere. Get some sleep."

God, where was she?

Jake remembered every cruel thing he had ever said to her. He regretted the times he had deliberately hurt her. Self-loathing tasted vile in his mouth. He would never forgive himself if something had happened to her. Never.

What if that farmer had shot her and dragged her back to his house? What if he let her bleed to death? What if . . . what if . . . what if . . . Jesus, the "what ifs" could drive him crazy.

He circled the camp one more time, his eyes spearing through the darkness looking for a trace of her. He was on his way back to alert the boys, wondering how he would break the news of Banner's death to Ross and Lydia, when he heard something that didn't belong with the other night sounds.

Humming.

A lilting tuneless song coming from the direction of the

creek was discordant with the environment. He came off Stormy's back and, pushing aside grapevines and thorny bushes, slashed his way toward the creek.

The gelding was tied to a cottonwood sapling near the bank. Banner's pants and boots were piled on a boulder. She was in the creek, about midstream, cupping handfuls of water over her shoulders.

Humming!

She heard Jake's spur strike a rock and turned her head in that direction. She was still wearing the chemise, but huddled down deeper in the waist-deep water just the same.

"You scared the life out of me," she said breathlessly.

"Me? Scared you? Where the hell have you been and just what the hell do you think you're doing?"

"I'm taking a bath."

"A bath!" he hissed across the distance between them. He threw his hat on the ground and began unbuckling his holster. "When I get my hands on you . . ." He let the threat dangle as he hopped first on one foot, then the other, tugging off his boots. He sent them flying into the tall grass lining the bank of the creek.

They spoke in whispers for reasons neither could explain. "Why are you angry with me? I didn't go riding off into the night like the boys did. Did you punish them?"

"Yes. Now it's time you got yours."

"What for?"

"You disobeyed me. I told you to stay in camp. What the hell were you doing out there, riding like a cavalry charge and . . . Where'd you get that gun?" he demanded.

"My papa gave me that pistol on my sixteenth birthday, and I couldn't obey you, Jake. Lee and Micah were in trouble. Did you expect me to stay here and do nothing? I thought I could help and I did. They got away safely."

He worked impatiently at the buttons on his shirt. When they didn't cooperate with his clumsy fingers, he began to tear at them. "Why didn't you ride back to camp with us? We got back and you were nowhere to be found."

"I had eaten about a pound of dust. I was hot and sweaty and wanted a bath. What difference could it make to you?"

"I'll tell you what difference it makes." He finished unbuttoning the shirt. Now he struggled out of it, balled it up, and flung it to the ground. "Didn't you hear me calling you?"

"No. I washed my hair too. I dunked my head several times."

He advanced into the water. Instinctively Banner began backing up. "Well, while you've been out here dunking your head and having a cool, leisurely *bath*"—he virtually spat the word—"I've been combing the countryside like a madman looking for your body."

"My body?"

"I thought you'd been shot! No one saw you after we rode into camp, no one remembered seeing you after you pulled that little stunt of yours at the ravine."

"And you thought I'd been shot? That farmer couldn't hit the broad side of his barn."

"He could have got lucky. You sure as hell made yourself a target. What possessed you to do such a damn fool thing? You could have gotten yourself killed."

"Well, don't sound so disappointed that I didn't. And you stay away from me, Jake Langston," she said, putting out a hand to ward him off. "What are you going to do?"

Water pulled at his pants as he waded through the creek. His tread was steady and underterred, as though he were on dry ground. He was intent on his purpose. The unwavering light in his eyes told her that much.

"I'm gonna give you the paddlin' you deserve. And I think Ross would back me up."

"Oh, no, you're not." She turned and began thrashing her way to the opposite bank. She slipped in the soft mud and clawed through the water until she gained firmer ground. She had almost reached the grassy bank when her ankle was clasped in an iron fist.

Softly she screamed and began to climb up the bank. But Jake was right behind her, making her efforts to escape him futile. Finally she fell face first into the deep grass, breathing hard from her struggles. He crawled over her body, grasped her shoulders and turned her over.

Their panting breaths echoed each other. He stared down into her face. She met his angry stare defiantly.

"I told you to stay in camp for your own good, Banner. You could have been killed."

She gazed up into his eyes and saw not only his fury but his fear. His hands were trembling slightly even as he held her shoulders anchored to the ground. Her lips parted slightly when the truth dawned on her.

Slowly she raised her arms. Her fingers sank into the white-blond hair that hung around his lean, rugged face. "And you would have cared, Jake," she whispered. "You would have cared."

He blinked. Then in a heartbeat, he lowered himself over her and his mouth came crushing down. Low, guttural, animal sounds emanated from deep in his throat. He was one with every male in creation, driven by that need to claim his female, to protect, to mount, to mate.

She clutched handfuls of his hair and held his head fast. His tongue slid along hers, deep, deep, into the sweetest depths of her mouth. He twisted his lips against hers, realigned them, tasted her again. His fingers softly gouged the flesh of her shoulders.

Restlessly she moved beneath him. When her thighs parted, he nestled himself between them. She was very soft and he was very hard. Woman and man. Fitting perfectly. Hungry for each other.

He lifted his head and smoothed the wet hair from her cheeks. "God, yes, I would have cared. I care. I've tried not to, but I do."

He sipped the water from her face, her ears, her neck. He levered himself up to look at her. The chemise was bunched around her hips, leaving her calves and thighs bare. The sheer cloth clung to her, molding to her body.

Her breasts were no longer a mystery. They were high and round and beautiful. The dusky aureoles were puckered around perfect nipples that were beaded with passion. His hand pulled the ribbon free at the top of her chemise. Five pearl buttons later his gaze burned down onto her wet, naked skin.

He touched her. Her eyes fluttered closed. "Jake," she breathed through kiss-dampened lips.

His hand was warm, a delicious contrast to her water-cooled skin. She opened her eyes when that warmth was momentarily withdrawn. Jake paused to study her, then carefully he covered each breast with a hand. His eyes drifted up to hers and they held that telling gaze for a small eternity.

Then he began gently to rub the sensitive tips of her breasts with the pads of his middle fingers.

She whimpered and he looked up at her again. Their gaze held for another long moment. Banner thought her heart would fly out of her chest and join his, so closely were their tempos timed. He smiled at her. It was the tenderest expression she had ever seen on Jake's face, an almost apologetic, gentle smile that rid his face of that cold cynicism that was part of him.

His attention was drawn back to his handiwork. His hand cupped one of her breasts. He reshaped the soft mound to fit his palm, pushed it up slightly and served it to his descending lips. He pecked tiny kisses on the nipple until it thrust its way between his lips.

Had Banner been able to draw a breath, she would have gasped. Never had she imagined such an intimate caress. Touching, yes. But with his mouth? No. Yet it was happening. She could feel the heat of his mouth closing around her snugly, the wet silkiness drawing her inside, the gentle rolling motions of his tongue over her nipple. He whipped it lightly, then lapped at it languidly.

"You have the sweetest breasts . . . the sweetest . . . the . . ."

His mouth moved over her, tasting and licking and kissing her until she feared she would go mad. She raised her hips against his and made a cradle for the hard ridge of muscle that his wet denims conformed to. Moist and warm, she flowered open, her body aching for him to fill that void. She was desperate for the feel of him and ran her hands down his chest.

"Yes," he groaned. "Touch me, Banner."

Her fingers combed through the golden pelt on his chest

and tested the firmness of the curved muscles. She followed that sleek ribbon of hair between his ribs to its destination and dipped her finger into his navel.

Making a low sound in his throat, he lifted himself over her again and fused her mouth to his. When her lips closed around his intrusive tongue, he growled with arousal. Rolling to one side, his hands moved frantically to unfasten his pants.

But when the first button slipped from it hole, he froze as he remembered his earlier words. "*Keep your pants buttoned up until we get to Fort Worth.*"

He lifted his mouth from Banner's and stared into the darkness, breathing hard. "*Then I don't care if you diddle every whore in Hell's Half Acre.*" He looked down into Banner's bewildered face. "*But stay away from nice girls.*"

His own words came back to haunt him. He was committing the very sin he had warned Lee and Micah against. He sat up. Drawing his knees to his chest, he laid his forearms on them, and bowed his head between them.

Banner lay perfectly still. Her eyes were round with misapprehension. Her body throbbed with longing. She didn't understand. She wanted to touch his naked back, smooth and dark in the feeble moonlight, but she didn't. When she tried to breathe, the air staggered from her lungs. "Jake, did I do something wrong?" He moaned, but only shook his head in answer. "Are you still angry with me?"

"No."

"Then why aren't you still kissing me?"

"I can't."

"Why?"

"I can't kiss you and stop."

The silence was tense and thick enough to taste. "You mean you want to make love with me again?"

His jaw knotted. "Yes."

"Then why—"

"You know why. It's wrong. Your parents trust me. I'm too old for you. I'm too . . ." His breath escaped on a long disgusted sigh. "I'm not good enough."

She crammed a fist against her lips to trap a sob, but tears flooded her eyes. "You just don't want me."

His head came around then and his eyes drilled into hers. "I want you. You could feel me against you. You know I want you. I want to be so deep inside you . . . oh, God." He covered his face with his hands.

"Then why?" she cried softly.

He dragged his hands down his face and stood. He raked his hair back with fingers that punishingly plowed through the thick mass. "For all the reasons I've said. It's wrong. Now that's an end to it."

He took a shallow dive into the creek and swam across. When he emerged on the other side, she was still lying in the tall grass, weeping softly.

FIFTEEN

Even the whiskey tasted sour. Where was the warm glow he wanted to feel in the pit of his stomach? Where was that buzzing in his head that was always so pleasant to experience at the end of the trail?

None of those satisfactions had come from the glasses of whiskey he had tossed down. He wasn't even getting drunk, and he wouldn't have been opposed to getting falling down, slobbery drunk. But he could have been made of wood for all the effect the liquor was having on him. If he didn't know better, he would think Pris had been watering it down. But every cowboy knew that the Garden of Eden had the finest, most potent whiskey and the coldest beer to be found.

The crowd was beginning to pick up. Men entered the pleasure palace singly, in pairs, and in rambunctious groups to fill the gaming rooms and parlors. A pall of smoke fogged the gas chandeliers overhead. The pianist thumped out lively tunes. The girls were becoming friendlier and more scantily dressed by the minute as they drifted through the crowd making themselves available. They were smiling and gracious, entertaining and alluring, as their madam had trained them to be.

Jake had to admit they were an attractive group. Some were pretty and sweet. Others were sophisticated, as though they knew all there was to know about the world, and what they didn't know didn't count. There was a whore to appeal to every taste.

He took another swig of whiskey. All it served to do was burn his throat. He supposed he should get in on a poker game, but he really didn't want to. So, for the time being, he would just lean against the bar and drink and hope that the whiskey would soon take effect and he would stop thinking about where he really wanted to be and with whom.

Sugar Dalton glided in front of him. "Well, hello, Jake."

"Hiya, Sugar." She looked more pathetic than she had the last time he was here, the night before Banner's wedding. Her face was puffy. Ineptly applied cosmetics did little to camouflage the lines of dissipation and unhappiness around her mouth.

But her eyes, in a forlorn way, were as kind as always. It was said that she treated her customers with maternal, loving care. That was what some men needed, especially the younger ones out on their own for the first time. Jake supposed that's why Priscilla kept Sugar as an employee.

"Drink, Jake?"

He already had one the bartender had just freshened, but he accepted her offer, knowing that the girls got a percentage of every drink they enticed a customer to buy. Among the younger, prettier competition, Sugar must have a hard time of it. "If you'll share one with me."

She knew she was being patronized, but she wanted a drink too badly not to accept Jake's generosity. Leaning over the bar, she whispered to the bartender, "Pour mine

out of the same bottle as his, not the one Madam Pris keeps
back there for us.'' She lifted soulful eyes to Jake. ''How've
you been?''

''Can't complain.''

''What are you doing in town? Didn't you go to east
Texas?'' She took a drink of the whiskey, holding it in her
mouth a long time, savoring it, before swallowing.

''I'm here to buy cattle. Starting up a herd.''

Her smile was genuine. ''That's good, Jake, real good.
I'm glad for you.''

''Thanks. It's not my own, I'm only foreman.''

''But that's fine. I'm glad to know you've got a good job.
When did you get in?''

''This afternoon.''

They had checked into the Ellis Hotel. If it had only been
him and the two young men, they would have settled for
more modest accommodations. But Jake stretched their
budget and checked into the Ellis as much for Banner's
protection as her comfort. He, Lee, and Micah were sharing
a room that adjoined her. Their rooms were on the third
floor.

''Look, Banner, there's a balcony out here,'' Jake had
said, opening the drapes. The window provided a view of
Throckmorton Street, one of the busiest in town. He had
hoped the pedestrian traffic and the constant parade of
buggies and horse-drawn trolleys would excite her.

She had merely nodded. Her weak smile could barely be
called such. ''Yes, this is nice, Jake. Thank you.''

There had been few words between them since they broke
camp early that morning. Because Lee and Micah were still
gauging Jake's reaction to their escapade the previous night
and wondering what effect it might have on their freedom in
Fort Worth, it had been a subdued group that had entered
the hotel lobby that evening.

They were trail dusty and looked none too reputable to
the clerk behind the registration desk. His manners improved greatly when Jake mentioned Mr. Culpepper, the
cattle broker. That and the fact that Jake paid him for two

nights' residence in cash, taken from Ross's safe to cover the expenses of the trip.

Now, with his head full of the smoke and noise of the Garden of Eden, Jake realized he didn't want to be here. He had thought he did. He had thought he couldn't wait to get out of those fancy hotel rooms and back to the element of society he knew best.

"You keep both doors locked at all times. Don't open them to anybody except me and the boys," he had instructed Banner before he left. Micah and Lee had already departed, saying they would eat supper out. Jake had seen to it that Banner had a supper tray brought to her room. He didn't even want her eating alone in the dining room downstairs.

"You've told me that a hundred times. I understand." She had been standing at the window, gazing out as though she were a prisoner in a cell. In a manner of speaking, Jake had to admit she was. "All I want is to take a bath and go to bed."

"All right then," he had said, suddenly reluctant to leave, "goodbye."

"Goodbye."

She had sounded so dejected and looked so sad he had almost been compelled to stay with her. Before he could talk himself into doing that, he had rushed out.

Now he wondered what the hell he was doing here. Even though Banner was barely speaking to him after what had happened last night, he preferred her company to this raucous crowd. He preferred looking at her face, even her *angry* face, to any of the painted whores who wandered past him with an invitation in their sultry eyes.

Sugar had finished her drink. Jake smiled down at her. "I have two boys with me."

"So where are they?" she asked.

In spite of his dreary mood, Jake laughed. "Out building up their courage, I reckon. They have work to do tomorrow, so I told them to restrict their fun to the shooting galleries. I'll bring them in tomorrow night and introduce them to you."

She laid a hand on his arm. "Thanks, Jake. I'll appreciate that." Her gaze grew warmer and her hand tightened around his arm. "I'm not doing anything in particular right now." It was an offer extended hopefully.

His lips turned down at the corners and he shook his head self-deprecatingly. "I wouldn't let you waste your valuable time on an old saddle tramp like me. Go find you a rich customer."

He was turning her down gracefully and she was gracious enough to accept the rejection in the same way. "Someday one of those rich customers might fall wildly in love with me."

"I wouldn't doubt it."

"And carry me right out of here. Away from her," she added under her breath. She tilted her head toward the portiere that separated the gaming rooms from the barroom. Priscilla was standing with one hand on her hip; the other held a scarlet plumed fan.

As she started forward, Sugar eased away from the bar. "'Bye, Jake. And thanks."

"Just a minute," Priscilla said as Sugar made to pass her. She gave the old prostitute a long, silent, reproachful glance, then slapped her hard across the cheek. The cracking sound stopped all other noise in the room.

Jake jerked erect, ready to defend Sugar, but Priscilla threw him a look as sharp as a dagger that dared him to interfere. He didn't because that would have only made things harder on Sugar after he left.

Sugar covered her cheek with a defensive hand. "What was that for?"

Actually it was for the tender expression Priscilla had seen on Jake's face when he looked down at Sugar and the soft kiss he had laid on her mouth. But she said, "There's a hole in the knee of your stocking. Get upstairs and don't come down for the rest of the night."

"But I need the money," Sugar whined.

"You heard me," Priscilla said coldly.

Avoiding the curious eyes the scene had drawn, Sugar slunk from the room and up the stairs. Priscilla arched a brow at the piano player, who immediately resumed his playing. Then eyes as cold and flinty as metal shavings slid back to Jake and Priscilla covered the remaining distance to the bar.

"Did the Colemans get tired of you already?"

"You're a real bitch."

"You're right. That's part of my job."

"The part you like best, I think."

"You know better than that, Jake," she said seductively. "You know the part I like best."

"Why'd you slap Sugar?"

"I have to keep my girls in line."

"Over a torn stocking? What's poor old Sugar ever done to you?"

"Poor old Sugar has cost me plenty of dollars when she was too drunk to accommodate the randiest cowboy."

"And that's all that counts with you, isn't it? Money?"

"And enormous cocks."

Jake shook his head in disgust. "As I said, you're a bitch."

"Are you going to answer my question or not?"

This was familiar ground and Jake began to feel better. Sparring with Priscilla was one of the things he liked to do best because she was so deserving of every insult he could throw her. "I'm here buying cattle for the Colemans."

"So things have worked out?"

"Yeah." He finished his whiskey, but didn't ask for another.

"Celebrating?"

He shrugged.

"Can't you do any better than Sugar?" Priscilla took a step closer, making certain he could see her exposed breasts to their full advantage. The red satin dress cinched her waist and pushed her breasts up until they were all but overflowing the black lace bodice.

Jake took it all in. Every detail was planned to seduce, to fulfill the desires of every man in the place. Except him. "The way I see it, one whore is just about the same as another," he drawled.

Priscilla's eyes narrowed with outrage. He was surprised she didn't claw his face with her viciously long nails. Her control was admirable. Instead of lashing out, she purred. "Why, Jake, is something wrong with you, honey?" Her hand slid down his front to his fly. She squeezed him. "Aren't you going to take any of my girls?"

Calmly he reached down and removed her hand. "Nope, not tonight."

In that instant he made up his mind. Why was he wasting his time here? He should be looking after Banner. It wasn't like her to be sullen and silent. He didn't recognize that mood and it scared him. He would rather have her fighting him toe to toe than see that blank, lifeless, hopeless expression on her usually animated face. Why had he left her alone? She shouldn't be left alone in a hotel room. Not in any town, but especially this one. "I'd better get back to the Ellis to check on Banner."

He didn't even realize he had spoken his thoughts aloud until Priscilla repeated, "Banner?"

"The Colemans' daughter. I told you about her. She came with me. We're buying cattle." He was distracted, fishing in his pocket for money to pay the bartender.

"Is her husband with her?" Priscilla asked in order to confirm what Dub had told her.

"Husband? Oh, no. She didn't get married. It was . . . uh, called off." He tossed down the coins. "Goodbye, Pris."

With a mixture of frustration and fury, she watched him walk away from her. Jake wasn't acting like himself. When she had been told he was in the building, she had rushed through her toilette. She had been surprised to find him, not at the poker tables, not in one of the beds upstairs, both of which would have been normal, but drinking alone, or as good as alone since Sugar had been with him.

That wasn't normal. And Priscilla was always atuned to people who acted out of character. One never knew when a grain of information was going to turn into a pearl of blackmailing ammunition.

The Coleman girl was with Jake? Traveling with him? Interesting. Priscilla promised herself to get acquainted with

Banner Coleman. She wanted to see what Lydia's daughter looked like and why she was capable of preoccupying Jake.

She watched him as he rounded the portiere. Just as he did, he collided with a man crossing the hallway. Apparently the stranger had won handily at the poker tables. His head was bent and he was counting his money. That's why he didn't see Jake until they literally ran into each other.

The hostility that sparked between them was instantaneous and had nothing to do with their collision. The other man stepped back as though he had seen a ghost. Jake automatically reached for his holstered pistol, though he didn't draw it. They stared hard into each other's eyes. Even from across the room, Priscilla could feel the antagonism between them. She recognized that expression on Jake's face. It was hard and closed. His eyes were as cold and implacable as frozen lakes.

The other man was the first to move away. He took several steps backward, his fear of Jake apparent. Without a word spoken between them, the stranger hastened toward the bar. Priscilla watched Jake's eyes follow him before he turned on his heels and stormed out.

Priscilla felt every nerve in her body relax. Only then did she realize just how tense she had been. Jake had looked like he was going to kill the man right on the spot. That's all she needed to bring the religious fanatics down on her head, another killing.

She fanned herself indolently, forcing down her temporary tension. This was promising to be an amusing night after all. Jake was definitely interested in this stranger. And whatever was of interest to Jake, interested her.

Knowing she looked tantalizing, she moved toward the man who was now gulping down a drink and demanding another. "Hello." Her voice was as smoky as her eyes.

He turned his head and did a double take. His eyes went wide as they toured down her body and back up again, lingering on her breasts. "Well, hello."

"I've never seen you here before."

"I've never been here before. I didn't know what I was missing."

"I see you won big. Your pockets are bulging." The fan drifted downward to the general vicinity of his pants pockets, but it tickled more than them.

"I guess I need to spend some of that money on somebody. Somebody pretty like you," he whispered.

Priscilla simpered and closed the fan with a snap. "My name's Priscilla."

His eyes bugged wide again. "*The* Priscilla?"

"You've heard of me?"

"There isn't a man in the state, big as it is, who hasn't heard of you."

She smiled. "Disappointed? Don't I live up to my reputation?" Her eyes slid down to his lips.

He turned to face her fully, letting his elbow slide across her ample breast. "That remains to be seen, doesn't it?"

"One hundred dollars." She flicked an imaginary piece of lint from his lapel.

He whistled. "That's a lot."

Her fingernail lightly scratched his lower lip. "I'm worth it."

Priscilla was breaking her own rule. She never took a stranger to her bed. A man had to be a customer for a long time before she entertained him personally. By then she knew his marital status, the names of his children and servants, where he lived, what his business was, which church he attended, what he liked to eat and drink and how much he did of both, what brand of cigar he preferred to smoke, what he liked to do in his leisure time, what he liked to do in bed, where he kept his money, and how much there was of it.

But this was an exception. Jake had behaved strangely. He had something against this man. She would make it her business to know just what that was.

"Well?"

The man reached into his pocket and took out the necessary bills. She closed her fingers around them and smiled invitingly. "This way."

Once the door to her private quarters was closed behind them, she wrapped her arms around his neck and kissed him, arching her body against his. The sooner she got this over with, the sooner she could get back to the nightly operation of the Garden of Eden.

"Goddamn, lady, you keep that up and I might die before I get my pants down."

"We can't let that happen, can we?"

With talented hands she began to undress him. She sighed when she found him hard and ready. "What's you name, winner?"

"Sheldon," he panted. "Grady Sheldon."

"Who's there?"

"It's only me."

Jake's silhouette filled the doorway between the rooms. Banner's room was in darkness. There was one lamp turned down low in the room he shared with Lee and Micah. But in the slice of light that arced across her bed, he could see her sitting up, clutching the covers to her chest.

Her hair was in disarray, catching the light on its wavy tumbled strands. Her eyes were round with apprehension, having just been awakened from a deep sleep when he opened the door.

Banner in bed, soft and mussed.

For the first time that night, Jake felt stirrings of arousal. How could this girl—yes, a girl only eighteen—dressed in an innocent nightgown a nun would have approved of, inspire desire in him when neither Priscilla's groping nor her whores, jaded and willing and partially naked, hadn't fazed him?

"What are you doing?" Her voice was a husky, sleepy whisper that reached through the darkness to touch him.

"I just got in, wanted to check and see if you were all right."

She lay back on the pillow and pulled the sheet up to her chin. "Have Lee and Micah come back yet?"

Jake shook his head and chuckled. "No. They'll probably be a while."

"What did . . . where did you go?" It cost her some pride

to ask. She wasn't looking at him, but kept her eyes trained on the ceiling.

"Nowhere."

"You went somewhere."

"No place you need to know about, Banner."

"To her?"

"Who?"

"Priscilla Watkins."

"Maybe."

"Did you finish with her what you started with me last night?"

"That's a helluva thing to ask!"

"Well, did you?"

"That's none of your business."

She sprang to a sitting position again. The cover slid to her waist. "It's my business," she said, thumping her fists against the mattress, "if you lock me in my room so you can go see her. The boys go out and carouse, you do, and I'm stuck here in this room."

"The boys can take care of themselves."

"So can I!"

He sighed. This wasn't going the way he had wanted it to. He had been glad she woke up. He had wanted to talk to her, to hear in her voice a trace of forgiveness for what had happened last night. Maybe he could have held her, touched her hair, kissed her cheek, told her he was sorry for hurting her again. Maybe he could have explained that he cared about her too much to treat her with no more regard than he would a woman he paid. And maybe, just maybe, she would have understood.

But they were arguing.

"Banner, you've got enough sense to know that you can't go traipsing all over Fort Worth unescorted."

"You could have escorted me. Instead you shoved me in this room, locked the door, and went off to visit your whore. That *is* where you went, isn't it? Tell me."

"Yes! I saw Priscilla. There, are you satisfied?"

She stared at him in injured silence for several seconds

before lying back down, pulling the sheet up high, and turning her back on him.

"Shit!" he muttered, slamming the door between them.

The hotel room closed around him and he paced. He considered going back into her room and apologizing for locking her in. He would offer to take her on a sightseeing tour of the city tomorrow after their business with Culpepper was settled.

But he couldn't trust himself to go back in her room. She thought he had slaked his desire with Priscilla. What she didn't know was that he was aching with it now.

Jake flopped down on the bed to remove his boots. Should he warn Banner that Sheldon was in town? He could easily have killed the man tonight. The strength of his hatred was frightful. Sheldon was a menace to the Colemans. That in itself was reason enough for Jake to hate him. But that he threatened Banner particularly, and the way in which he threatened her, made Jake's attitude toward him murderous.

Sheldon hadn't seemed in mourning over the deaths of his wife, unborn baby, and father-in-law. Nor had he the bearing of a man anxiously awaiting the acceptance of his marriage proposal. He had acted self-confident and sure, like the answer he wanted was a foregone conclusion. Such arrogance rubbed Jake the wrong way.

And what the hell was he doing in Fort Worth?

Jake glanced at the door connecting the rooms. Had Sheldon heard about their trip? Banner couldn't have gone unnoticed in Larsen as she prepared to follow them on horseback. Could Sheldon have followed her here on purpose, thinking she might be more likely to accept his proposal when she was out from under the protection of her family?

Well, whether Banner was mad at him or not, tomorrow Jake planned to stick to her like glue. He would make it impossible for Sheldon to get anywhere near her.

Jake looked down at his hands and was surprised to find them clenched into whitened fists. He had been imagining them around Sheldon's neck. That's what he would want to do to any man who touched Banner. He couldn't stand the thought of anyone's hands on her.

Except his.

Cursing, he flung himself back on the bed and tried to rid his mind of thoughts of them together, him and Banner.

Banner, her hair and skin damp and smelling of soap.

Banner, her mouth responsive beneath his.

Banner, her thighs bracketing his.

Banner, her breasts melting against his tongue like sugar.

The images persisted tormentingly until his own hand gave his loins relief.

Scalding tears continued to roll down her cheeks in incessant rivulets. Thank heaven she hadn't cried in front of him. Had he known she was crying when he left her alone on the bank of the creek last night? When was she going to stop humiliating herself like that? When would she learn?

Oh, but last night he had come close. He had come close to loving her, and she knew he had wanted to. The passion with which he had kissed her couldn't be fraudulent. The loving way his mouth had moved over her breasts couldn't have been a product of her imagination, because she could never have imagined such a sweet caress.

Then why had he stopped?

He had said because he was too old, because he wasn't good enough, because this and because that. Banner knew them all to be lame excuses. The real reason was that she wasn't Lydia. Jake might desire her, but he still loved her mother. He wasn't willing to settle for second best.

She listened to the sounds he made getting ready for bed. She heard the splashing of water he washed in, heard the thud of his boots hitting the floor, heard the sagging of the bedsprings when they took his weight.

Had he undressed? When he was alone, what did Jake sleep in? Not a nightshirt. He wasn't the type. His underwear? In the hot summertime?

Nothing?

She went weak with the thought of him lying naked only

a few yards away and rolled to her stomach in hopes of quenching the small flames igniting her body.

Why was she tormenting herself like this? Didn't she have any pride? Jake's body wasn't on fire, was it? He had put out whatever fires of desire Banner had started with another woman.

Priscilla Watkins. Without ever having met her, she detested the woman.

She lay awake for a long while, wondering if Jake was asleep. Was he reliving those moments of passion they had shared last night, or was his mind reviewing his evening spent with Priscilla?

In the wee hours the boys came in, tripping, giggling, and stumbling with drunkenness. In loud whispers that penetrated the walls, Jake told them to be quiet and get into bed before the management of the hotel threw them all out. She heard them settle.

And still she lay awake, wondering what a woman like Priscilla Watkins could do for a man like Jake that she couldn't.

"Ah . . . ah . . . ah!" Grady Sheldon climaxed. Priscilla pretended to. He was a lousy lover, taking all, giving nothing. Not that she was easy to please. She wasn't. But she hadn't been aroused in the slightest by Sheldon's rapid, sweaty lovemaking.

She ran her long nails up and down his back languorously. "Hmm," she sighed, "that was nice." Without his quite knowing how she had done it, she had separated them and rolled aside. Exhausted, he nestled his head on her shoulder.

"Good?"

She rolled her eyes ceilingward. The ones who had to ask were never good. "Very," she said, blowing gently in his ear. His hand found her breast and squeezed too hard. She allowed it. Grady had gotten what he wanted from her, but she was far from satisfied. She wasn't through with him yet and until she was, she would go on stroking his pride, and whatever else she had to stroke.

"Will you be coming to see me often? Are you from around here?"

"No. Larsen."

Her hands stilled for only a second. Grady didn't even notice. "Larsen? In east Texas?"

"Uh-huh." He nibbled her neck. "I've got a sawmill there. Biggest one in ten counties. They float timber down the Sabine, right to my back door."

She laid her hand on his thigh. He might have more potential than she had first thought. In financial circles it was known that the next growing industry would be lumbering in east Texas's piney woods. "Be gentle with those teeth, darling." The last thing she wanted was teeth marks. That was another rule she laid down to the lovers she took: Do what you want, but don't leave any traces for the next man to see.

"Sorry," Grady mumbled. "I get excited about my business. Now that we have the railroads, it's easier to ship lumber all over the country."

"I see," she said meditatively. "Aren't you worried about leaving it?"

"I have a dozen employees to run the business for me."

Yes, Sheldon's might be a friendship worth cultivating. She wasn't foolish enough to believe that the Garden of Eden could go on indefinitely. The vigilant church groups would put it out of business sooner or later. Even if they didn't, she didn't want to live out her days a madam. She wanted years of ease, years to live off the profits she had saved. Investments were the way to make money these days.

"How did you come to know Jake Langston?" Grady's head popped up and he peered into her guileless face. "Am I mistaken? You do know him, don't you?"

"I don't know him. I know who he is," he said bitterly.

She cradled his head and guided his mouth back to her breast. "I wouldn't have asked if I'd known it was going to upset you. Please don't stop what you were doing. It felt so good."

He kissed her breast bruisingly, taking his frustration out on her. "I first saw him on my wedding day."

"He was a guest at your wedding?"

"Not my guest. My wife's. Or at least she was supposed to be my wife."

It couldn't be! No wonder his name had rung a bell. She had heard it first from Dub. Could it be that she had the Coleman girl's former fiancé in her bed? Rarely was fate that benevolent. Priscilla had difficulty controlling her glee. Before she jumped to conclusions, she had to make sure.

She trilled a laugh and said, "Grady, you're not making any sense."

He grinned lopsidedly. "Guess I'm not. Well, you see, I had some trouble on my wedding day. It was called off, right there in the church."

She sat up slightly, her eyes rounding with wonder. "No! Tell me what happened."

He repeated the story she had heard from Dub. "That bastard moonshiner said it was me who gave his daughter a kid," he finished his tale heatedly.

Priscilla gave him a knowing smile. "I've had you, Grady. I wouldn't be surprised."

He laughed complacently. "Well, I reckon I'm potent enough to have done it."

"You should have come to me sooner. We don't let little accidents like babies happen."

She kissed him, using her tongue like no other woman he had ever known could, not even Wanda. "And where did Jake fit into all this?" she asked, when at last she pulled away. Her heart was pounding with excitement. Not over the kiss, surely, but over what she was about to hear.

"He rallied to the cause of my fiancée's family. The Colemans. Banner, that's her name, stormed out without letting me explain."

"You poor thing." Priscilla settled back against the mound of pillows and drew him to her in pity. Her eyes were dancing, but she was careful not to let him see.

"I was stuck with Wanda and her pa."

"Was?"

"They died in a fire a few weeks back."

"How sad."

He raised his head and winked at her. "Not for me."

Silently he communicated what he didn't dare speak aloud. Priscilla's eyes narrowed with a new appreciation for Grady Sheldon. Like her, he didn't let anything stand in the way of getting what he wanted. "Fires are such ghastly things, aren't they?" She scratched his ears.

"They sure are."

They both laughed. He butted her breasts with his head, then began kissing them ardently. But Priscilla didn't have the complete picture yet. "What does Jake have to do with you now?"

"He's the foreman of Banner's ranch, the one her daddy gave her. It was supposed to be mine too. She's got acres of timberland going to waste."

"And you want it," she said intuitively.

"I like you, Priscilla. We think alike." He grinned slyly. "Since my wife's untimely death, I've gone to Banner on bended knees begging for forgiveness and asking her to marry me in spite of what happened."

"And what does she say?"

"Not much." His lips thinned bitterly. "I can't get near her. Jake Langston keeps an eagle eye on her."

Priscilla brushed her fingers through his hair and said offhandedly, "Then you know she's here, in Fort Worth, with him."

"What!" Grady sat upright. "Banner's here? How do you know?" Priscilla repeated what Jake had told her. "Well, I'll be a sonofabitch. The sheriff in Larsen was getting a little too curious about the cause of the fire that killed the Burnses. I thought it would be prudent to get out of town for a while, but I hated like hell leaving without having a definite answer from Banner."

He threw back his head and laughed. "With Jake so busy buying cattle, maybe I'll just mosey over to the hotel and see her." He gazed down at Priscilla, who had watched the workings of his mind with growing admiration. She adored men who turned every event to their advantage, just as she did.

And what a weapon she had! Banner Coleman's scorned

fiancé. Only one thing troubled her—Jake's protective attitude toward the girl. She didn't like that one bit. What did it mean? According to Grady, he was practically living with her on that ranch. He had run off tonight to check on her, turning down her poker tables, her liquor, her girls, even *herself*, to get back to that girl.

Well, she wouldn't have it! She'd see to it that the affair, whatever it was, was brought to ruination if it was the last thing she ever did. It was about time Jake got his comeuppance for rejecting her all these years. She would use Banner Coleman to bring it about.

"How do you know this Langston fellow?" Grady asked, a shade suspiciously. Maybe he had talked too freely about that fire.

Priscilla's slow, easy smile assured him. She drew his head down for a long, lascivious kiss. "I've known him for years. Since we were kids. He's nothing but a saddle tramp who buys his drinks on credit."

Grady seemed satisfied with her answer. Besides, he was too befuddled to think straight. She had pushed his head back to her breasts and he was drowning in the musky scent of her perfume. His mouth slid wetly from one nipple to the other, sucking hard. She didn't seem to mind anything he did to her.

His pulse pounding, he came to his knees and straddled her shoulders. His eyes were hot as they poured down on her face. She raked her sharp fingernails down his chest, drawing blood in two places. His chest heaved.

"It'll cost you extra," she said softly. Priscilla always fairly informed her customers what they would have to pay.

"How much?" he asked thickly.

She made a silky fist of her hand and slid it from the tip of his penis to the root. "Another fifty dollars."

"Yes, good God, yes, anything."

Smiling bewitchingly, she raised her head to his lap. The information he had provided her had been invaluable. He deserved a treat.

SIXTEEN

Jake and Banner breakfasted early the next morning. Their appointment with Mr. Culpepper was set for ten o'clock.

"You two look like hell," Jake said to Lee and Micah when they staggered forward to join Banner and him at their table in the hotel's dining room. Their faces were gray and pasty. Red lines rivered through the whites of their eyes.

Lee fell into the chair adjacent to Banner's. Propping his elbows on the table, he held his head in his hands, groaning. "I feel like hell. Banner, would you please pour me some coffee. My hands are shaking so much I could barely shave."

Sniffing her disapproval, she poured cups of strong black coffee for him and Micah, who had yet to say anything.

"If you can't handle it, you'd better not drink it," Jake said sagely.

He smiled conspiratorially at Banner and winked. She only stared back at him with a cool disdain that indicted the male population in general. He had spent a helluva night over her, and her condescending attitude rankled. He took his sudden bad mood out on the boys. "Hurry up and get some coffee down you. I don't want Mr. Culpepper to think he's dealing with drunkards."

They decided to walk from the hotel to the cattle broker's downtown office. Fort Worth bustled with activity. Banner, despite her determination to pout all day, was caught up in the excitement of the city. The shop windows were full of tempting merchandise. The streets were clogged with traffic, farm wagons loaded with produce and gawking children, smart buggies driven by smartly dressed ladies, cowboys on horseback, trolleys loaded with people who had places to go and things to do.

It was a town radiating energy, and that energy was infectious. By the time they reached the building that housed Mr. Culpepper's offices, Banner's eyes were sparkling. Even the mood among the men seemed to have improved.

Jake caught Banner's eye as he held the door for her. As she went past him he said, "You're looking right fetching this morning, Banner."

Her head came around. Was there some underlying derision in his compliment? No. The blue eyes burned steadily into hers. "Thank you, Jake."

She was wearing the same ensemble he had smirked at two mornings before. She had folded it carefully into her saddle-bag, knowing she would have to have it for their interview with Culpepper. This morning she had smoothed out the wrinkles as best she could and reshaped the hat over her hair, which she had piled high. There were pearl earrings in her ears. She knew she looked businesslike, but still feminine.

And Jake had noticed!

"You look nice too," she told him as they took the stairs. He was dressed in the same clothes he had worn to her wedding.

"Thanks," he mumbled self-consciously.

A harried clerk ushered them into Mr. Culpepper's office on the second floor of the building. The broker was obviously surprised when Banner came in with the others, but he covered it by offering her a chair.

His was the office of a busy man. The furniture was a trifle dusty and his desk was littered with papers and documents and bills of sale, all of which looked very difficult to read and awfully official. The shelves behind his desk were cluttered with books and piled with ledgers and cattle registers.

Lee and Micah took seats on the horsehair sofa against the wall, gratefully out of the sunlight that poured in through the tall windows. They were content to let Jake conduct the business transactions.

At first Mr. Culpepper addressed everything he said to

Jake, but after Banner asked several incisive, intelligent questions and he learned that she was indeed the owner of the ranch for which they were buying the cattle, he reversed his opinion of her as being merely a pretty young lady who shouldn't have to be bothered with dull business details.

Within a half-hour they had agreed on a price for the small herd. "Twenty-nine Hereford cows and a bull." Culpepper considered for a moment. "I have a Brahman bull that has proven to be of a . . . uh . . . romantic nature," he said in deference to Banner. "He's valuable, but I could give you a price break on him. Would you be interested?"

Jake shook his head. "They do better in south Texas. I'll stick with the Herefords to start."

"Very well. Are we ready then to draw up the bill of sale?" Mr. Culpepper asked.

"Everything sounds all right," Jake said. "But I want to check the cattle first. Right down to their hooves." His smile was congenial, but his eyes said that he meant business.

The cattle broker was taken aback. He had thought Jake Langston a likable enough fellow, but only a cowboy. Now he was showing traits of a careful businessman, which Culpepper had to admire.

"Of course, of course. Shall we go to the stockyards and inspect them? Would that be convenient right now? We can take my buggy."

Jake stood. "That'll be fine."

Culpepper summoned his clerk and asked him to have his buggy brought around to the front of the building. They all went downstairs. Jake turned to Lee and Micah. "Take Banner back to the hotel. It won't be necessary for all of you to go."

"I'm going," Banner said.

Before Jake had time to respond, Lee said, "Banner, you can't go down there."

"Aren't women allowed at the stockyards?"

"It's just no place for them, that's all," Micah said diplomatically. "All kinds of riffraff hang out around there."

"I'm not going to look at the riffraff. I'm going to see the cattle I've bought." She looked at Jake, her eyes daring him to forbid her to go.

"Go on, git," he said to the boys. "We'll see you later."

Taking Banner's arm, Jake led her out to the boardwalk where Culpepper was standing by with the buggy. He watched Lee and Micah walk away without Banner and turned back to Jake. "Will the young lady be going with us?" he asked dubiously.

"Yes, the young lady will be going with us," Jake said grimly as he helped her into the buggy. He hoped he wouldn't have to kill somebody for getting fresh with her before the day was out.

As it turned out they concluded their business without mishap. Banner was delighted with the white-faced cattle. Their curly red coats gleamed in the sunshine. She fell in love with each cow, though she gave the bull wide berth.

"They're breed cattle, Banner," Jake said, smiling at her as she patted one cow between the wide-set eyes, "not pets."

"I know. But they're mine and I'm going to name each one."

He laughed indulgently. A bill of sale was tucked safely in his pocket. Ross would be pleased with the deal he had struck. There was good news from the railroad. The strike was expected to end at midnight. He had already made arrangements for their herd to be loaded on to cattle cars on the first train going to Larsen.

Feeling as lighthearted as Banner, he clasped her around the waist and lifted her off the ground. "Well, Banner girl, we have us a herd."

"And it's only a start, Jake, only a start."

"You bet it is."

"I was holding my breath," she said excitedly. "I didn't know if Mr. Culpepper would accept your final offer or not. You were wonderful. You sat there so calm and collected. I wanted to kick you on the shin for driving such a hard bargain."

She squealed with laughter as he whirled her around,

disregarding the odd looks being cast at them. "I'm a real big deal maker, didn't you know that?"

When he set her back on her feet, he didn't release her, but left his hands encircling her tiny waist. Nor did her hands leave his shoulders. He gazed down into her sunlit face. Her eyelashes looked iridescent as she squinted against the glare of the sun. He could enumerate each freckle scattered randomly across her nose and cheekbones.

The hot, dusty, smelly atmosphere of the stockyards could have been Paradise and he doubted he would have felt any better about life than he did right then. Looking into Banner's expectant face he didn't feel old and tired and cynical, but young and energetic and ambitious. He felt good about himself; he could almost believe that he might turn out to be worth something after all. Hell, at the moment he felt like he could take these first thirty head and, with just a half-smile from fortune, multiply them into the finest herd of beef cattle in the whole damn state.

For the first time in a long time, Jake's smile came from his soul. It erased the caution that always lurked in his eyes, and eased the lines of bitterness around his mouth.

"What would you like to do?"

"Do?" Banner repeated. While his mouth was smiling and happy, she would like to taste it, to know this rare joy that was inside him. But her pride wouldn't let her ask him to kiss her.

"Today is your day," Jake said when she seemed at a loss for something to say. "Name it and you've got it. What would you like to see and do? Let's start by taking a trolley ride."

She didn't really care what they did. She had Jake's undivided attention and that was enough.

They rode around Fort Worth, taking in the expansion of the city. They ate a roast beef lunch in a classy restaurant and toasted their new herd with a bottle of wine. Laughing tipsily himself, Jake refused to let her drink a third glass.

They shopped. Banner dragged him into one store after another, but he was grudgingly permissive. She picked out an embroidered handkerchief for Lydia, a new apron for Ma, and a pipe for Ross.

"Does he smoke a pipe?" Jake asked.

"He will now."

She tilted her head back and smiled up at him. If she had asked him to eat the pipe, he would have. She was thoroughly captivating with those dancing, chameleon eyes that seemed to change color with her mood. Her smiling red lips were capable of demonstrating tremendous passion and the least reminder of her kisses sent his heart to racing. A man could look at that animated face for a hundred years and never get tired of it. Only the discreet cough of the salesclerk brought him around. He paid for the purchases and they returned to the hotel to freshen up and eat a light supper.

He had consented to take her to the opera house for the evening performance of *My Sister's Escapade*. "Lee and Micah aren't joining us?" she asked as they made their way to their balcony seats. She had heard a furtive conversation going on beyond their adjoining door before they left the hotel, but couldn't distinguish the words.

"They had other things to do," Jake said obliquely.

"Wouldn't you rather be doing those 'other things' and not watching over me?"

He clasped her arm and led her down the aisle toward the row number printed on their tickets. "No." When she raised her eyes doubtfully, he repeated softly, "No." They smiled at each other and barely had time to locate their seats before the play began.

She didn't make further comment, though she hoped he was telling the truth. This had been one of the happiest days in her life.

When they returned to the hotel, he unlocked the door to her room and followed her in. "I'd better check around." She lit the lamp and removed her hat, gloves, and jacket while he opened the door to the wardrobe, looked behind the drapes and under the bed. Dusting off his hands, he stood. "Everything's all right."

"Good."

"Well . . ."

"Thank you for today, Jake. I had a wonderful time."

"I'm glad. You deserved a day of fun." She looked so beautiful standing in the golden pool of lamplight. He wanted to touch the front of her blouse just to see if the lace was as soft as it looked. And her hair. And her cheek. And her mouth.

Banner twisted the program she had gotten at the opera house, forgetting that she had intended to take it home to show Lydia and Ma before storing it in her box of keep- sakes. "You didn't stay with me for that reason alone, did you?"

"What reason?"

"Because you felt I deserved it, that you owed it to me." She lowered her eyes. "To make up for something else."

Jake tapped his hat against his knee. "I'll never make up for that night in the barn, Banner. I'm trying real hard to live with that." He stepped closer to her and gazed down at the top of her head. "I spent today with you because I wanted to."

And that was basically true. Sure, he had kept her away from the hotel so Sheldon wouldn't have a chance to see her. But underneath that noble gesture Jake knew his real reason was that he had enjoyed her company. And he had had a damn good time. Even sitting through the silly play hadn't been so bad because Banner had been close beside him in the dark, her elbow resting beside his on the armrest, her knee occasionally bumping his.

Now, when she raised her head, tears were making her eyes luminescent. "Thank you for saying that." Coming up on her toes, she lightly kissed his cheek.

Jake battled with himself. If he took her in his arms and kissed her, really kissed her, he wouldn't let her go. The room was too private and the bed too convenient. And even though she might fancy herself ready to make love to him now, she would hate herself all over again in the morning.

So he reached for her hand and kissed the back of it softly. Then, because Jake was more sinner than saint, he turned her hand over and planted a hot, heartfelt kiss in the cushion of her palm. Before he could talk himself out of it, he left her, closing the door firmly behind him.

Banner watched him leave with mixed emotions. She had been disappointed that he hadn't embraced and kissed her passionately. But he hadn't gone to meet Priscilla or any other woman tonight. He had chosen to stay with her. All day he had treated her in a courtly manner, but she had sensed his desire simmering just beneath the surface even as hers was.

She had two things on her side, time and proximity. They had the ranch in common. They had to work on it together. While they were at that, he would fall in love with her. She would see to it. It would take some doing, but she thought he was getting close. Satisfied with the day's progress, she dropped off to sleep immediately.

Hours later, she was awakened by shuffling sounds coming through the connecting door. Rolling over, she smiled into the darkness. Lee and Micah were returning after a night of debauchery. She heard a quick, whispered conversation, then the opening of a door followed by a soft click when it closed.

Someone had gone out.

Without thinking, she threw back the sheets and flew to the door of her room. She opened it quietly and stuck her head out. Jake was retreating down the carpeted hallway, buckling on his holster. He was in a hurry. At the landing he turned and disappeared from sight.

Despair settled over Banner like a heavy, limb-paralyzing, debilitating cloak. Dejectedly she returned to bed.

He had waited until the boys returned, waited until he thought she was safely asleep, then sneaked out like a thief to go to his whore. Everything he had said and done today had been a lie, a lie to placate her. He had known her feathers were ruffled after last night, and he was only smoothing them to put her off guard.

Oh, she hated him! She beat her fists against the pillow, imagining it to be his lying face.

"I hate him!" she vowed softly.

But in her heart she knew that she loved him. That's why his deception hurt so much.

"I'm sorry, sir, we're closed."

"Not to me you're not." Jake shoved his way past the bouncer at the door of the Garden of Eden.

"Miss Priscilla—"

"Will kick your ass if you don't let me in." The bouncer had been hired for his brawn rather than his brain. He was twice as big around as Jake, but not nearly as agile and he knew it. Besides, he had heard of this man's temper and readiness with a pistol. Most mind-swaying of all, he knew that Priscilla Watkins's eyes lit up whenever this particular cowboy was in the place. "Is she alone?" Jake asked.

"Yeah. I think she's taking a bath," he said dully. "I saw the maid hauling in hot water a few minutes ago."

"She won't mind if I go in." Jake said the last words over his shoulder. He was already on his way into Priscilla's private quarters. He heard the languid splash of water as soon as he opened the door. He lifted his heels off the floor, not wanting his spurs to alert her that he was there until he was ready for her to see him.

At the door leading into her bedroom he paused. She was reclining in the tub which had been moved from behind the screen in the corner. A lazy hand was squeezing a sponge over her breasts. Her head, with her hair piled high atop it, was resting on the tub's arm. Her eyes were closed.

Jake leaned one shoulder against the doorjamb and silently watched her for several minutes. Something finally alerted her that she wasn't alone. She opened her eyes and saw his reflection in the mirror. She sprang up, splashing crazily, whipped her head around and gave a small cry.

"Hello, Pris." He spoke softly, intimately, letting his eyes drift over her wet breasts.

"Jake," she breathed.

In the doorway, he stood tall and rangy and dangerous, though his posture was slouchy. From beneath the brim of his hat, which he had had the bad manners to leave on, something Priscilla wouldn't have tolerated from another guest, his eyes were steady and assessing.

For just an instant, Priscilla felt a flash of modesty. The way his sapphire eyes seemed to flay the skin right off her body made her want to cover herself from his penetrating stare. Recovering, and cursing herself for acting like a schoolgirl in the throes of her first romance, she said, "What the hell are you doing here?"

Pushing himself away from the door frame with a casual shove of his shoulder, he sauntered toward her. "Aren't you glad to see me?"

She followed his progress warily. She wanted to believe he had come for the purpose she had always dreamed he would, but she couldn't trust herself to think that. "I'm always glad to see an old friend."

He grinned arrogantly. "We sure are that, aren't we, Pris? Old friends?"

Her heart leaped wildly when he straddled the tub with his long legs, standing over her like a conqueror. His pants were black and fit the muscles of his legs like a second skin. His shirt had been pulled on in haste. Most of the buttons had been left undone, revealing a carpet of thick blond hair over coppery skin. No bandana, no tie, no vest. Jake had been in a hurry to see her. Well, it was about time!

It was exciting, the hot, passionate way he stared down at her, as though he might hurt her a little before giving her immense pleasure.

"I'd like to think we're friends," she said softly. For once her heavy-lidded eyes and breathy voice weren't manufactured. They were genuine. She wanted to touch his thighs, to run her hands up them, but she didn't quite have the nerve. His eyes were glowing with a sensual light, but his bearing intimated untouchability.

Jake leaned down and braced himself over the tub with one hand. Reaching into the water, he groped for the sponge, which Priscilla had dropped when she saw him in the mirror. Finding it near her thigh, he lifted it from the water and squeezed it over her breasts. "You look as pink and plump as a baby, Pris."

Her body was reacting. He was dripping water onto nipples hard with desire for him. But she didn't want him to know how anxious she was. She smiled up at him cunningly. "I hear you like them young these days. Eighteen? Like the Coleman girl."

Good, Jake thought, *she's going to make it easy for me.* He had asked the boys about their adventures upon their return from the Garden of Eden. But he had found out more than he had bargained for.

"It was great," Lee had said, falling on the double bed he shared with Micah. He was satiated. "Sugar was great." He sighed. "Not real pretty and a little old, but she sure as hell gave me a workover."

"And after her we had"—Micah snapped his fingers, searching for a name in his sex-besotted brain—"what was her name, Lee?"

"Betsy," he said dreamily. "She was so sweet. I think I love Betsy."

Jake, groaning over the misguided notions of youth, reached to turn out the light. "Better wipe that sappy grin off your face before Lydia sees it, Lee, or she'll never let you go anywhere with me again. And that goes double for you, little brother."

Micah was tugging off his boots when he said offhandedly, "You'll never guess who we saw there. Sheldon. Grady Sheldon."

Jake's hand paused in the act of turning out the lamp. "Oh? Did he see you or Lee?"

"No. He was on his way to see the madam herself."

"How do you know?"

"I pointed him out to Betsy and told her he was from our hometown. She was impressed, said he had spent most of the day with Priscilla and that she didn't usually favor a man for that long."

Jake switched out the light, but he was suddenly wide-awake. Priscilla and Grady Sheldon. A dangerous combination if he'd ever heard of one. It bothered him to think of what those two could cook up together. He got out of bed and dressed. The boys were already snoring softly by the time he left the room.

Now he looked down into Priscilla's snide face and knew all his suspicions had been confirmed. He'd been right to come and was glad she had mentioned Banner first. "Her name is Banner," he said.

"Oh, yes, Banner. You were seen all over town with her today."

"Was I? Who told you that? My friend Sheldon?"

The flash of panic in her eyes gave away her surprise. Priscilla hadn't wanted him to know she'd been "favoring" Grady. That was even more cause for Jake to worry.

"You and Grady are friends?" Priscilla said. "That's not what he told me." This time she yielded to the temptation and laid her hands on his thighs. They were as hard as they looked.

"And just what did he tell you?"

"That Banner was considering marrying him." She threw the barb to see if it struck home. It did. Jake's eyes went cold and hard. The muscles beneath her hands flexed before relaxing again.

"Did he tell you about his wife?"

"Yes."

"How she died?"

"The fire?"

Just as Jake suspected. Sheldon was the kind who would brag to a whore. "Clever of him, wasn't it, to get rid of her and his kid that way?"

Priscilla's hands crept up his thigh, coming to within touching distance of what she ached to know again after almost twenty years. "I thought so, but then I admire ingenuity. Grady's ambitious. And he wants Banner Coleman. No doubt he'll get her."

So, Sheldon *had* set that fire. He wasn't beyond murder. And he wanted Banner. "Not if I have anything to do with it," Jake growled.

Priscilla laughed and came up out of the water. Her hands slid over his crotch, up his stomach and over his chest. She pressed her body against his. "So it's true. Grady told me you watch that girl like an eagle. Isn't that carrying loyalty to the Colemans a bit far?''

Sinuously, she moved against him, rubbing her pubis against the juncture of his straddled legs. One hand curved around the back of his neck; the other slipped inside his shirt. "Or is it more than that? Don't tell me the big bad Jake Langston has fallen in love with a child?''

Jake refused to be provoked. "I've loved Banner all her life.''

Priscilla's laugh rumbled up from her magnificent breasts. "Just like you've loved her mother, your best friend's wife?''

Before she could blink, he had her wrists manacled in his fists. "I won't have you talking about either one of them with your filthy whore's mouth.''

She only smiled. "My, my, aren't you touchy? Sure you aren't falling for the daughter the same way you did the mother?''

"Shut up.''

"Isn't it tough on you, Jake, loving and never having, slaking your passion on whores because you can never have the women you love? It's a rotten shame, isn't it? Hmm?''

"I said to shut up!''

"Do you love Banner Coleman?''

"Not like you mean, no.''

"Sure?''

"Yes.''

"Prove it.'' Her breath struck his lips, hot and heavy. "Take me.''

His arms went around her and he lifted her from the tub. His mouth swooped down hard and cruel on hers as he carried her toward the bed. Priscilla, thrilling to her victory, twisted against him, imprinting her wet body on his clothes. She wrapped her legs around his and searched for his tongue with her own.

His hands slid to her waist and closed around it like pinchers. Then he shoved her down on the bed and wiped her kiss from his mouth. "Never, Priscilla. Never. Because every time I look at you I remember that first afternoon we diddled away. An afternoon I should have been with my brother. He's dead because of me. I'll never forgive either one of us for that. And I'll never forget that you're anything but a whore. As sorry as I am, I'll never dirty myself with you again.''

Priscilla lay there, panting hard, propped up on her elbows, thighs spread, chest heaving. She watched him leave, her eyes dilated with hate. He had scorned her for the last time. If she died trying, she would hurt Jake Langston, hurt him so bad he would never recover.

And the way to him was through Banner Coleman.

Banner slept late. When she woke up, she knocked on the connecting door of the rooms and when she didn't get an answer, opened it. The room was empty. The men were out and about.

Well, she wasn't going to stay cooped up in the hotel room indefinitely. If Jake could deceive her, she wouldn't worry about angering him by going out.

She dressed quickly in her suit and ate a hearty breakfast in the hotel dining room. It was a bright sunny Saturday. Traffic jammed the streets. Banner left the hotel and stepped out onto the boardwalk. She glanced up and down the street, trying to decide where to go first. Maybe if she waited for the next trolley . . .

''Banner Coleman?''

At the sound of her name, she turned around. She knew who the woman was instantly. Maybe it was her eyes that gave her away. They were brittle and peevish. Banner thought life held few surprises for those cool gray eyes. There were no telltale lines in her face, but an indefinable stamp of experience that made her look every day her age and older.

Her clothes surprised Banner. She would have expected tarty baubles and bangles, a glittery fabric, an overabundance of everything. Instead the woman was wearing a well-tailored blue suit. The only dashing thing about the costume was the black plume in her hat that curved over her brow. Her hands were gloved with kid. A tiny reticule was hanging from her wrist by a silk braid. She carried a parasol that matched her suit, but it was left unopened as she stepped forward from the shadows beneath the covered boardwalk.

"I'm—"

"I know who you are, Miss Watkins," Banner said.

One of Priscilla's brows arched, but she said nothing. Banner Coleman was a disagreeable surprise. She was prettier than Lydia. And more exotic. Her coloring was even more vivid. She had all of Lydia's femininity, and all of Ross's dashing good looks. It was a strong face that stared back at her, not one to be intimidated easily. She had hoped the Coleman girl would cower from her in horror. Instead she was demonstrating a spunk inherited from her mother.

Priscilla peddled female flesh. She could have made a fortune off Banner Coleman. The thought infuriated her. Banner was young. The rosy blooms in her cheeks were real. She had a respected name. People didn't snub her in the streets. Youth, natural beauty, respect. She had everything that Priscilla scorned, but secretly envied.

"So you've heard of me."

"Yes." Banner didn't elaborate. She wasn't offended because a notorious whore had confronted her on a public street. She hated the woman for being Jake's bed partner, but she was consumed with curiosity about her too.

"From Jake?"

"For one."

"Ah, Jake." Priscilla closed her eyes for a moment and drew a deep breath. When she opened her eyes again, she triumphed at the seething expression on Banner's face. So the chit was in love with him. This was going to be marvelous fun! "Jake and I have been . . . friends . . . for a long time."

"Yes, I know."

"He was just a boy when I met him." Her eyelids lowered. "But not for long," she added softly. "He's become such an exciting man, don't you agree?"

"He's always been exciting to me."

"Of course," Priscilla said, almost sympathetically. "You never knew him as a boy. How are your parents? You knew that I met them years ago too?"

"Yes, on the wagon train. They told me about you."

"Did they?"

Banner blushed. "I've heard them mention you."

Priscilla was amused. "I'll bet you have." She cocked her head to one side. "You resemble them both. You're a very attractive girl."

"Thank you."

"So is your brother. Attractive, I mean."

If she wished to shock Banner into knowing that Lee had been to the Garden of Eden, she failed. "I know he went to your whorehouse last night, Miss Watkins. Thank you for your compliment. I think he's attractive too."

Priscilla wasn't enjoying this as much as she had hoped. The girl had more gumption than she had expected and fencing with her was becoming more of a challenge than Priscilla had anticipated.

Banner didn't notice the arrival and departure of the trolley. Nor did she notice the furtive glances cast in their direction as pedestrians eddied around them. Her eyes held those of the woman who was her enemy. Priscilla Watkins posed a threat to her. It was as yet unrevealed, but it was there. Banner felt it in every fiber of her body.

Priscilla was like a beautifully polished apple, tempting, captivating, stunning in her external perfection. But Banner perceived the rottenness on the inside.

"Of course he's only your half-brother, isn't he?" Priscilla said, picking up that thread of conversation.

"Yes. His mother died when he was born. That was before my mama and papa knew each other. But you know all that, Miss Watkins. You were there."

"Yes, I was there." Her eyes slid up and down Banner assessingly. Just how much fortitude did the girl have? She was about to find out. "I was there when Jake and his brother Luke found your mother in the woods. She was nearly dead, you know."

"That's what Jake told me."

"It was to be expected I suppose after the ordeal she had been through." Casually she adjusted the feather over her brow.

"Ordeal?"

Priscilla's eyes homed in on Banner like a hawk spotting a wounded rabbit. "Giving birth out in the open like that." Then she pretended embarrassment and laid a gloved hand on her chest. "Oh, I'm sorry. Perhaps I shouldn't have said anything. You *did* know about your mother's first baby, didn't you?"

"Baby?" Banner whispered just before all the blood drained from her head.

SEVENTEEN

"Baby?" Banner repeated the word. There had to be some mistake. She was her mother's only child.

Wasn't she?

The traitorous thought invaded Banner's mind as she stood there, trying to ward off waves of dizziness. Priscilla Watkins had finally succeeded in shocking her.

Baby! Was this the secret that Lydia and Ross had kept from her and Lee? Was this the key to their past that Banner had waited for? Suddenly she didn't want it. Let the secrets of the past remain intact. If this Watkins woman had imparted the news, it couldn't be pleasant, and Banner thought she was better off not knowing.

But like a bird mesmerized by a snake, she stared back at Priscilla. Her eyes were trained on the woman's painted lips, as though convincing her ears that she wasn't hearing properly.

"Nobody ever knew who Lydia was or where she came from, much less who that baby belonged to."

"You're lying. There wasn't a baby," Banner rasped. "My mama never had another baby."

"Of course she did, my dear. It died out there in the woods somewhere in Tennessee. Ma and Zeke Langston buried it. Word had spread through the wagon train by noon that the Langston boys had found a girl and her dead baby in the woods."

"I don't believe you."

Priscilla laughed throatily. "Oh, yes, you do. You're an intelligent girl. You've always known there was more to your parents than what you saw on the surface, haven't you?"

"No!"

"Didn't your mother ever tell you that she was taken to Ross Coleman's wagon to wet-nurse baby Lee?"

Banner's lips thinned stubbornly. She shook her head furiously. "It's not true."

"Ask her," Priscilla whispered with the taunting inflection of the serpent offering Eve the apple.

"Ma Langston only took her to him to help with Lee."

"She nursed him. My mama was in the Coleman wagon when Ma brought Lydia in. She said her breasts were leaking milk."

"No."

"And you know if she had milk, that means she had a baby. Besides, I saw her nursing him myself plenty of times."

"You're lying!"

"Or is your mother? Ask her. See what your mother says about that other baby. I wonder who fathered it. And ask your papa about his past too. I never did believe—"

"Priscilla!"

Jake barked her name from the doorway of the hotel. He had entered the lobby on the Third Street side and gone immediately to their rooms. When he discovered Banner wasn't there, he had dashed out to Throckmorton Street, only to be brought up short at seeing her engaged in conversation with Priscilla Watkins.

That in itself was shocking enough. But the paleness of Banner's cheeks and the chalky line around her mouth made his heart constrict with dread.

Damn the whore! Damn the day he ever met her. If she had hurt Banner, told her something she didn't need to know, he would kill her.

"What the hell are you doing here?" he demanded as he came striding toward them. He wedged himself between the two women, acting as a shield for Banner.

"Having a pleasant little chat with Miss Coleman. I was just inquiring into the well-being of her parents."

Jake's eyes hardened menacingly. He didn't believed Priscilla's honeyed explanation for one moment. In the first place, she didn't give a damn about anybody's well-being but her own. It had been no accident that she met Banner on the street. She had probably hired someone to point Banner out to her. Ordinarily Priscilla wouldn't have exposed herself to the madness of a Saturday morning in Fort Worth's commercial district. No, this meeting had been carefully calculated, and it boded no good for Banner.

"Banner, get inside."

Jake kept his deadly blue stare on Priscilla. He spoke softly, but no less emphatically to Banner, who was still spellbound by what Priscilla had told her. "Banner, get inside," Jake repeated when several seconds passed and she didn't move.

Like a sleepwalker, she stepped around him and went into the hotel. Only when she was well out of hearing did his eyes slice back to Priscilla.

"What did you tell her?"

"Why, nothing, Jake. I—"

"What did you tell her?" he shouted.

"Why don't you ask her?" Priscilla said, drawing herself up haughtily.

"I intend to. And you'd better hope to God I don't find out you've hurt her."

She smiled scornfully. "Poor Jake. First the mother. Now

the daughter. You're a champion for lost causes, aren't you? When you've run out of them, you can always come back to me." She laid her hand on his chest. "I've got what you really want."

He threw back his head and laughed. "No, Priscilla. It's the other way around. I've got what *you* really want."

Her face became ugly with hate and she snatched her hand back as though he had bitten her. She turned on her heel, popped her parasol open and strode down the sidewalk, her skirts angrily swishing.

Men had fought over her, drunk themselves sick over her, a few had even killed themselves over her. None had ever laughed. That bastard had laughed!

How she hated him. She had seen the way he protected the girl. The fool probably fancied himself in love with her, just as he'd been with her mother years ago. Priscilla wouldn't have traded places with either Lydia or Banner, but it galled her that Jake preferred both of them over her. When had he ever rallied to her cause? Since that day his brother got killed, she had meant nothing to him but something to wipe his feet on. And isn't that what all men did to her?

They used her. Oh, yes, they liked to work out their frustrations on her, fulfill their wildest desires with her, but when had she ever gotten more from a man than the crumbs of his life left over from his family and business? When had a man, any man, ever looked at her with gentle protectiveness the way Jake had that Coleman girl?

She despised them all.

Just as she arrived at that conclusion, one of her nemeses materialized. Dub Abernathy was crossing the street with his buxom wife and horse-faced daughter in tow. He was tipping his hat to those whom they met. The gauche daughter simpered stupidly when her father introduced her to one gentleman. The wife looked well fed and complacent. And why shouldn't she? She was the wife of one of the city's leaders. Priscilla wondered if Mrs. Abernathy would look quit so smug if she knew the depravity her husband was capable of in bed.

Without an instant's hesitation, Priscilla daintily raised her skirt and stepped off the boardwalk and into the street. She crossed it slowly, attracting as much attention as she could while her eyes stayed on the Abernathys as Dub helped first his wife, then the graceless daughter, into their shiny black carriage pulled by a magnificent gray. Dub was just stepping in himself when Priscilla reached them.

She took supreme satisfaction in the look of absolute horror on Mrs. Abernathy's face. Her flabby jaws hung slack. The daughter's whey face collapsed in disbelief. They knew who she was and that delighted her.

"Good morning, Dub." Her voice was husky, intimate, but loud enough for anyone nearby to hear her address him by his first name.

He froze in the act of stepping into the buggy. Then slowly he turned his head. His eyes beaded in on Priscilla. If they had been swords, she would be dead from the lancing look he gave her. Then, without saying a word, he climbed into the buggy and gave the horse a smart rap on his rump with the whip.

Priscilla glanced around and smiled craftily. She had an audience. Good. Dub Abernathy needed some humbling. She would love to be privy to the explanation he gave his wife once they reached their mansion.

Feeling somewhat mollified after Jake's rejection, she stepped on to the boardwalk and headed home, back to Hell's Half Acre.

Banner was sitting motionless in the chair nearest the window when Jake came in. "Banner?"

He crossed the room and knelt down in front of her. Her hands were lying listlessly in her lap. He covered them with his own. "Banner, what is it? What did she say to you?"

She turned her sightless gaze from the window and looked into his face. Several seconds ticked by before she really saw him. Then she shook her head and smiled tremulously. "Nothing, Jake, nothing."

He didn't believe her. He had seen that terrible look on

her face. "Tell me what she said. So help me God, if she said or did anything to upset you, I'll—"

"No," Banner said quickly. She didn't want anyone to know what Priscilla had told her, not until she had had time to digest it herself and form her own opinions about it. Jake knew about that other baby. He had found her mother in the woods with a dead child. Was that the extent of the secret?

Had her mother been married before? If so, why hadn't she told Banner about it? Or had she not been married before she had that other baby? No! That was unthinkable. But what other explanation was there?

She couldn't pretend it didn't hurt. It did. If she had found out any other way, it would have been shattering enough, but to have found out from Jake's whore, that ugly, spiteful woman whose bed he frequented, had added insult to injury.

"I'm fine, Jake, really. It just surprised me that she would accost me on the street."

"Accost you?"

"That's too strong a word," she said, and restlessly stood up. Now that the encounter was over, she wanted to forget it. She certainly didn't want to rehash their conversation for Jake's benefit. Now Banner knew why he so faithfully kept her mother's secret. He didn't want anyone to think badly of Lydia. He adored her. That hurt too.

"Priscilla just spoke to me, and asked about Mama and Papa. And she mentioned Lee. I think she wanted to shock me by telling me he had been to her whorehouse. I told her I already knew. That's all. You came out then." Uncomfortably warm from lying, she shrugged off her jacket and laid it on the bed. (She wasn't going to ride the trolley again after all.) She would find no joy in the excursion now.

Jake wasn't convinced that she was telling the extent of her conversation with Priscilla, but he knew that was all the information he was going to get out of her. If Priscilla had told her anything about Grady, Banner was keeping it to herself. "I rushed back to tell you we're leaving."

"When?"

"Soon. The trains are running again. I've already bought

our tickets. We pull out right after noon. I left the boys to see that the cattle and our horses got loaded. I came to tell you to pack."

"All right." Normally she would have argued to stay a few days longer, but nothing was normal anymore. She wondered if it ever would be.

Why were lies and secrecy necessary? Why hadn't her mother told her and Lee about that other baby? Why hadn't anyone? Moses? Ma? Jake? Unless it was something to be ashamed of.

"Will you be all right if I leave you alone?"

Jake was standing close to her now. She raised her head and looked up into his blue eyes. What secrets did they hide? They were so seldom open to the world. Rarely did they reveal anything Jake was thinking or feeling. "Yes, I'll be all right."

He looked like he might touch her. His hands came up a fraction, then lowered back to his sides. "I'll come back for you around eleven."

She nodded, but didn't speak. She longed for him to hold her. His deceit last night, even the fact that he didn't love her, had no bearing. She wanted to be held against him, consoled, petted. Her soul yearned for the solace of his strength. Her body craved the secure warmth of his. She felt chilled to the bone.

But she had asked for his loving more than once and had been rebuffed. She wouldn't ask again.

He went to the door. After opening it, he paused. "Banner?" He waited until her eyes met his. "Sure you're all right?"

"Yes." She forced a little laugh. "Will you get to that train and take care of my cows? If you don't, I'll fire you and get me another foreman."

He tried to smile at her, too, but it was no more convincing than her joking. He doffed his hat and left her. As he took the stairs to the lobby his jaw was firmly set. This trip had been nothing but one nightmare after another. They couldn't get out of Fort Worth fast enough to suit him.

Banner refolded her clothes into the saddlebags and packed the rest of her things. She kept her suit on, knowing that once they reached Larsen, she would exchange the borrowed horse for their wagon at the livery.

When everything was ready she returned to her seat beside the window, watching the passing traffic and wondering if those people busily going about their lives had problems as she did.

Was it necessary to experience this kind of adversity to reach maturity? Apparently her mama had. What had Lydia's life been like before that day Jake and Luke discovered her in the woods? Why had they all kept the secret of the stillborn baby?

Why had Jake sneaked off last night after being such an affectionate companion all day? Why would he prefer Priscilla's bed to hers?

Why, why, why?

The questions rolled like tumbleweeds through Banner's mind, never snagging themselves on an answer. Would she ever have all the answers?

It was nearing eleven o'clock. When someone knocked on her door, she said, "Come in," without hesitation.

She heard the door open behind her, then close. She turned around. It wasn't Jake who stood on the threshold as she had expected. Nor Lee, nor Micah.

"Grady!"

"Hello, Banner."

"What in the world are you doing here?"

"Langston didn't tell you I was in town?" He tossed his bowler hat on a table. He was dressed in a checked suit. His white shirt was spotless and had a high starched collar. But his face looked sallow. Dissipation had etched fine lines around his puffy eyes.

"No. When did you see Jake?"

"The night before last. I've been trying to see you ever since. He's kept you busy."

Unaccountably she was afraid of Grady. It wasn't at all seemly for a gentleman to come to an unmarried woman's hotel room. She hadn't even thought about convention when she and Jake had been alone, but she wanted to point it up to Grady now in the hopes he would leave. The way he was looking at her, with a resolute light in his eyes, made her nervous.

"What are you doing in Fort Worth?"

"Business," he answered evasively. "It couldn't be avoided or I never would have left Larsen without notifying you." He came further into the room. "Have you thought over my marriage proposal, Banner?"

"Yes, I've thought about it."

"Well?"

She edged around the chair she'd been sitting in, unconsciously placing it between them. "I haven't made up my mind yet." She was playing for time, hoping Jake would return. Why hadn't he told her Grady was in Fort Worth?

"You had already made up your mind to marry me months ago. What's changed?"

She stared at him incredulously. "What's changed? Everything. The situation. Me. You. Everything."

"I haven't. I'm the same man. You're the same woman. The situation, as you call it, has been remedied."

How could he speak so casually about the horrible deaths by fire of his wife and unborn child? "I wouldn't call the way it was remedied a blessing."

"Nor I," he said, bowing his head momentarily. "But I told you before, Banner, that I feel like I've been given a second chance. I still love you and want you for my wife. Don't you feel anything for me?"

She realized then that she didn't. Not liking or loving, not hate or even the pity she had felt before. Where Grady Sheldon was concerned her heart was a void. How had she ever considered herself in love with him? Why hadn't she recognized his shallowness before?

He was reasonably good-looking, but he held no appeal for her. Sleeping in the same bed with him, sharing her body with him? No! There was only one man she could be intimate with and that was Jake.

Jake.

She loved him.

No matter how he had hurt her, she loved him. Even to

consider spending her life with another man was incomprehensible. She would rather live alone than be with any man except Jake.

But she couldn't blurt out her true feelings to Grady. That would be cruel. And she still didn't trust his newly acquired arrogance. He had never been this way before. He had always been humble and meek, especially when her parents were around. Was she seeing him as he really was? Had he only been trying to impress Ross with his mild manners and humble demeanor?

This dual personality frightened her, so she answered cautiously. "Naturally I still have feelings for you, Grady. They're just not clearly defined any longer. After all that's happened . . ." She foundered. "I need time to straighten out my emotions, time to sort through all that's happened and determine what I want for the future."

He stared hard at her. She was the first to look away. Taking one determined step after another, he closed the distance between them. Banner stayed rooted to the floor. She felt an inclination to back away from him, but only the window was behind her.

"I wonder what changed your mind. Or should I say *who* changed your mind?"

She wet her lips. What time was it? Where was Jake? "What do you mean?"

Grady's eyes wandered around the room, taking in every detail. "This is a large room. Almost too large for one person."

When his eyes returned to her, they were insinuating. And what they insinuated made Banner furious. "Clarify your point, Grady," she said tightly.

"My point is that Langston stays as close to you as a shadow. I just wondered if he was exceeding his duties."

Her hands curled into fists and her eyes flashed dangerously. "Jake is an old family friend. He is the foreman of my ranch. He promised my father to look after me and that's what he's doing."

Grady smirked. "He's also legendary where women are concerned. As randy and rowdy as they come. You ought to hear the way the girls talk about him in all the whorehouses in town.''

''So you've been to them.''

He was temporarily nonplussed, then he continued in those deceptively dulcet tones. ''Yes, I've been to them. I'm a man, Banner.''

''Barely,'' she said through clenched teeth. ''How dare you come in here smearing dirt on me just because your sins have been found out.''

He laughed, a low laugh rife with threat. ''You look beautiful when you're angry, Banner. Maybe I should thank Langston. Maybe you've wanted it rough all along and I just didn't know it.''

He lunged for her and caught her shoulders. Pulling her against him, he sealed his mouth over hers. Her screams were trapped in her throat, but she struggled against him, not so much frightened now as enraged.

''That's right, Banner. Fight me,'' he panted as he slid his mouth down her neck. ''Is that how you do it with Langston? Huh? You think I'm stupid? You think I don't know what's plain to anybody who sees the two of you together?''

''Let me go!'' She fought him in earnest, slapping at his face and shoulders every time she managed to work a hand free from his grasp.

''Marry me, Banner. We'll have a great time.''

She tried to cry out, but his mouth came down hard on hers again. His arms were like steel bands closing around her and giving her no room to maneuver. She was gasping for breath, trying to free her mouth from the suffocating strength of his when the door crashed open against the wall.

''Let her go or you're dead, Sheldon.''

Grady froze at the distinct click of a pistol's hammer being drawn back. If that hadn't been enough to forestall him, the frigid, emotionless tone of Jake's voice would have.

Still keeping his arms around Banner, Sheldon turned his head and looked at the man who had promised before to kill him. ''I'll kill you if you don't let her go. Now.'' When

Sheldon still hesitated, weighing the validity of Jake's threat, Jake added, "Don't make the mistake of thinking I won't. I've done it before."

Priscilla's interest in him had made Grady bold, but his newfound courage evaporated beneath the blue fire in Jake's eyes. He released Banner and garnered his slipping courage. "This is no business of yours, Langston. It's between Banner and me. I've asked her to marry me."

Jake's eyes didn't veer off Sheldon. "Banner, do you want to marry him?"

Weak with relief, she leaned over the back of the chair. Her hair fell forward like a dark curtain as she hung her head and breathed deeply. "No. No."

"The lady said no, Sheldon. Now get out."

Grady evaluated his circumstance and wisely decided that now wasn't the time to argue. With as much dignity as possible he crossed the room and retrieved his hat. Jake's eyes followed his every move. When he reached the door, he turned to Banner. "Ride the cowboy. See if I care."

Jake's gun hit the floor as he launched himself at Sheldon. One fist crammed the man's nostrils up to his eyesockets. Another gouged its way through his middle almost to his spine. Grady doubled over in pain, but Jake grabbed a handful of his hair and jerked him upright. His mouth was dealt another punishing blow that drew blood and rattled teeth. His cheekbone caught one well-placed fist and cracked on contact.

Then his lapels were grasped in steely fists and he was slung against the wall. Jake's knee rammed into his groin and Grady prayed for death.

"I'd love to kill you just for the hell of it, Sheldon, just because I want to. I won't for the same reason I didn't before, because of the embarrassment it would cause Banner and her family. But if you ever come near her again, I'll kill you. Understand?" Jake shook the man like a dog shakes a rat held in its teeth. "Understand?"

Sheldon's head flopped up and down in a pathetic semblance of a nod. Jake released him so abruptly he slid down the wall, barely catching himself on rubbery knees. He slunk from the room, dripping blood on the carpeted floor.

By the time he reached the landing at the end of the hall, his head had stopped ringing, though his face and gut and crotch ached abominably. He wondered if his ribs were broken. He sent a murderous glance down the hallway toward the room where his hopes of ever acquiring Banner and her timber-rich property had died at the hands of a worthless cowboy.

He vowed that Jake Langston and the Colemans had humiliated him for the last time. "You'll pay for this," he pledged between swollen lips as he made his way painfully down the stairs.

Priscilla's mood was none too reliable by the time she returned to the Garden of Eden. She kept remembering the genuine mirth in Jake's laugh and the look of loathing Dub had shot her. She was spoiling for a fight. Her disposition didn't improve when she spotted Sugar Dalton nursing a glass of bourbon in one of the parlors. The drapes were drawn against the sunlight. The room was dim. Sugar sat in one of the corner settees like a small nocturnal animal hiding from the day.

Whipping off her hat and gloves, Priscilla bore down on the other woman. She really should get rid of Sugar. She attracted few customers and was becoming more of a liability than an asset.

"Why aren't you upstairs resting? We have a big Saturday night coming up."

"I needed a drink more than I needed sleep," Sugar whined. Since the night Priscilla had slapped her in public, she had stayed out of the madam's way. She cursed her bad luck for getting caught now. "Besides, I can't sleep."

Priscilla pinched her chin between her thumb and finger and yanked her head up. She studied the bloated face, the vacuous eyes, the lackluster, limp hair. "You look like hell. If you don't improve by nightfall, you don't work tonight. And if you don't work tonight, you're out by tomorrow."

Sugar eased her head back, warding off Priscilla's hand. "All right, all right." She hauled herself to her feet.

"And bathe, for crissake's. You stink."

Sugar only laughed and pulled the flimsy robe tighter around her. "No wonder. I had quite a night last night. If you hadn't been so busy yourself you would have noticed." She shuffled toward the portiere. "Young Micah reminds me of Jake a few years ago. And Lee Coleman's just about as good-looking as his daddy."

Priscilla, her mind already on other avenues, snapped to attention. "What did you say?"

"I said—"

"Never mind. When did you ever meet Ross Coleman?"

Sugar gaped at her blankly. "Don't you remember me telling you about that? When I first hired on, we discovered our paths had crossed before. Remember us saying what a coincidence it was? I was working in Arkansas for that bitch who called herself LaRue," she said, jostling Priscilla's memory. "And you were with that wagon train that passed through."

Priscilla's mind was whirling. "Tell me about it again," she said, motioning Sugar into a chair and pouring her another drink. She vaguely remembered mentioning one day soon after Sugar had started working for her that she had come to Texas from Tennessee with her parents on a wagon train. Sugar's face had lit up. She had asked Priscilla if a man named Coleman had been in that same group. Then she had gone off at a tangent that Priscilla had thought was no more than the drunken ramblings of a whore she had had reservations about hiring in the first place. "Tell me about the time you met Ross Coleman."

Sugar smiled and reached for her glass. "That was just it. His name wasn't really Coleman, you see."

Priscilla's eyes were alight as she watched Sugar take a long thirsty drink. Her lips curved into a malicious smile. When Sugar finished that drink, Priscilla poured her another.

Banner swayed with the rhythm of the train. The rocking motion was relaxing; the very incessancy of it was lulling. It was growing dark in the coach. Only a few lamps, strategically placed, were dimly burning.

She glanced at the man sitting on the seat beside her. He was staring out the window. As though sensing her eyes on him, he turned his head toward her.

His eyebrows showed up whitely in his shadowed face. From beneath them those incredibly blue eyes gazed back at her. For long moments, they stared at each other. Banner knew that every bleak thought was registered on her face. Her turmoil over her mother's past, the news that she had had a stillborn half-brother or sister, Grady's degrading treatment of her, had all combined to form a maelstrom in her soul. She was being sucked down into its misery.

But when she looked into Jake's face, she basked in her love for him. She would hold on to that, forget all else, and think only about how much this man filled her heart.

"Thank you." Her lips barely moved. The words were sighed more than spoken. But he heard them and smiled with only one side of his mouth.

"For beating the hell out of someone who deserved it?" He flexed his fingers. "You don't have to thank me for that, Banner. The pleasure was all mine."

She shook her head. "You were there when I needed you."

"I always want to be."

Jake realized as he spoke the words aloud that he meant them. There was no use fighting this thing, and he was tired of running from it and pretending that it didn't exist. She had gotten her hooks in him and he had become a willing victim.

Damned if he knew what he was supposed to do about it. But he had to do something, even if it meant going to Ross with his hat in his hand and, at the risk of getting shot, confessing everything.

He had used Sheldon's own violence, his physical abuse of Banner, as an excuse to fight the man. He had to admit now, after hours of thinking about it, that he would have wanted to do it anyway out of sheer jealousy. He had been blinded by it. Had Sheldon been holding Banner tenderly, kissing her softly, he still would have felt the same flash of rage, that lust to kill Sheldon for so much as touching her.

What would Ross and Lydia, his own Ma, think when he announced that he wanted to marry Banner? They would be shocked speechless. But it didn't matter. None of it, not them, nor their opinions mattered as much as the woman staring up at him now, awakening his senses to every nuance of her. Not even Lydia's opinion would matter. He couldn't quite reconcile himself to that, but he didn't try. Banner was all that mattered now and she was speaking to him again.

"Do you?"

"Do I always want to be around when you need me?" She nodded. "Yes, Banner." He bent his index finger and rubbed his knuckle back and forth over her lips. "Did that sonofabitch hurt you?"

"No."

"Anywhere?"

"No. You got there just in time."

Jake cupped her cheek tenderly and she turned her face into his palm. If he kept on touching her, he was liable to do something stupid. But, hell, people probably kissed on trains all the time and the sun still rose and set on schedule.

He glanced across the aisle where Lee and Micah had been sitting together playing cards. Now their hats were covering their faces as they rested their heads against the seats. They were asleep.

Jake lifted his arm around Banner's shoulders and drew her against him. He lowered his head. His mouth met hers. Their lips clung. His tongue went seeking hers and found it. They made love to each other. Her hand crept up his chest and closed around the folds of his bandana. His hand spread wide over her ribs as he held her tight. The kiss was long and thorough. It was the sweetest kiss either had ever had.

When at last he lifted his mouth from hers, he smiled at her gently. "Go to sleep. When you wake up we'll be home."

He tucked her head into the hollow between his chin and

collarbone. He stretched his long legs out as far as the seat in front of them would permit and held her close.

The word "home" took on new significance to Banner as she snuggled against Jake. For the first time in days, she didn't feel cold and alien. The warmth of his hard, lean body seeped into hers, chasing away all the dismal thoughts and dread of the future. She loved the scent of tobacco that clung to his clothes. She welcomed the feel of his breath in her hair and on her cheek.

Even the rain that ran relentlessly down the windows of the train was welcome after months of drought.

EIGHTEEN

It was still raining when Jake nudged Banner awake. Whisking an airy kiss over her temple, he whispered, "We're pulling into Larsen."

She shifted and stretched and yawned, all before opening her eyes. When she did, she smiled up at Jake. He smiled back and lifted his arm from around her. Micah and Lee were beginning to stir across the aisle. Other passengers were gathering their belongings in preparation for arrival at the depot.

Banner sat up straight and smoothed her hands over a hopelessly wrinkled suit. She was flustered and invented activities for her hands to cover it. She wanted to study Jake, to test his reaction to having held her in his arms for an extended period of time while she slept peacefully.

But now wasn't the time. They had to see to unloading the cattle, picking up their wagon, and traveling home. Everything was complicated by the inclement weather.

Micah summed up the situation when he stepped from the

tall steps of the train onto the loading platform of the depot. "We sure need the rain, but it picked a helluva time to start coming down in buckets."

Jake surveyed the sheets of rain that slanted against the near horizon just beyond the overhang. He grimaced and made a smacking sound with his mouth. "I didn't figure on driving those cows to the ranch tonight anyway and I sure as hell don't want to attempt it in this."

He gnawed his bottom lip while the rest of them stood by awaiting his instructions. Lee couldn't stop yawning and rolling his head from side to side to work the crick out of his neck. His eyes blinked monotonously.

Jake turned to Banner. "You've buttered up that man at the livery. Do you think he'd let us pen the herd in one of his corrals till we can come back and drive them to the ranch?"

She grinned broadly, glad that he had asked her for something she could grant. "I think I can talk him into that."

Jake winked at her, but mumbled, "Brat" under his breath. "All right, you two," he addressed the sleepy younger men, "look alive. Banner, while we're seeing that herd off the train, you go to the livery. Will you be all right in this rain?"

She shot him a scornful look. "Ask them." She turned and sashayed down the platform and stepped off into the driving rain.

"Well?" Jake asked Micah.

"She used to force us to play in the rain with her. She's got skin like a duck's back. Water rolls right off her."

Jake's smile was quick and personal. He pulled it back before it could become a full-fledged affectionate grin that the boys would notice. "Let's go."

They saw to their horses first, making sure they were saddled before leading them off the train. After consulting with the depot manager to make certain no passengers were lingering about, which might cause an accident, they pulled down the side of the cattle car and formed a ramp. Its edge settled heavily into the mud with a soft squish.

"How long has it been raining?" Jake shouted to the railroad man as the Herefords began ambling down the ramp.

"Since early this afternoon. We needed it, but hell, not so much at one time." He spat a string of tobacco juice into a puddle and made his way back under cover. He didn't like or trust beef cattle. He would leave working with them to the cowboys who knew how.

Lee and Micah were overzealous. They were whistling and shouting and wheeling their horses about. "Calmly, calmly," Jake said over the din of falling rain and bawling cows. "We don't want them spooked. It wouldn't do to have them stampede Main Street."

They arrived at the livery stable to find everything in order. Without mishap Jake and the two younger men drove the Herefords into the pen made ready for them. The owner of the livery even had the insight to provide a separate pen for the bull. His borrowed gelding was returned with thanks from Banner.

"Do you want to spend the night here in town, Banner?" Jake asked solicitously. Despite her bragging about playing in the rain, she looked sodden, bedraggled, and her teeth were chattering.

"No. I want to go home."

He considered her for a moment. Rain dripped heavily from her clothes. If she were as wet as he, she was soaked to the skin. Even his boots had rainwater sloshing in them. "Let's leave the wagon for now. We can come get it when things dry up. I doubt it would make it over the roads in the state they're in anyway."

"You want the gelding for a while longer then?" the livery owner asked.

"No thanks. Banner can ride with me," Jake said. "We'd appreciate a blanket though, if you've got one to spare."

When they rode out of town a few minutes later, they were a sad-looking group. Micah and Lee were huddled morosely in their saddles, reminiscing about their trip and regretting that it was over. Rainwater dripped from the brims of their hats and ran down into their collars.

Banner had been tucked in front of Jake on his saddle, wrapped in the borrowed blanket. His arms held her securely, but even the warmth of his body couldn't dispel the wet chill that had seeped into her bones, making her feel miserable. At any other time she would have loved riding double with him, his arms holding her close and his head bent protectively over hers. But she felt too bad to enjoy it.

When they reached the bridge that separated River Bend from Banner's property, they reined up. "Which way?" he asked her. "River Bend or your place?"

The thought of her dry warm bed in the upstairs bedroom where she had known such childhood happiness was enticing. But she was bone-weary and didn't feel like recounting the details of her trip, which she knew she would be pressed to do. Besides, she longed for her own small quaint house. "I want to go home."

He didn't have to ask her what she meant by home. His eyes bored into hers for an instant, and he knew. "Banner want to go on across the river," he told Lee and Micah. "Tell everybody she's fine and that the trip was successful. If it's raining this hard tomorrow, tell Jim and Pete and Randy not to report to work. I think we all deserve a day off, especially Banner."

"Be careful crossing the bridge, Jake," Micah cautioned. "The river's up."

Jake had already noticed that. There were only a few scant feet between the bridge and the churning, rushing waters of the river. "We'll take it slow. Get on home now and be sure to tell everybody we're fine and not to worry."

He watched the boys ride out of sight, then, gathering Banner tighter in his arms, he led a reluctant Stormy toward the bridge. The stallion picked his way carefully. Jake kept tight control.

Even in the darkness, Banner could see the dizzying swirls and eddies of the water beneath them. She shivered in the damp blanket and snuggled closer to Jake. If only she were warm and dry. She didn't feel well, though she couldn't actually pinpoint the source of her misery. As soon as she was safe in her own house, she would begin to feel better. At least that's what she told herself.

They reached the other side of the river and Jake let out a sigh of relief. In the morning, if the weather permitted, he'd see to that bridge. Even if it meant leaving the herd in Larsen an extra day, he and the hands needed to give that bridge some overdue attention.

The tiny new house looked forlorn in its clearing, valiantly taking the brunt of the rainstorm. To Banner, it had never looked better. Jake dismounted first, lifted her down, and carried her the remaining steps to the house. Taking the key from her reticule, which was secured to her wrist, Banner unlocked the door. They all but fell inside. Jake's fingers fumbled to light the lamp on the nearest table.

"I'm tracking up your floor." He left a chain of puddles as he made his way to the fireplace.

"I don't care," she said, shivering. "Please get a fire going. Is there any dry wood?"

He checked the box. "Loaded. Jim must have seen to it. Go get out of those clothes. By the time you're back I'll have a roaring fire going." He smiled over his shoulder at her from where he was hunkered down in front of the grate.

His smile was almost enough to warm her, but not quite. She went into the bedroom, groping for the lamp and matches. Her hands were shaking so badly she could barely strike the match. If only she were dry and warm, this debilitating trembling would stop. She knew it. Her head would clear. Everything would stop looking muzzy. And her stomach would stop its roiling.

She stripped out of the wet clothes and conscientiously draped them over a chair to dry. Her teeth were chattering as she plunged her head into the neck of a flannel nightgown and pulled it down over limbs blue with cold and pebbled with goosebumps. She wrapped herself in a winter robe and pulled on a pair of socks whose only merit was that they were warm against her numb toes.

Did she have fever? Is that why she was so chilled? This was summertime. Even with the rainfall she shouldn't feel this cold. Was she hungry? Is that why her stomach felt funny? But the thought of food was revolting. She was rarely sick. Such symptoms were as irritating as they were uncomfortable.

She went back into the living room to find that Jake had been true to his word. Orange and yellow flames were licking the logs stacked in the fireplace. He was rearranging them for better ventilation with the iron poker. When he heard her approach, he turned around.

"Come over here by the fire." Taking her hand, he drew her forward. He thought she might have fever. Her eyes looked glassy and unnaturally brilliant. He chafed her upper arms. "How's that?"

"Better." She sighed and leaned against him slightly, only to realize that he was still wet. "You should change too."

"I'm on my way out now."

Her heart sank. She hadn't thought of him returning to the barn. It seemed so distant. The rain looked like a curtain separating the house from the barn. He would be so far away. Feeling as bad as she did, she wanted him to hold her, stroke her hair, murmur that she would feel better soon, as her parents had done on the few occasions she had suffered childhood illnesses. But she couldn't ask that of him. He would think it was just a female wile, or that she was behaving like a child frightened of a rainstorm.

"Are you sure you'll be all right?" he asked.

"I'm going to brew a cup of tea and take it to bed with me."

"Good idea. What you need is a full night's rest." He stroked her cheek with the tip of his finger. "It's been an unsettling day."

Her physical ailments had superseded her emotional ones. She nodded. "Yes. You're right. I need some sleep."

"I won't be far away if you need me."

He dropped a soft kiss on her cheek, then left on a gust of damp air. Sprinkles of rain showered the threshold. Banner stared at them sightlessly long after he had closed the door behind him. Her stomach twisted with a cramp and she realized she had been standing motionless for several moments.

Forcing herself to move, she carried the lamp into the kitchen and filled the kettle with water. She lacked the energy to build a fire in the stove, so she brought the kettle back to the fireplace and set it as close to the flames as possible.

She was feeling worse by the minute. The cramping in her stomach was coming at regular intervals. She needed to vomit, but held it back with an iron will. She alternated between shivering in her robe and sweating so much that she pulled at it in a frenzied effort to discard it.

The kettle was just beginning to boil when Jake knocked on the door. "Banner?" He swung the door open and then kicked it shut behind him. She stared up at him from the low stool she was sitting on in front of the hearth.

"There's something about the barn I didn't know until tonight."

"What?" she asked raspily.

"The roof leaks." One corner of his lip lifted into a wry grin. "Stormy and I tossed for the only dry stall. He won. Would you mind if I bed down in here?" he asked, indicating the couch with his head.

"I'll feel better with you in here with me." Even as she spoke the words, she was hoping with all her heart they would prove to be true. She certainly couldn't feel any worse.

"Have you had your tea yet?" He dropped a heap of bedding and dry clothes on the floor beside the sofa.

"I was just about to. The kettle's boiling."

He pulled a bottle of whiskey from the pile of bedding. "I'll add some of this to it. That'll warm you up. You stay where you are. I'll go in the kitchen and change while I'm brewing your tea."

He carried the steaming kettle and a change of dry clothes into the kitchen with him. Banner gripped her stomach and bent forward at the waist as soon as he was out of sight. She had had tummy aches before, but nothing to equal this one. Thankfully the worst of the pain had passed by the time

Jake came back wearing dry clothes and carrying two fragrant cups of tea. Steam rose from their brims. He handed one to her, folded his legs beneath him Indian fashion and sat down. Setting his cup between his thighs, he reached for the whiskey bottle. He uncorked it and held it over her cup.

"This is for medicinal purposes only, you understand."

She frowned at him as he poured a meager portion into her cup. "Ma's been sneaking whiskey to me all my life. Every time I had a cough."

He laughed as he added the whiskey to his own tea. "She used to pour it down us too. Corn liquor distilled in the hills of Tennessee." He shuddered and made a face. "One time when Luke had the croup, he got to liking it so much, he started asking for it. That's when Ma knew he was getting well." He smiled, shaking his head with the fond memory.

Banner's world shrank to consist only of him. The firelight gilded his hair and cast his face into shadow. It highlighted the lean bone structure, the bladelike sharpness of his cheekbones, the stubbornness of his jaw. The shadows scooped out the hollows of his cheeks and made them more pronounced. He was smiling, relaxed, and talking to her about the brother he had loved.

If she didn't feel so ill, this would have been a treasured moment in her life. They were encapsulated in this softly glowing, warm cocoon while the rain beat down around them, separating them from everyone else in the world. Damn! She was too sick to enjoy it. That made her angry with this unnamed sickness and she vowed to will it away.

She sipped the whiskey-laced tea, hoping that its burning punch would banish the nausea and cramps in her stomach and abdomen.

Jake added another log to the fire. He had left half the buttons of his shirt undone and hadn't tucked the shirttail in. He was wearing only socks. He looked comfortable and cozy and showed no haste to leave her to her own devices and go to bed.

"Feeling better now?" He stretched out on his side in front of the fireplace and propped himself up on one elbow.

The shirt fell away, giving her a heart-stopping view of his throat and chest.

"Yes, I'm fine," Banner lied. She wanted to stretch out beside him breast to breast, belly to belly, hip to hip. It would feel absolutely glorious to lie that way with him, their mouths touching frequently, until passion overcame them and he rolled her to her back and lay atop her.

A heat wave rolled through her that had nothing to do with her fever. If she made such a brazen move to lie down beside him, would he deter her this time?

But even as she thought about it, a rush of scalding, sour bile surged to the back of her throat. Shakily she set her cup down on the stone hearth. The last thing she wanted to do was disgrace herself by throwing up in front of Jake. That would be too humiliating.

"I was already sleepy and the whiskey only made me more so. I think I'll go to bed, Jake."

He raised himself to a sitting position. His expression was a mixture of bewilderment and hurt. "Sure, Banner. Good night."

Somehow she managed to pull herself to her feet and make it to the door of her bedroom without giving away how weak and woozy she was. At the door she turned back to him. He was pouring another portion of whiskey into his cup, without tea this time. By the stern set of his jaw, she could tell he was angry or disappointed or both, but no more so than she.

"Thank you, Jake, for everything."

He lifted his eyes to her and nodded brusquely, but said nothing. He finished his drink in one swallow and reached again for the bottle. Sighing with regret, Banner went into her bedroom and closed the door behind her.

The room was damp, the sheets clammy, but she crawled between them and huddled under the covers until she began to warm and her teeth stopped clicking together. But she couldn't straighten out her legs. She kept her stomach protectively cradled between her knees and her chest. Her muddled brain decided she must have a fever. Maybe she had influenza. She thought she was going to vomit, but again she forced it down.

She drifted in and out of consciousness. She slept, but was continually aware of the nagging overall discomfort and the frequent spasms of pain in her abdomen. Each time she awoke from a bad, painful dream and discovered it was real, she groaned into her pillow, praying for oblivion.

The rain continued to fall. The long hours of the night stretched out into the wee hours of the morning, then into the pale, ghostly predawn when the outdoors became only a slightly lighter shade of gray.

In her sleep, Banner clutched her middle and uttered a sharp cry. She came awake, knowing that this wasn't some ailment she would sleep off. Panting with the effort, she raised herself and hung her head over the side of the bed. Her body was bathed with a film of sweat, but she was shivering with cold. Her ears seemed on fire. They pounded with each beat of her heart.

"Banner?"

The door to her bedroom was flung open when she didn't answer. Jake stood there dressed only in his pants, as though he'd just pulled them on. "Banner!" He saw the greenish tint to her face and the hollow, sunken dullness of her eyes.

He ran into the room, ducked down beside her bed and cradled her head in his hands. "What's wrong? Are you sick?"

"Go away," she said miserably. "I'm going to . . . to . . ."

He dragged the procelain chamberpot from beneath her bed just in time. She vomited into it with spasms that wrenched her body as though she were a rag being wrung between giant fists. Jake had seen cowboys puke up three nights' worth of debauchery, but he had never seen anyone as wretchedly ill as Banner. Nor had he ever seen anything as vile as what her stomach voided.

When she was done, she collapsed, exhausted, on the pillows. Jake covered the pot with its lid and sat down on the edge of the bed. He clasped her hands. They were cold and moist and lifeless. Her face was as pale as the sheet she lay on.

He smoothed her hair back from her damp, pallid cheeks. "That pissing whiskey." He cursed, hating himself for giving it to her. He should have known she couldn't tolerate even a thimbleful.

She opened her eyes and focused on him. She tried to shake her head. "No. I was feeling bad before that."

Panic stabbed through him like an icepick. "Since when, Banner? When did you start feeling sick?"

"Just after . . ." She stopped to allow an agonizing pain in her abdomen to subside. "Just after we got to town," she finished on a wheezing breath.

"Why didn't you say something? You've been like this all night? Why didn't you call me? Never mind, don't talk. What can I do? Do you want something?" Desperately he pressed her hands, trying to knead life back into them.

"Stay with me." She tried to squeeze his hand, but lacked the strength to do it. She was afraid she would die and no one would be there with her. In a rational corner of her mind, she knew she must be delirious, but she couldn't curb the panic that seized her at the thought of dying alone.

"I will, sweetheart, I will. Wild horses couldn't drag me out of here."

For hours he tended to her, holding her head as she retched into the chamberpot he had to empty after each bout of nausea, bathing her sweat-beaded face with a cool cloth, talking to her in loving, soothing tones.

He cursed his ineptitude, the weather, everything and anything. He cursed himself for giving the hands the day off because of the rain. It was coming down as fast and furious as ever. No one would venture across the river today.

He had never felt so useless in his life. All he could do was watch Banner writhe in agony while he stood by, impotent to do anything to relieve her suffering.

As the hours dragged by, one thing became clear. He was unqualified to take care of her. This illness was life-threatening. He had to go for help.

"Banner." Once his mind was made up, he knelt beside

the bed and took her hand. When her eyes struggled open, he said, "Sweetheart, I've got to go get help."

Her watery eyes instantly cleared as panic shot through them. "No!" She clutched at his shirtfront. "Don't leave me here to die."

"You aren't going to die," he stated firmly, and wished to God he could convince himself of that. "I've got to find a doctor and bring him back."

"Don't leave me, Jake. Jake! You promised. Don't go."

Steeling his emotions, he pried her fingers from the material of his shirt and left her. Tears flooded his eyes and her pleading cries filled his ears as he ran to the barn to saddle Stormy. He argued with himself to go back, to stay with her, but he knew he couldn't. She wouldn't be alone long. He would ride to River Bend and notify her folks of her condition. Someone would come stay with her while he went to Larsen and brought back the doctor.

Despite the slippery roads that were barely distinguishable in the downpour, he made it to the river in record time.

"Sonofabitch!"

He sent the scathing curse hurling toward heaven, not even caring if God heard it. Where the bridge used to be was only a rushing current of muddy water. All that was left of the bridge were fragments of its supports on each bank. The lumber was torn. Water swirled around the jagged edges of wood. The rickety bridge had been ripped apart by the force of the flood.

He deliberated and weighed his options in the time it took to turn Stormy around and head toward town. He could search for hours along the banks of that flooding river and still never find a place he could cross. The folks at River Bend would have to remain ignorant of Banner's condition for the time being. Paramount now was locating the doctor and bringing him back.

The town was battened down against the weather. More businesses were closed than were open. The streets looked like lakes. The postmaster had run up the national and state flags, but they clung sodden to the flagpoles. It was at the post office that Jake dismounted and went in to inquire about the doctor.

The postmaster, involved in a novel about a Pinkerton detective on the trail of train robbers, glanced up querulously when Jake came in.

"I need a doctor in a hurry."

"You don't look sick."

"Not for me. For my... wife."

"Well, which one do you want?"

"How many have you got?"

"Two. Ol' Doc Hewitt and a younger one named Angleton."

"Angleton."

"He ain't here. Out of town for a week. Went to see his wife's folks in Arkansas."

"Where does the other one live?" Jake asked tightly, wondering how long he could control his temper without exploding.

The postmaster gave Jake directions to the doctor's house. As soon as Jake left, the postmaster frowned at his rain-splattered floor and went back to reading his novel.

The doctor's house had a white picket fence around it and organdy curtains at the windows. Jake looped Stormy's reins over the hitching post and ran up to the door.

He whipped his hat off and shook water from it after he knocked. He had on a slicker, so he wasn't as wet as he might have been. The door was answered by a plump matron with iron-gray hair and pillow-sized bosoms.

"Is Dr. Hewitt at home?"

The woman eyed him suspiciously. "I'm Mrs. Hewitt. May I help you?"

"I need to see the doctor," Jake said with diminishing patience.

"He's eating lunch. His clinic will reopen at three o'clock."

"This is an emergency."

She rolled her mouth and nose around once, showing her aggravation over his interruption of their meal. Jake speared her with intimidating blue eyes and she thought better of arguing with him further. "Just a minute."

She closed the door in his face. When it opened again, a

man, who matched his wife in girth, was wiping his mouth with a checked napkin. He frowned at Jake, assessing him immediately as an outlaw who had come to seek help in removing a bullet from a wounded partner. At least that had been the description his wife had given him of their caller and Dr. Hewitt thought that, as usual, her first impression was correct.

"Mrs. Hewitt said you have an emergency."

"A young woman vomiting the worst-looking and smelling stuff I've ever seen, complaining of cramps in her belly and nausea in her stomach. She's sick. She needs you."

"I'll see her this afternoon whenever it's convenient for you to bring her in."

When he tried to close the door Jake's hand was splayed wide over the whitewashed surface, forestalling him. "I didn't say she needed you this afternoon. She needs you *now*."

"I'm in the middle of my lunch."

"I don't give a good goddamn what you're in the middle of!" Jake shouted. "You're coming with me now."

"Look here, you just can't come in here demanding—"

"Do you know the Colemans?"

The doctor's lips wobbled uselessly for a moment. "The Ross Colemans? Yes, of course."

"This is their daughter, Banner. Now, unless you want to face not only my gun should anything happen to Banner, but her father's as well, I suggest you get your little black bag or whatever the hell you need and come with me." For good measure, Jake drew his gun. "Now."

Mrs. Hewitt had come into the hall when she heard the shouting. Now she cowered against the wall, her hand fluttering at her throat. "Well, I never," she said over and over.

"It's all right, dear," Dr. Hewitt assured her with a calmness he didn't feel, as he dropped the napkin and began pulling on his coat and hat. "This, uh, gentleman, is a friend of the Colemans. He's distraught, though I plan to discuss his rude behavior with Mr. Coleman the first chance I get."

He glared at Jake, who was indifferent to what they thought of his manners. All he could see was Banner's deathly pale face and all he could hear was her begging him not to leave her to die alone.

"Do you have a horse?"

"A buggy. In the barn in back."

"Let's go."

Jake sheathed his pistol and stepped back into the downpour only after the doctor went before him. He followed him to the barn, helped him harness the horse, and then led the buggy through the streets of town. The doctor's caution on the muddy roads was commendable, but Jake's insides were screaming with impatience. Every minute that ticked by was another minute of agony for Banner.

It seemed that centuries had gone by before he led Stormy into the shelter of the barn and rushed to drag the reluctant doctor into the house.

It was quiet. Too quiet. Jake dashed into the bedroom, dreading what he might find. Banner lay unconscious beneath the quilts, but he saw the discernible rise and fall of her chest and almost sobbed with relief. He shoved the doctor forward.

With maddening slowness, Dr. Hewitt took off his coat and carefully folded it over a chair. He balanced a pair of spectacles on his nose and began to peel back the covers. When Jake leaned in closer, the physician looked over his shoulder censoriously.

"I can't examine the young lady with you in the room."

If he hadn't needed the doctor, Jake would have rubbed the pious expression off the man's face with his fist. As it was, he gave the doctor one telling look and left the room.

He paced, praying and cursing with each step. For lack of anything else to do, he laid a fire in the stove in the kitchen and lit it. Maybe she would want more tea, maybe... maybe... maybe...

The possibilities paraded through his mind, each one more grisly than the last.

Finally the doctor came out of the room polishing his

eyeglasses with a large white handkerchief. He was shaking his head sadly and staring at his shoes.

"What is it? What's wrong with her?" Jake demanded impatiently when the doctor's concentration seemed to be solely on his eyeglasses.

"Perityphlitis. Stomach fever to you."

Jake let out a long gust of breath, his eyes lifting to the ceiling. "Her appendix, I thought so."

"I'm sorry, young man," the doctor said, laying a conciliatory hand on Jake's sleeve, "for you, for Banner, and for her folks. But there's simply nothing I can do but make her comfortable until . . . until it's over."

NINETEEN

Unblinkingly Jake stared back at the man. "What do you mean there's nothing you can do?"

"Exactly what I said. I'll make her as comfortable as possible, of course, but—"

"What are you babbling about?"

"I'm trying to expla—"

"You'll cut it out, you fool."

"Now see here, young man. I won't permit you to address me in that tone of voice!" Even huffily pulling himself up to his full height, the doctor was still dwarfed by Jake. "I don't think you appreciate the complications involved in an operation of this sort."

"Explain them to me."

"No use in that. I won't do the surgery," he pronounced firmly.

"Why not?"

The doctor told him. The skin across Jake's cheekbones became taut.

"You smug, sanctimonious bastard. I brought you out here to do whatever was necessary to save her life and that's what you're going to do."

"I'm of the school of thought which believes that some parts of the body should remain inviolate, namely the chest, the brain and the abdomen."

Jake wasn't impressed by his pedantic lecturing. He grabbed the doctor by the lapels and jerked him forward and up until his feet dangled an inch off the floor and his face was on a level with Jake's. "Where'd they dig you up? Relics like you were laughed out of existence long ago."

He shoved the doctor against the wall, drew his pistol and rested it against the end of Hewitt's nose. He pulled back the hammer with a slow confidence that coaxed sweat from the doctor's brow. "Now you're going in there and you're going to open up Banner Coleman, you're going to take out her appendix . . . or you're going to die. Got it?"

"You'll answer to Mr. Coleman for this," the doctor sputtered.

"If Ross were here, he'd do the same thing. Now, am I going to have to blast your brains against this wall, or not?"

"All right, I'll do it."

Jake released his hold on him and backed away so abruptly, he knocked Dr. Hewitt's eyeglasses askew. They rolled down his face and chest. He caught them at his knees.

He had never been so unhinged. He set his eyeglasses back on his nose and tugged at the bottom of his vest nervously. "I don't even know if I have ether with me. Putrefaction is our worst enemy. We will need to place an antiseptic barrier between the wound and the germ-containing atmosphere. Carbolic acid is in my bag, some bandages too. Get that out, please," the doctor said hurriedly. He wanted to appease this barbarian. His eyes were sharper than any lancing implement the doctor owned. As Jake disappeared into the other room, the doctor deliberated running from the house and getting in his buggy. But he knew he could never outrun a man on horseback and he feared Jake's wrath should he catch him trying to flee.

He almost feared the surgery more. He hadn't kept up with modern medicine and the strides being taken in surgical procedures. He was content to pat the hand of a woman delivering a baby, to suture cut fingers, and dispense pills for dyspepsia.

George Hewitt couldn't be bothered with keeping up with innovations like those in asepsis. This was a wild land he lived in, alien from the hallowed halls of medical research. He could dig out bullets in record time if they didn't threaten a vital organ. He could amputate limbs almost as quickly. But the interior of the human body mystified and terrified him.

When all was ready, he gazed down at Banner Coleman's flawless white skin and a cold sweat broke out over his face. He looked up at the man who had insisted on being present. Hewitt had consented. He would need someone to drip the ether onto the cloth covering her nose should she begin to come around.

"I won't be held responsible for what happens as a result of this," he said with much more bravado than he felt. "If the appendix has already ruptured, she'll likely die no matter what I do. I want you to understand that."

Jake didn't flinch. He only stared back at the doctor with glacial blue eyes. "And I want you to understand this. If she dies, so do you, doc. If I were you, I'd make damn sure she doesn't."

The man was a ruffian and a heathen, of that Hewitt was certain. He was also certain the cowboy meant what he said. He drew upon what little professional skill he had and lowered the razor-sharp scalpel to the expanse of smooth flesh covered by a carbolic-soaked cloth on the right side of Banner's navel.

Jake's heart all but stopped beating as he watched the knife go through the fabric to etch an oozing red line on Banner's body. Was he doing the right thing? *Yes!* What choice did he have? She was going to die without the surgery. The chances of her dying in spite of it were awesome, but he had to try to save her.

She couldn't die. She couldn't. He wouldn't let her. God wouldn't let her.

As Dr. Hewitt's clumsy fingers pried apart the incision in her abdomen, Jake prayed earnestly for the first time in years.

Hewitt secured the bandage, lowered Banner's nightgown, and covered her with a quilt. Only then did he hazard a glance at Jake. His fearsome eyes were on the girl.

"Her color's not good," Jake observed worriedly.

"Her body has undergone a shock, one I personally and professionally thought was unnecessary, if you'll recall." The doctor thanked God the girl hadn't died under his knife, though he seriously doubted she would live through the night. Luckily the appendix hadn't yet burst, but it had been close. He thought such cases were hopeless and that it was much more benevolent to let the patient die without having to suffer surgery. "Try to keep her fever down with cool sponge baths. Put carbolic acid on the bandage now and again and give her laudanum if she's in pain."

He gathered his things, tossing them helter-skelter into his normally well-organized bag. He wanted to leave the house before the girl died, to get away from this gunslinger before he exacted his revenge for something Hewitt had had no control over. Some people just wouldn't let God go about His own business of giving and taking life without interference.

He couldn't leave the house fast enough, but he did have a few words with Jake before he made his escape. He didn't know what Ross Coleman was thinking of to leave his daughter in the care of a ruffian, but then there had been that scandalously aborted wedding. Was the girl totally without discipline?

He couldn't wait to get home and tell Mrs. Hewitt the latest chapter in the life of Banner Coleman. He would swear her to secrecy, of course. This was a tale that couldn't be repeated to the town gossips and traced back to him. It wouldn't do to offend the Colemans, though the company their daughter kept was suspect and her conduct less than exemplary.

He hoped his wife had kept the chicken and dumplings warm.

And damn this rain that still came down in torrents.

Jake had pulled the straight, ladderback chair to the edge of Banner's bed. His elbows were propped on his knees. His hands were clasped in front of his mouth. His eyes never wavered from her face.

Her breathing was so light and shallow it barely stirred the covers over her chest. It scared him. He didn't know whether to be worried that she hadn't shown signs of coming around or glad that she was sleeping through the worst of it. Frequently her eyelids fluttered as though she were having a bad dream. Otherwise she lay motionless, soundless, limp.

He came out of the chair, willing away the thought of death. He laid his callused palm on her brow and told himself that it was definitely cooler than the last time he had checked it. When had the doctor left? He hadn't noticed or cared. All he cared about now was saving Banner's life.

In the corner of the bedroom he spotted the pile of blood-stained linens he had insisted they replace after the surgery was completed. The sight of them made him sick to his stomach. That was Banner's blood. He wadded them together, carried them through the dark house and threw them out the back door. He would wash them later.

Pulling on his slicker and hat, he went to the barn to attend a sorely neglected Stormy. Since the other horses had been transferred to River Bend while he was in Fort Worth, the stallion had the barn to himself.

"Hey, boy. Did you think I'd forgotten you?" Jake rid him of the heavy saddle and gave him a well-deserved rub down and a ration of oats.

Out there, in the stillness of the barn, with the soulful sound of rain dripping from the eaves, the gravity of the situation hit Jake like a tidal wave. He had known it was on the horizon, moving closer, threatening, but he hadn't wanted to acknowledge it. Now it engulfed him.

Banner might die.

His fingers knotted in Stormy's mane and he laid his forehead against the tough flesh. "No, no," he groaned. "She can't." Not like Luke. Not like Pa. Heavy tears rolled down his cheeks. He would be devastated if he lost Banner. And not because he had loved her as a child, or because she was the daughter of his dear friends. He didn't want to lose her because a light in his life would be extinguished.

God, he had caused her pain. He had deliberately hurt her, insulted her repeatedly. He had told himself that it was for her own good. Now he had to admit the real reason. She had become too important to him.

Twenty years ago he had shut himself off from emotional attachments because they were too risky. You loved someone, you lost them. Better not to love at all. Loving Lydia all these years had been easy because that love was secret and demanded nothing of him. Lydia was already lost to him. But loving Banner . . .

Did he love Banner?

"I don't know," he whispered to Stormy.

All he knew was that he would move heaven and earth to see her face animated and laughing or haughty and angry or shining and flushed with passion. Anything, *anything* but in the stillness of death.

He left the barn at a run, hurdling puddles and wading through a sea of mud to reach the house. Haphazardly he hung his hat and slicker on the rack at the back door and tugged off his boots, dropping them heedlessly on the floor. He dashed through the house on stockinged feet. The bedroom was as sepulchral as when he had left it. He crossed to the bed and knelt beside it.

"You're not going to die, Banner. You're not going to leave me. I need you to want to go on living myself and you won't desert me. I won't let you," he whispered fervently, grasping her hand and pressing it to his mouth. Her only response was a low moan, but it was music to Jake's ears.

Laughing and crying in relief, he surged to his feet. He

wasn't going to let her wake up in these dim, dismal surroundings. In a frenzy he raced through the house lighting lamps. Things had to look cheerfully alive when she woke up. The death angel wouldn't dare lurk in a house with all the lamps burning. He knew he was thinking like a madman, but he wasn't going to take any chances.

He stoked up the fire in the fireplace and refueled the one in the kitchen stove. He heated a tin of beans for himself and kept the kettle hot should Banner want something when she came around.

After that flurry of activity, he was exhausted. He sat with Banner until he couldn't hold his eyes open, then he went into the parlor, peeled off his clothes, and wrapped himself in a blanket on the sofa. He fell asleep almost instantly.

She was hot. So hot. Something was pressing her down, sealing her to the bed. Her mouth seemed to be lined with cotton. There was a throbbing pain coming from some point on her body, but she couldn't seem to locate it. She willed her eyes to open. The light was exceedingly bright. It struck her eyes as though they were virgin. It pierced. It hurt.

Gradually she accustomed her eyes to the light and let them come open all the way. They drifted toward the windows and she saw her bedroom reflected in the glass. It was dark outside, and still raining.

She tried to orient herself and pin down her last memory, but her random thoughts wouldn't be collected. Her room loomed large, then shrank. The foot of her bed seemed no farther than the end of her nose, then looked as though it stretched away for miles. These wavering ballets made her nauseous and she panted through open lips to ward it off.

She tried sitting up, but the pain bit into her middle and she collapsed back onto the bed with a muffled cry of alarm.

"Banner?"

Jake, his hair rumpled, stood framed in the opening of the door. His arms were widespread, bracing him in the doorway. She was delirious. She must be.

He was naked.

He rushed forward and dropped to his knees beside the

bed, clasping her hands. His eyes wouldn't be still, but
moved rapidly over her face. "How do you feel?"

She looked at him fearfully. "I don't know. I feel odd.
What's happened to me?"

"You've had surgery."

Her pupils dilated in spite of the light pouring into them.
"Surgery? You mean cut open? Jake?"

"Shh, shh. Here, I'll show you." He carried one of her
hands beneath the covers and rested it lightly on her bandage-
wrapped stomach. She winced with even that much pressure
being applied to it. "Gently," he cautioned. "The cut is
still fresh. Don't you remember being sick?"

Her memory came back in snatches. The trip home in the
rain. The feverish ache in her bones. The nausea. The
gripping cramps. The sickness while Jake held her.

"Your appendix became inflamed."

"Stomach fever." Tears of terror filled her eyes. "You
can die of that."

"But you're not going to," he said fiercely. "The doctor
came and took it out. I'm going to take care of you. In a
week or two you'll be as good as new. Better."

She tried to absorb all this, keeping her hand over the
sore place on her abdomen which was making her ache all
over. "It hurts."

"I know." He kissed the back of the hand still clasped in
his. "It will be for a few days. How are you otherwise?"

She blinked. "The light is awfully bright."

He smiled self-derisively as he reached to turn off the
lamp on the bedside table. "That's my fault. I didn't want
you to wake up in the dark and be afraid."

"You're taking care of me?"

"Yes?"

"Where's my mother?"

He touched her cheek. "I'm sorry, Banner. I tried to get
across the river and bring your folks back, but the bridge
washed out. The river's impassable. Until the rain stops and
the floodwaters go down, River Bend is isolated. I'm afraid
you're stuck with me."

She lay still for a moment, staring up at him. "I don't

mind that, Jake." She lifted a hand to touch his cheek, but it fell back weakly. "I'm dizzy."

"That's from the ether and your fever. You should go back to sleep. Would you like a drink of water?"

She nodded and he poured a glass from a pitcher on the table. "Just a sip." He cradled her head in his hand and tilted the glass toward her lips. It clinked softly against her teeth. She swallowed a sip, then another. "That's all for now." He returned the glass to the table and noticed the vial of laudanum the doctor had left. "Are you in pain? I can give you laudanum."

"No, but stay with me."

"Stay . . . ?"

"Sleep with me. Like on the train."

"But, honey, you—"

"Please, Jake."

She was battling to keep her eyes open, but she made a feeble gesture to reach out for him. It was enough to banish his objections. He came to his feet, lifted the covers, and slid beneath them. He placed one arm under her shoulders and pressed her head against his bare chest. She rolled toward him. "No, no, lie still or you'll hurt yourself." He laid his other hand on her upper thigh so he would be alerted if she moved the lower half of her body. Her fingers curled into his chest hair and her gentle breathing blew through it.

Oh, God. What heaven. What hell. What delicious torment.

But miraculously, within moments of the time slumber reclaimed her, he fell asleep too.

In the morning, Jake crept around the house, not wanting to disturb Banner's healthful sleep. He tended to Stormy, carried in wood, stoked up the fires, cooked a breakfast of bacon he had found in the springhouse, biscuits of a sort, and strong, hot coffee.

When all that was done, he took up his post at her bedside. The imprint where his body had lain was still on the sheets. He closed his eyes as undiluted pleasure washed through him. He had never spent the entire night with a woman before. He had used them and left them. But there was something to be said for sleeping beside one, sharing body heat, exchanging breaths.

Not just any woman. Banner.

He gazed down at her. There was even more to be said about waking up beside her. Lord a'mighty, she was soft, and warm, and sweet. He had awakened to find her hand curved over his heart, her slightly parted lips pressed against his chest. And his hand . . .

He swallowed, remembering where his hand had been. The softest, warmest, sweetest place of all. He had been cupping it protectively. But who was going to protect her from him? Not that he would ever hurt her again. Never. The need inside him to protect her was almost painful.

How long he sat there staring at her sleeping face he didn't know. It didn't matter. That was where he wanted to be.

When she awakened, she was more alert, but also more aware of her soreness. "I don't think I'll ever move again."

He smiled. She wasn't going to die. Whether God's intervention or his cussedness had prevented it, he didn't know. But Banner wasn't going to die. "You'll be riding Dusty in no time." She groaned and he laughed. "It will take time, you understand. Would you like some tea?" She nodded and he went to fetch it.

When he came back, she was squirming beneath the covers. "Uh, Jake, there's something . . ."

"What?" Instantly concerned, he set the tea on the table.

"Nothing, never mind," she said, not meeting his eyes.

"What? Are you sick again? Do you need to vomit?"

Her cheeks flared red and this time he knew it wasn't from fever. "No."

"Then what? Are you in pain? Do you need some laudanum? Take it if you need it, that's—"

"I don't need laudanum."

"Then goddammit, what is it?" he said, losing patience. "Tell me!"

"I have to go to the bathroom!"

Jake took on the stupid expression of someone who had

just been hit in the face with a wet tow sack. "Oh. I never thought of that."

"Well, think about it. And *hurry*."

"I'll be right back." He ran to the kitchen and came back with a shallow pan. "Until you can get up and use the chamberpot, you'll have to use this."

"What are you doing?" she cried as he flung back the covers.

"Well, we have to get it under your, uh, under there, don't we?"

"I can do it."

"You can't move."

"I'll manage."

"Banner, don't be silly about this. I held your head while you puked your guts out the other night and—"

"Thanks for reminding me."

"—and I stood by and watched the surgery. I changed your nightgown when that prissy doctor refused to. I've seen you, all right? Now let me slide this pan under your bottom before you wet the bed."

"I'll do it myself or I'll hold it," she said through gritted teeth.

Jake didn't know how he could want to hold and comfort her one minute and choke her the next. He turned on his heel and stamped out. "Women!" he said in disgust as he slammed the door behind him.

Banner noticed that she had graduated from being a "brat" to being a "woman." She supposed that was an accomplishment of some sort.

Five minutes later when Jake knocked on the door, he was greeted with a weak, "Come in."

He peered around the door and was alarmed to see her arm lying limply, outstretched across the bed. "Are you all right?"

She opened her eyes and saw his concern. "I'm fine, really. Just tired."

"You wore yourself out." Indifferently he removed the bedpan and set it on the floor. "And I didn't help. I'm sorry I yelled at you. Go back to sleep, sweetheart."

"All right, Jake," she whispered obediently. Eyelids lined with the darkest lashes he had ever seen came down over her eyes and she was immediately asleep.

He nursed her throughout that day and into the evening. "You'll stay with me again, won't you?"

He paused in the act of straightening the covers around her. "I shouldn't, Banner."

"Please."

"All right. But you go to sleep. I have some things to do around here."

"Promise you'll—"

"Yes. I promise."

She slept through the night, awakening only once when she tried to turn over. She moaned softly, rousing Jake immediately. His arms tightened around her. "Shh. Remember to lie still," he whispered in her ear. He kissed her cheek. And to keep her from moving again, he lifted his thigh to cover both of hers. She cuddled against him. This time he moaned.

He didn't go back to sleep for a long time.

The following morning, she complained of being hungry. "This tea wasn't enough," she said, handing him the empty cup.

"That's a good sign."

"Is that bacon I smell?"

"Yes, but I don't think you should have that."

"Jake, I'm starving!" His brow puckered. "What's wrong?"

"There's very little in the house to eat. I need to ride into town and buy some fresh meat, some eggs and milk, get a few staples. Ordinarily we'd depend on Lydia and Ma to cook for you, but the rain hasn't let up. We're just damned lucky we're on this side of the river and can get to town." He looked at her closely. "Will you be all right if I leave you alone for an hour?"

The thought of being alone and immobile filled her with dread, but she couldn't whine to Jake about her fears. He was doing his best to take care of her. The least she could do was not make a nuisance of herself.

"Of course."

He made the trip in record time, battling the elements all along the way. The time dragged for Banner, though she dozed through most of it. When she heard him opening the back door, she almost forgot her soreness and sat up.

"You're back?" she called out.

"Why aren't you asleep?" he answered from the kitchen, where he was leaving his wet outer clothes.

"I'm tired of sleeping."

"You're getting ornery so you must be getting well." If his smile were medicine, she would have been healed immediately when he entered the bedroom. "Did you miss me?"

"What did you bring me? Steak and potatoes? Ham? Turkey?"

"Some beef to make a broth."

"Broth!"

He sat down on the edge of the bed. "Broth today. Maybe chicken stew tomorrow. And if you don't wipe that pout off your mouth, I won't give you your treat."

Her irritability fled. "What treat?"

He fished two candy sticks from his breast pocket and passed them to her. "One cherry, one sarsaparilla. Your favorites."

She clutched the candy sticks to her breast. "You remembered."

"Hell, when you were a kid I wouldn't've dared come to River Bend without bringing you those candy sticks."

Her hand touched his cheek. "The candy sticks had little to do with why I was glad to see you, then and now. But thank you just the same."

Jake's loins filled with a desire so explosive it rocked his whole body. He moved away from her before he remembered the way she felt against him in the night, before he remembered how sweet her mouth tasted. She was better, but she was still ill, and he didn't ever want to be accused of taking advantage of her again.

"I'd better get that broth started," he muttered as he left the bedroom.

He didn't sleep beside her that night. And she didn't ask. Tacitly they admitted that it would be foolhardy.

TWENTY

The next day she showed marked improvement. She was able to sit up against the pillows. She hadn't had fever for twenty-four hours. There was no putrefaction of the cut. Her body only needed time to recuperate.

"Do you feel like getting up and walking around a bit?" Jake asked, lifting her breakfast tray off her lap. She had eaten a scrambled egg with the ravenous appetite of a scavenger.

Banner had thought she would welcome leaving the confines of her bed. But now that the time had actually come to try out her legs and see if they still worked, she hesitated. Her stomach was incredibly sore. Getting up, walking, getting back into bed seemed insurmountable tasks.

"Do you think I should? What did Dr. Hewitt say?"

Jake looked away. "He, uh, he didn't mention this. But that soreness is never going to work itself out if you stay in bed."

"Maybe tomorrow."

Placing his hands on his hips, Jake faced her challengingly. "Have you come to like that bedpan?"

Her eyes sparkled with the familiar militancy he had hoped to provoke. "All right, I'll do it."

"I kinda thought you would," Jake said dryly, trying to keep the self-satisfaction out of his voice.

She cast him another murderous look as she threw back the covers and edged her legs to the side of the bed. The lower region of her torso painfully protested and she winced.

"Banner, wait," Jake said contritely. "Maybe I am rushing you. We'll wait until tomorrow."

She shook her head. Her face was pale, but her eyes were bright with determination. "No. You're right. I've got to start using these muscles again sometime. Whenever it is, it won't be easy."

By now she had inched to the side of the bed. Jake was anguished over how frail and small she looked, with her legs poking from the hem of her nightgown, bare toes searching for the floor.

He put his arm around her waist. "Lean on me."

She did. As her feet found the floor, she pulled herself up with the support of his strong arm. "I'm so weak," she gasped, as the room started a slow spin around her.

"From lying in bed so long. Can you take a few steps?"

Together they hobbled to the door and back with Jake trying to reduce his long stride to match her short steps. She clung to him, mindlessly pressing his arm against her breasts.

Jake wasn't unmindful of it. His head spun as dizzily as hers, as her breasts reshaped themselves around his biceps. Her hair, a tangled mass of waves and curls, kept getting in the way of his chin and nose as he bent over her, constantly asking if she was in pain.

When they came back to the bed, he eased her down on the chair beside it. "Can you sit here long enough for me to change the sheets?"

She smiled up at him, feeling victorious. "Yes. It's not as bad as it first was." He held her gaze for a heartbeat and tucked a wayward strand of hair behind her ear before turning toward the wardrobe to get the fresh linens. "Do you think I'll ever stand up straight again?" Her posture had been almost at a forty-five-degree angle.

Jake stripped the linens from the bed and smoothed on the clean ones. The room was suddenly filled with the smell of summer sunshine, captured in the sheets as they had dried on the clothesline weeks before.

"Sure you will, when you're certain you won't pop open if you do." He grinned at her as he plumped her pillow.

"It's silly of me, I know."

"But normal."

Suddenly she covered her mouth with her hand to trap a giggle. "What's so funny?" he asked. He had the pillow tucked between his chin and his chest and was struggling to work the pillowcase up over it.

"Maybe you could get a job in a hospital as a nurse. Only half of the time, of course, so it wouldn't cut into your cowboy work."

He frowned at her as he dropped the pillow back onto the bed. "I'm only letting you get away with remarks like that because you're convalescing. But once you're well, look out," he threatened with a soft snarl.

He helped her back into bed. When she was propped up on the pillows, she asked for her hairbrush. Her arms collapsed tiredly to her sides after a minute or two of brushing. "I'll never get all the tangles out."

"Want some help?"

Jake had been standing at the foot of the bed, idly watching as she lifted her arms over her head and pulled the brush through her hair. She was so beautiful. And he had almost lost her. His gut knotted every time he thought of how close he had come to losing her.

"Would you mind?"

Mind? He invented excuses to touch her. He came around to the side of the bed and levered her up. His hip barely settled on the corner of the mattress, but he propped himself there by planting his booted foot flat against the floor. He lifted the hairbrush out of her hand. "Tell me if this gets too uncomfortable for you."

"Hmm, it won't," she sighed, as he dragged the brush through her hair. "It feels good."

"It's pulling."

"A little, but it doesn't hurt."

It took several minutes of concentration just to work the brush through the matted strands on the back of her head. But after freeing them of tangles, he could comb the brush through the thick skein with ease.

Her hair was thick, wild, luxurious. He wanted to bury

his face in it, to whisper endearments into the midnight density and express all that was in his heart.

Banner's neck went boneless. Her head moved with the movements of his hands. Each pull of the brush was like a lover's caress. Hands that were accustomed to twisting barbed wire, branding cows, and roping mavericks were as gentle as a mother's with her babe. She could feel his breath on her neck when he scooped her hair up with the brush, dragged it through the bristles, and let it sift back down. Listlessly, she settled against his chest.

"Are you getting sleepy?" he murmured.

"No. Just pleasantly drowsy."

Every cell in his body was wide-awake. The curve of her hip pressed against his thigh. Her back was supple and conformed to his chest. Even beneath the voluminous nightgown he could distinguish the delicate way she was shaped. He longed to reach around her and lay his hands on her breasts. Each time she drew a long, languorous breath the cotton covering them trembled enticingly. He ached to touch her, see her, taste her.

He grew hard.

He laid the brush on the bedside table. Closing his hands around her shoulders, he drew her against him. His face nuzzled in the glory of her hair. He closed his eyes against the spasm of emotion that rushed through him. He wanted her. He wanted to be inside her, loving her.

One arm slid around her. Her head fell back against his shoulder. Her face tilted up to his. Their mouths met in a whisper-soft caress. Briefly, briefly.

Then with tremendous self-sacrifice, Jake set her away from him and eased off the bed. "Your hair looks real pretty now, Banner."

"Thank you." Her voice was small. She couldn't keep the disappointment out of it. For a moment, she had thought, hoped, that he was going to make love to her again. There was a new gentleness in his touch, in his whole attitude toward her, that hadn't been there before. She wanted to capture it while it was there. With a woman's intuition she knew his rugged exterior hid a deep hurt he had experienced in his youth. He was capable of loving, but wouldn't risk it. He safeguarded himself against letting his love for other people show. But there were cracks in the wall he had built around himself. Banner intended to probe each one until she was allowed inside, behind those implacable blue eyes.

"Where are you going?" she asked softly as he made for the door.

He turned and gazed at her with longing. She lay against the pillows, her hair spilling like dark ink over the linens. Her eyes were misty. "You're all spruced up." He ran a hand over his jaw. "I haven't shaved yet."

"Do it in here," she suggested spontaneously.

"What?"

"Shave in here, over there at my dresser." She pointed toward the bureau with the vanity table on top.

"Banner," he said, rolling his eyes, "I can't."

"Why?"

"Because, uh . . ." He searched for a viable reason. "Because there's nothing to shaving, that's why."

"If there's nothing to it, then why do you mind me watching?"

"I don't mind you watching. It's just that . . ."

"Well?"

"Oh, hell. If it'll make you happy."

He stamped out and she lay back, smiling complacently. When he came back in he was carrying a mug and brush, a razor and a towel. "I hope you realize I'm going to a lot of trouble to entertain you," he grumbled. He set his shaving tools on the vanity and left to fetch a pitcher of hot water from the kitchen.

"Don't think I don't appreciate it," she called after him.

He muttered something, but she didn't catch any of the words beyond "brat." He was scowling when he brought in the hot water and poured it into her porcelain washbowl. The yellow roses painted on it caught his attention.

"You'd better never tell anybody I shaved out of a bowl with flowers painted on it."

"My lips are sealed."

Her eyes were sparkling mischievously. That sign of

health was the only reason Jake was putting up with this nonsense. She was improving every hour. Her normally sound body was emerging, replacing the one racked with pain and delirious with fever. He was committed to seeing that she went on healing.

She watched him unbutton the first few buttons of his shirt and tuck the collar inside. "Why don't you take your shirt off?"

He dipped his brush into the water, then into the mug of shaving soap, and began to work up a rich lather. "Why don't you mind your own business?" He slapped the foamy white lather on his jaw and painted it around until his lower face was covered. "I've been doing this for a number of years without needing a coach."

"I only thought that you might drip or something."

Just as she said that a dollop of the sudsy lather dropped to his shirtfront. He cursed, picked up a towel, and blotted it off. She giggled; he frowned darkly into the mirror. Somehow it didn't come off as a very threatening expression with his face covered in shaving soap.

He picked up the razor. "Aren't you supposed to strop the razor first?" she asked.

He ignored her. Angling his head to one side, he raked the razor from his sideburn to his jaw. He swished it clean in the bowl of water and made another pass. He rolled his lips inward to shave his upper lip. "You're making me very self-conscious." The words came out garbled from the way he was holding his mouth, and Banner giggled.

"It's fascinating."

"Oh, yeah, fascinating," he mocked.

When the lower part of his face had been scraped clean, he reached for the brush again and lathered under his chin and down onto his neck. Rearing his head back, he placed the edge of the razor at the base of his throat and dragged it upward over his Adam's apple.

"Jake?"

"Hmm?"

"Would you say your pecker is larger than most?"

"Shit!" A bead of blood appeared in the area of his

jugular. He whirled around. "That's a helluva thing to ask a man when he's got a razor at his throat."

"It just now came to my mind."

"Well, maybe you shouldn't say everything that comes to your mind. Did you ever think of that?"

"Well?"

"Well what?"

"None of your business!" He turned back to the mirror, picking up the towel to staunch the trickle of blood running down his neck. "What kind of question is that coming from an unmarried young lady? Or even a married one. Where'd you even hear that word?"

"Isn't that what it's called?"

"Sometimes, but where did you— No, let me guess," he said, raising his hands, palms out. "Your brother and mine."

"I came up behind them one time when they were relieving themselves in the woods. I think they were comparing their—"

"Don't say it again."

"Until then, I thought they were all the same. I guess they're like women's breasts. Some are just naturally bigger than others."

"Oh, God." Jake's face took on a pained expression.

"What's the matter with you? There's no modesty between us, is there?"

"Apparently not." He finished shaving and began sluicing water over his face.

"Our situation hardly conforms to the laws of propriety. Otherwise you might have thought twice about sleeping with me naked."

His head came up and, regardless of the water he was dripping onto the floor, he faced her again, stupefied.

"Do you always sleep like that?"

"How do you know I do?"

"I saw you."

"When?"

"That night after my surgery."

"You were crazy with fever and pain."

"Not *that* crazy. Don't you think I would remember a naked man climbing into bed with me?"

He turned to the vanity table again and dried his face with the towel. Then tossing it aside, he flipped his collar out and began rebuttoning his shirt. "I'm not going to talk about it anymore."

"I've never seen a totally naked man before. Wouldn't you expect me to be curious?"

"Sure, I guess so. But I would rather you not tell *me* about it."

"Why? You're my first naked man."

"Will you stop saying that!"

"Well, you don't have to get so mad. You've seen me naked, too."

He pointed a finger at her and spoke sternly. "Only because it was necessary, Banner. I was assisting the doctor."

"I understand," she said primly, lowering her eyes. "But I didn't exactly go chasing after you and rip off your clothes. I didn't know when I woke up and cried out that you were going to come charging in here as naked as a jaybird."

"I always sleep like that!" he shouted defensively.

She stacked her arms beneath her head, settled back against the pillows, and smiled the proverbial smile of the cat that has just swallowed the canary. "Do you?"

Jake was furious at being tricked. He had told her what she wanted to know. The triumphant gleam in her eyes was as seductive as her reclining form on the bed.

To save face, he had to pull her smugness out from under her like a rug. His expression ceased being fulminating and became arrogant. His eyes toured her body insolently as he sauntered forward.

"We can't have you going around with an unsatisfied curiosity, can we?"

"What do you mean?" she asked, her complacency suddenly giving way to uneasy caution.

"I mean that we had just as well lay your mind to rest about everything."

Banner's eyes went wide with shock as he unbuckled his belt. She wet her lips. "Just a minute."

He paused. "Why?"

"What are you doing?"

He smiled, and the hard, strong fingers continued working the buttons on his pants. "I'm unfastening my britches."

She sat up straighter, no longer the temptress but the demure maiden. "Wait, Jake!"

He undid the last button on his fly. "You want an answer to your question, don't you?"

"I—"

"Well, here it is."

She slammed her eyes shut when his hands moved again.

"No, I don't always strop my razor before shaving. Just when it needs it. About once a week."

Her eyes popped open. He was calmly tucking in his shirttail. She watched in mounting rage as he finished the task, then refastened the buttons and rebuckled his belt.

"Any more questions?"

Stormy eyes lifted to his. "You . . . you . . ."

He made a *tsk*ing sound. "Now don't get yourself all riled up, Banner. Remember you need your rest." He dodged the pillow that came sailing toward his head and raced for the door.

His booming laughter drowned out the vitriolic name-calling.

"Knock, knock. Am I going to get a pillow in my face if I come in to check on you?" Jake stuck his head around the door a few hours later. He had cared for Stormy, carried in firewood, and started soup for their supper. Years of cooking on the trail came in handy now. The food he prepared might not be superb, but it was filling.

"No."

He had expected her to be sulking, but as he swept the door open and moved nearer the bed, he could tell she wasn't even thinking about their earlier skirmish. She showed signs of discomfort.

"What is it, Banner?"

She moved her head fitfully on the pillow. "I know this sounds crazy, but my incision is itching like mad."

"Itching? That probably means it's healing." He paused for a second too long not to be noticed. "But we had better take a look."

She raised her eyes to his trustingly. "Whatever you think, Jake."

He peeled back the quilt and sheet. When he saw her small frame clothed only in the nightgown that molded to every rise and dip of her body, his throat constricted. He cleared it loudly. "Do you want to, uh . . . ?" He made a descriptive motion with his hands, then turned his back.

Banner raised her nightgown and adjusted it to cover her feminity, baring only that part of her abdomen that needed his attention. Of course it left bare one leg and hip and much of her side, but there was no help for that.

"All right," she said softly.

Jake turned around. His eyes didn't meet hers, but kept themselves trained on the bandage that crossed her middle. As gently as he could, he removed the wrapping.

Banner gasped. His head snapped up. "Did I hurt you?"

"No." She stared down at the thin pink line with its sprouting sutures. "I just realized that I really was cut open." Closing her eyes and swallowing hard, she fought off the revulsion that shivered through her. "It's so ugly."

"Compared to some of the wounds I've seen stitched up, Hewitt's work is a masterpiece." He probed the area around the incision gently. He could find no traces of swelling or redness. "See these little flecks of dry skin? That's what's itching. It's healing properly."

"I'm surprised Dr. Hewitt hasn't come out to see to me. Even with the rain and flooding, you would think he would."

Jake decided she didn't need so large a bandage and replaced the original with a soft square of gauze the doctor had left. As he worked, he said, "Banner, there's something I should tell you."

She stared at the crown of his head, which reflected the

lamplight like a new sun. She could feel his breath falling lightly on her stomach. "What?"

"About the doc."

"Yes."

"I brought him here at gunpoint." Her lips parted slightly, but she had been rendered speechless. Jake felt the need to elaborate. "He came willingly enough when I told him who the patient was. But once he had examined you and diagnosed stomach fever, he was ready to dose you with laudanum until you died."

"He wasn't going to do surgery?"

"Not until I pulled a gun on him and threatened to kill him if he didn't."

She put her hand on his shirtfront. If she didn't love him for any other reason, she would now. She owed her life to him. He covered her hand with his own and pressed it against the hard curve of his breast.

"That damn quack was going to do nothing but let you die and then console your parents afterward," Jake said tightly, his eyes going hard and cold with the memory. "When it was over, he scuttled out of here like a possum. He didn't give me any instructions about your recovery because he didn't think there would be one."

"But you did."

His eyes delved into hers. "Yes."

Their gaze held for long moments, then she said, "The doctor might press charges of assault later, Jake."

"Let him. I'd do the same again. I would have killed him if he hadn't done that surgery."

Her eyes filled with tears. "You went to all that trouble to save me, Jake. Why?"

Cupping her face in his hands, he scanned her face, taking in every lovely feature. "I wasn't going to let you die. I would have given my own life to save yours."

Then, surrendering to the craving that had plagued him for days, he slanted his mouth over hers. His lips were parted, damp, and she matched hers to them. His tongue probed her mouth with slow, gentle thrusts that pitched her senses into chaos.

Her arms curled and locked around his neck. He pressed her deeper into the pillows and covered her upper body with his. Her breasts felt the urgent pressure of his chest. The pounding rhythm of his heart echoed hers.

His lips plucked lightly at hers, lifting the dew of their kiss off her mouth. "Banner, Banner," he whispered into her neck, "I wasn't about to let you die. I need you too much."

They kissed again tempestuously, heads twisting, mouths rubbing hard, tongues mating, until they were breathless. Jake raised his head, saw the full, bruised look of her mouth and smiled. It was a mouth designed to give and receive passionate kisses and he planned to see that it was granted its due often.

"I almost forgot to ask if you were hungry." He picked up a strand of her hair and watched as it wound around his finger, as surely as she had wound an invisible cord around his heart.

"I'm starving. Do I get some real food tonight?"

He got off the bed and headed for the kitchen. "Hot soup."

"Jake?" He turned around. "I didn't need Dr. Hewitt or anyone else to take care of me. You've done a wonderful job."

His eyes filled with emotion, but he only bobbed his head once before going out to prepare their dinner.

Things changed between them after that night. They didn't hide their feelings from each other. He kissed her good night, but the caresses went no further than that. Nor did either of them suggest he sleep beside her. The time for them to make love wasn't right, but it was coming. Both of them knew it. In the meantime, they were waiting and letting the anticipation build.

Each morning with her tea she was given a kiss. Whenever he moved close to the bed, she reached for his hand and held it as they gazed into each other's eyes. He continued to shave in her room. He brushed her hair. They shared innumerable small intimacies.

In the evenings he sat in the chair within arm's reach of her bed, reading books about cattle breeding he had purchased in Fort Worth. She worked on needlepoint cushions for the dining room chairs she hoped to have someday.

"Jake?" He raised his head from his book. "Is it interesting reading?"

"Not when I can talk to you instead."

"I don't want to distract you."

He smiled roguishly. "Miss Coleman, you've been distracting me for months." She blushed.

He closed the book and laid it aside. It had been a special night. She had walked as far as the kitchen and back twice, standing up straight. There was only a remnant soreness in her abdomen when she moved too hastily.

"When did you learn to read?" she aked him. "'Don't be insulted, please, but most cowboys don't know how."

He grinned. "That was Lydia's doing. She started teaching Anabeth on the wagon train. Once we got to our homestead, Anabeth was damned and determined that I learn, too." His eyes drifted toward the window as he recalled the intensity with which his sister had taught him and the others their letters and the confusing combinations that fashioned them into words.

"At first I thought it was a waste of time, but she reminded me that Ross knew how to read. Anything Ross did was what I wanted to do."

"Why did you go to her?"

The question was so out of context and asked in such a broken voice that his head snapped around. "Who?"

"That Watkins woman. Why did you leave me in the hotel after that lovely day we spent together and go to her?"

He was both baffled and alarmed by the tears standing in her eyes. He went down on his knees beside the bed and took her hands.

"You saw me leave?"

"Yes."

"I didn't go for the reason you think, Banner."

"What other reason could there be for a man to sneak off

to a whorehouse in the middle of the night? You could have had it with me. All you had to do was ask."

"Shh, shh, Banner. No, I couldn't. Not then. It wasn't right."

"And it's right with a whore?"

"Listen to me," he said forcibly, shaking her hands. "Micah and Lee came in. I woke up. Micah told me he had seen Grady Sheldon in the Garden of Eden. It bothered me that he was in town. I had warned him to stay away from you. For all I knew he had followed you to Fort Worth and planned on kidnapping you or something. I left immediately and went to Priscilla's place to see if I could find out what he was up to." He felt it wise not to mention at this point that Grady and Priscilla had been keeping such close company.

"And that's the only reason?" she asked gruffly. "You didn't . . ."

He laid his hand on her hair, filled his hand with it. "No, I didn't."

"But the next morning she made it sound like, well, you know."

His mouth thinned with irritation. "Whatever she said was a lie. She only wanted to hurt you to get back at me."

"I thought you were friends."

"Not in the way you think. I've told you before I didn't sleep with Priscilla."

She tweaked a loose thread on the quilt. "Grady said the girls in the bawdy houses talk about you. That you're a legend."

He showed his amusement with a smile. But when he saw Banner's shattered expression, he drew a serious face. "Banner, I haven't had another woman since that night you came to me in the barn."

"Is that true?" she asked in a hoarse whisper.

He carried her hand to his mouth and kissed the palm. His lips moved against it as he spoke. "I can hardly believe it myself, but I swear it's true."

"But is that the extent of it? That one night?"

"That depends on you," he said quietly. "What do you want?"

"I haven't made a secret of it, Jake."

He studied the floor between his boots. Days ago, when she lay on the brink of death, he had realized that it wasn't just physical desire that had a stranglehold on him. He longed to lose himself in her body, yes, but he wanted a merging of their hearts as well.

She had long ago ceased to be Ross's and Lydia's daughter. She was Banner, a woman, *the* woman he needed to fill the emptiness in his soul. If anyone could heal him of cynicism and bitterness, it would be Banner. He was tired of fighting himself. Besides, their future together was already sealed, though only he knew it.

When he looked up again, he was smiling. "Would you like a bed bath?"

TWENTY-ONE

"A bed bath?"

She watched with unblinking eyes as he went to the vanity and returned carrying a washbowl of warm water and two soft cloths. These he set on the bedside table. He lowered himself to the edge of the bed. His eyes roved her face. He reached out and touched the tip of her impertinent nose with the end of his finger and smiled.

"Have I ever told you what I really thought about you that night in the barn?"

Speechlessly, she shook her head. Silence permeated the house. She was aware only of the sound of his breathing, the rustle of clothing when he moved, the hypnotizing gruffness of his voice.

"I thought you were one helluva woman. Not many would come to a man and ask him to do what you did."

"You were shocked."

"Yes, I'll admit that. To me you had always been little Banner, the cute tomboy with untidy braids and skinned knees. Even the day of your wedding I was thinking of you like that."

His fingertip settled on the point of her chin and skimmed down the center of her throat to its base. "But that night, I saw you in a new light. You were all woman, Banner. I knew that I would never again mistake you for anything else. It's been hell, living near you and remembering that night. I've regretted it."

His mouth lifted in a wry grin. "I've relished it, too, wishing a thousand times that it would happen again." He leaned down and kissed her. His kiss was tender, but possessive. His mouth moved over hers, separating her lips for the gentle plunder of his tongue.

When he raised his head and gazed down at her, her eyes were lambent. "I want you to be comfortable. I thought I'd give you a bed bath."

"Do you want me to take off my nightgown?"

"No," he replied, smiling tenderly, "I want to take it off."

Her heart leaped to her throat as his hands moved toward the front of her nightgown. It had a row of buttons that extended from her neck to below her waist. He had buttoned her into it while she was unconscious. Even now, she blushed to think of that.

His nimble fingers undid the buttons, but he didn't open the nightgown. His eyes burned their way along the narrow ribbon of skin that showed through the opening, but he didn't touch her. Instead he said, "Can you sit up without it hurting?"

She came to a sitting position. He moved behind her, into the corner of the mattress as he had done the day he brushed her hair. He put his hands on her shoulders and lowered the nightgown inch by slow inch over her shoulders and down her arms. Banner pulled her arms free of the long sleeves, but held the fragile shield of embroidered batiste over her breasts.

Jake eased the garment down to the first gentle swell of
her hips below her waist. Her skin looked creamy in the
lamplight, golden and soft. He dipped the cloth in the
washbowl and wrung it out. Sweeping her hair aside, he laid
the cloth on her shoulder and washed in slow, measured
circles. He moved it down the length of her back to the twin
dimples on either side of the base of her spine, back up. Her
head lolled to one side, making her hair fall forward in a
black cascade over one shoulder.

"Feel good?"

"Yes." She moaned. He increased the pressure, massag-
ing away the soreness one acquires from days of lying
inactive in a sickbed.

He exchanged the washcloth for a dry one and blotted her
skin until it was again dry and glowing. The back of her
neck was too vulnerable to resist. Leaning forward, he
encircled her waist with his arms and laid his lips against
the velvety skin.

"You're so beautiful," he whispered as his lips tasted and
his tongue took liberties with her ear.

His mouth meandered around her neck, up to her cheek,
to find her mouth. Her head fell back over his arm and he
drew her down until she was angled backward, half across
his lap and half across the bed. He kissed her hungrily,
sending his tongue deep into the honeycomb of her mouth.
As the kiss intensified, he eased himself around until she
was lying fully on the pillows again. Her fingers were
tightly gripping the bunched nightgown that covered her
breasts, but not out of fear or modesty, out of passion.

She wanted more of his mouth. When he kissed her, she
felt it all over her body. Sensations tingled along every
nerve, touched her everywhere, stung, burned, stroked. The
world and all its problems dissolved. She became entrapped
in a chrysalis of rapture where adversity wasn't allowed and
where Jake was master and donor of all joy.

But once again he dipped the cloth into the bowl. He
washed her neck and chest, going no further than the
nightgown she still clutched to her breasts. He lifted one of
her arms and rubbed the cloth down its slender length. The

other arm received the same meticulous treatment. Much to her chagrin, he even washed her underarms. Modestly, she turned her head aside. "All parts of you are beautiful, Banner," he whispered. "Don't be ashamed."

After he had dried her again, he lifted one of her hands to his lips. He kissed her palm, each finger, then startled her by closing his lips around her little finger and sucking it into his mouth. His teeth gently ground into the fleshy pad, which until now she had never known was sensitive.

"Jake!" Her cry was softly alarmed. The unheralded caress set off tiny explosions in the lower part of her body. Rivers of sensation swirled through her breasts, causing the peaks to stiffen. She would never have guessed that her fingertips were linked to the parts of her body that were throbbing warmly.

Now he was kissing the inside of her wrist and his lips began working their way up her arm. He opened his mouth over the inside of her elbow and she felt the wet friskiness of his tongue. He turned her arm so that the underside was available to his nibbling lips. His teeth sank lightly into the soft, sweet flesh of her upper arm and she groaned. He trapped that groan with a mind-stealing kiss that started at her mouth and ended with a trail of fervent kisses down her throat and chest.

He sat up. His eyes looked extremely blue as he gazed into hers. Slowly he moved her hands aside. The cooler air caressed her fevered skin as he lifted the nightgown away from her breasts. "Good Lord, Banner," he said in a raspy voice, "you're so pretty."

What he had only seen by moonlight was now gilded by the lamp's wavering glow. So lovely. So milky white. So rosy pink. So perfect.

Gently he lifted her right arm and folded it above her head, then the left one, until her arms framed her head. Her hands lay open, vulnerable, with the fingers slightly curled toward the defenseless palms. Breasts, too, were without covering, easy victims.

Yet she wasn't afraid.

She lay quietly and let him adore her.

He could barely tear his eyes away long enough to dampen the cloth again. Then he bathed her, moving the cloth gently over the mounds of her breasts, her ribs, the plain between them. With the other cloth, he dried her. When he was done, he admired her as an artist does his lifetime's best work.

"I can't believe I'm here with you like this. That it's so damn good. Any minute I expect someone to come barging in here and take you away from me."

"I wouldn't go, Jake."

"I've never had a time like this with a woman, Banner. Tender and peaceful. I've taken them, used their bodies, but never enjoyed them. I might not be able to do it the way it's supposed to be done, loving like. I might be too old to learn how. But I'd like to try. Let me play with you."

Her heart swelled with love until it overflowed, just as her eyes did with tears of profound emotion. She *was* more to Jake than the whores he had had. He hadn't said he loved her. But he had spoken of loving and that was close.

Each of his hands covered a breast and molded her to fit his palms. He squeezed, drawing all the fullness into twin globes that epitomized womanhood.

"Banner, Banner." She saw his lips move but hardly a sound came out.

"Does that mean you like me?" she asked timidly.

"Like you?" He laughed softly. "Yeah, I like you."

His eyes lowered to her breasts again. His fingers were combing over them tenderly now. He marveled at the soft texture of her skin, the responsiveness of her nipples. When they became velvety pebbles beneath his caressing fingertips, he dipped his head.

She was transported with the first touch of his lips. She had been born for this moment, to give this moment's pleasure to Jake as a gift. For that's what it was. The sounds he emitted were whimpers of starvation and satisfaction, sighs of longing and appeasement, growls of desire and fulfillment.

Banner's head ground into the pillow with every rolling stroke of his limber tongue. The gentle tugging of his lips struck a chord in the heart of her womanhood. The yearning it engendered was akin to pain.

She lowered her arms and threaded her fingers through his hair, loving the feel of it against her skin. The sensations he evoked were exquisite. The place between her thighs was melting with want, aching with need, pulsing with pleasure.

She felt the trembling in his limbs and knew that his torment was just as great as hers. "I've needed you for so long, Banner. For years. All my life."

He levered himself up and stormily kissed her mouth again. When they fell apart weakly, he brushed soft kisses across her lips and ran his fingers through her hair. She looked up at him inquisitively.

"You're not going to—"

"No, I'm not. Not while you're still weak and there's a danger I'd hurt you." His lips were soft against hers. "But I would like to hold you through the night."

"Oh, yes," she murmured.

He left the bed and turned out the lamp. She heard the rustle of his clothes. When he lay down beside her beneath the cover, he was naked.

"Oh, God," he groaned into her hair. Rather than readjusting the nightgown, she had taken it off. His nakedness touched hers, the silkiness of her bare thigh caressed his. "Be careful," he urged as she stretched to get closer to him.

"You won't hurt me, Jake," she whispered, curling her hand around his neck and pressing her lips against the pounding pulse at its base.

His arms held her tenderly, but at tremendous cost to his sanity. "For godsakes, Banner, be still," he grated.

She snuggled against his warmth and he felt her yawn against his chest. "Good night, Jake," she mumbled sleepily.

"Good night, sweetheart."

While he was still contemplating the miracle of holding her, another occurred. He fell asleep.

"Good goda'mighty!"

Jake leaped from the bed, cursing when his long legs

tangled in the covers. He stumbled across the floor and
glanced out the window. Just as he thought, horsemen were
riding into the yard. Sometime during the night, the rain had
stopped. A weak sun was shining.

Banner sat up, her eyes groggy. The sheet fell to her
waist. She was as gloriously naked as the man clumsily
pulling on his pants.

"What is it, Jake?"

"The men. They've crossed the river." He glanced at her
tumbled disarray, at her breasts, rosy and sleep-warm, and
groaned. "If they find out about last night . . ." He let the
sentence dangle unfinished as he worked his arms into the
sleeves of his shirt.

Taking up his socks, boots, and ripping a quilt and pillow
from the bed, he raced into the parlor and closed the
bedroom door behind him. He flung the bedding down on
the sofa, rumpling it to look as though it had been slept on.

He went to the door just as Jim called out, "Hey,
anybody home?"

Faking a huge yawn, Jake pulled open the door of the
house. He was idly scratching his chest as though he'd just
awakened. It wasn't all that uncommon to find a man early
in the morning without his boots and with his shirt unbuttoned. "Keep your voices down," he warned with a frown.
Glancing over his shoulder toward Banner's closed bedroom door, he gave the three riders plenty of time to see the
sofa. Then he stepped out on the porch and shut the door
behind him. Speaking softly he said, "Banner's been very
sick."

"Sick?" Randy was the first to speak up. He and the
others had been stunned speechless by Jake's appearance in
Banner's house. Three pairs of eyes looked at him suspiciously.

"I had to fetch Doc Hewitt from town. Her appendix was
about to burst. He did surgery on her and took it out."

"The hell you say," Peter murmured in awe, glancing
back at the house. "And her folks didn't even know?"

"There wasn't any way to notify them without finding a
place to cross the river and I was afraid to leave her alone
that long." He shook his head, evoking their sympathy.

"She's been poorly. I can't tell you how bad. I thought we were going to lose her."

The three cowboys were chagrined. They had thought the worst when Jake came out of Banner's house, but here he was telling them that were it not for his care, she would have died. Properly subdued, Pete asked, "Is there anything we can do for her?"

"Nope. Just get this place back in shape after the rain. Have you ever seen such a wet June? I haven't."

He directed them into a conversation about the uncanny flooding. "How'd you get across the river?" he asked.

"We've been working on a raft and finished it last night. Ain't much of one," Pete said, spitting tobacco juice into the mud in the yard. "But it's enough to get a man and horse across. Ross is coming over later."

"Yeah?" Jake's reply was studiously casual, but his heart jumped fearfully. "Well, I'd better get inside and check on Banner. If one of you will see to Stormy and saddle him for me, I'd be much obliged. We'll ride out and inspect the fences, make sure there wasn't any damage done." He grinned winningly now. "You ought to see the herd, prettiest cows and the randiest bull you ever saw."

Randy whooped. "Where are they?"

"In town. We'll drive them home tomorrow. Let's give the ground one more day to dry out."

Having received their instructions, the cowboys made for the barn. Jake went back into the house to find Banner hovering near her bedroom door. Her hair was still wild, but he was relieved to see she had put on a robe. Even with sleep-puffy eyes, she looked sexy as all get out and tempting as hell and he resented that he'd risked his job and his life by spending the night holding her in his arms.

"How do you feel?" he asked brusquely. Beyond her sexiness, she looked as innocent as a babe. He felt as loathsome as a pervert who molested children. And no doubt that's what Ross would think of him.

"Fine."

"You sure?" For once he had exercised sound judgment. Last night he could have had her, but he didn't. But maybe if he had, his body wouldn't be putting him through hell right now. His uncontrollable arousal made him angry with her and more so with himself.

"Yes, I'm sure. Jake, what's wrong?"

Banner stubbornly refused to let him see the threatening tears in her eyes. Her throat was hurting with the effort to keep them back. She had expected him to be as gentle, tender, and loving this morning as he had been last night. Instead he was scowling angrily. She was too well acquainted with the closed, hard expression on his face not to dread it.

"Nothing's wrong. But Ross is on his way." He shoved his feet into his boots. Banner watched mutely as he pulled on his socks, buttoned his shirt, tucked it in, slipped into his leather vest, and tied a bandana around his neck.

"Papa?" she asked on a high note.

"Yes, Papa. Now for godsakes go put on a nightgown and get back into bed." If he was going to sell Ross on how infirm she had been, then by God she needed to look infirm!

He stamped into the kitchen and made an unnecessary amount of noise brewing a pot of coffee and preparing a breakfast of oatmeal for Banner. When he carried it into her, he noticed his shaving things spread out on her vanity. "Damn!" He swept them against his chest and carried them into the parlor. He dumped them on top of his other belongings, hoping to convince Ross that they had been living close, but separately.

During all his comings and goings in the bedroom, Banner wouldn't look at him. She avoided his eyes, wouldn't even glance in his direction as she ate her oatmeal in sullen silence. No doubt she was feeling ashamed, sorry that she had ever invited him to share her bed.

After making certain no traces of him remained in the feminine room, he stalked out and went into the kitchen. There he stayed, even when he saw Ross ride up.

"Banner?" His bass voice thundered through the house, reminding Jake of God's Old Testament brand of wrath.

"In here, Papa," Jake heard her answer weakly.

"Still in bed, you lazybones?" That's all Jake heard after

his ears tracked Ross's booted footsteps across the parlor toward the bedroom.

He remained in the kitchen and sipped his coffee. When he was finished, he set the cup on the drainboard and, garnering all his courage, went toward the bedroom.

"I don't remember much after that," Banner was saying when he entered the room.

Ross was sitting in the chair beside the bed, which Jake had frequented of late, leaning forward, his eyes on his daughter's face. He had clasped both her hands between his. His dark brows were lowered into a stern frown.

"The next thing I knew," Banner continued, "I was waking up, and Jake"—her eyes flitted to where he stood framed in the doorway—"told me the doctor had done surgery to remove my appendix. He's been taking care of me all this time."

Ross turned his head in the direction of Banner's gaze and saw Jake. He came to his feet and walked forward. When he was but a few feet from the younger man, he raised his arms. It took a conscious effort on Jake's part not to flinch.

But Ross merely laid his hands on Jake's shoulders and said a heartfelt, "Thank you."

Jake only shrugged. "Don't thank me yet, Ross. I might have caused you some trouble. That damn quack was going to let her die, said he didn't believe in violating the abdomen. I pulled a gun on him and threatened to kill him if he didn't do surgery on her."

Ross's mouth thinned beneath the brush of his mustache. "I would have done the same thing."

Jake nodded. "I thought you would."

"We've been trying to drum Hewitt out of town for a long time. There's a new doctor—"

"Yeah, but he was out of town. I had no choice."

"Don't fret about it. I'll take care of Dr. Hewitt if he raises a fuss."

Ross turned back toward the bed. "Lordy, Princess, I can't believe you have suffered through this without your mother and me to take care of you. Lydia will have a conniption fit when she finds out about it. She wanted to come over and see you this morning. But as you well know, she's terrified of water and wouldn't think of crossing the river on a raft.''

Clancey Russell, Lydia's stepbrother, had given her her fear of water. He had knocked her into a river when she was only a girl and terrorized her by almost letting her drown before he pulled her out. Ross had wished for twenty years that he had been the one to kill Russell. He hoped before he died to find out who Clancey's killer had been so he could thank him.

"Jake took very good care of me," Banner said quietly.

Ross faced Jake. "I'm grateful, Jake. You saved Banner's life."

Jake shrugged indifferently again and pushed himself away from the door frame. "Ross, we go back a long way. If we start thanking each other for favors rendered, we'll be here all day. I've got to see to the business of ranching."

Assuming correctly that Banner would be taken care of, he left, pausing first in the parlor to collect the rest of his cowboy paraphernalia, a lasso, a pair of leather gloves, his chaps, spurs, and his hat.

Banner heard the front door close behind him. He hadn't even looked at her before he left, hadn't said goodbye, waved, nothing. Was he so glad to be rid of the responsibility of nursing her? Had everything he told her last night been a lie? Or had Ross's appearance reminded Jake of the woman across the river, the one he really loved? Her tears wouldn't be held back any longer. They collected in the corners of her eyes and her father saw them.

He sat on the edge of the bed and hugged her. "My little Princess. Are you still in pain?"

She was, but not of the sort Ross could imagine. She cuddled within the safe arbor of his arms and buried her nose in the hollow of his shoulder. "I'm all right, Papa. I'm just awfully glad to see you. I've missed you all so much. Tell me what's been happening at River Bend."

Ross sat with her for the better part of the morning, fetching and carrying, creating an atmosphere anything but restful and making her nervous with his awkwardness. He wasn't an ideal nurse, but his efforts to help her were endearing.

At noon he left her to nap and returned to River Bend. When Lydia and Ma were informed of what had happened, they whirled about like two busy tornadoes. Before the afternoon was out, Micah and Lee were packed down with food and commissioned not to drop it into the river as they crossed it.

Despite her terror of water Lydia wanted to go to Banner, but was convinced by both Ross and Ma that the raft wasn't a safe means of crossing and that to avoid another catastrophe in the family, she was better off staying at home. Ross assured her repeatedly that Jake was giving their daughter good care.

As soon as he saw the boys safely across the river, Ross rode into Larsen. He consulted with engineers about building a new bridge, this time with steel supports. He wanted to get it underway as soon as possible.

Afraid he would finish what Jake had started with Dr. Hewitt if he met the man face to face, he left payment for Banner's treatment in the doctor's mailbox.

Banner was brushing her hair when Lee tapped on her bedroom door. "Banner?" he called softly.

Immediately she pulled open the door and he nearly fell inside. "I thought you were sick in bed," he said crossly when she and Micah burst out laughing.

"I am, or rather I was. But I'm better. It's good to see you."

"Did that ol' sawbones really cut you open?" Micah asked indelicately.

"He really did. Or so Jake tells me. I have the scar to prove it. Wanna see?" she taunted.

Both young men, knowing the approximate location of one's appendix, flushed to the roots of their hair, and Banner laughed again.

"Aren't you supposed to be in bed?" Lee asked.

"I'm tired of this room!" she cried in frustration.

She had put on a peach-colored silk dressing gown that

had been part of her trousseau. Ecru lace lined the deep V in the front and hung over her wrists from bell sleeves. She had brushed her hair until it shone like the wings of a raven and pinched some color into her pallid cheeks.

"I don't reckon it would hurt if you sat out on the porch for a spell," Micah said. He glanced toward Lee for his opinion and only got a bobbing head as agreement. "We could move that rocker in the parlor out there. If you sit in the shade it wouldn't be so hot."

Banner's eyes lit up. "That would be wonderful."

Their solicitousness was extreme and comical, and before long aggravating and patience-taxing. "Will you get that quilt off my lap," Banner said irritably, shoving it away even as Lee tried to tuck it around her knees. "I don't have rheumatism."

"If we don't go back and tell Lydia and Ma we treated you like a queen, we'll catch hell," Lee said defensively. But at Banner's fulminating look, he folded the quilt over the porch railing.

"Your concern is duly noted. And I do appreciate it," she said, softening considerably. "Forgive me if I'm testy. It's just that I've been cooped up in the house for so long. I'm tired of being an invalid."

"We understand," Micah said sympathetically. He had never known anybody who had had surgery beyond a pulled tooth or an extracted bullet. He looked at Banner with new respect.

"Thank you for bringing all the food. I don't know how I'll eat it all."

"It's for Jake, too."

"Yes, Jake." Her heart tore in two at the thought of the indifference he had shown toward her that morning.

"Speaking of food, it's getting close to suppertime," Lee said.

"It sure is." Banner smiled up at them again. "I'd feel better if you cross the river on that raft I've heard so much about while it's still daylight. I just hope Papa doesn't rebuild the bridge before I have a chance to ride the raft!"

The boys were laughing as they rode away. They could

report to the folks at River Bend that Banner might have suffered an ordeal, but she was her old feisty self again, wanting to cross the river on a raft.

She was still sitting on the porch in the rocker when Jake and his three hired hands rode into the yard and reined in their mounts at the edge of the porch.

"What are you doing out here?" he asked without preamble.

"Getting some fresh air," she snapped.

Jake was vexed that she was sitting in plain sight of the other three men wearing a dressing gown that would turn the stoutest man's heart to mush. She looked so damned feminine, touchable, with her skin glowing from the warmth of the sun and a breeze lifting her hair around her face. The sinking western sun formed a halo around her.

The men spoke to her respectfully and inquired how she was feeling. Randy, typically bolder, slid from his saddle and stepped onto the porch carrying a bouquet of roses in his gloved hand.

"I'm glad you're out here, Banner. These roses were brave enough to poke their heads out today after all that rain. I was going to ask Jake to give them to you. Now I can give them to you myself."

Delighted, Banner reached for the flowers. She carried them to her nose and sniffed daintily. "Thank you, Randy. They're beautiful." She blessed him with a dazzling smile so potent he stumbled on his backward desent down the steps. Jake ground his jaws together.

Banner knew damn good and well that she looked as pretty as a picture sitting there, swathed in lace and bathed in sunlight. She had done it on purpose to drive him crazy, and she was playing the scene to the hilt, looking as vulnerable, helpless, and frail as those damned roses that he should have picked for her himself.

"We've got a busy day tomorrow. Meet me here at dawn. We'll ride into Larsen and herd the cattle back." That was a foreman's dismissal and the three cowboys recognized it as such. They doffed their hats to Banner and rode off, the hooves of their horses tossing up clods of drying mud.

Jake dismounted. Banner stood up. For the first time that day, they looked each other straight in the eye.

"How are you feeling?" he asked at last.

"Better. Much stronger."

"Is your incision bothering you?"

She shook her head and turned toward the door. "I'll get supper on the table while you wash up."

"You don't have to, Banner."

She whirled on him angrily. "Our mothers sent over enough food to feed an army. You might as well eat." With that ungraciously extended invitation, she went in, slamming the front door behind her.

Jake entered the kitchen by the back door a while later, having taken care of Stormy, and washed. The atmosphere in the kitchen was thick with hostility. Banner glanced at him when he came in, but didn't speak. He glared at the roses which had been placed in a vase and given a position of prominence in the center of the table.

He had spent so much time in the kitchen recently, cooking for her, he was at home in it. He went to the stove and poured himself a cup of coffee. Bracing his hips against the dry sink, he sipped it. "We didn't find any permanent damage from the storm, though the ground will be soggy for a while in the shady spots."

"You're bringing the herd there tomorrow?"

"Yeah, but the horses will have to stay at River Bend until the new bridge is built."

"Well," she said, sighing, "I can't ride for a while anyway."

"You weren't kidding about all the food," he observed. There were several napkin-lined baskets scattered around the kitchen.

"We're having fried chicken tonight. Ma plucked it fresh this morning, Micah said. By the way, she asked about you. I sent her your regards and told Micah to tell her you were fine."

There was a question in her eyes as she looked at him. He only nodded and took another sip of coffee. She turned back to the chore of getting food on the table.

The baskets contained jars of preserved vegetables and fruit, a ham, a crock of pinto beans, pickles and jellies, several loaves of bread, a pound cake, and teacakes sprinkled with sugar the way Banner liked them. She had already sampled them and they had melted on her tongue like butter. Only Ma could bake them like that. But her pleasure in the mouthwatering food was diminished by Jake's reticence.

From beneath her lashes, she studied him. He hadn't taken off his chaps. They disturbed her. The chamois flopped against the outsides of his legs when he walked, but where they buckled onto his lean hips, they fit with disturbing accuracy. The opening framed his sex, called attention to it, emphasized the bulging fly of his pants. Thinking back to the way he had held her close the night before made her stomach feel weightless when she looked at that spot.

Aggravated with herself for remembering so vividly what he had obviously forgotten, she lashed out. "You could at least have taken off your chaps before coming to the dinner table."

"Do they bother you?"

Yes, they bothered her, but not in the way he meant. "Oh, leave them on. I don't care."

"No, no," he said gratingly. He wrestled with the buckle, then yanked at the lacings around his legs. "I don't want to upset the princess."

He tossed the chaps on the floor by the back door and flung himself into a chair at the table. Banner ground her fists into her hips as she glowered at him. "Why are you being so mean to me? Didn't last night mean anything to you? Hasn't this week changed things between us?"

He stared at her incredulously. "Me? You wouldn't even look at me this morning."

"Because you wouldn't look at me. You were short tempered and grouchy. You acted like you wished I would just disappear."

"Now just a minute," he came back angrily, "you were acting like you were ashamed of having me in your bed. I'm sure you think you've been dirtied, that the Princess of

River Bend has lowered herself by sleeping beside one of the hired hands.''

Fury engulfed her and made her eyes spark. "Oh!" She stamped her foot. "You are the most infuriating man. I could kill you for being so stupid. I love you, Jake Langston. I love you."

Tears glistened like diamonds in her eyes. Her body quivered with emotion as she stood ramrod straight with her hands still planted firmly on her hips. She looked more gorgeous than ever and desire speared through Jake like a white-hot brand.

With one swift motion his arm shot out, caught her around the waist, and pulled her forward. His arms locked around her and he pillowed his head between her breasts. "Do you, Banner? Do you?" His voice had a serrated edge. It came from the depths of his soul, working its way up through years of disillusionment and despair, hopelessness and bitterness, self-recrimination and regret.

She bent over him, sheltering him with her hair. Her arms clasped his dear head and held it tight. "Yes, yes. Are you blind, Jake? How could you not have known?"

His head came up and if his incisive eyes had ever demanded the truth from anyone, they did so now. He saw it shimmering in the tigerish depths of her eyes. His hand cupped the back of her head. He embedded his fingers in her hair and pulled her head down for a kiss that seared their souls. It was hard, almost brutal in its passion.

"Banner, Banner." He tore his mouth free and nestled his face beneath her chin. His mouth worked its way down. Hot and moist, it moved over her skin. He pulled free the tie belt of her dressing gown and, laying his hands over her breasts, moved the silk aside. She was wearing a chemise beneath the robe. The sheer cloth did nothing to hide her loveliness. Her breasts with their dusky crowns beckoned to him, thrusting against the fabric in brazen invitation.

He touched her, moving his hands over her front in an attitude of reverence, but too wildly to be religious. His head rutted against her, like a child seeking sustenance. Her body responded. She arched her back and offered herself up for his seeking mouth. It scoured her, rubbing, gently gnawing, nuzzling, kissing randomly with a pagan hunger.

She raised one of her knees to the rim of the chair seat and pressed it to his groin. She ground it lightly against his erection and he nearly vaulted out of the chair.

Tongue flicking, he touched the tip of one breast and a bolt of lightning shimmied through her. Her head fell back on her shoulders; her hair swung down her back. It was as free and untamed as the hands that opened the tiny pearl buttons of her chemise.

He worked a magic on her breasts with his mouth. His hands slipped inside her robe and cupped her derriere. He urged her closer and she responded. He nipped at her waist with his teeth.

Jake steadied her as he rose from the chair and slipped the dressing gown off. It fell unheeded to the floor. He swept her into his arms and carried her through the twilit house into the bedroom made rosy by the sunset.

He laid her on the bed with a carefulness that was belied by the way he tore off his shirt and vest and hurled them to the floor. His boots were kicked aside as he worked his feet free of them. He unbuttoned his pants and came to her, lying beside her, facing her, and drawing her precious body to his.

Their mouths met in another fiery kiss. He caressed his way down her side and lifted the hem of her chemise. Her thigh was smooth beneath his palm.

Banner rolled on her back. She reached for his hand and lowered it over herself, cupping his palm to fit the feminine delta.

"My God," he whispered, squeezing his eyes closed. He felt an urgent need to confess his small transgression. "The other morning . . ."

"Yes?"

"When I woke up . . ."

"I know."

His eyes came open and rained blue fire over her. "You knew?" She nodded. "I swear I didn't do it on purpose, Banner. I guess I just reached for you in the night and . . ."

She stilled the flow of words by laying three fingers against his lips. "Why didn't you say something?"

"I thought I was dreaming."

"I thought I was too."

"What would have happened if I hadn't been sick and if you had known I was awake?"

"Like now, you mean?"

"Yes, like now."

His hand wedged itself between her thighs. They eased apart. His fingers began to move. He separated and probed, lightly and gently, until he found her wet and warm. She sighed his name.

He lowered his head and covered the peak of her breast with his mouth. His fingers, sliding inside her, were as deft as his tongue on her nipple. Together they caressed until she was twisting restlessly, her legs sawing against his. He moved carefully, positioning himself between her thighs.

Her eyes were hazy, but they opened to gaze deeply into his when she felt the tip of his manhood breaching the petals of her sex. "Tell me if I hurt you." She nodded her head.

He penetrated her.

Then her eyelids sank closed. The emotions were too riotous to contain. Jake filled her, Jake, Jake hard and thick and warm and smooth. Moving. Stroking.

He whispered instructions. She complied and felt even more of him. Of their own accord, her hands moved to his hips, his buttocks. She slid them inside his clothing. The sleek muscles rippled against the palms of her hands as his body rhythmically pumped into hers.

Jake gritted his teeth against reaching his peak too soon. He watched Banner's face, loving the rapture he saw there. He absolved himself of taking an untutored virgin before. This was a woman, his woman, moving with him, responding, quickening beneath him even as, against his control, he felt his own climax rushing toward him.

Banner's eyes opened wide and clutched at his back. She called his name in a moment of panic as her body tightened around his. He reached as deep as he could, scaling the very gate of her womb.

"Yes, yes, yes," he chanted as he felt her body shudder. His own release was long and scalding and splendid.

TWENTY-TWO

"You liar." When she opened her eyes, they were deeply green, but alight with gold flecks.

"What?" he laughed.

"You said you were no larger than other men."

"No, I didn't. I said it was none of your business."

"You're huge," she whispered.

"Who are you comparing me to?" he asked, scowling.

She laughed gustily and he winced. He couldn't bring himself to leave her yet. He was still snugly burrowed in that silken sheath. "No wonder all the ladies talk about you."

His face became serious. "I've never been with a lady before you."

Her voice dropped to a mere breath. "You're a legend at making love."

He kissed her softly. "And this is the first time I've ever made love."

Eyes tearing, she reached up to touch his face, his mouth. "Is it always like this the second time?"

"It's never like this, Banner. Never before."

He bent his head to kiss her again and, despite her protesting groan, eased himself away from her and rolled to his side. Their eyes met and locked across the pillow. His fingers lightly plucked at the buttons on her chemise. "You're beautiful, Banner Coleman."

"So are you, Jake Langston."

Self-effacingly he shook his head. "I'm old and beat-up, scrawny as a scarecrow. A saddle tramp."

She leaned forward and kissed him softly. "Not to me. You've always been my Lancelot."

"Who's he?" One white eyebrow cocked.

She traced its arch with her fingertip and laughed softly. "You'll have to read about him sometime. But I assure you, you'll be pleased with the comparison."

Then her smile turned into a frown. Lancelot had loved the king's wife. Would Jake still love Lydia after tonight? Banner pushed the thought away. She wouldn't let anything distress her tonight. Jake was here, loving her, accepting her love. For now that was enough.

She touched his shining hair. "It makes me angry for you to talk about yourself that way."

"What way?"

"Old and scrawny. You're not. You're beautiful. And why do you say you're a saddle tramp?"

He looked away, uneasy. "I don't think too much of myself."

"But why?"

He shifted, putting one arm behind his head and gazing at the ceiling. "It all happened a long time ago, Banner. In another lifetime. You don't want to hear about it."

"Yes, I do."

He turned his head, caught the love so evident in her eyes, and sighed. She would probably think less of him than he did himself when he told her, but it was better to destroy her image of him now rather than later. He had kept things to himself all these years. With her, at this moment, he felt compelled to talk about them, get them off his chest once and for all.

"I lost my virginity and my brother on the same day. It was my fault that Luke was killed."

Banner lay quietly, unmoving. Jake sought her face to gauge her reaction. When she returned his gaze steadily, he expounded.

"Priscilla had me pegged from the day we started out on that wagon train. I was sixteen and randy as a spring bull."

Calmly, tonelessly, he related the story of how Priscilla had worked him into a sexual frenzy that summer, taunting and tempting him. "One afternoon I bribed Luke to do my chores and sneaked off to meet her. When I came back to the train hours later, my Ma lit into me. She asked me where Luke and I had been. Then Moses came into the circle of wagons carrying my brother in his arms. His throat had been cut."

A tear rolled down Banner's cheek. Still she didn't speak. Jake was opening himself up to her as he never had to anyone else. Now was the time to remain silent. He desperately needed someone to listen. Neither to condemn nor to commiserate. Only to listen.

"I've had to live with that all these years. If I hadn't been diddling Priscilla, my brother would probably still be alive."

He rolled to a sitting position and draped his arms over his raised knees. "I know you and everybody else think I've been one of Priscilla's studs. The fact of it is, I haven't touched her. I took her a few times after that day, but every time I did, I hated myself more.

"We parted company when the train broke up and I didn't see her again for years. I met up with her in Fort Worth when I was passing through on a long drive. It didn't surprise me to find her working in a whorehouse. She wanted to pick up where we left off. But every time I look at her, all I can see is Luke's face, dead, pale, with his shirt stained brown with blood."

He came off the bed and went to the vanity, pouring himself a glass of water from the pitcher and wishing it were whiskey. "That's not all of it. You might as well hear the rest. I found out who murdered Luke."

He paused in his tale. This is where he and Lydia had formed such an unbreakable bond. His brother's killer had been her stepbrother, her rapist, her tormentor. Jake had settled the score on both accounts. "I killed him, knifed him in an alley and took pleasure in doing it. I was sixteen years old. Sixteen," he said through clenched teeth.

His head dropped forward. Banner, heedless of her recent surgery, lunged off the bed and came to stand behind him.

When he heard her, he whirled around. "That's the kind of man you just took to your bed," he said, pointing toward it.

"And I'm not sorry for it. The man you killed deserved to die."

"Did Luke?"

"That wasn't your fault! You weren't responsible. A bizarre set of circumstances, coincidence. You can't carry that guilt with you the rest of your life."

Couldn't he? Hadn't he for almost twenty years? And for every day of that time, he had scorned women too. He had punished each and every one he had ever encountered for Priscilla's part in Luke's murder.

Until tonight.

Banner wasn't cringing from him in revulsion, but looking up at him with understanding and love. Her body had cleansed him when he hadn't felt clean since that first fateful afternoon with Priscilla Watkins.

"There were others, Banner. Two. Men with names and faces and I killed them."

"Tell me about them."

"One of them killed a friend of mine. He was a wet-behind-the-ears kid on his first cattle drive. I had taken him under my wing. He reminded me of Luke. This other guy was a bully. He beat the kid to a pulp for stumbling and spilling coffee on his bedroll. The boy must have been bleeding on the inside. He died later that night. I fought with his killer. Fought him for what seemed like hours. Finally I . . . I broke his neck."

Banner laid a hand on his chest. "And the other?"

"The other was a gambler in Kansas City who had cheated me and nearly every other cowboy out of his pay. He suckered us into poker games, let us win a few hands and then bled us dry by cheating. I challenged him to a gunfight. He drew on me. I was faster."

He stared down at the woman standing close to him. A bitter smile curled one corner of his mouth. "So there you have it. The sordid, sorry life of Jake Langston."

Boldly she wrapped her arms around him and rested her

cheek against his chest. "Those men were hurting other people, Jake. You're no killer."

Taking her arms, he pushed her away. "But don't you see? I might do it again, if I deemed it necessary."

"I would expect you to. I would expect my father to. I don't know if he's ever killed anyone before, but I know he would if he felt it was justified."

"Is it ever justified?"

"Yes," Banner said with soft emphasis. "Yes, Jake. I believe sometimes it is."

He hugged her to him then and buried his face in her hair. "I don't know if we're right or wrong, Banner, but thank you for saying that."

"I'm not saying it just because I think it's what you want to hear. I think all of us are capable of violence if provoked. You killed in defense of your family and friends."

"I've never even told Ma."

"Maybe you should. She's wise, Jake. She would know what to say better than I do." She reached up and framed his face between her hands. "But I know she loves you and would go on loving you no matter what you've done. And so do I."

He brushed her hair away from her cheek. "I feel better having told you."

"I'm glad." She rubbed his back, opening her hands wide over the smooth skin and pressing her fingers into the firm flesh.

He bent down and found her mouth with his. His kiss thanked her. Why he had been able to tell Banner things he couldn't tell anyone else, he didn't know. He had opened his heart and the words he had found so difficult to say before had come pouring out. He felt a freedom he hadn't felt since that summer he had lost his innocence. And he had found hope again in the tiny package of womanhood who snuggled against him trustingly.

"You didn't get any supper."

She laughed. "It *was* interrupted, wasn't it?"

"You won't hear me complaining."

"Me either," she said just as his mouth covered hers for another kiss.

When they pulled apart, she said, "I appreciate your gallantry, but I know you're hungry. And it would be a shame to let all that food go to waste."

"Come on." He lightly smacked her on the bottom, and led her from the bedroom.

"Is there more than one way?"

Banner lifted shy eyes across the table which was littered with the meal they had just finished. She moistened the tip of her finger and pressed it against the cookie crumbs on her plate. When they were collected, she licked them off her finger.

Jake watched in affectionate amusement and growing arousal. She had rebuttoned her chemise, but had chosen not to put her dressing gown back on. Several times during the meal, he had found it hard to swallow while looking at her. "More than one way to what?"

"You know what I mean."

He grinned. "What do you think?"

"I don't know," she said, saucily tossing her hair over her shoulder. "How could I? You've been my only lover."

Reaching across the table, his grin faded.

His thumb massaged the back of her hand as his eyes held hers. "I'm sorry about that first night, Banner. I should have been easier with you. I tried but . . ." He shrugged helplessly. "You took me by storm."

She leaned forward, loving the way the light reflected off his eyebrows and cast the rest of his face into shadow. "And now?"

"You take me by storm," he whispered roughly.

Leaving her chair, she rounded the table. He moved his chair back and made room for her to sit on his lap. One of her arms draped around his shoulders, the other hand sifted through his hair. He encircled her waist with one arm. The other hand once again unbuttoned her chemise and covered a breast. It was still flushed from their recent loving.

They kissed long and leisurely, tasting each other, drinking their fill. When Banner drew away she tweaked at clumps of his chest hair. He had worn his shirt to the table, but had left it unbuttoned. She moved the cloth aside, never wanting that magnificent chest to be hidden from her view again.

"Jake?"

"Hmm?" He was concentrating on the lushness of her breasts, their size, their creamy smoothness and firm peaks.

"I want you to teach me."

"Teach you?"

"How to . . . you know, how to do things."

Her hand drifted down his chest to touch the copper disk of his nipple. He caught his breath. "Banner, you don't need any instruction."

"Don't patronize me. It's important to me to know how to please you."

Jake had always imagined that Lydia was a loving wife who had never left her husband dissatisfied. Ross had never confided to Jake about his marital bed, but anyone who knew him saw a happy man. Ross Coleman was lusty and virile. Yet since his marriage to Lydia he had never sought another woman. On that Jake would bet his life.

Banner was the daughter of two people who had enjoyed an active marriage bed. Still Jake was amazed at the extent of her ardor. It transcended anything he had experienced from whores, who faked their responses most of the time. Other women didn't even know they were capable of such passionate release.

"I don't want you to go to anyone else for something I'm not giving you."

"Banner . . ."

"Will you teach me how to love you?"

He touched her hair, sliding his hand down from the crown of her head to her shoulder. It was a damned tempting proposition, but she was still recovering from her surgery. Lord a'mighty, when he thought of the way she had writhed beneath him, arching and . . . It's a wonder she hadn't popped her stitches. What the hell had he been thinking about?

"Not tonight," he said, easing her off his lap. The round pressure of her hips against him was making it harder to stay resolved. "You look tired. Go on to bed and let me clean up the dishes."

It wasn't tiredness that weighted down her shoulders as she left the kitchen. It was disappointment.

She was still awake when Jake pushed open the bedroom door a half hour later. "I thought you'd be asleep by now."

"I was waiting for you." Her shoulders were bare above the counterpane. The lamp was turned down low. She looked lovely. The bruises of fatigue making violet smudges beneath her eyes only added to their haunting quality.

Jake felt a twinge of guilt for having taxed her strength. At the same time, desire surged through him. "We can't sleep together anymore, Banner. We almost got caught this morning."

"I'm willing to take the risk."

He shook his head adamantly. "But I'm not. For your sake, not mine. I won't have your name bandied about in the bunkhouse."

"Will you at least kiss me good night?"

He smiled, his teeth catching the lamplight and shining whitely in his dark face. "That I'll do."

The mattress sank with his weight as he sat down on its edge. Gravity, and her own desire to be close, dragged Banner toward him. The sheet covering her was pulled aside, so that when Jake gazed down at her after a deep, evocative kiss, he saw one pink nipple peeping at him teasingly.

He groaned softly. "You don't play fair, Banner."

"I've always broken the rules."

He lowered his head. "Why can't I get enough of you?"

His mouth didn't hesitate, but closed around the tip of her breast. He laved it with his tongue. One taste wasn't enough. He moved to the other breast and polished it as well with long, delicious licks that left Banner gasping with desire.

"Please, Jake. Haven't we waited for each other long enough?"

He pondered her. She was so incredibly lovely, with her hair tumbling down over her creamy shoulders. Her breasts, still shining moistly from his kisses, peeped through the wavy raven strands. Her mouth was swollen and red from being well kissed.

Slowly he came off the bed and peeled off his shirt. He unbuttoned his pants. Banner stared, awestruck by his furred chest and the muscles in his arms. Surely no woman was lucky enough to have a lover as handsome as hers. He was lean, every rib pronounced, but the muscles in his stomach were corded and hard. Veins showed in his arms that bunched with developed muscles every time he asked the merest motion from them.

He eased the pants down his hips and legs and bent slightly to pull them off. When he straightened, Banner gasped softly. Her attraction to his nakedness was purely carnal, for he was beautiful with the lamplight gilding his bronzed skin and golden-white body hair.

Her eyes tracked his tapering chest into a flat stomach and narrow hips. His thighs were long and lean, his calves as hard and round as apples. Her eyes fluttered back up to his sex, where the blond hair clustered darker and denser and curlier around his impressive organ.

Jake leaned down and drew the covers back, finding her, as he had thought, naked. He lay down beside her and gathered her close, holding her tenderly, aware of her bandaged incision. But the personality of their kiss wasn't restrained. It was savagely intent, totally undisciplined, passionately unbridled.

He took her breast beneath his hand and loved it, first with his fingers, then with his mouth that followed close behind. His lips skated down between her ribs. He kissed her navel with an intimate introduction of his tongue and a light scraping of his teeth. His lips drifted toward the bandage on her abdomen. He kissed it with utmost tenderness.

The fever in his blood heightened. His heartbeats accelerated and thrummed against his eardrums.

Banner's fingers tunneled through his hair. What would have previously alarmed her, now elicited thrills that rushed through her body as unchanneled as a flooding river. Feeling the foreign touch of his lips on her body was shocking, but his caresses promised only joy and indescribable ecstasy.

He nuzzled her belly with his nose and chin. He kissed the white square bandage again, then moved to the shallow groove between her thigh and abdomen. He dragged his tongue down it.

Raising his head slightly, he focused on the nest of silky black curls. His breath touched her first, then his lips, whispering endearments.

Breathing hard, he lifted his head and gazed up at her. "Banner, I've never done this before, but . . ." The words hung in the air like an unfinished question.

"Done what?" Her voice was smoky with passion.

Jake dropped to his knees beside the bed. He eased her toward the edge. He kissed the point of the triangle where her femininity funneled together. Her back arched and she grasped the sheets beneath her in restless hands.

Slowly he parted her thighs and draped them over his shoulders. Turning his head he pressed his mouth to the soft inner lining of her thigh. Again. The sweet caresses went on endlessly. He charted the length of each thigh from the knee up with kisses as light and soft as those to the top of a newborn's head.

Then he allowed himself to taste her. He savored her essence, branding it into his memory forever. He covered her with his mouth, softly sucked. His tongue was an adventurous explorer that delved deeply and sweetly. When it withdrew, it glazed the pulsing flesh with swirling strokes that robbed her of thought.

That blessed black velvet abyss yawned wider and drew Banner closer. Sobbing his name, she fell into it, into an explosion of brilliant light. Her whole being was shaken by the ultimate human experience.

Jake had sworn that he wouldn't take her again that day, but he was powerless to resist when her arms came up, searching for him. He stretched above her and buried himself deep.

"Taste how wonderful you are." He kissed her.

Her hips undulated against the thrusts of his body. His climax came quickly, just as she reached another summit. Jake trembled with an outpouring of emotions as his seed filled her. They clung together, survivors of a turbulent storm.

When at last he regained enough strength to pull away from her, he looked down into her face. He ran a finger along the shadows beneath her eyes, but could feel no regret. The moment had been too precious.

"I never knew..." she whispered.

"Neither did I."

They kissed tenderly. He covered them both and she curled against him. Their bodies fit in a way only heaven could have designed.

As she drifted to sleep, he heard her whisper, "I love you, Jake."

He lay awake for a long time, listening to the soft cadence of her breathing, feeling it fan the hair on his chest where her head nestled.

There was no other decision to make.

Tomorrow he would have to tell her.

Her eyes took a long time coming open. When they did, she blinked to bring him into focus. The bedroom was foggy with the gray of predawn. "What are you doing up?" she asked groggily.

Jake, fully dressed and geared for a day's work, sat on the edge of the bed. He was winding a strand of her hair around his finger. He had been tickling her nose with it to wake her up. "The men are coming early. We're driving your cattle home today, boss lady." He cuffed her on the chin. "I didn't want to leave without saying goodbye."

Her mouth formed a delectable sulky pout. "I only wish I were going to drive the cattle with you."

"Next time." He leaned down to kiss the end of her nose, a kiss that extended down to include her lips, then her mouth as his tongue slipped inside. "I love waking up with you beside me, Banner."

"Me too."

"But we can't go on like this." He left the bed and went to stand at the window where the gray on the horizon was giving way to pearl pink.

Banner, her heart thudding like a death knell, threw off the covers, groped for her robe and came off the bed. "What do you mean?" She wrapped the robe around her and lifted her hair out of the back of it.

"We can't go on sleeping together. I care too much for you to cheapen you like this. Besides that, I'm lying to Ross and Lydia every time I touch you. They entrusted you to me."

Her heart was pounding at an alarming rate. He couldn't be telling her he was leaving. If he were, she would die on the spot.

Slowly he turned. Nervously he shifted the brim of his hat through his fingers. "Banner, I think . . ." He stopped to clear his throat. She stifled a sob. "I think we should get married."

Her relief was so profound that she let go of her pent-up breath with one huge gust. She launched herself at him, throwing her arms around his neck and showering his face with kisses. "Oh, Jake, Jake. I . . . oh, yes, yes."

"You want to?"

"Good Lord, yes. If you hadn't asked me to be your wife, I would have asked you. I thought you were going to tell me you were leaving."

He grinned at her enthusiastic acceptance. Dropping his hat on the floor, he returned her bear hug. "Careful. You'll pop a stitch yet."

"Oh, Jake, when? *When?*"

"As soon as possible." He pushed her away from him slightly and peered down into her face, his smile suddenly becoming strained. "Banner, we don't have time for a fancy wedding. I've already got the license. I handled all that the day I rode into town for food. Do you mind if we just find a preacher and get married without the fuss, without even telling our folks until it's done?"

"No, of course not," she answered in bewilderment. "I don't want the fanfare of another formal wedding. But why shouldn't we tell our parents? Why do you say we don't have time?''

He set her from him then, but kept his hands tightly on her shoulders. ''There's a baby, Banner.'' She stared back at him, too stupefied to respond. ''You're carrying my baby.''

A baby! Jake's child!

''It must have happened that first night in the barn,'' he went on. ''The doctor told me when he was here. That was one of the reasons he didn't want to operate. He was afraid the surgery would endanger the child.''

I'm going to have a baby. A baby Jake and I made.

Undiluted joy rushed through her, bubbling and gurgling like a fountain, sparkling through her system like expensive champagne.

But then the impact of what he had said struck her, immediately and effectively damming the rivers of happiness flowing through her. She shrugged off his hands and backed away from him. Her face went from joyful to blank, to angry, to furious. Before Jake could brace himself for it, she let her hand fly and cracked him smartly and painfully on the cheekbone.

''You bastard! I don't need your pity *or* your charity. Oh, when I think . . .''

She sputtered incoherently. That he had made love to her, proposed marriage to her out of pity was too humiliating to tolerate.

''Pity? Charity? What the hell are you talking about?'' he demanded, nursing his jaw.

''Just get out of here and leave me alone. Get out!'' she screamed. Jake had seen too many of her childhood temper tantrums to know she wasn't joking. And the choice was taken from him when he heard the men riding into the yard reporting for work.

''We'll talk about this later.''

''You go to hell.''

He stalked from the house.

Banner followed him as far as the bedroom door, which she slammed with an impetus that made the window panes rattle. Then, covering her face with her hands, she slid down the cool wood until she reached the floor. Heavy sobs wrenched through her.

She felt more humiliated than she had the day of her wedding, more than she had felt after the incident in the barn, more than she had ever felt in her life.

Humiliated and miserable.

TWENTY-THREE

Grady Sheldon had recovered. His ribs didn't knife into his entrails every time he moved or inhaled. The loosened teeth seemed to have reanchored themselves in his gums. The bruises on his face had gone through the various purple hues and were now jaundiced splotches which were detectable only in certain light.

The physical injuries were healing. But the hatred inside him was as raw and oozing as an open wound.

A goddamned cowboy

Ross Coleman had threatened his life in front of the whole town. That had been humiliating enough. But for a chit like Banner Coleman to prefer a saddle tramp to him, Grady Sheldon, was unthinkable. Langston was years her senior. He probably didn't have two nickels to rub together. It wasn't only unthinkable, it was unforgivable.

For days he had hibernated in his hotel room, nursing his wounds and his hatred. The former because it was necessary. The latter because that hatred had become the focal point of his life. They were all due a comeuppance, and if it was the last thing he did, Grady Sheldon was going to see that they got it.

He had terrorized the hotel parlor maids, snarling at them like a beast lurking in his cave every time they knocked on his door asking if he needed their services. He had lived on whiskey, at first to blur the edges of his pain, then out of laziness. He didn't bathe, didn't shave, didn't do anything but wallow in his hate for Jake Langston and all the Colemans.

This day he had awakened from a drunken sleep with a monumental hangover that hurt everything from his hair follicles down to his toenails. He had pulled himself out of the sweat-dampened sheets, requested a bath in his room, and gradually evolved back into a human being.

Now, as he entered the Garden of Eden, he felt confident again. He had had a run of bad luck that rivaled any in the annals of mankind. It would change.

His cheeks were pink with the first shave in two weeks. His checked suit had been sent out and returned to him pressed and brushed. The black youngster who solicited customers on the street corner had polished his shoes. The bowler sat at a jaunty angle on his head.

Grady shuddered at the thought of whiskey, but asked the bartender for a beer. As he surveyed the crowd in the smoke-filled parlors and gambling rooms of the notorious saloon, he missed the bartender's signal to one of the bouncers, who in turn spun around and headed for the proprietress's chamber.

Priscilla responded to the summons by entering the barroom with less theatrical leisure than usual. She had anxiously awaited word of Grady Sheldon's whereabouts. No one had seen him for weeks. She had mailed a letter to Larsen but had received no answer. What she had to tell him wouldn't keep much longer. Now, when she saw him leaning against the bar, sipping the foamy head off his beer, she rushed toward him.

"Grady!" She tapped his arm with her fan. "You naughty thing, you! Where have you been? I've been dying to see you."

He beamed down at her. She had missed him that much, had she? His heart swelled with pride. He had the most salacious and insatiable whore in the state lusting after him.

"I met with some trouble." For an instant his brown eyes

clouded with the memory of every blow he had received from Jake's fist, as well as Banner's final rejection of his marriage proposal. No doubt they had had a good laugh at his expense afterward.

Sensing his troubled mood, Priscilla laid a comforting hand on his arm and pressed her bosom against his chest. "I hope it's over now."

The words came soft and soothing to his bruised spirit. "Not yet." Then he smiled lazily. "But you can take my mind off my problems, can't you?"

Seductively she lowered her gaze to his lips. "You bet I can. I've missed you."

In a way that was the truth. Male companionship had been notably lacking in her life recently. Apparently Dub Abernathy was angry with her and keeping his distance. He hadn't been to the Garden of Eden since she had approached him on the street.

She hadn't had a man since . . . since Jake had rejected her. She called him a filthy name in her mind, but her body flamed hot with sexual hunger at the memory of his long, hard thighs straddling her bathtub.

She arched her neck and gazed up at Grady with smoldering eyes. Her fingers wandered inside his coat and vest to scratch his shirtfront lightly. "Come with me, Grady. I'm going to make you a happy man tonight." She wet her lips with a wicked tongue. "In more ways than one."

She led him toward her private quarters. At the door, she spoke softly to the bouncer who had informed her that Grady was in the saloon. Grady preceded her in, but the moment she closed the door behind them, he turned to face her. She melted into his arms, curving her body against his enticingly.

"God, you look beautiful," Grady said breathlessly when the long kiss was finally reduced to a moist meeting of their mouths.

Her lips lightly whisked his, but her mind was furiously working. "If I did something for you, Grady, would you do something for me?"

"Like what?" he said thickly.

"Oh, I haven't decided yet. But would you?"

"Sure." He would agree to anything while her tongue was lashing at his lips that way. "One favor deserves another."

"I knew you'd say that."

She was gowned in peacock blue satin. Her breasts swelled above the low neckline. Grady's hands skimmed the creamy mounds; his lips followed. "Damn!" He raised his head from that most engrossing occupation when someone knocked on the door.

Priscilla stroked his cheek. "Someone important to us both, darling. Trust me. No matter what I say, play along." She lowered her hand to his hard erection and squeezed. "Then we'll take care of that."

Her whisper held such provocative promise that Grady didn't even have the willpower to object when she slipped from his embrace and went to answer the door.

He was somewhat surprised when Priscilla admitted one of the whores. He couldn't imagine that the woman with the puffy face and lank hair would be of any interest, much less any importance, to him.

But Priscilla reached for the prostitute's hand and ushered her in, closing the door behind her. She led her to one of the ridiculously spindly chairs around a small tea table. The woman made full use of the decanter of whiskey there. She poured herself a liberal portion and raised the glass to her lips, suspiciously eyeing Grady over its rim.

"Sugar, this is Mr. Grady Sheldon, the lawman I told you about."

Grady shot Priscilla a look of pure disbelief, but she was as cool as a cucumber as she took a seat opposite Sugar and indicated that Grady should take the other. "Would you care for a drink, Mr. Sheldon?"

Plumping down in the chair, he forgot his earlier resolve and croaked, "Yes, please."

"I've seen him in here before. I thought he was one of yours." Sugar mumbled the words dourly. Lately Madam Priscilla had been treating her better. She got to drink all the whiskey she wanted. If she didn't feel like taking on the customers, she could stay upstairs in her room. She'd even been given the new gown she was wearing tonight as a token of Priscillia's appreciation for years of dedicated service.

Sugar wanted to take these special considerations at face value. But if she knew anything about life, and she knew plenty, it was that nothing came without a price. What was Priscilla up to, introducing her to this lawman? He didn't look like any lawman Sugar had ever seen. Too nervous and pale. Was Priscilla going to pin some trumped up crime on her and have her carried off? Had she only been buttered up for a roasting?

"Mr. Sheldon is one of my favored customers," Priscilla said silkily, "but tonight he's here on business. As you know, the Garden of Eden and Hell's Half Acre in general, attract a certain criminal element. Mr. Sheldon often combines business with pleasure since the pressures of his job are so tremendous."

"What's his job?" Sugar sloppily tilted the decanter over her glass and splashed more whiskey into it.

"To track down wanted criminals, of course."

Prisicilla could see the growing suspicion in Sugar's bleary eyes as she surveyed Grady. Priscilla rushed on. "Do you remember the story you told me about Ross Coleman? Mr. Sheldon would like to hear it."

"How come?" Sugar asked insolently.

"He wants to know if it bears checking out. It would be a shame to let that reward go to waste."

"Reward?" For the first time since coming into the room Sugar displayed some interest. Her glass was even halted midway between the table and her flaccid lips.

"How much did you say the reward was, Grady?" Priscilla asked innocently.

"Uh, uh, five hundred," he improvised.

"I thought you said one thousand."

"Oh, yeah, yeah, one thousand." Grady had no idea what all this was about, but if it concerned the Colemans, it concerned him. And from the way it sounded, with Priscilla passing him off as a lawman, it boded ill for Ross Coleman.

His interest was as sharpened as Sugar's. He would gladly pay a king's ransom to hear what the old whore had to say.

"You'll give me one thousand dollars for telling that story about Ross Coleman?" Sugar shrieked. She planted her hand over her chest. "Jesus. Why?"

"It could be very important," Priscilla said obliquely.

Sugar's momentary enthusiasm subsided and she looked at them warily. They resembled two birds of prey about to swoop down on her. "I don't want to get nobody in trouble."

"Would you rather let a criminal go free?"

Grady's head snapped around and his eyes bored into Priscilla. Coleman was a criminal? God almighty!

He cleared his throat and tried to sound authoritative. "If you know any information vital to the apprehension of a wanted outlaw and withhold it, you could be considered an accomplice."

Priscilla looked at him with new respect. Her smile was secret and congratulatory.

"I don't want to get anybody in trouble," Sugar repeated tremulously. Her eyes filled with apprehension. She thought of the two dear boys who had showed her some respect even while releasing their lusty passions. And Jake, who had always treated her kindly.

But she wanted to live out her days in the Garden of Eden. Between it and starvation were the flophouses and the cribs behind the livery stables. She didn't want to die a crib girl. At least at the Garden of Eden she had a roof, a bed, and an occasional bottle of whiskey.

She had prostituted herself nearly all her life. One more time wouldn't matter. "What do you want to know?"

Priscilla laid a comforting hand on Sugar's shoulder. "Just tell Mr. Sheldon the story you told me."

Sugar eyed Grady again. He drew his most foreboding expression, though he wanted to smile elatedly. Priscilla's promise hadn't been an empty one. She was providing him with the ammunition to bring the Colemans to their knees.

"I was working in a dirty railroad town in Arkansas," Sugar began in a small voice. "During Reconstruction."

"1872," Priscilla supplied, knowing the year she and her parents had migrated to Texas from Tennessee. The year of her liberation.

Sugar nodded. "I worked for this madam named LaRue. It wasn't her real name. She was—"

"Just stick to the part about Ross Coleman," Priscilla urged, trying not to let her impatience show. "When did you first see him?"

"Well, we, uh, our wagon had broken down outside of town. A wagon train of folks had camped near the creek there. A man was sent for to help us. Once he got us pulled out of that mudhole, he rode back to town with us. We all wanted a go at him on account of how handsome he was and all. But I don't think he took any of us. Anyway we got busy with those railroad men. They were as randy as a herd of buffalo bills. I didn't see him anymore."

Grady looked at Priscilla inquiringly. One visit to a whorehouse wasn't incriminating. If it were, nearly the entire male population would be behind bars. Priscilla smiled complacently.

"Go on, Sugar," she said.

Sugar fortified herself with another belt of whiskey. "We would have forgotten this Ross Coleman, except that a lawman came looking for him later. A Pinkerton man. Don't remember his name, but he had Coleman's daddy-in-law with him."

"Lydia's father?" Grady asked.

Priscilla shook her head. "No. It must have been Ross's first wife's father."

"Lee's mother," Grady mused. "Why were they looking for Coleman?"

Indelicately Sugar scratched under her arm. "One of our whores had been killed. No one ever knew who did it. Mr. Coleman hadn't because he hadn't been there that night."

"I still don't understand," Grady said, shaking his head in puzzlement.

"Well, the strange thing was that they said Coleman's name wasn't really Coleman."

"Wasn't Coleman?" Grady sat straighter in his chair and leaned across the table.

"Nope. It was Clark, I believe. Sonny Clark. Rode with the James brothers. You can imagine how excited we girls got over knowing that we'd rubbed shoulders with one of the James gang. They were in their heyday then. That bitch LaRue made a fortune advertising the fact that he'd been in her place. 'Course, after he was killed she—"

"Killed?"

"This is where it gets interesting," Priscilla purred. "Tell him what you told me, Sugar."

"A while later, maybe a month or two, Madam LaRue got a letter from this Pinkerton man saying that Sonny Clark had died of gunshots. We all thought it was real sad, his being killed and being so good-looking and having that pretty wife and all."

She drank from her glass again. "I didn't think about it for years. Then when I hired on with Priscilla and found out she had been on that very wagon train, we started talking about it. I thought it was odd when she mentioned that the Colemans were living in east Texas." She shrugged. "But it wasn't none of my business. I only saw him and his wife that one day. If such a commotion over his name hadn't been raised later, I wouldn't have even remembered that."

Grady Sheldon sat perfectly still. He tried to organize the information Sugar had given him into some sort of logical order and digest it. Ross Coleman, a rider with the James brothers? A robber? A killer? Living under an alias all these years?

He wanted to crow with glee, to fall to the floor and roll with hilarity. But he pulled a serious face as he addressed Sugar. "Is there anything else?"

"No."

"You've been most informative and helpful, Miss . . . ?"

"Dalton," she said primly.

"You'll get your reward tomorrow."

"Thank you, Sugar," Priscilla said, rising and indicating that the interview had concluded. She led the other woman to the door. "You look tired, dear. I know this has been an ordeal. Why don't you go to your room and rest?"

"I could use a drink."

"I'll have one of the boys bring you a bottle."

After she closed the door behind Sugar, Priscilla turned to her guest slowly, her grin feline and villainous. "Well?"

Grady rushed across the room, took her in his arms, lifted her up and whirled her around in a mad dance. "Priscilla, I'll smother you in furs and cover you in diamonds for this!"

She laughed. "All I ask for is a partnership in your timber business. I think your ideas are innovative. I have some of my own. And I can bring a considerable amount of cash into the coffers to finance our expansion."

Grady stopped walzing and slowly lowered her to the floor. He had never considered taking on a partner. He had certainly never considered going into partnership with an infamous whore. But he'd work all that out later. Right now he felt like celebrating. "I'll give you anything you want, Priscilla. You've made me the happiest man alive." Then his smile collapsed. "What if she's just a drunken slut who's making up fairy tales to get attention?"

Everything Sugar had said fit. It had always been curious to him that the Colemans didn't have any in-laws. Ross's temper wasn't that of an ordinary man. Grady could well imagine him a trigger-happy outlaw. Still, he couldn't take any drastic action until Sugar's story was checked out.

"I've already documented it," Priscilla assured him. Her eyes grew animated as she told him what she had uncovered. "The sheriff here is a friend of mine. He checked his file of wanted papers, but they didn't go that far back. I had him wire Memphis. There *was* an outlaw named Sonny Clark.

"He was no more than a wild kid when he rode with the Jameses. He disappeared and was given up for dead in '69. Three years later, his name resurfaced and lawmen were on the watch for him living under the alias Ross Coleman. He was reported to have been killed by a Pinkerton detective named Majors."

"That would have been 1872."

"The year coincides with Sugar's story."

Grady paced the room, slamming one fist into the opposite palm as he concentrated. "There are still gaps a mile wide in the story. Why would the Pinkerton man report Coleman dead and close the file forever?"

Priscilla had come this far. She wasn't going to let a panty-waist like Sheldon get cold feet and ruin everything. She needed him to do her dirty work, to get back at Jake for his rejection of her and to get even with that cat-eyed, black-haired girl he fancied himself in love with.

"Who knows?" she cried. "Who'll care when you bring him down? Imagine," she said, firing his imagination, "all those people who laughed at you for having to marry that moonshiner's daughter will respect you and look at you with fear and awe. You'll bring one of the James gang to justice. You'll be famous." She thrust herself against him and let her eyes shine up into his face. "It makes me breathless just to stand close to you."

His mouth swooped down on hers. Sex, power, and lust for revenge surged through his body and concentrated in his loins. He carried her into the bedroom and virtually ripped the satin gown to shreds getting it off. In no less a frenzy, Priscilla disrobed him.

As their heaving, naked bodies came together on the bed, Priscilla panted, "You know what you have to do, don't you, Grady darling?"

He plowed into her yielding body, bucking wildly. "Yes. I'll leave for Larsen tomorrow."

She clutched his hair, pulling so hard tears came into his eyes. Her teeth sank into his meaty shoulder and they screamed together as their fulfillment blazed, forging them in a covenant of hate.

Ma Langston didn't like it. Not one bit. Something was amiss. She could smell it, sense it like an animal senses the change of season.

She arrived at Banner's front door the morning after the cattle had been herded to the ranch. She had stubbornly insisted on taking the raft across the river and walking the distance to the house.

Alternately she scolded and sympathized as she deftly relieved Banner of her stitches with a pair of manicure scissors. She examined the incision and pronounced it was healing well considering a sawbones like Hewitt had done the surgery.

When Banner fell onto her enormous bosom and began to weep copiously, Ma patted her back and comforted her, thinking she was still upset over the surgery. They had shared a cup of tea and a chat. Banner was composed by the time Ma hauled herself up for the trip back across the river.

She was uneasy, knowing something else ailed the girl, but as yet unable to figure out what. Did she miss her mama? Was that the reason for Banner's tears?

But when Jake rode up beside Ma as she made her way back to the river, she got her first inkling that it amounted to much more than homesickness.

"Ma, why don't you ride Stormy the rest of the way?" Jake offered as he dismounted.

"Hmph! I reckon my legs is as strong as his. I'll walk, thank you."

"How is Banner?" Jake matched his pace to hers, leading Stormy by his reins.

"Don't you know?"

"I didn't see her last night. This morning I was too busy for breakfast."

"She's fair to middlin'. Healing right nicely. A little out of sorts." Ma shaded her eyes with her hand as she peered closely at her son. "You look a might peaked yourself. And swelled up like a bullfrog. What's wrong with you?"

His teeth clamped down his cheroot. "Nothing."

"You got a bellyache?"

"No."

"You mad at somebody?"

"No."

"Hmph!" Ma repeated, letting him know she didn't believe him.

When they reached the river, he made sure she was safely

on the raft. Before she took up the long pole to push herself across, she said, "Take care of that girl, ya hear?"

"She can take care of herself," he muttered beneath his breath.

"No, she can't," Ma snapped, wondering if her son was too old to get a well-deserved whipping. "She ain't strong enough yet to see to herself. She's weak in body and soul. Bawled her eyes out this morning."

Jake wouldn't meet his mother's eyes as he threaded Stormy's bridle through his fingers. "Did she say anything?"

"Should she have?"

He shrugged, automatically alert to his mother's keen perception.

Ma dipped the long pole into the water and when it found the muddy bottom, she leaned her weight on it. Something was wrong all right. And it had to do with the two of them. She'd stake her life on that.

Well, whatever it was, they each seemed determined not to talk about it. Best just to leave them alone and let them work it out by themselves. She left Jake with one last instruction. "See to it that she don't do too much."

Neither of them would have been pleased to see Banner lift the tub of wet clothes and haul them toward the clothesline. The morning after her visit with Ma, she decided that the laundry couldn't pile up for one more day. It had to be washed. Besides, activity kept her from thinking.

She didn't want to think about it.

It was all she thought about.

Jake didn't love her. He pitied her. All his tenderness, his gentle concern, his soul-rending kisses, had been born of pity, not passion.

Oh, the gall of him!

What was she to do now?

Banner knew what people thought of girls who got themselves "in the family way" before they were married. They were no longer stoned in the streets, but their reputations were. As often as not the man who fathered the child went unnamed and unscathed while the girl was sent away in shame. Her family invented trips to Europe or sick relatives back east as an excuse for her absence. But everyone knew she had gone away to give birth to an illegitimate child. Often neither the girl nor the child ever returned.

Banner's parents would never forsake her. She was too confident in their love for her to fear banishment. No matter how she disgraced them, they would never cast her out. But they would be disillusioned beyond repair. Hadn't she hurt them enough with one disastrous love affair? Could they withstand another?

Could she?

She must. Even though she felt like dying, she would live because of her baby. Setting the tub beneath the clothesline, she paused to run her hand over her abdomen. It was awesome and wonderful and thrilling to think that she was carrying a child inside her. Jake's child.

She sniffed as a tear trickled down her cheek. He would probably think no more of it than he did her. It would be a liability to him just as she was. He hadn't become her foreman because he wanted to. He had stayed out of a sense of responsibility for what had happened in the barn. He felt he owed it to her parents for tainting their daughter. He was making recompense for taking her virginity.

Well, she didn't need pity from a sorry sort like Jake Langston! Who did he think he was to pity *her?*

He had ruined everything for her. She couldn't even find joy in seeing her herd of curly, red-haired Herefords being driven into the fenced pastures. For the benefit of the hands, she had smiled and waved and whooped from the front door as they drove the cattle past the house. For Jake she had had nothing but a cold stare, full of all the contempt she felt for him. He had taken the hint. He hadn't shared a meal with her since their argument. He hadn't even approached the house.

Jake, Jake, Jake.

Why wouldn't he leave her mind? Why couldn't she forget his sweetness as he tended her, his soft voice, the touch of his hands, the taste of his lips? She had no pride.

Her body yearned for him even as her mind rejected him. Why was she so stupid as to go on loving him when she should despise him?

She bent at the waist and reached into the basket for a garment, wincing as she stood up too quickly and pulled at the tender flesh surrounding her scar. She laid the petticoat over the line and held her hands there, resting, drawing in deep breaths to ward off the fatigue which would weigh her down into immobility if she surrendered to it.

Of course she had wondered about the cessation of her monthly periods. She had dismissed it as being due to the stress she had been under after the wedding and the exhaustion of moving to her own ranch and setting up her household. That she was carrying Jake's child had never occurred to her.

But as though to prove to her it was real, her pregnancy had begun to make itself manifest now that it had been acknowledged. Her shortness of breath and debilitating lassitude weren't only remnants of the surgery or the after-effects of ether. Sometimes she was rocked by waves of dizziness.

As now...

TWENTY-FOUR

"What the hell was that?"

The three men, occupied with notching the ear of a cow for identification, straightened from their task. They froze, while the cow wrested herself free of their loose ropes. Randy had spoken aloud the question uppermost in their minds.

"Sounded like three pistol shots," Pete offered.

"It was." Jake started running toward Stormy, tethered just outside the fence. He scrambled under the barbed wire. When he noticed the others were right behind him, he said, "Stay here. The shots are coming from the house. If Jim or I aren't back in five minutes, one of you cross the river and fetch some riders from River Bend, the other sneak up to the house and see what's going on."

He vaulted into the saddle and spurred the stallion into a gallop. Only a few minutes earlier he had sent Jim to the barn for some pliers. Were the gunshots a summons for help? Had something happened to Banner?

The thought thundered through his mind with each of Stormy's hoofbeats on the turf. The worst possibility was realized when he rode into the yard. The older cowboy was bending over a prostrate form beneath the clothesline. Jake was off Stormy's back and running before the horse had come to a complete standstill.

"What happened?"

"Don't know, Jake. I seen her a'lyin' like this when I come out of the barn. She sure looks poorly. I fired the pistol to git you here quick."

"You did the right thing," Jake said, relieved that the gunshots had only been a signal. He knelt on the ground, his chaps stretching over his knees. "Banner?" He put one hand behind her head and raised it slightly. "Get some water." Jim rushed to do his bidding.

Jake was struck by how pale she looked. There were dark violet smudges beneath the fans of her eyelashes. He remembered his mother's warning. Banner wasn't supposed to be doing any hard work. Why the hell had she taken it into her mule head to do the wash?

When Jim returned with a pail of cold well water, Jake dipped his hand in it and sprinkled it over Banner's face. Her eyes fluttered and she moaned slightly. He sprinkled her again. This time she lifted the back of her hand to her face and brushed the droplets away.

"She's comin' 'round," Jim said.

Her eyes struggled open. Then she squinted against the bright sunlight that fell on her face. "What happened?"

The iron ring of panic around Jake's heart eased its pressure. "She's all right," he said to Jim. "Just fainted I guess. Ride back and tell the others before they rouse the whole countryside."

Jim left them. Jake placed an arm under Banner's knees, another behind her back and lifted her against his chest.

"I can walk."

"You couldn't crawl."

"Put me down."

"No."

"I'm all right now."

"Shut up," Jake growled down at her.

"Don't talk to me like that."

"I'll talk to you any damn way I please."

When they reached the porch, he set her down, then pushed her lightly into the rocker, which had been left there for her. He wasted no time, but launched right in. "Why the hell were you out here in the sun doing the wash?"

"I needed some clean clothes."

"You couldn't wait and ask me to wash them tonight?"

"No. I wouldn't ask anything of you."

"Why?"

"Because I don't want to be beholden to you. I don't want your pity! I can take care of myself."

"*And* the ranch? *And* the baby?"

Her chin went up a notch. "If I have to."

He cursed beneath his breath, then pointed an imperious finger at her. "Now you listen to me, young lady, and you listen good. You're a spoiled brat. Stubborn as a mule. Headstrong. Reckless. And proud. But this is one argument you lose, Banner. We're getting married. You fainted today, for godsakes. You might do it again. The hands'll start to talk and your surgery will be an excuse for only so long." He paused to draw a breath. "Pretty soon someone will figure it out. And what about when you start showing? What did you plan to do then?"

Her lip had begun to tremble. "I'll think of something," she said bravely.

"You won't have to. Because by then we'll be married."

His eyes took on a fierce, possessive light. "And as your husband, I'll kill any man who breathes a bad word against you."

He pulled himself up to his full height and said sternly, "Now go put on whatever frock you want to get married in, because we're going into town. Today. That's all there is to it. And one more thing," he said, punching the air with his finger, "if you ever smack me again the way you did the other day, there'll be hell to pay."

"Do you love me, Jake?"

Her soft question took all the starch out of him. His posture wilted. His eyes warmed. The firm lines around his mouth softened appreciably. He came down on one knee in front of the rocker and covered her hands with his, mindless of the leather work gloves he still wore.

He shook his head, chuckling softly. "If I didn't love you, how the hell could I put up with you the way I do?"

She fought a battle with a smile and lost. "If I based my acceptance solely on the proposals, I should have accepted Grady's. His was much more romantic and flattering." She reached down and took off his hat. Her fingers combed through the hair as white as moonlight. "He came courting me with flowers and candy, telling me how pretty I was. He said God had robbed heaven of one of its angels when He sent me to earth."

Jake was skeptical. "That jackass said all that?"

"Words to that effect."

He studied her face. He caught the middle finger of his glove between his teeth and pulled it off, then laid his hand against her wan cheek. When he spoke, his voice was vibrating with emotion.

"You know I think you're pretty. You're more woman than I deserve. I love sharing a bed with you. For the first time in my life that means something. I want to go to sleep with you every night and wake up with you lying beside me. I want to see you nursing my baby."

He leaned forward and kissed her breast softly, then pressed his face into the soft fullness. Moving his head down, he nuzzled her lap. "I couldn't believe it when the doc told me. I was so worried I was going to lose you, I couldn't even think about the baby. But later, when I sat with you while you were sleeping, I'd think about him and get to feeling so warm and mushy on the inside I'd want to cry.

"I never thought I'd have a kid of my own. If he's a boy I hope he takes after Luke. And if it's a girl, well, I'd kill any sonofabitch that did to her what I've done to you." He kissed her stomach lingeringly, then raised his eyes to her face.

"I'm not very good husband material, Banner. I haven't got anything to offer you. But I'm willing to break my back to make something of this place for us and our baby. Now if you're willing to take a saddle tramp on those terms, you'll be Mrs. Jacob Langston by nightfall."

His words were poetry. They fell on Banner's ears like the lyrics to the sweetest love song. She should take him now so he wouldn't have time to reconsider, but her pride wouldn't let her.

"You're not just marrying me because of the baby, are you? I don't want a martyr sitting across the hearth from me on a cold winter's night, Jake, miserable because he isn't out carousing with his cowboy friends."

"Do you know one red-blooded man who would rather be out carousing with his cowboy friends than going to bed with Banner Coleman?" His teasing worked to soften the frown between her brows, but he answered her seriously. "No, Banner. It's not because of the baby."

He ducked his head with an endearing shyness. "To tell you the truth, I'm glad I've got the baby as an excuse for us getting married. I had given some thought to the idea, but it seemed impossible."

She slid from the chair onto her knees so that she was kneeling with him on the porch. "Jake, I love you so much."

They kissed, lightly at first, testing their truce. Then the desire that seemed an ever-present, living, and vital part of them, urged their mouths to meld with heat.

When at last Jake pulled away, he smiled down at her.

"Go do whatever a bride should do before her wedding. I'll tell the men we're going into town."

"How long do I have?"

"Half an hour."

Banner dashed into the house to wash and dress. It was while she was brushing her hair that she realized he hadn't actually professed to love her.

"Where are we going?"

"Just sit pretty, will you Mrs. Langston? I want to show you something." They were in the wagon.

Jake was driving. He was taking a different route home.

"A surprise?"

"Consider it a wedding present."

"I already have one," she said, proudly holding up her left hand on which Jake had placed a thin gold ring when the preacher had called for it. "When did you get it?"

"The same day I got the license."

"You certainly were confident that I'd say yes."

"Hopeful," he countered, and leaned over to plant a soft kiss on his bride's parted lips. He groaned when he felt the warm, wet touch of her tongue on his lips. "Have you no shame?"

"Not where you're concerned. I never have." She pondered the scenery for a moment. "I guess I'm no better than Wanda Burns."

Jake's head swiveled around. "I ought to paddle your butt for comparing yourself to her!"

"It's true. She was having a baby with a man she wasn't married to. So was I. What's the difference?"

"There are hundreds of them," he shouted. "You were with only one man. That's the main difference."

The fight went out of her. It was too lovely a day and she was too happy to argue. Banner snuggled against his arm and rested her head on his shoulder. "Yes, I was with only one man. And I must have already loved you when I came to the barn that night. Otherwise, I never could have done that."

"I'm glad I was available," he whispered into her ear before kissing it.

Moments later he pulled the horse to a halt in front of an arch made of two stout tree trunks joined by a crossbar at their tops. The arch bridged the road leading to her house. They hadn't come this way on the trip to town so she hadn't seen it earlier.

"What is this?"

"The surprise."

When she would have jumped from the wagon with her usual exuberance, Jake rushed to lift her down. "You'll have to be careful from now on, sweetheart." She thrilled to the way his dark hand moved to her stomach and pressed lightly. He kissed her mouth gently while his fingers caressed the place where his baby slept. The warm sensations were still dancing in her body as he ended the kiss and led her beneath the arch, then turned so she could gaze back at it.

"Jake!" She clapped her hands over her mouth. Tears sprang into her eyes. Branded into the wood of the crossbar were the words PLUM CREEK RANCH. "You changed your mind about the name?"

"No," he said, shaking his head ruefully. "I still think it's a damn silly name for a cattle ranch."

"Then why? I can't believe you went to all this trouble."

With his hands on her shoulders, he turned her to face him. "I wanted to do one thing that would make you happy, one thing that would make you smile instead of cry. I've brought you a lot of misery, unintentionally, but misery just the same. For once I wanted to make you happy."

She fell into his arms. Had he not been so strong they would have toppled backward. His arms went around her and hugged her possessively. He buried his face in her neck, breathing deeply of her perfume which smelled like jasmine and sunshine. They held each other for a long, quiet while before he set her away.

"Should we picnic out of the basket that preacher's wife fixed us?"

She nodded her head eagerly and watched as he led the horse off the road and stationed the wagon under a tree.

Reaching beneath the seat, he took down the basket. "How did you bribe her into doing that?" Banner wanted to know.

Jake had wisely sought out the minister of a country church outside Larsen. If he had consulted the pastor of the church where the Colemans were members, word would have spread like wildfire and Ross and Lydia would have known about the wedding before he was ready for them to know. Thankfully the pastor hadn't recognized him or Banner and had been only too glad to officiate.

His stout wife had played the organ while his spinster daughter acted as witness. As they left, the wife had handed him a basket and blessed him with best wishes for a long and happy life.

"I didn't bribe her. I think she just liked my looks," he said arrogantly as he located an area of thick, soft summer clover beneath a grove of pecan trees. Honeysuckle and pine scented the air. A mild south breeze and the shade provided by the sprawling branches of the trees warded off the heat.

"Are you talking about the wife or the daughter?" Banner quipped tartly. "She was looking at you with covetous calf eyes."

"I didn't notice. I was looking at you."

He dropped on to the clover and pulled her down beside him. He didn't even give her time to regain her balance before pushing her into a reclining position. His lips moved hotly and surely over hers. His tongue stoked passionately, evocatively. He massaged her breast gently.

Beneath him, Banner moved, restless and wanting. When he sat up, she complained with a whine, "Jake, come back."

"If I tumble you here in the clover you'll mess up your pretty dress."

Sighing discontentedly, she let him pull her to a sitting position. She yanked off her hat and tossed it aside. "I don't care about my dress."

He tweaked her nose. "Then you haven't grown up much. I remember when every dress you owned was missing a button, or had a tear, or had its hem straggling down."

She laughed as she took the pins from her hair and let the

coil on the back of her head free itself into a cascade of ebony waves and curls. "I kept Ma's mending needle busy, but it's unchivalrous of you to remember."

The basket that had been so graciously prepared for them proved to be filled with goodies—slices of smoked ham, a loaf of oven-warmed bread, a jar of plum jam, and fresh peach tarts, the pastry of which was so flaky they licked the crumbs from their fingers.

As Jake sucked the crusty flecks from his fingertips, he said, "You look like a buttercup sitting there."

She had worn a yellow dress as pastel and soft as the flower he compared her to. "Thank you, husband."

How could she ever have imagined herself to be in love with a man like Grady, any man for that matter, when Jake Langston walked the earth? He was tall and lanky, all lean muscle and sinew. He moved with the loose-jointed, hip-rolling saunter of his profession, but beneath that indolence lay a dormant power that made her shiver with expectation.

His brows, almost bleached white by heredity and years in the sun, shielded the world from eyes so blue it was sometimes sweetly painful to gaze into them. She loved every weather-etched line in his face, his strength of character, even his stubbornness.

Watching him, she sighed languorously.

"Tired?" She shook her head. "Ready to go home?"

"Not necessarily."

Smiling, he propped his back against the tree trunk. "Lie down." He pulled her head into his lap. It was summertime. They were warm, but not hot. They had just eaten a delicious meal and were pleasantly full. Bees buzzed nearby in a thicket of honeysuckle. The breeze unambitiously stirred the leaves of the tree. Clouds as white and puffy as cottonballs drifted in idle suspension.

The two lovers surrendered to their lassitude, but were far too aware of each other to be sleepy. Banner's thick hair was spread across his lap like a black silk mantle. Her breasts rose and fell with each quiet breath. Jake's index finger adoringly charted the planes of her face.

"I should go home and get back to work, but I'm lazy," he confessed.

"I'm seriously considering firing you."

He smiled, then whispered. "Your gorgeous, Banner Coleman." He bent down to kiss her.

Just before his lips captured hers, she corrected him. "Banner Langston."

He kissed her with unleashed passion, letting his tongue plunder her mouth. Her arms crept up to encircle his neck and, as she urged his head down closer, she arched up to meet him.

Unfastening only a few of the buttons on her bodice, he shifted the material until the tip of her breast rose up to him like the center of a delectable flower from its cushion of sheer batiste, lace, and satin ribbon.

"You sweet, sweet girl." He caressed with his fingertips. Then his lips. Then his tongue. Softly, Erotically. Wetly.

Banner whimpered with animal pleasure and twisted her head with sublime agitation.

Suddenly Jake's head came up. His back pressed rigidly against the trunk of the tree while his head ground the bark beneath it to powder. Moaning in protest that he had stopped, Banner turned her face into his lap.

Then she knew the reason for and extent of his agony. "Jake?" Her voice wavered. Tentatively she touched the fly of his pants.

His breath hissed through his teeth. "I'll be all right in a minute, only . . ."

"Only what?"

"Banner," he said hoarsely, "lift your head away from me."

"Why?"

"Every time you move . . . ahhh, God . . . and I can feel your breath. That's not helping the situation, sweetheart."

She gazed up at his tortured face for a moment, then lowered her eyes to what was directly in front of them. Her hesitation lasted no longer than a heartbeat. She kissed him softly.

"Ahh—"

His fingers tunneled through her hair until all ten settled on her scalp and held her head. But he didn't push her away. Nor did he urge her forward. He looked like a man who couldn't decide what to do, like a man torn by agony but experiencing ecstasy. His breath rushed raggedly through gnashed teeth. His eyes were pinched shut.

Banner kissed him again. This time her lips stayed. And stayed. And moved.

Incoherent sounds slipped through Jake's lips until they finally formed her name. He repeated it over and over with every unselfish pass of her lips up and down that ridge of his masculinity.

Her hands were as light and quick as the beat of a butterfly's wings. Buckles, buttons, cloth didn't deter her. Even the sky heard the low mating sound Jake made when he felt her breath against his flesh, the first glance of her soft, soft lips, the timid touch of her tongue.

"Banner, Banner."

The name was chanted in the dearest tones. So sweetly did she caress him he wanted to die, for life would never again afford him such pleasure.

One of his hands disentangled itself from her hair and combed down her throat and chest to fondle her breast. Then, working his way under the layers of petticoats, he found her knee above her garter, the smooth length of thigh, the lacy edge of her pantaloons. His hand wandered blindly upward, grappling with ties and buttons until he met with flesh as smooth as warm satin.

The nest of dark hair ensnared his caressing fingers as surely as her being had trapped his heart. Then he found her soft and yielding, liquefying against his fingers, responding to his caresses with movements as elemental and old as time.

Her mouth gave him a prolonged glimpse of heaven. But man can only stand so much bliss and Jake's heart and loins were bursting with it. When he had almost exceeded his limit, he repositioned them and covered her body with his. He found that sweet channel with one swift thrust.

Their eyes met and locked while long, slow strokes

carried him deep within her, brought him back to the portal, only to sink into her again.

Never had their loving meant more. Her body echoed each loving motion of his. It was as though they were being rocked in a giant cradle. It overturned and tipped them into a shining new universe when the time was right. They sailed, they soared, their hearts sang. The celebration seemed endless. Then they gently glided back into this world.

They roused to find themselves wrapped in each other's arms, their clothes sticking to them uncomfortably, due to the sheen of perspiration that glossed their bodies.

Weakly, Jake raised his head from her shoulder. Her face was an ever-changing pattern of shadow and sunlight as the leaves of the tree overhead shifted in the breeze. Her eyes came open languidly. Swirling combinations of green and gold captured each sunbeam.

Still sheathed by her, he whispered earnestly, "You are my woman, Banner. None else. You."

Her smile was unsteady, her fingers shaky, as she reached up and touched the lips that had spoken the words. Love for him spilled through her like a river of golden wine.

But like an imp that wouldn't be banished or laid to rest, a thought nagged her. Did his vow include her own mother?

It took some doing, but they set their clothing aright. Banner did her best to brush twigs and leaves from her hair. There was no help for the green stains on the yellow dress. She helped Jake gather the remains of their picnic and walked with him hand in hand back to the wagon where the horse stood by peacefully grazing.

"I think we ought to go tell your folks." Jake had waited until they were on their way to make the suggestion. As soon as the words were out, he turned his head to gauge her reaction.

"I'd like that. I want to shout it to the whole world."

He was less optimistic. "They might not take it too well, Banner. We'll have to break it to them gently, maybe tell them about getting married, but save the news about the baby for another day."

"They love you, Jake. They have since they've known you."

"Not as a son-in-law. I'm particularly worried about Ross's reaction," he said grimly.

Banner smiled confidently. "Let me handle Papa if he proves difficult." Then she laid her hand high on his thigh. "It won't make any difference if they approve or not. You're my husband and nothing's going to change that."

Her optimism was infectious. By the time they parked the wagon and poled across the river on the makeshift raft, Jake was feeling relieved that he wouldn't have to hide his feelings for Banner any longer. He could touch her whenever he wanted to without glancing over his shoulder first. By God, she was his wife, and he couldn't wait for everyone to know it.

He assisted her up the incline and kept his arm around her as they walked toward the yard. When they reached the gate, he bent down and softly kissed her mouth.

"Does my hair look too bad?"

He plucked a clover from the recalcitrant strands. "No."

"Liar. Do you think they'll know what we did between here and town?"

He leaned down and laid his mouth against her ear. "Do you care?"

"No." She giggled. He hugged her to him tightly.

"Just what the hell is going on?"

Ross's voice boomed around them. They jumped apart guiltily. Ross had been sitting on the porch, smoking the pipe Banner had brought him from Fort Worth, when he saw them coming up the lane. Delighted that they had come in time for supper, he had made his way toward them. But before he could hail them, he witnessed the intimate exchanges.

He didn't see his daughter with his old friend. He didn't see the tender, loving expression on their faces. All he saw was his daughter in the embrace of a man who had no right to be touching her like that. Ross's blood had already reached a boiling point long before he strode through the gate and faced them like a warlord.

"Get you hands off her."

"Papa, that's Jake you're talking to!"

"I know damn well who I'm talking to."

"Ross—" Jake began.

"Banner, go in the house," Ross ordered. He intended to beat the hell out of Bubba Langston and he didn't want his daughter to see it.

"I will not. And stop glaring at us. I'm not a child, Papa, and—"

"You're *my* child," he roared. "And I won't have any man pawing you like some common crib girl."

"That's enough, Ross," Jake said tightly. "Calm down and let me explain."

"I don't need an explanation. I know what I saw."

"We're married," Jake announced quietly. "I married Banner this afternoon."

Ross was in the act of stepping forward threateningly. He came to a halt so suddenly he swayed. "Married?" His eyes sawed back and forth between them. His chest began heaving. He dropped the pipe into the dirt and his fists clenched at his sides. "You're old enough to be her father."

"But I'm not. I'm her husband. Let's go in the house—"

"You must have had a damned good reason for getting married," he snarled. "I know how you feel about women. They're all fair game for that pecker of yours."

"Papa, stop!" Banner cried.

Several cowboys had heard the shouting and had come from the bunkhouse to see what the commotion was. Banner's cheeks flushed scarlet as she glanced around.

"Having a wife would cramp your style, Bubba. There's only one reason why you would take a wife and by God that better not have happened. Have you . . . ? Did you . . . ? You bastard, I believe you did!" He came rushing toward them. "You were supposed to be taking care of her, you low-down sonofabitch."

He took a swing at Jake that connected with a sickening thud against the younger man's jaw. Banner screamed and hastened out of the way as Jake went reeling back and careened into the fence.

"What's going on?" Lydia, her skirts hiked almost to her

knees, came running down the steps of the porch. Ma was close behind her, a dishtowel still in her hands. Lee and Micah rushed forward to take Banner by the hands and pull her protestingly out of the way.

Jake hadn't had time to recover from the first blow before Ross's fist found his belly and sent him flying sideways into the dirt. He rolled to his knees and shook his head to clear it. He hurt all over, but thought he should be grateful that Ross wasn't wearing his gun. He would be dead for sure by now. And, he supposed, it was just as well he hadn't strapped his holster back on after his and Banner's picnic. Any minute now he was going to get mad.

"Ross, I don't want to fight you, but if you hit me again—"

He never got to finish. Another powerful fist came flying toward his head. He deflected it before it could do more damage than split his lip open.

That was all his temper would let him take without fighting back. Doubling over, he barreled into Ross with a vengeance. They fell to the ground, a melee of thrashing limbs, flying fists, kicking feet, gouging knees. Blood and sweat mingled in the dirt beneath their twisting, grappling bodies.

Their spectators stood in speechless dismay at seeing the two friends fighting. Lydia twisted her hands. Tears rained from Banner's eyes. Micah stood with a pained expression on his face, knowing intuitively what the fight was about. Ma shared his intuition, her mouth set. Lee couldn't believe his eyes.

Everyone was so engrossed in the fight that no one noticed a horseman who reined up just beyond the gate. He was surprised himself by the spectacle that greeted him. But he smiled. In a few moments, their fight would be of little consequence. He went unnoticed until he called out in a loud voice:

"Sonny Clark!"

Ross's head snapped up. Befuddled, his eyes scanned the half-circle of faces surrounding him. They stopped on Lydia. Dreamlike, everything went into slow motion. He saw her eyes go wide with disbelief, saw the color drain from her face, saw her look of horror as she raised her eyes from his to gaze at a point beyond his shoulder. He saw her lips form the word no.

Ross leaped to his feet in a crouching positon. Even as he turned in the direction of Lydia's gaze, he slapped his hip, instinctively reaching for the holstered pistol that wasn't there. He got a vague impression of a man on horseback with a rifle raised to his shoulder.

Then the blast rent the air.

Lydia and Banner screamed.

Some of the hands ducked for cover.

Others groped for weapons.

Jake was the only one who acted reflexively. He lunged for Micah. As he knocked the unsuspecting boy to the ground, he whipped Micah's pistol out of its holster. Rolling over twice, he came up on one knee.

With an aim Ross Coleman had helped him perfect, he planted a bullet square between the eyes of Grady Sheldon.

TWENTY-FIVE

Sheldon was dead. His gloating expression became his deathmask.

Jake didn't wait to see how long Sheldon's body sat astride the horse before it finally toppled to the dusty ground. He wheeled around and rushed to Ross's side. Lydia was bent over him, screaming his name as she frantically clutched at his hand. Jake shoved the dumbfounded ranch hands out of the way.

"Oh, Jesus," Jake breathed. It amazed him that Sheldon could have gotten off such an acurate shot. If the bullet missed Ross's heart at all, it couldn't have been by more than a hair. The bullet had punctured a small neat hole in the middle of his chest, close to another scar above his left breast. Jake shuddered to think what his back looked like.

"Lydia?" The garbled, liquid sound bubbled from Ross's mouth.

Lydia raised her head. Her face was devoid of color. Her eyes looked vacuous and sightless. "He's hurting, Bubba. Do something," she pleaded almost silently.

Jake looked down at his friend. Ross's eyes were closed. But he wasn't dead. Yet.

"Let's get him in the house." He motioned his brother and some of the other hands forward for assistance. Lee seemed to be petrified with shock. He was standing nearby, looking at his father as though he had never seen him before. Banner stood beside her half-brother, clutching his arm. Her face was white.

Jake knew the risk they were taking in moving Ross, but he wasn't going to let his friend die in the dirt. With a man at each shoulder, two at his hips, two at his feet and Jake holding his head, they lifted Ross up and with slow, measured steps carried him into the house. Lydia followed them like a sleepwalker.

They didn't dare take the stairs, but carried Ross into his office. Ma, as though perceiving beforehand what Jake had inteneded to do, was already spreading a quilt over the leather sofa. The men lowered Ross onto it gently.

"Go get a doctor, that younger one," Jake ordered no one in particular. He tore open Ross's bloodstained shirt. "And the sheriff. Let Sheldon rot in the sun till then." The cowboys shuffled out respectfully, muttering softly among themselves.

"What do you need?" Ma wedged her way to the couch where Jake worked over Ross. He was unaware of the bruise over his own eye, his swelling lip, and the bleeding abrasion on his cheek. He didn't even remember their fight.

Jake glanced up at his mother. His eyes told her that there was nothing they could do. Then they shifted to Lydia, who looked as pale as her husband and as severely wounded. Her face was shattered and bleak. For her benefit he said, "Hot water, some bandaging."

Ma, without comment, headed for the door. She called upon that strength within her that was as enduring as the mountain that had spawned her. She had buried five children and her husband. Just when she had been sure she would die of grief, she had surprised herself by continuing to live. She glanced back at Lydia and offered up a prayer that the younger woman would find some source of courage to survive what fate had deemed she must.

"Will you cut the bullet out?" Lydia asked Jake in the small, high-pitched voice of a child.

His eyes locked with hers. "No, Lydia. It's too close to his heart. That would kill him for sure."

A sob escaped her trembling lips and she collapsed to her knees beside the couch. Again she pressed Ross's hand between her own. "He's strong. He'll live. I know it."

Ross had blessedly slipped into unconsciousness. Now his eyes fluttered open. He seemed to have difficulty focusing on anyone except his wife. His eyes went to her unerringly. Somehow he found enough strength to reach up and touch her hair.

"Stay . . . with . . ."

"I will. I will." Tears ran down her cheeks and into her lips. She licked them away and leaned over to kiss Ross. "I'll never leave you. I'll always be with you. Always."

Banner was standing at the end of the sofa with her hands clasped beneath her chin. She stared at her father's massive chest. The skin that was usually tanned and healthy now looked spongy and pale. The carpet of black hair covering it was a stark contrast. The wound was below the scar that she had always been curious about. Her parents had told her he had been wounded in the War Between the States. Now she wondered. Because everyone had heard Grady call out another name just before he fired the rifle.

Sonny Clark.

Her father had raised his head. He had recognized that name. Mama had too. What was the secret that bound them? Who had fathered that baby her mother had borne in the woods before Jake found her? And who, really, was Papa?

Did it matter? Lord, why had she dwelled on that for all these years? Why had she let such a trivial thing bother her? Her papa was about to die and it didn't matter what his name was or how he had come to marry her mother. She loved him and a vital part of herself would die when he did.

Life without Papa, without his strength, without his flashing white smile beneath the mustache that tickled when he kissed her? No!

And, oh, God, they had been arguing just before Grady shot him. *Grady, Grady, may you burn in hell!* her mind screamed. Tears blurred her vision. She closed her eyes. The tears ran unchecked down her cheeks in twin streams. This was her second wedding day to end in tragedy.

Jake bathed the wound with the water Ma carried in in a tin bowl. He stanched the flow of blood as best he could with strips of an old sheet. Ross's chest lifted and fell like an unreliable bellows. He struggled for each breath and his respiration rattled in his throat.

But he was alert now, aware of what was going on around him. And as a consequence, aware of the pain as well. He gazed up at Jake. The green eyes were fogged with pain, but not vacant with delirium. Ross had several things to do before he died. He was going to see that they were done.

"Call Lee and Banner," he gasped. It cost him his strength to say even that, but no one dared dispute him. Ma motioned Lee forward, and he came on stumbling feet, made even more clumsy by the tears standing in his eyes. He couldn't reconcile that his father, who had always seemed as tall and sturdy as an oak, able to ward off any danger or threat, was precariously clinging to life.

Banner sank to her knees on the floor beside her mother and laid her hand on her father's shin. Lee took up her position at the foot of the couch. Jake and Ma moved aside.

Ross's eyes focused on Lee. He nodded his approval of the fine son he had sired out of Victoria Gentry. Lee himself had struggled to live those first few days after he was born. It had made him strong.

The green eyes traveled to Banner. Ross smiled, remembering all the times she had crawled into his lap, begging him to tell her a story. He could still smell her flannel nightgowns fresh from the clothesline and remember the feel of her little pink toes as he warmed them in his hands. Now she was a woman, a beautiful woman, as vibrant as her mother.

Lydia. He looked at her now. It seemed he had been engaged in that occupation for as long as he could remember, looking at Lydia. Her face filled his declining vision. God, how he loved her! How he hated to leave her. Nothing in heaven would compare to the joy he had found with her.

For the first time he was angry about what had happened. Furious, impotent rage surged through his dying body. If he hadn't been fighting Jake, if he had been wearing his gunbelt, if he had had nothing to hide in the first place . . . If, if, if.

That was an exercise in futility and he didn't have time to indulge it. He should have died over twenty years ago, riddled with gunshots after a bank robbery. God had seen fit to let him live, had granted him a second chance, had given him the marvelous gift of the life with Lydia. He had no argument with Divine will.

"Tell them." The words came out on ragged breaths that required all the strength he could garner.

Lydia didn't have to ask what he meant. "Are you sure?"

He blinked once in affirmation. Better that his children understood why he had had to die violently than to remain forever in the dark. What good was keeping the secret now? Would they love him less? He gazed at their tear-glossed eyes. No. He didn't think so.

Lydia touched his hair. Her fingers barely sifted through the raven strands sprinkled with silver, but she loved the texture of it. A smile ghosted over her lips. "I love you, Sonny Clark." She kissed his forehead, then looked at her children. "Your father's real name was Sonny Clark. His mother was a prostitute and he was raised in a brothel. After the war, he became an outlaw who rode with Jesse and Frank James."

In a steady voice, almost emotionlessly, she told them the unbelievable story of Ross's life, how he had been left for dead and nursed back to health by a hermit in the hills of Tennessee, John Sachs by name.

"When he was well enough, he changed his appearance and went down into the valley to find work. He was hired on at the Gentry stables. That's where he met your mother, Lee. She was from an aristocratic family, but she fell in love with the stable hand. I don't blame her," Lydia added gently, glancing down at her husband.

She related how Ross had married Victoria much to her father's displeasure and how they decided to migrate to Texas and assume ownership of some land, the deed of which had been given to Ross by John Sachs. That land had become River Bend.

Victoria hadn't been as confident in their future as she had pretended and had taken a pouch of jewelry from her home when they left. Her father assumed Ross had stolen it and went after them. Since Victoria had convinced Ross to leave in her father's absence, he hadn't known their destination.

"He didn't even know she was pregnant with you," Lydia told her stepson. "Nor did he know that she had died until he caught up with us in Jefferson. In the meantime, he had found out about Ross's past. He didn't believe that you were his grandson and tried to kill your father out of vengeance for Victoria's death. A Pinkerton detective named Majors shot and killed him."

Ross nudged her arm. "Shot . . . you," he rasped.

Lydia ducked her head, then faced her children's incredulous faces again. "The scar on my shoulder . . ." she said uneasily. "I tried to save Ross's life."

The room was still. The only sound was the ticking clock in the corner.

"What happened to this detective, this Majors?" Lee asked huskily.

"We never saw him again," Lydia answered softly, and smiled down at Ross. "He let Ross go. I think he could see that your father wasn't an outlaw anymore. He wasn't Sonny Clark. He was truly Ross Coleman. And, Lee, we have that jewelry. We saved it for you because it belonged to your mother and her family. We planned to give it to you when you turned twenty-one."

"And no one ever knew about Papa's past?" Banner asked.

"Not even Ma," Lydia said, looking toward the older woman as she stood quietly weeping. Micah was patting her shoulder.

"And Jake?" Banner whispered, seeking her husband's eyes.

"I knew some of it," he replied softly. "Not all."

"How did Grady find out?" Banner asked the question uppermost in all their minds. No answer was forthcoming. Then Banner asked another question. "Mama, did you have another baby, before me, before you met Papa?"

What little color remained in Lydia's face drained. Wildly, she looked inquiringly at Ma, who shook her head in denial. Jake answered her unspoken question. "Priscilla must have told her."

"Priscilla?" Lydia repeated. "Priscilla Watkins? When? How?"

"In Fort Worth. She cornered Banner on the street. They were having a conversation before I interrupted it."

Everything inside Lydia sagged. She slumped forward. Her greatest shame, one she had wanted to outlive, was back again to haunt her on this, the worst day of her life. She felt Ross's hand on hers, squeezing.

She laid her ear against his lips. "It . . . never mat-mattered to me." Her tears dripped saltily onto his face. She wept openly now with love. Her heart and soul overflowed with it and it had to come pouring out. "Ross, Ross," she cried out in a pleading voice. Momentarily she rested her head on his stomach.

It was Banner who drew her mother's head up. She smoothed down Lydia's hair, which, except for the color, was identical to hers. "It's all right, Mama. It doesn't matter. Really it doesn't. I love you. I was just curious, that's all."

Lydia shook her head. "No, it's best if it's all told." She

paused to draw in a deep breath. "I was running away when I collapsed in the woods and gave birth to the baby. I thought I had killed its father. He was my stepbrother. Not by blood," she rushed to say when she saw the horror register on their faces. "My mama married a man named Otis Russell when I was about ten. He and Clancey made our lives hell."

She explained about Russell's death and Clancey's abuse. "He . . . he . . . I got pregnant by him. When Mama died, I ran away. He came after me. When he found me, I knocked him down and he hit his head on a rock. I thought he was dead, so I kept running, afraid someone would blame his death on me. I was glad when the baby was stillborn and wanted to die of shame myself. But when I woke up, Bubba was there."

Lydia looked at him and smiled. Something inside Banner snapped, painfully, like a dry twig.

"The Langstons took care of me," Lydia continued. "Then I was taken to Ross when my milk came. Victoria had just died, leaving him with a hungry newborn. I nursed you, Lee. I've always loved you like my own."

"I know that." The young man was fighting a losing battle with unmanly tears.

"But Clancey wasn't dead. He caught up with the wagon train and found me married to Ross. Somehow he had discovered Ross's identity too. He knew about the jewelry Ross had supposedly stolen. He threatened me. I was terrified of him. I was afraid he would hurt Ross or Lee." She glanced up at Lee. "There was even a time when he suspected you were his child and that I had lied about his baby dying. He was capable of brutality, I knew that."

She stood and went to Ma. Taking the older woman's hands between her own, she stared into the lined face she had loved for so long. "Ma, it was my stepbrother Clancey who killed Luke. Forgive me for not telling you. But I couldn't. I was so ashamed."

Ma's only reaction was a brief puckering of her lips. She reached out and drew Lydia to her, patting her back in comfort and reassurance. "Weren't none of your doin'.

Don't see that it rightly matters who killed him. Didn't then, don't now.''

Lydia pushed herself away. "Clancey killed Winston Hill, too. He died protecting me. That's another thing I've had to live with."

"What happened to him?" Banner asked, hating the man she had thankfully never known.

"He's dead." Lydia's voice held a finality that no one dared breach. Save one.

"I killed him."

The three words echoed in the room. All eyes turned to Jake. Even Ross reacted. His whole body twitched and he tried to turn his head toward Jake.

"I overheard him threatening Lydia to bring the law down on Ross that night we arrived in Jefferson. He bragged about killing Luke. I tracked him into town, waited until I caught him alone in a dark alley and slit his belly open with Luke's own knife."

He turned to his mother. "Ma, if it's any consolation, Luke's murder was avenged years ago."

She came forward and touched her oldest son's cheek. Then, losing her composure, she wrapped her bulky arms around him. This explained so many things, his bitterness, his wariness of people, his self-imposed loneliness. He had taken the burden of the family on himself when he was still a mere boy and she suffered for him.

"Bubba."

The raspy voice called to him from the couch. Jake rushed to Ross's side quickly. As though tacitly agreeing on their need for privacy, everyone else fell back out of hearing. Jake knelt beside the couch. "Yes, Ross?"

"Thank you." The words, though barely spoken, were heartfelt. The emerald eyes were clouded by more than pain now. They were shiny with tears of gratitude. "Wish . . . I'd . . . killed him."

Jake smiled wryly. "Sounds to me like you already had your hands full."

Ross tried to smile back, but it was more a grimace of pain. "Sorry about . . ."

Jake shook his head. "I know you didn't mean to fight me, Ross. It's not worth apologizing for. We gave you quite a shock."

"Banner... you'll..."

"I love her, Ross. Didn't count on it happening, but..."

"Yeah, well"—he cast a glance at Lydia—"it happens like that sometimes."

"You were right, though. She's carrying my baby." The green eyes cleared instantly, then filled with tears again. Jake rushed on. "I can't tell you how proud I am about having a child from your seed, Ross. He'll be special."

The older man's lips trembled, but he smiled. "You and me, huh? Reckon he'll be sonofabitchin' mean."

Jake laughed. "Reckon he will."

"Keep... keep the happy news for Lydia. She'll need it." Jake's own eyes glossed with tears. He nodded. "You turned into... a fine man, Bubba."

Jake closed his eyes, squeezed them shut, trapping in tears. When he opened them, he saw his friend's face through wavering moisture. "Remember me telling you that I never liked a man as much as you, except maybe my brother?" Ross smiled and moved his head in a facsimile of a nod. "That still holds. I'm going to miss you like hell."

The two men clasped hands, years of friendship and unspeakable understanding passing between them. "Watch over Lydia and—"

"I will."

"Goodbye, friend."

"Goodbye, Ross."

"Lydia"—Micah spoke from the door—"the doc just got here. And, Jake, the sheriff wants to see you."

Priscilla moved the file around the tip of her nail, shaping it to a sharp point. She had bathed, scented, and powdered herself in preparation for her visitor. Her peignoir was a frilly confection in her favorite shade of lavender. She had piled her hair high, but loosely, on the top of her head. She looked exquisite.

A gloating smile curved her mouth and her eyes narrowed

cunningly. To think that just a few weeks ago she had been concerned about the future. Now everything pointed to bright years ahead.

If Grady Sheldon thought he would leave east Texas alive after boldly shooting Ross Coleman as he claimed he would do, he was a greater fool than she suspected. She had pumped him full of confidence, stroked his pride, and stroked his hatred until he was as fanatic about killing Ross Coleman as a samurai warior bent on a suicidal mission.

Priscilla had heard that River Bend was impressive. Coleman wasn't a land baron compared to many in the state, but he would no doubt have his small army of riders who wouldn't stand by and see him murdered without recourse. And even if that weren't so, Jake wouldn't let Sheldon draw another breath after killing Ross.

Priscilla was certain that her partner wasn't long for this world.

And partner she was. She had made sure of that before letting him leave her boudoir the day before. With the aid of an attorney, a loyal patron of hers for years, they had drawn up a contract. Grady had been so drunk on power and lust that he hadn't read all the clauses she had surreptitiously instructed the lawyer to include in the document. One stated that in the event of the death of a partner, all capital assets and the ownership of the company reverted to the other. She could confidently predict that without ever having spent one dime toward the investment, she would own and control a thriving timber business by this time tomorrow.

She hummed softly as she laid the nail file aside and picked up a buffer. "What is it?" she called out when a knock sounded on the door.

"Your guest is here, Miss Priscilla," the bouncer announced.

"Send him in." The music and raucous noise from the saloon swelled, then diminished to a low rumble as the door was closed. Priscilla said nothing, but kept her buffer poised over her nail until she saw Dub Abernathy's shadow cross her parlor. She was a picture of docile feminine perfection when he entered the bedroom.

She tilted her head up and gazed at him through her lashes. "Are you angry with me?" she asked softly.

He had been. For weeks after their encounter on the city street, he had fumed. The audacity of the strumpet had appalled him. He could easily have wrung her neck. She had made his life hell at home. He had only this week gotten back into his wife's good graces after promising her a vacation to New York. Then this afternoon he had received a decorous, hand-delivered note asking him to come see her.

Repentance was written all over Priscilla's features as she languidly put the nail buffer aside and came to her feet. She made certain that the folds of the violet peignoir fell just right as she took a few hestitant steps toward her former mentor. "I'm sorry, Dub. I was jealous," she said, spreading her arms wide in appeal. "Your wife has you all the time. I saw you lifing her into that buggy and I got livid. It's just not fair that she gets to live with you and I have to wait until it's convenient for you to see me." She moved forward again, stopping just short of touching him. "I'm sorry if I embarrassed you or caused you any hardship. Please forgive me."

Her breath filtered up to him. It was brandy-scented. His favorite label of brandy. Her body looked as smooth as ivory, but as warm as fresh cream. Her lips were wet and shiny and sulky. She was wearing the high heels and stockings he loved, but she wore nothing beneath the corset. Overflowing its satin cups were the mounds of her breasts. If she breathed deeply, he would be able to see their tips as they popped free. The thought sent a geyser of heat into his loins and his upper lip began to sweat. She was a whore, but she was one without equal. As long as she recognized and acknowledged who had the upper hand, they would get along just fine.

He tossed his hat and cane on the chaise. With an amazing alacrity for a man of his size, he seized Priscilla and jerked her to him, embedding one stubby hand in her hair, twisting painfully, and with the other held her back arched and her stomach pressing against him.

"Don't ever do anything like that again." His lips swooped

down on hers. He showed not a trace of caring or tenderness, but ravished her mouth with a bruising tongue. When they pulled apart, Priscilla's eyes were alight with excitement.

She shrugged out of the robe and let it slither down her body to the floor. Dub reached for the hooks on her corset and jerked them open. The backs of his knuckles dug creaters into the soft flesh. As in his fantasy, her breasts spilled into his waiting hands, the redly rouged nipples already hard and eager. He sucked on them ruthlessly, causing pain, but she reveled in it.

Her hands worked frantically to get him out of his clothes. When he was naked, they moved to the bed. He fell on to it on his back and pulled her down to straddle him. He impaled her brutally, but with no more savagery than she rode him to a clawing, biting, gasping climax that left them both weak and breathless.

Minutes later, Priscilla, clad only in the sheer peignoir, came back to the bed carrying a snifter of brandy. She passed it to Dub. He sipped, watching as she reclined against the pillows next to him. He reached over and flicked open the ruffled panels of the negligee.

She stretched her arms above her head and arched her back in brazen disregard for the heated eyes that roved over her nakedness. "You like?" she purred.

He dipped his finger into the brandy, spread it around her nipple, then licked it off. "I like."

Priscilla's hands rested lightly on his head as his mouth wandered further afield, stopping to sample morsels of her flesh on the way. "Too bad this is our last time together."

He was so involved in his activity that several seconds passed before he raised his head and peered into her eyes. They were no longer glowing with passion, but with something much more explosive. "What do you mean?"

She pushed him off her and stood. Going to the dressing table, she picked up a hairbrush and, after pulling the pins from her hair, idly began to brush it. "I'm selling the Garden of Eden and leaving town."

"Selling? I don't understand. Where are you going?"

"That's my business, Dub," she said to his stunned

reflection in the mirror. He really did look ridiculous, sitting there naked in bed, with a stupid expression on his face like a toad caught in a lantern light.

She had decided to move to Larsen. Whether Grady managed to stay alive or not, she planned to oversee the timber company from now on. Besides, Larsen was where Jake was. He might think they were finished once and for all, but she sure as hell knew better. She wouldn't stop until Jake came to her bed like a beggar pleading for a crust of bread.

"I'm going into another line of work."

Dub laughed as he came off the bed and began pulling on his clothes. "Well, good luck to you, but I doubt you'll be as good at it as you are at this."

Priscilla's back went rigid and she faced him with smoldering eyes. "I'm glad you're amused tonight. You might not be laughing so hard tomorrow, Mr. Abernathy. There will be a letter from me to your preacher in tomorrow's mail. I've confessed everything, especially how I've led prominent members of his flock astray."

Dub froze in the action of pulling on his vest. "You didn't," he growled.

She smiled sweetly. "Oh, yes, I did. I petitioned his prayers, of course, for my damned soul. But at the same time, I named names. Yours topped the list in capital letters." She tossed her head back and sneered at him. "I was good for an afternoon tumble, but you wouldn't help me when I needed to get those crusaders off my back. You would have seen me in ruination before you would have stuck our your neck to help me. On a public street you looked straight through me. Well, it's about time you and those of your ilk, you hypocritical sons of bitches, paid a premium for my services."

"You goddamned bitch," he yelled.

"If you hit me, I'll go see that preacher in person wearing the bruise you gave me." The words tripped out in a rush as he came toward her with his arm raised ready to strike. The threat forestalled him. He lowered his arm, but his face was mottled with fury and his chest was heaving with pent-up rage seeking an outlet.

He finished buttoning his coat with fumbling fingers. "Don't forget your hat and cane, dear," she called sweetly as he stamped toward the door. Her laughter trilled after him as he slammed the door behind him.

Priscilla waltzed around the room and collapsed on the bed in a heap of ruffles. The apoplectic expression on his face had been worth the weeks of planning, the hours spent tolerating Grady Sheldon's sloppy lovemaking, the humiliation of being snubbed in the streets.

She laughed out loud, hugging herself. It would take more than the pious city fathers of Fort Worth to bring down Madam Priscilla Watkins.

For his part, Dub Abernathy's whole world was bathed red with rage as he elbowed his way through the boozy crowd in the saloon. His eyes scanned the sweaty faces until they lit on the one he sought. He made an understood motion with his head and moments after he left the Garden of Eden he was joined in the shadows outside on the boardwalk. The conversation was terse, the instructions given explicit.

The man returned to the saloon. Dub Abernathy walked to where he had left his buggy parked several blocks away. Climbing in, he clicked his tongue to the horse. He drove through the balmy night toward home, where his family was waiting for him.

Sugar Dalton woke up earlier than usual. It wasn't even dawn when she rolled over with a sour taste in her mouth and a pain in her left arm that was keeping her from sleep.

She edged to the side of her bed and sat up groggily. Shaky hands clasped her head as she bent almost to the waist in an effort to haul herself off the sagging mattress where she had spent years entertaining too many men to count.

What had she eaten last night to give her such heartburn? Or when had she eaten last? Since she had gotten that reward, she'd been spending it on whiskey.

She stumbled down the dark stairs, having decided that

all she needed was a trip to the outhouse. She went through the dim rooms and let herself out the back door.

The dew was cold and wet against her bare feet as she stepped onto the narrow stretch of grass between the back door and the outhouse. She raised the hem of her gown and tiptoed lightly. When she glanced up to measure the distance remaining, a scream congealed in her throat and was never uttered.

The gray, misty morning light added an even more phantasmogoric quality to the horror that greeted Sugar's eyes.

The madam of the Garden of Eden had been nailed to the outhouse wall. The garrote which had been the instrument of death was still twisted around her neck. Her face was blue. Her lips and tongue, which protruded, were purplish. Her eyes were bugging obscenely. Wisps of ash-blond hair stirred eerily in the faint wind, looking as mournful and gray as Spanish moss dripping from the branches of a dead tree. Her arms and legs were spreadeagled against the faded wall of the outhouse. Blood had dried to a rusty residue on her palms and feet where the nails had been hammered in.

She was naked.

Sugar tried to scream. It came out a hoarse croak as her left arm seemed wrenched from her body with the pain that tore through it. She tried to run, but her knees buckled beneath her. The heart that had been taxed with years of alcohol abuse had stopped beating before the soft, damp earth cushioned her fall.

The preacher was irritated later in the day when his mail failed to be delivered to the parsonage. Such oversights were inexcusable and he told the postmaster so. But he was somewhat mollified by the headlines in that day's newspaper. The ghastly deaths of Priscilla Watkins and Sugar Dalton would provide him with fuel for the hellfire and brimstone sermon he was writing for this Sunday's service.

Citizens all over Fort Worth shook their heads sadly over the grisly accounts they read in the newspaper. Two soiled doves had died, one violently. The were to be pitied, but it was written that one reaped what one sowed. Later in the day, the two deaths were old news.

It was nothing new really. Whores died with lamentable frequency in Hell's Half Acre.

It was a miracle. Ross was still alive.

The hours of the night crept by slowly. Lydia heard the clock chime, but she didn't move from his side. With every passing minute his breathing became more labored.

Only a supreme effort had kept her from screaming when the doctor sadly shook his head after probing the wound and softly declaring there was nothing he could do. Even Jake, whom the doctor gave a wide berth after hearing of the man's temperament from his colleague, didn't argue. It was obvious to everyone, even to Lydia if she admitted it to herself, that had Ross not been so strong he would have died instantly from the bullet's impact.

Ross knew it as well. Hours ago he had bade his children goodbye. Banner had wept copiously, clinging to her father. Lee had tried to maintain more reserve, but there were tears in his eyes when he fled the house after leaving his father's side. Micah had followed him saying, "I'd better stay with him." They had ridden out of the yard and hadn't been seen since.

Lydia didn't fear for Lee. He would be all right.

She was more concerned about her daughter. They had had a tearful reunion. Lydia ached for Banner, knowing that she could find no joy in her wedding day. Lydia had been thrilled with the news that Jake was officially a part of her family, though she felt that he had been for years. When Jake quietly announced that he and Banner were married and explained why he and Ross had been fighting, there was much weeping and hugging all around.

Lydia had laid a hand on Jake's arm. "Ross was reacting like a father. When he has time to think about it, he'll be as glad as I am."

"We've made our peace," Jake had told her.

When Ross last spoke to Banner, he took her hand, patted it, and smiled at her. "I'm glad about you and Jake. Be happy," he whispered. Rather than making Banner happy, her father's words only served to deepen that haunted, stricken look in her eyes.

She couldn't be comforted, even by her husband. Ma had finally coaxed her to lie down in the parlor on the sofa. Jake sat nearby. Ma kept vigil in the kitchen, brewing tea nobody wanted and insisting that everyone should eat to keep up their strength. But she wasn't eating either.

Lydia had retreated to Ross's office and shut out the rest of the world. If this were to be their last night together, they would spend it alone.

Now, as if she had silently beckoned him, he opened his eyes and looked at her clearly. God granted small favors. Ross had been granted the privilege of thanking Jake for killing Clancey. Now he was being blessed with enough strength to say goodbye to the woman he loved more than his life.

Seemingly without effort, he raised his hand and threaded his fingers though her hair. "Remember... how I used to make fun... of it?"

She bowed her head, willing herself not to waste these precious moments weeping. When she lifted her head, her eyes were sparkling. "Yes. You were a bully."

"I love it now." He fingered the wayward strands.

"I love you," she whispered.

"I know," he responded quietly. His hand moved from her hair to her cheek. "I remember the first instant I looked into your face. I got lost in you, Lydia."

A sob tore through her throat. She forced her trembling lips into a smile. "You needed a shave."

"I remember everything."

"So do I. Every moment with you has been precious. I didn't live until I met you." She rubbed her forehead against his. "If Jake hadn't killed Sheldon I would have. Why did he do this?"

"Shh, shh. It could have happened any time in the last twenty years. We've had so much time together we didn't expect. Let's not be selfish."

"Where you're concerned I've always been selfish. I'll never have enough of you." Ardently she kissed his hands.

His body spasmed with pain and she sank from the chair on which she sat to her knees. She laid one arm across his stomach. The other she enfolded around his head. His hair was mockingly crisp, lively against her hand.

When the worst of the pain passed, he gazed up at her. "How will I bear heaven until you get there?"

"Oh, Ross!" Her face crumpled and the agony she had tried so hard to hide couldn't be concealed any longer. Her tears gushed out. "The time will pass quickly for you. But *me*. How will I live without you? I can't. Let me come with you."

He shook his head and reached out a hand to comfort her. He was thinking of the grandchild she didn't even know about. "You can't. Our children need you. Lee will be confused and hurt. See him through this for me. Banner . . ."

"Banner has Jake. They love each other."

"I wish for them . . . what we had."

"No one will have what we had."

He smiled. "All lovers think that."

"It's true in our case," she insisted as her fingers skated over the lips she loved, over his thick mustache. "Because of you." .

His eyes dimmed with pain. "No, my love, because of *you*." He reached for her blindly. She grasped his hand and laid it against her breast. "Lydia . . . Lydia . . . Lydia . . ."

She let him slip quietly into the other life because she couldn't stand to see the pain he was suffering in this one. But for hours she continued to hold him.

Banner awakened suddenly. Sleep deserted her with a brutal severance. She was instantly aware of everything at once, the pink dawn light seeping around the parlor draperies, Ma's gentle snores coming across the room from the chair in which she had finally allowed herself to rest. She also knew that her father was dead.

And she became aware that Jake was no longer in the parlor. She threw off the quilt he had spread over her when she finally consented to lie down and walked on silent, stockinged feet toward the hall.

At the portiere she was brought up short.

Standing in the hall, with the timid new sunlight filtering through the beveled glass of the front door were her mother and her husband.

Lydia clung to him as she wept into his shoulder. Jake's arms were holding her tight, his hands were comforting her tenderly, and his lips were moving in her hair.

Banner retreated before she was noticed.

TWENTY-SIX

"Lee and I are taking a trip to Tennessee. We're leaving tomorrow."

The quietly spoken statement had a profound effect on those eating breakfast in the kitchen at River Bend.

Lydia dabbed at her lips with a napkin and took a sip of coffee while Jake, Banner, Ma and Micah stared at her speechlessly. Only Lee wasn't surprised by the announcement.

Jake put down his fork and propped his elbows on the table, clasping his hands loosely over his plate. "Tennessee? What for?"

Lee cleared his throat noisily and avoided looking at his friend Micah, who was staring at him as though he'd just sprouted antlers from the top of his head. They shared every confidence. There hadn't been a secret between them since Micah and Ma Langston came to live at River Bend.

"I want to see where my mother came from," Lee said self-consciously. "I might have distant kin still living back there. Lydia said she wanted to go with me and show me places Papa had told her about. We might be gone for several months.''

It had been two weeks since the funeral. Every mention of Ross still created an uneasy silence while everyone experienced the pain of loss all over again.

''Lydia, are you sure you want to leave? Now?'' Jake asked her.

Banner lowered her eyes to her plate while her hands gripped each other tensely in her lap. What little appetite she had fled and she felt mildly nauseated. Her pregnancy was responsible for only a portion of her sickness. Every time Jake looked at Lydia, his eyes probing and concerned, Banner sustained a painful blow to her heart.

''I'm sure,'' Lydia replied softly. ''This trip will be good for Lee. He needs to have a sense of his mother's background.'' She sighed. ''And getting away will be good for me too. This house, this land . . . they are Ross.'' Her eyes began to cloud with fresh tears. ''The memories are too fresh.''

Lee shoved his chair back and stood. ''Micah, will you ride into Larsen with me today? I need to get some things for the trip.''

Together they went to the back door. They reached for their hats hanging on the pegs at the same time and their heads bumped.

''Excuse me,'' they said politely in unison. Ordinarily there would have been boisterous bantering between them, jests about one or the other's clumsiness. Instead their eyes met awkwardly. Lee was feeling guilty because he hadn't discussed the trip with his friend, but Lydia had sworn him to secrecy. Micah was feeling rejected and betrayed.

But when they looked at each other, their friendship was reconfirmed. Micah slapped Lee on the back and said, ''You'll let us know where you are and what you're up to, won't you? I hear there are some mighty pretty girls in Tennessee. Maybe you'll bring me back one, huh?'' With their arms around each other's shoulders, they left through the back door.

''Jake, as soon as you're finished, I'd like to go over

some things in the office," Lydia said, standing. "I want to make sure everything's in order before I leave."

"I'm finished." He scraped back his chair and tossed his napkin down beside his plate.

His hand was riding on the small of Lydia's back as they left the kitchen and went down the hall toward the office in which Ross had died.

With an aching heart, Banner watched them leave. She sipped her tea. It had gone tepid and tasteless. Listlessly, she shoved the cup aside. She stared out the window vacantly, aware of nothing but her own misery until Ma lowered her bulk into the chair next to hers.

"What's ailin' you, girl?"

"I miss Papa."

"What else?"

"Nothing."

"And pigs can fly." Ma planted her meaty hands on her knees and leaned forward. " 'Member when I tied you in that very chair until you ate your collard greens? Well, I just might try that again if you don't tell me right this minute what's wrong with you."

Banner's head came up haughtily. "I lost my father two weeks ago. I saw him shot before my very eyes."

"I won't take sass from you either, young lady. I know your pa's death was godawful. It goes without saying. But you're still a bride and you ain't actin' like one. Leastways a happy one. Now sumpin' ain't right and you're goin' to tell me what it is. What's wrong between you and Jake?"

"Nothing," Banner averred. She wasn't going to discuss Jake's feelings with anyone. It was bad enough knowing them herself.

"Have you told him about the babe?"

Banner's eyes rounded as she stared at Ma. "How did you know?"

Ma snorted. "I been there enough times myself to know the signs. If your ma hadn't been so upset lately, she would have noticed too. Does Jake know?"

"Yes," Banner answered in a small voice. She twisted her napkin until the corner of it made a fine point, then squashed it with the pad of her index finger. "That's why he married me."

"I doubt that."

"It's true! He doesn't love me. He loves—" She bit back the words that had been pounding in her head like tomtoms ever since her father's death. *He loves my mother.*

"Who does he love?"

"Oh, I don't know," Banner said impatiently and shot from her chair. She moved to the window before Ma could see her tears. "But it's not me. We fight like cats and dogs."

"So did your ma and pa when they first got married."

"That was different."

"What was different about it? The only two people I know who're more ornery and bullheaded than the two of them are you and Jake."

She came to Banner and none too gently spun her around. "You get out of this house today and get some sunshine in those cheeks. Brush your hair right proper. Smile at Jake every once in a while. You've been slinkin' 'round here like a haunt. You figurin' to tell your ma about the baby?"

Banner shook her head. Jake had told her that Ross had died knowing about the baby and was glad about it. Together they had decided they would keep the news from Lydia awhile longer.

"I didn't want to tell Mama just yet. Expecially now. She might cancel her trip, and I know how important it is to her and Lee."

Ma patted her shoulder. "I'll take care of you. She'll be proud as punch when she gets back."

"She'll be angry with us for not telling her."

"But it'll occupy her mind. And that's what she needs right now. You know, don'tcha baby, that your mama ain't ever gonna be the same without Ross Coleman?"

Banner's throat constricted. "Yes, Ma, I know."

Ma gave her a light push. "Go sit on the porch for a spell. The fresh air will do you good."

As Banner went through the quiet, cool rooms of the house, she knew that Ma's advice was sound and had merit.

She was married to a man who loved someone else. Things like that probably happened with more frequency than people admitted to.

She couldn't spend the rest of her life moping around or her soul would atrophy. Banner Coleman Langston would become an empty shell. She had the rest of her life in front of her. She would just have to make the best of it, continue to love Jake, and accept the fact that she was second choice in his heart.

Her resolve lasted only until Lydia's leavetaking the next morning.

A sad group collected in the shade of the pecan tree. "I selected this spot for the house because of this tree," Lydia said, gazing up through the dense branches. "It wasn't near this tall then. Ross laughed at me, saying we'd have pecans dropping on the roof all the time." She smiled shakily through her tears. Everybody stood solemnly around her.

"Well," she said briskly, sniffing back her tears, "we'd better be off. We don't want to miss the train."

She hugged Ma. As always, Lydia seemed to draw strength from her and held her close for long moments. "Watch over everything while I'm gone."

"Don't worry 'bout nothin' here. We'll be waitin' for you to come home."

Lydia turned to Jake. Wordlessly, they went into each other's arms. Lydia buried her face in the collar of his shirt. His eyes closed tight as he hugged her. When they stepped apart, no words were necessary. They merely stared at each other long and hard.

Then Lydia took Banner into her embrace. Banner's heart was breaking over what she had just witnessed between her husband and her mother, but that didn't diminish the love she had for both of them. She clung to the woman who had given her life and made it such a happy one. Separate from her own grief over Ross's death, she was anguished for her mother.

Lydia set Banner away and scanned her face. She reached up to stroke Banner's eyebrow that arched like a black wing

over her eye. "Your eyes look more like Ross's every day."
Her lip began to tremble uncontrollably and she clamped it
tightly. "You won't forget to tend his . . . his grave."

"Of course not, Mama."

"I know." Then her gentle smile collapsed and she
hugged her daughter hard again. "Oh, Banner, I miss him
so much. I pray to God that you and Jake will always be
together, that you'll never have to know this kind of pain."

Mother and daughter held each other and wept for their
private reasons. At last Lee said softly, "Mama, we're
gonna be late."

The two women broke apart. Banner wiped her eyes
unashamedly, smearing tears over her cheeks. Lee helped
Lydia onto the wagon, then climbed up himself. Banner
noticed a new maturity about her brother. He was solicitous,
much more serious-minded than before Ross's death.

Earlier, Banner had told her half-brother goodbye by
flinging her arms around his neck and dampening his shoulder with her tears. "We'll be back before you know it,
Banner," he had said. "By the way, I'm surprised about
you and Jake, but glad, too, ya know? I mean, hell, if I
could have chosen a big brother it would have been him."

"Thank you, Lee. Take care of yourself. And Mama."

Now, Micah jumped into the wagon bed. He was going to
drive it back to River Bend after seeing them off. Lydia had
persuaded the rest of them not to come to town. Banner
suspected it was because she wanted to leave with a picture
of them near Ross in her mind.

Lydia turned to wave to them as they drove through the
gate. Banner saw her kiss her fingers lingeringly, then blow
the kiss toward the fresh grave on the hill to which she had
already carried fresh flowers earlier that morning.

Banner realized how difficult it must be for her mother to
leave the man she loved. But how much harder for her to
stay.

"What are you doing out here in the dark, Jake?"

Micah came up beside his brother at the fence and hooked

his boot over the bottom rung, resting his forearms on the top one, as Jake was doing.

"Thinking. Want a smoke?"

"Thanks." Micah took the cheroot Jake offered him and cupped his hands around the match. "They got off without a hitch," he said, puffing smoke and fanning out the match. Jake only nodded. "Lee and I acted like a couple of damn fools. Got all teary-eyed."

Jake smiled at him, his teeth shining whitely in his dark face. The moon had just topped the trees. "There's nothing wrong with a few tears. Especially for a friend," Jake finished quietly, and returned his gaze to the pasture. The tip of his cigar glowed redly as he drew on it.

"I'm awful sorry about Ross, Jake. For your sake, I mean. I know he was your best friend."

"Yeah, he was. Helluva way for a man to die, to be gunned down in his own yard." Despairingly, his head dropped forward as though hinged at his neck. "At least I got the sonofabitch that killed him."

"What did the sheriff say?"

Everyone had been so concerned about Ross that afternoon, it wasn't until later that anyone inquired about Grady Sheldon.

"He said it was clearly self-defense. Grady's fingers were still around the trigger of that rifle. The sheriff said I had no choice but to shoot him." Jake laughed without mirth. "In fact he said I had done him a favor. He never had been satisfied with the explanation Sheldon gave him about the fire that killed his family."

"You read about Priscilla Watkins, I reckon."

"Yeah. I can't help but think there was some connection between her and Sheldon's killing Ross."

"In that case they both deserved to die."

"That's the way I see it."

They smoked in silence for a while. When Jake at last turned, he hitched his elbow over the top rail. "Lydia and I spent days in the office going over the books. She wanted me to know all there was to know about River Bend since the day she and Ross moved here. She made me foreman of it and Plum Creek.''

"What the hell is Plum Creek?"

Jake smiled around his cigar. "That's Banner's ranch and if you know what's good for you, you won't say anything insulting about the name. Anyway, I'm going to have my hands full running both places until Lee comes back and decides what he wants to do. Will you help me out?"

"Sure, Jake. You don't even have to ask. Reckon I'm gonna miss Lee something fierce. I'll need work to keep me busy.''

"Lydia wants Ma to move into the house until she gets back. It wouldn't hurt you to spend a night or two a week with her instead of in the bunkhouse." Micah nodded. "Banner and I are going home tomorrow. The hands have been keeping an eye on things, but I went over today to air the house out so it would be ready."

Micah shifted his weight from one foot to another, then back again. "I, uh, well, what I mean is . . ."

"Spit it out."

"I was surprised about the two of you getting married," Micah blurted.

"Well, I was kind of surprised about it myself," Jake said with a wry smile.

"How long . . . I mean when . . . when did it start?"

Jake shrugged. "A while back." He studied his brother in the moonlight and was vividly reminded of himself at that age. Micah just as well get a bitter taste of the real world now as later. "She's pregnant, Micah." He saw his brother swallow hard, but he said nothing. "The baby's mine, but that's not the reason I married her. I love her. Do me a favor. If you ever hear anybody making a remark about—"

"You don't have to ask me that either, Jake," Micah said adamantly. "If any sonofabitch says anything about her, I'll set him straight if it means cutting out his tongue."

Jake laid his hand on his brother's shoulder. "Thanks. You know, it looks like my future is sewed up here. Banner and I will never leave Plum Creek and River Bend. I don't have any use for that hundred and sixty acres down in the hill country that Anabeth's husband is holding for me. Why don't I sign the deed over to you?"

Micah gaped at him. "You mean it, Jake?"

"Sure I mean it. You've spent more time on that place than I have. I need you around here for a while, but when and if you ever get ready to start out on your own, let me know and I'll make it all legal."

"Lord o'mercy. I don't know what to say."

"Say good night. It's getting late and we've got a lot of work to catch up on—starting early tomorrow."

"Thanks, Jake." Micah stuck his hand out and Jake shook it solemnly. Then Micah dropped his cheroot and ground it out. "G'night." He headed toward the bunkhouse, leaving his brother with only the soft stillness of the night for company.

Banner sat curled in the window seat of her upstairs bedroom and watched her husband.

How many times had she sat here as a child, contemplating the stars, the moon, her future, and wondering what promises it held for her? How many times had she thought about Jake Langston? She would wonder where he was and what he was doing and when she would see him again.

But never, during any of that daydreaming, had she imagined herself marrying Jake. Loving him. Having his child.

She covered her lower abdomen with her hand. A part of him was growing inside her. She was still awed and humbled by the miracle of it. Every day her body grew fuller with the new life. Apparently the surgery hadn't affected the baby. She knew, with a mother's intuition, that her child would be robust and healthy and the most beautiful baby in the world.

Would it have dark hair like hers and Papa's? Or would it be fair and flaxen-haired like the Langstons, like Jake? She envisioned a towheaded younster with bright blue eyes scampering around the yard, tagging behind Jake, leaping to plant its chubby feet in its daddy's widely spaced footprints. Banner hugged herself with the thought. It would be a wonderful baby. She couldn't wait to hold it against her, smell its sweet smell, nurse it from her breasts, love it.

But her moment of happiness was snuffed out as surely as the cheroot she saw painting a fiery arc on the darkness as Jake threw it away. What was he doing out there? Did he prefer solitude to sharing a room with her?

It had been strange to have Jake sleeping beside her in the bed which had previously been hers alone. No one seemed to consider it awkward that they now shared her bedroom. No one but the two of them. They rarely spoke when they were in this room together.

As often as not she was already in bed when he concluded his quiet discussions in the office with Lydia and climbed the stairs to join Banner. He treated her with consideration. She was polite in turn. But there were no intimacies exchanged. They slept with their backs together, facing away from each other, as wary of accidentally touching as strangers.

One night, he had turned to her. Softly he spoke her name. She had pretended to be asleep. She felt his hand sifting through her hair, felt his light caress on her shoulder, felt his warm breath on her neck. She longed to turn into his embrace. Her body ached for the touch of his.

But she couldn't foget that he spent every waking hour with Lydia; she couldn't forget the way he had held Lydia, whispering into her hair the morning after Ross died.

Oh, nothing improper had happened between them. Banner didn't entertain that thought. Jake knew that Lydia had loved Ross with her whole being. He had loved Ross himself and would do nothing to insult either Lydia or Ross's memory.

But it was no less painful for Banner to know that Jake longed for what was still unattainable. And on this night of Lydia's departure, Jake was morose, abjectly depressed if his . posture were any indication. For hours Banner had watched him out there by the fence, staring into the darkness as though longing to pierce it and catch sight of Lydia.

Poor Jake. What irony. He had married the daughter only hours before the mother, whom he really wanted, had become available. How he must be cursing the fates.

Suddenly Banner was enraged with the fates as well. Their dirty trick had been played on her too. And it was the second one she had been dealt.

Well, she was tired of being the butt of fortune's jokes. She was tired of Jake's long, sorrowful face too. And sick to death of his mealymouthed platitudes,

"How do you feel, sweetheart?"

"You look tired. Why don't you go lie down?"

"Sure you're all right? You look pale."

She wouldn't have it! She couldn't, *wouldn't,* live with him the rest of their lives and have him yearning for another woman. She had told him once she didn't want a martyr across the hearth from her. Well, she damn sure didn't want one in her bed either. If he couldn't have Lydia, let him find another substitute for her. Banner Coleman wasn't going to serve as one.

She bounded off the window seat, flew to the door of the bedroom and ripped it open. She took neither shawl nor robe to cover the white nightgown that trailed after her like an airy veil as she raced down the stairs.

Banner had watched her mother bravely leave the man she loved cold in the ground. She had realized then that Lydia couldn't stay and look at that fresh grave every day. It was a constant reminder of the reality that was too agonizing to bear.

Banner didn't want to leave Jake either. It would be like cutting out her heart and walking away from it while it still beat. But she would leave him before sacrificing her life by staying. She couldn't stand by docilely and watch him love her mother until they were all old. What kind of miserable life would that be? When would the resentment set in? When would he begin to hate her? Or worse, when her body was heavy and awkward with their child, would he begin to pity her?

No! She had more pride than that. She had chased him, thrown herself at his feet, argued and pleaded, but no more. Never again would she subject herself to humiliation. She couldn't make him love her. No power on earth could do that. Better to let go now than spend years in a fruitless pursuit.

She ran up behind him, panting with exertion. He heard her even before she caught his sleeve and yanked him around. He blinked in surprise. Her nightgown showed up against the darkness like the sail of a ghost ship. The moon caught her eyes and they glowed like a cat's in the night. Her hair was a wild wreath around her head, coiling and curling like a black flame. She looked unworldly, a beautiful and furious goddess from Greek mythology.

"If you want her, go after her," she cried. "I won't stop you. I love you. I want you. But not like this. I don't want to see your face across my pillow with that naked yearning on it for somebody else. So just go!"

She spun around and went marching back toward the house, but was jarringly halted when he grabbed a handful of white lawn nightgown. "Let me go!"

"Uh-uh," he said, pulling her backward, reeling her in. "It's about time somebody jerked a knot in your tail, Princess Banner. You started this fight, now by God you'll see it to the finish."

Giving him a mutinous look over her shoulder, she wrenched her nightgown free of his hold but made no move to run away.

"All right then," he said in a considerably lower tone of voice. "What's on your mind?"

"For starters, I'm sick of you sulking around all the time."

"Me sulking? You haven't put three words together in days."

"And I'm tired of you being nice to me all the time. I'd rather have you ranting and raving than putting cushions under my feet."

"I haven't . . . what the . . . cushions!" he sputtered.

"I think you ought to move into the bunkhouse since you obviously prefer the company of the horses in this pasture to mine."

"Who says? And I'll sleep in the house, thank you."

"You don't want to share a bedroom with me."

"The hell I don't! Why do you think I've been sulking and treating you like goddamned royalty? Huh? I want my wife back."

Her rebellion dissolved and she stared back at him blankly. "What?"

"I said I want my wife back. What happened to her? On the day we were married, her father died. So, all right. I could understand her acting standoffish for a few days, but it's been two weeks!" He made an effort to keep his rising volume under control. "I'm about at the end of my rope, Banner. It's time you started acting like a wife. I wish we could go back to that afternoon after we got married and start all over again."

He shook his head agitatedly. "You *do* remember that picnic after our wedding, don't you? What you did to me? What we did together? God almighty, Banner, you run hot and cold. One day you're making love to me like that, the next, every time I come close, you shrink away. I don't understand. How the hell am I supposed to be acting?"

"But you love her."

"*Who*, for crying out loud?"

"My mother."

He fell back against the fence. The rails caught him at shoulders and hips. His arms dangled loosely at his sides as he stared at her in disbelief.

"How do you expect me to play the role of wife, make love with you, when I know you love her? I saw you holding her the morning after Papa died. You haven't been three feet from her side since then except when you're forced to sleep beside me."

Tears were rolling down her face. She dashed them away with her fists. "I watched you say goodbye to her today. It was heartbreaking the way you looked at her. You know how proud I am. You've reminded me of it enough times. How can you think that I want to spend the rest of my life with a man who is in love with another woman? Especially since that woman happens to be my mother. She's had your heart for twenty years. I can't compete with that. I won't."

"Are you finished?" he asked quietly when she had

wound down. His only answer was a long, liquid sniff of her nose and another swipe at her tears. "So that's what all this is about? You think I love Lydia."

"You do."

"Yes, I love her. I'll always love her, just as I did Ross. We shared something that is impossible to explain. I'm closer to Lydia than I am to my own sisters. On the day Ross died, we grieved together. Why shouldn't we? We held each other to give each other what comfort we could."

"That's not the kind of love I'm talking about and you know it."

He lightly slapped his thighs in exasperation. "Sure, as a kid I put Lydia up on a pedestal. I thought she was pretty, everything a woman should be. She became my ideal woman, and for years I fancied myself in love with her. Yeah, and I was jealous of Ross for having a woman like that in his bed every night." He drew a deep breath. "But I'm not in love with her now, Banner. Not like I am with you. I was never in love with her like I am with you."

Her whole body shuddered and she drew in a ragged little sigh. She opened her mouth to speak, closed it, tried again. "You're in love with me?"

He raised his eyes toward heaven imploringly. "What did you think? I have been ever since that night in the barn. Why do you think I acted meaner than hell all the time? I was fighting it. That night I felt like I'd been poleaxed and couldn't shake myself out of it. I didn't want to feel that way about any woman, but especially not about you. You were just a kid, and the daughter of my best friends." He extended his hand and said softly, "Come here."

She drifted toward him, a waif in a long white nightgown. Clasping her hand as soon as she was within reach, he drew her to him and pressed her body along his.

"Banner." He inhaled the fresh sunshine scent of her hair that he had missed so much. "God, you were sweet that first time. You shook me right down to my boots. I've been crazy in love with you ever since. Probably long before that. Probably all the time you were growing up, but I couldn't let myself see it."

"You've never said you love me."

"I haven't?" She shook her head. "Well, I'm saying it now. I love you, Banner."

He pressed his mouth down on hers. Swiftly their lips parted and tongues touched. Jake groaned deep in his chest. His arms went around her, lifting her until her bare toes stood on the tips of his boots. Her arms locked around his neck and she ground her middle against his.

When he raised his head from their lengthy kiss, he gazed down into her eyes where the moon was reflected. "For years I pretended to be real tough. I was bitter about everything, having to grow up so fast, Luke's death, everything. It showed. I guess some men respected me for being a good cowboy and handy with a deck of cards and a gun, but no one saw the real me. Only you did, Banner."

"Yes, I did. I saw the man behind those cold, blue eyes." She kissed his throat. "Your temper didn't scare me a bit."

He chuckled, smoothing his hands over her derriere. "You're a fine one to mention tempers. I've enjoyed our fights."

"So have I."

"I was so lonely before you. God, I don't ever want to be like that again." He burrowed his face in her neck.

"You wouldn't let anyone get close to you. But now you'll have me and the baby."

"I guess I'll have to start enlarging the house." He slanted her away so he could look down at her body with loving eyes. "I still can't believe it."

"I can. My body's changing."

"Oh, yeah?" He slid his hands over her breasts. "I think you're right," he said, winking.

Their lips met for another kiss. When they pulled apart, Banner laid her head on his chest and moaned, "Jake, I'm so randy."

With his thumb beneath her chin, he snapped her head up and peered down into her smoky eyes. "You know what *that* means?"

"Sure. I heard it from—"

"I know, I know. Kiss me again before you say something else dirty."

She complied, inching her body up his until she could press his hardness between her thighs. Having abstained these past two weeks, he throbbed with the need for release. He eased his lips free of hers. "Banner, sweetheart, if we don't stop, I'm going to have to take you standing up against this fence."

Her eyes sparkled and she smiled with delight. "Can we?"

He swatted her bottom. "Shameless hussy. Not on a moonlit night like tonight."

"Some other time?"

His wicked grin shone in the darkness. "Yeah, but for now, come on. I have a better idea."

He lifted her in his arms and carried her across the yard. When she realized that their destination was the barn, she buried her head bashfully in his collar.

"What did you really think of me that night?"

"At first I thought you were a hurt little girl looking for sympathy. Then I thought you were a witch sent by the devil to tempt me, or maybe an angel God was using for the same purpose. In any event, I was giving some serious thought to the unthinkable."

He pushed the barn door closed behind them and found an empty moonlit stall filled with fresh, fragrant hay. He set her down but kept his arms around her.

"And afterward?" she whispered against his mouth.

His tongue flirted with the corners of her lips. "Afterward I thought surely I had imagined it. Because it was the best thing that ever happened to me." He clasped her tighter. "Love me, Banner." He whispered the urgent plea into her hair.

Together, they fell on to the hay. Their mouths fused. The buttons of her nightgown fell away beneath his fingers. He slipped his hand inside the fabric to cup her breast. Its center was swollen with passion even before his mouth moved over it. Soft and wet, his tongue caressed until Banner thought she would die of the pleasure.

He pulled the nightgown over her head and drank in her nakedness.

Standing quickly, he removed his clothes. When he finally moved to cover her, he found her a creamy, tight sheath that gloved him perfectly.

"I love you, I love you," he whispered as he gave himself to her. She echoed the words fervently.

The fulfillment was swift and tumultuous.

Later he made a pallet of their discarded clothes. They slept naked and close. And in the morning, just as the new sun was peeking over the horizon, Jake reached for his sleep-flushed wife again. This time they made love without the thunder . . . softly, sweetly, in celebration of the dawn that would last the rest of their lives.

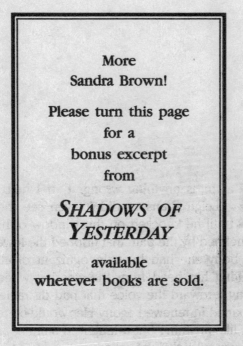

More
Sandra Brown!

Please turn this page
for a
bonus excerpt
from

SHADOWS OF
YESTERDAY

available
wherever books are sold.

M a'am, is anything wrong? Can I help you?"
Leigh Bransom didn't even see the man
until he knocked on the window of her car.
Overwhelmed by the pain that gripped the lower part
of her body, she had been incognizant of all else.
Now, lifting her head from the steering wheel and
swiveling it toward the voice that had distracted her,
she moaned in renewed agony. Her would-be rescuer
looked like anything but a knight in shining armor.

"Are you all right?" he asked.

No, she wasn't, but she didn't want to admit it to
this rough-looking man who could easily get away
with any crime he chose to commit on this lonely
stretch of highway. His clothes were filthy, stained with
grease and sweat. His large brass belt buckle with the
state seal of Texas on it was at Leigh's eye level as he
bent from what must be a height of at least six feet
to peer at her through the window. The well-worn

jeans and short-sleeved plaid cotton shirt fit a large muscular frame. A battered straw cowboy hat cast a sinister shadow over the man's face. Amid the pains Leigh felt her heart contract with terror.

Perhaps if it weren't for the dark sunglasses that prevented her from looking into his eyes—

As though discerning her thoughts, the stranger took off the glasses, and Leigh stared into the bluest eyes she'd ever encountered. She saw no threat in that anxious blue gaze, and the spasm of fear passed. The man might be dirty, but he didn't seem to be dangerous.

"I'm not going to hurt you, ma'am. I only want to know if I can help." Leigh heard the concern in the stranger's voice, which, like his eyes, was oddly reassuring.

Another pain rippled through her, starting at her spine and creeping around her middle to her abdomen. She caught her bottom lip between her teeth to bite off the scream she felt rising in her throat and slumped forward, bumping her head on the steering wheel.

"Godamighty," she heard on an anxious rasp before the door was flung open. When the man saw her distended stomach, he whistled through his teeth. "What in the world are you doing out here by yourself in your condition?" he asked. Carelessly he tossed the sunglasses onto the dashboard over the steering wheel.

Leigh panted, trying to count out the seconds until the contraction subsided. His question was apparently rhetorical, as he seemed not to expect her to answer it. He laid his hand on her shoulder. It felt hot and dry against her cool, damp skin.

"Take it easy now. Okay? Easy. Better?" he asked when she sighed and leaned back against the seat.

"Yes," she said. For a moment she closed her eyes, trying to regain some strength, some dignity, with which to face the stranger while in the throes of labor. "Thank you."

"Hell, I haven't done anything yet. What do you want me to do? Where were you headed?"

"Midland."

"So was I. Do you want me to drive you there?"

She looked at him quickly, cautiously. He had squatted on his haunches between her and the car door. One strong, tanned hand was on the car seat, the other on the steering wheel. Now that the sunglasses were gone, she could study the deep blue eyes looking up at her with solicitude. If the eyes were truly the windows to the soul, Leigh knew she could trust this man.

"I . . . I guess that would be best."

He glanced over his shoulder. "I think I should drive your car and leave my truck here. It's—Oh God, another one?"

She had felt the contraction coming even before the pain hit her. Pressing her hands against the taut sides of her abdomen, she tried to remember to pant, forcing relaxation and control. When the contraction was over, she sagged against the seat.

"Ma'am, it's forty miles or so to Midland. We're not

going to make it. How long have you been in labor?" He was speaking soothingly, calmly.

"I stopped about forty-five minutes ago. I had had some pains before then, but I thought they were indigestion."

He almost smiled, and she saw a hint of laugh lines around the startling eyes. "No one stopped to help you?"

She shook her head. "Only two other cars drove by. They didn't stop."

His eyes scanned the interior of the car to assess its limited space. "Do you think you can walk? If not, I'll carry you."

Carry her? To where? He read the panicked questions in her eyes. "You can lie down in the bed of my pickup. It's not a delivery room, but the baby won't know any better."

This time the smile was for real. The laugh lines were prominent and deep, the creases white in contrast to the rest of his skin, which was darkly tanned. His teeth flashed white and straight in the coppery face. Leigh realized that under other circumstances she would have found the face disarmingly attractive.

"I think I can walk," she said, sliding her legs from under the steering wheel as he stood up and moved aside. His hard, strong arm went around what at one time had been a slender waist. She leaned into him gratefully.

Taking tentative, short steps, they walked toward the rear of her car. The heat rolled up from the west Texas plains in suffocating waves. Leigh could barely breathe the scorching air into her lungs.

"Hang in there. Not much farther." His breath struck her cheek in warm, staccato puffs.

She focused on their feet. His long legs were comically matching her short, unsteady gait and he wobbled with the effort. Dust from the gravelly shoulder of the highway rose in clouds that powdered the well-manicured toenails that peeked out from her sandals and the scuffed, cracked leather of the stranger's boots.

His pickup was as dirty as he, covered with a fine layer of prairie dust. The blue and white paint had faded together into one dull beige. It was a dented rattletrap, but Leigh noted with relief that there were no obscene or suggestive bumper stickers on it.

"Lean up against here while I lower the tailgate," the man instructed, propping her against the side of the truck. Just as he turned away, another pain seized her.

"Oh!" Leigh cried, instinctively reaching for the stranger.

His arm went around her shoulders and a callused palm slid down her tightening abdomen to support it from beneath. "Okay, okay, do what you have to do. I'm here."

She buried her face in his shoulder as the contraction split her in two. It seemed to go on interminably, but at last diminished. She heard herself whimpering.

"Can you stand up?"

She nodded.

A scrape of rusty hinges, a clang of metal against metal, and then he was back, supporting her, gently lifting her into the bed of the truck. She sat with her back against the side while he hurriedly spread a tarpaulin out onto the ribbed floor of the vehicle. It looked none too clean, but it was better than the rested bed of the truck. He cursed softly and muttered self-reproachfully as he spread out the army-green canvas.

"Now," he said, taking her shoulders in his hands and lowering her to the tarpaulin. "This is bound to feel better."

It did. She sighed as her back settled on the hard surface, not even minding that it was hot. Her body was filmed with perspiration that made her sundress stick to her cloyingly.

"Have you been taking classes to teach you how to breathe like that?"

"Yes. I couldn't attend as regularly as I wanted to, but I learned a few things."

"Feel free to apply anything you've learned," he said ruefully. "Do you have anything in your car that might be useful?"

"I have an overnight bag. There's a cotton night-gown in it. Kleenex is in the glove compartment." Her mother would be proud of her, Leigh thought wryly. Ever since she could remember, her mother had drilled into her that no lady was ever without a tissue.

"I'll be right back."

He vaulted over the side of the truck and Leigh noticed distractedly that for a man his size, he moved agilely. When he came back into her field of vision, he had her nightgown slung over one shoulder like a Roman toga. He handed her the box of Kleenex.

"I bought this newspaper this morning. I saw in a movie once that a newspaper comes in handy during an emergency birth. I think it's supposed to be germ-free or something. Anyway, you might want to slide this under your . . . uh . . . hips." He handed her the folded, unread newspaper and then turned his back quickly and climbed out of the truck again.

She did as he told her, feeling acutely self-conscious. Her embarrassment quickly dissolved when her abdomen cramped with another strong labor pain. Suddenly he was there, kneeling beside her, squeezing her hand between the two of his.

She stared at the watch he wore on his left wrist as she panted. It was stainless steel with all sorts of dials and gadgets, and ticked loudly. The intricate, expensive instrument was incongruous with the mud-caked cowboy boots and dirty clothes. Leigh's gaze slid from the watch to the stranger's long, tapering fingers, and she noted the absence of a wedding band. Was her baby to be delivered by a man who was not only not a doctor but not even a father?

"Are you married?" she asked as the lingering pain slowly ebbed.

"No." He took off the cowboy hat and tossed it against the cab of the pickup. His hair was long, and dark brown.

"This must be terrible for you. I'm sorry."

He smiled as he reached into his back jeans pocket and took out a bandanna, which he tied around his forehead like a sweatband. Leigh was startled into an awareness of how handsome the man was. His shirt front hung open where he had unbuttoned it for coolness. Over the dark skin, his chest hair was spread like a finely spun web. "Aw, hell, this isn't so bad. I've done worse." His teeth gleamed behind his wide, sensual lips.

He popped a tissue out of the box and with gentle fingers dabbed at the perspiration beading her forehead and upper lip. "Only next time, you might pick a cooler day," he teased, coaxing her to smile.

"It was Doris Day," she said.

"Pardon?"

"It was a Doris Day movie. James Garner was her husband. He was an obstetrician. Arlene Francis went into labor in a Rolls-Royce and Doris Day helped him deliver the baby."

"Is that the one where he drives his car into the swimming pool?"

She laughed. "I think so."

"Who would have thought that a movie like that could be educational?" He ran the Kleenex around her neck.

"What is your name?"

"Chad Dillon, ma'am."

"I'm Leigh Bransom."

"It's a pleasure, Mrs. Bransom."

When the next pain came, it wasn't so bad, because Chad's capable hands stroked the hard, torturous ball her abdomen had become. As the contraction subsided, he said, "You're close, I think. Luckily I have a thermos of water in the cab of the truck. I'm going to wash my hands with it."

He got the large jug of water and, hanging his hands over the side of the truck, washed them as well as he could.

"What were you doing this afternoon?" Leigh asked tactfully, wondering how his clothes could get so dirty.

"I was tinkering on an airplane engine."

So he was a mechanic. Funny, he didn't seem . . .

"You'd better take off any underwear you have on," he said softly.

Leigh closed her eyes, too humiliated to meet his gaze. If only Chad weren't such an attractive man . . .

"Don't go shy on me now. We've got to get that baby here."

"I'm sorry," she murmured. She raised her dress. Having worn no slip or bra because of the heat, she had only panties to take off. With Chad's assistance, she peeled them down her legs and pulled her sandaled feet through them.

"Would you feel better without the shoes?" he asked.

"No. They're fine . . . Chad," she cried on another pain.

He quickly knelt between her raised knees. "I can see the head," he said with a relieved half-chuckle. "Are you supposed to push or . . . or something? What?"

Panting, she pushed with all her might. "That's the way," he encouraged her. "You're doing fine, ma'am." His low, steady voice was like a balm over her twisted insides.

"We're almost there, Leigh," he said, leaning forward to blot up her perspiration with another tissue. The bandanna he had tied around his forehead was wet with his own sweat. He swiped across his thick brows with the back of his hand. The hair on his chest was damply curled.

Quickly he took a pocket knife out of his jeans pocket, straightening his leg to work his hand down between the tight fabric. He poured water from the thermos over the knife, then cut a shoulder strap off her nightgown. "You're something, you know that?" he said. "Most women would be crying and carrying on. You're the bravest woman I've ever met."

No, no, I'm not! her mind screamed. She couldn't let him think that. She must tell him what a coward she really was. But before she could form the words, he went on, "Your husband's going to be proud of you."

"I . . . I don't have a husband," she said through gritted teeth as another labor pain bore down on her.

Stunned, Chad stared at her for a moment before her contorted features alerted him. His eyes dropped to the birth area, then opened wide in delight. "Oh, this is beautiful. That's it. A little harder. The head's out," he cried, laughing.

The baby choked, spat, then began to wail.

"Come on, Leigh, you're doing great. All we need

is to get the shoulders out. There, there, that's it. Now! Oh, God!" he said, catching the slippery new baby in his capable hands. "Look at what you've got. A beautiful baby girl."

Tears of relief were rolling down Leigh's cheeks as she looked at the man beaming down at her. "Let me see her," she breathed weakly. "Is she all right?"

"She . . . she's perfect," he said gruffly. "Just a minute. Let me take care of this cord." She felt the beating of fists and feet against her as he laid the baby between her thighs. "How are you doing?" he asked anxiously after a moment. He didn't look up. He was concentrating on what he was doing. A bead of sweat clung precariously to the tip of his chiseled nose.

"I'm wonderful," she said drowsily.

"I'll say you are. You're terrific."

Crouched between her legs, he worked. He raised his arm so his sleeve could absorb the perspiration on his face. Then he was lifting up the red, wet, wrinkled, squirming, squalling infant and laying her tenderly on Leigh's breast.

"Oh, Chad, thank you. Look at her. Isn't she a miracle?"

"Yes." His voice was rough.

The mellow look in her eyes changed to one of pain again.

She felt a gentle tugging, then relief.

"There. Is that better?" Chad wrapped the newspaper around the afterbirth.

"Yes."

The knife sliced deftly through the cotton of the

nightgown. The baby mewed against her mother. Leigh was no longer aware of the heat, only of the wiggling flesh that she held in her arms. Her hands examined the baby's damp body. She counted toes and fingers. She kissed the beating soft spot on her daughter's head. Her daughter! Leigh was awed to think that this tiny, perfectly formed little girl had come from her body.

Chad was pressing the pad he had made of the nightgown between her thighs. He secured it with a makeshift belt around her waist.

"It feels strange to have a flat stomach again." She sighed.

He chuckled. "I'll bet it does. Are you too uncomfortable?"

Only now was she beginning to realize the throbbing ache. "No," she answered, but she knew hesitancy told him that she was.

"We've got to get you two to a hospital." Chad spoke almost to himself.

To read more, look for *Shadows of Yesterday* by Sandra Brown.